Praise for Sue Miller's

THE ARSONIST

"Provocative, suspenseful and emotional. . . . [Miller's] portrayal of the fragility of relationships and fear of the unknown—of the things that happen to and around us that we can't control—are spot-on."
—*Star Tribune* (Minneapolis)

"[Miller] has an elegant way with prose. Her descriptions never feel writerly, but intricate and real, and her sentences flow like a summer river. . . . There's a kindness to her writing, a sort of authorial gentleness; though never saccharine or sentimental, we see the goodness in the people she creates. . . . She's the kind of author who creates, for us, a home on the page."
—*The Seattle Times*

"Moving and convincing. . . . [Miller] is an eloquent chronicler of the complexities of ordinary relationships, whose informal language belies the depths of her insights. . . . [Her] prose, narrated in the third person . . . is colloquial and homely. . . . [She] nails the contradictory emotions and desires that are responsible for people so often bypassing the seemingly easy road to happiness."
—*The Independent* (London)

"Miller [eschews] easy cliff-hangers or narrative deceits. The momentum grows instead from her compassionate handling of these characters. . . . Not all questions are answered, nor all mysteries solved, but the end of the book is imbued with the same quiet energy that's been building throughout; it's not happy, exactly—that would be too easy—but, in true Sue Miller fashion, it's triumphant."
—*Elle*

"Written in a style that is both graceful and accessible, this enthralling novel grabs your attention and never lets it go." —*Real Simple*

"Moving . . . profoundly satisfying. . . . In another writer's hands *The Arsonist* would be a thriller, but Miller is concerned with deeper mysteries of human motivation." —*The Daily Telegraph* (London)

"Miller writes with penetrating honesty. . . . With a deft, homespun acuity." —*The Guardian* (London)

"This isn't a conventional mystery book. . . . It's intense, building toward resolutions that answer some questions but not all. Miller's pacing is perfect, making *The Arsonist* a pleasurable slow burn of a read." —*San Antonio Express-News*

"Sue Miller's acclaimed first novel, *The Good Mother*, was published in 1982; now, almost thirty years later, *The Arsonist* reminds us, if we needed reminding, of her remarkable achievement in fiction." —*Commonweal*

"Miller's prose . . . keeps you reading. Her sentences have a sumptuous quality to them." —*Providence Journal-Bulletin*

Sue Miller

THE ARSONIST

Sue Miller is the bestselling author of the novels *The Lake Shore Limited*, *The Senator's Wife*, *Lost in the Forest*, *The World Below*, *While I Was Gone*, *The Distinguished Guest*, *For Love*, *Family Pictures*, and *The Good Mother*; the story collection *Inventing the Abbotts*; and the memoir *The Story of My Father*. She lives in Cambridge, Massachusetts.

THE ARSONIST

Sue Miller

Vintage Contemporaries
Vintage Books
A Division of Random House LLC
New York

FIRST VINTAGE CONTEMPORARIES EDITION, APRIL 2015

Portions of chapter three first appeared, in significantly different form,
as "From Burning Summer" in *Ploughshares* vol. 37, nos. 2 and 3 (fall 2011).

The Library of Congress has cataloged the Knopf edition as follows:
Miller, Sue.
The arsonist / By Sue Miller.—First edition.
pages   cm
1. Arson—Fiction.   2. Arson investigation—Fiction.   3. Pyromania—Fiction.
4. Psychological fiction.   I. Title.
PS3563.I421444A89 2014   813'.54—dc23   2013041004

Vintage Books Trade Paperback ISBN: 978-0-307-74179-0
eBook ISBN: 978-0-385-35170-6

Book design by M. Kristen Bearse

www.vintagebooks.com

Printed in the United States of America
10 9 8 7 6 5 4 3 2 1

For Bob
August 1941–November 2013

THE ARSONIST

1

LATER, FRANKIE WOULD REMEMBER the car speeding past in the dark as she stood at the edge of the old dirt road. She would remember that she had been aware of the smell of smoke for a while. *Someone having a fire,* she had assumed then, and that would turn out to be correct—though not in the way she was imagining it. She had the quick thought, briefly entertained amid the other, rushing thoughts that were moving through her tired brain, that it was odd for someone to be doing this, having a fire this late—or this early—on an already warm summer night.

But in the moment she didn't go beyond her quick assumption, her fleeting thought. She smelled the smoke, she saw the car approaching, and she got quickly out of the road, stepping first into the ditch that ran alongside it, and then, because it was night and she worried that the driver might not see her in the dark, onto the scrubby bank, pulling herself up between two trees that stood there. By the time she turned around to face the road again, the car had passed her. She stood for a moment watching as the wink of the red taillights disappeared behind a rise in the road, appeared again, dropped from sight, and appeared once more; and then was gone, the car's sound fading into nothing, into the rustle and odd croak of the night. She'd been walking for more than an hour by then, awash in memories and images of the life she'd just left behind.

She'd waked, as she'd known she would, at about one-thirty, and in her jet lag and confusion, she didn't know where she was, or even, for just a second or two, *who* she was. She'd felt this way only a few times before in her life—in childhood mostly—a disorientation so profound that it momentarily wiped her consciousness clean. It left her breathless now, too, her heart knocking hard in her chest as she lay there slowly feeling the room and her life—her sense of being precisely *herself*, Frankie—return and settle around her. It took her a few seconds longer than that, though, to understand why she might be here, in this room that meant summer, family.

She lay still for a while, feeling her body grow calm again, taking in the familiar shapes in the dark around her. The clock next to her on the bedside table glowed greenly—now 1:40, now 1:45. She turned on her back and stretched. She heard an animal screech somewhere far off and the tick of something shifting somewhere in the old house.

Two o'clock.

Okay, sleep wasn't going to come again for a while. She got up. She dressed in the dark, pulling on the same clothes she'd shed onto the floor five hours earlier when she'd come, exhausted, upstairs to bed. Carrying her shoes in her hand, she went into the black hall, found the stairs, then the smooth wooden handrail, and descended slowly, each step loudly protesting her weight, even though she tried to stay at their edges on the way down.

The bright moonlight fell into the living room, clearly delineating the furniture. She could see the deep old slipcovered chairs hunkered companionably by the fireplace. This was where her parents sat on chilly nights, usually reading. The couch was turned toward the view of the mountains. Behind it, the globe of the earth with its obsolete borders and nations was bulbous in its wooden stand. The chest of drawers that held dress-ups and puzzles and games—Monopoly and Clue, Parcheesi, Scrabble—was a large dark block in the far corner of the room. She could hear her parents' twinned snoring from their bedroom in the new wing down the hall from the kitchen, the wing they'd built this past year because they were retiring—retiring to this farmhouse they had used as a summer home for as long as Frankie could remember. She stood still and listened for a long moment. She thought she could distinguish one from another, her father's snores low and regular, the proverbial sawing of logs; her mother's more intermittent, more fluttery.

She thought of their faces as they'd looked at the dining room table earlier tonight, both turned to her inquisitively, both seeming to ask to understand something of who she was now, both seeming to want something from her, something she could feel herself pulling against giving, as usual.

She had a sense, suddenly, of how useless it was, that reflex. Probably they were just being polite. Probably the questions they were asking had been designed to keep the sense of a conversation going. Her resistance seemed to her now the residue of some childish impulse that had stayed with her into adulthood, the impulse to keep her life from them, not to let them own it.

She sat down in one of the chairs by the fireplace. As she bent to pull on her shoes, the smell of old ashes rose toward her, and she felt flooded with a sense of nostalgia—but a kind of aimless nostalgia. She couldn't locate its source. Nostalgia for this place? For something in her past here? Or, perhaps, lost to her, in her past elsewhere? She sat there for a long moment, swept by this formless, hungry feeling.

Then she stood up, walked through the dining room, the kitchen, and came outside, setting the screen door of the little porch carefully, soundlessly, back into its wooden frame.

The moon was bright here, bright on the grass around the house and the field beyond it, bright on the gravel driveway that led to the blackness of the trees at the driveway's end. The air was cool and smelled fresh after the closed-in warmth of the house. The noise of the gravel under her shoes seemed explosively loud.

When she got to the road, she turned left, away from town, and emerged from the dark well under the trees. The moon made a glowing white band of the road in front of her, made the woods on each side of the road read as more deeply black. As she walked, she was going over the steps that had brought her here the day before, a day that had gone on and on, that had lasted more than thirty-two hours as she traveled north and then west, across continents and oceans and time zones.

She saw herself in Lamu, climbing down onto the old wooden ferry that plied the water between the island and the airport, holding the hand of the weather-beaten, skinny ferryman as she stepped from the pier to the boat's edge, then to the built-in bench that curved inside along its hull, a bench covered in fresh straw matting. There were assorted other travelers waiting to be helped on, too, including a few tourists and a fat woman wearing a *buibui*. She looked ancient, her heavy, sallow face deeply lined, but Frankie knew from experience in Africa that she might have been only a few years older than she herself was. The woman was carrying two live chickens, white and plump, held upside down. This seemed calming to them. They were quiet anyway, they jerked their heads back and forth, looking around with a mild disinterest at everything within their purview.

The last to arrive were two younger women in head scarves. Once the boat had pushed off from the dock, once the ancient motor had caught and they were out on the choppy gray water, the girls pulled their scarves off, and the breeze lifted their thick dark hair. One of them closed her eyes and shook her head slowly in pleasure.

During the short trip across the channel, Frankie watched the dhows heading out to sea or returning, the one belling lateen sail turned this way or that to catch the wind. She looked back at the stone town rising behind the dusty waterside quay. She'd stayed for just four days this time, alone in one of the tall town houses. She'd slept out on the rooftop under a lattice covered with jasmine and bougainvillea and waked before dawn each morning to the electronically amplified call to prayer, to the rich erotic smell of the jasmine. She'd walked the streets slowly, avoiding the open-water channel, the meandering donkeys. She looked into the open shops, she bought food and trinkets from the street vendors. She'd wanted to mark what she thought might be the end of her life in Africa, and this was a place she had particularly loved.

On the other side of the wide channel, everyone disembarked in nearly perfect reverse order and walked up the sandy path to what constituted the airport—a few thatched-roof pavilions and huts where others were waiting, a short runway with a small plane parked on it. Everyone, including the chickens, got into this plane, each person having to lower her head when she passed through the narrow, low door hatch.

As they flew, Frankie leaned against the window and watched the plane's winged shadow move across the steady brown and green of the savanna below. Occasionally they passed over a village with thatched roofs, or tin roofs winking in the sunlight, and Frankie could see the rising smoke from cooking fires and people standing in the cleared spaces of red dirt, looking up, shading their eyes.

In Nairobi, she took a taxi home. She repacked her small bag quickly. Then she carried it, wheeling her larger bag, too, out to where the taxi driver waited at the gate by the guardhouse, talking in Kikuyu to Robert, the day guard. As the cab took her back to the airport, the sun set quickly, undramatically, equatorially: day, then night.

The driver helped her into the chaos of the brightly lighted airport with her large bag, and she checked it through to Boston. Then there was the long wait in uncomfortable orange plastic chairs for the plane to Amsterdam, delayed for some reason or other, as planes in and out of Nairobi often were. It was almost midnight when she finally boarded and settled into her seat. A tall blond flight attendant with thick, almost clownish makeup came by with a warmed hand towel, then with a packet containing socks, a miniature toothbrush with a tube of toothpaste, and a sleep mask. Frankie had the sense of the beginning of different rules for life, different expectations. The note of improvisation was falling away, the developed world was beginning to encircle her.

The sky outside the plane was dark, and she slept, a broken, uncomfortable sleep, alternately too hot and too cold and full of vivid, disturbing dreams she couldn't remember when she woke. The plane was squalid as they disembarked, blankets and pillows thrown on the floor along with trash, newspapers. She saw little empty nip bottles wedged into seat-back pockets here and there.

In Amsterdam, where it was morning, the airport smelled of espresso, there were expensive first-world goods for sale in the shops, there were people at computer stations and on cell phones, there was real luggage—not boxes taped and tied, not old suitcases held together with ropes. Frankie had a two-hour wait. She wandered in and out of the duty-free shops for a while, though she didn't buy anything. She startled herself with her reflection in a mirror in front of a perfume shop. She stopped and stepped toward it. She didn't look particularly American—a tall woman wearing a white blouse and khaki pants, her long wavy red hair pulled back, her pale face washed out without makeup. *A missionary from Scotland,* she thought. *A dour anthropologist from the Netherlands.* A very tired missionary or anthropologist. She went into a women's bathroom and washed her face with the odd-smelling soap. She brushed her hair. She put on fresh eye makeup. She didn't look very different, but she felt better.

On the flight to Boston, there was a movie, astonishing to Frankie in its stupidity and crudeness. Was this *all right* now in the States? Had she lived in Africa too long? She looked around at the others watching it with earphones in, watched as their faces changed in amusement. From time to time, she heard the ripples of light laughter sweep through the plane.

The sun was bright as they came in for the landing in Boston. There were sailboats and motorboats on the dark blue water, their wakes making curling white lines behind them. There was the familiar urban skyline off in the distance and the closer village one across from the airport, the toylike old-fashioned wooden houses seeming to look out benignly over the water at the boats and the airport activity. Frankie was struck, as she often was on the return to the States, particularly in good weather, at how pretty everything was, how fresh-looking, how clean. Tears rose to her eyes.

The bus north to New Hampshire was loading up as she arrived at its bay. There were only twenty or so scattered passengers, so Frankie had a seat to herself. She fell into it with a great sense of relaxation and relief. The driver came on board and started the engine.

The bus passed quickly through the streets around the station, and then they were on the highway. Frankie watched the sprawl around Boston fall away. She settled back for the long ride into a green that seemed vast and unused compared with Africa. She watched it rolling by, emptied, only occasionally a house, a farm, a gas station. She thought suddenly of Sam, one of her colleagues at the NGO she worked for. He had seen a photo of her family's country house once, with the overgrown, blooming meadows stretching out forever beyond it. "What crops are you raising here?" he had asked, pointing. When Frankie said, "Nothing," he shook his head in wonderment. "All that land and no farming." And here she was, she thought—back where she belonged, in the prodigal Western world of no farming. Undeniably an American after all. She felt this in some pointed way, since, for the first time in the fifteen years she'd lived in Africa and come home to visit her family in the States, she didn't have a return ticket. She didn't know when she was going back. Or if she was.

She leaned her head against the cool glass and dozed, then woke, then dozed again. The sun was getting lower in the afternoon sky when the bus pulled off the highway. They were approaching Winslow, and then they were there, at the little grocery-store-cum-gas-station that served as a bus stop. As they rounded the corner to the parking area behind it, Frankie saw several people waiting outside. It took her a few seconds to realize that one of them—the old woman sitting alone on a bench in front of the big glass window under a faded sign that advertised Salada tea—was her mother.

This had happened to Frankie with Sylvia before in recent years, this lag in recognition. *I must have a picture of her,* Frankie thought, *maybe at forty-five or fifty,* the same way you're supposed to form a persistent image of yourself that stays indelibly the same, in spite of the years that pass. The wear and tear.

Wear and tear indeed. Sylvia's face looked ravaged in repose, and yet she also still looked powerfully strong, in what was to Frankie—always had been—a slightly frightening way. The bus pulled into its spot, and Frankie watched her mother stand up from the bench. Watched her face come to life, watched as some energy, willed or not, animated it, and it became, somehow, beautiful.

Sylvia was there at the foot of the steps as Frankie stepped down from the bus. "Darling!" she cried, and threw her strong arms around Frankie.

And there was a part of Frankie that wanted it: to be held, to be taken care of, to be *mothered.* Though this was illusory, Frankie knew—mothering wasn't a gift of her mother's. But for the moment she welcomed the illusion, she leaned into it, into her mother's austere, slightly lemony smell, feeling her mother's breasts soft against her as she returned the hug.

They broke apart. The bus driver had come down the steps and was opening the luggage compartment at the side of the bus. He began pulling out bags to get at Frankie's. When he yanked it to the ground and deposited it in front of them, Sylvia took hold of it and tilted it toward herself.

And then made a face. "Good *Lord,* Frankie!" she said. "You'd think you were some kind of hit man, getting rid of the body." The driver laughed as he was flinging the other bags back in. Sylvia smiled at him, pleased.

"I'll take it then," Frankie answered, reaching for it.

"No, no, it's all right. I've got it. I'm just amazed, that's all." Her mother gestured to the car, the old green station wagon Frankie's parents had driven for years, parked at the side of the lot.

"What on earth is in here?" Sylvia asked.

"Just the usual." This was a lie. Frankie wasn't sure why she hadn't yet told her parents that she didn't think she was going back. Mostly, probably, because she wasn't absolutely certain she'd decided yet. And she didn't know what else she wanted to do. What else she could do, really. If she were going to stay, she'd need to *do* something, and the blankness that rose in her mind when she considered this frightened her.

"Then I'm getting older," Sylvia said. "Weaker anyway."

"No. Not you," Frankie answered. "No way."

Together they heaved the duffel into the back of the car. Then each of them came around and got in. As Frankie was fastening her seat belt, she said, "No Daddy. Boohoo."

"Boohoo, indeed. He's mired in his own world, as ever."

They were pulling out of the parking area onto the paved town road. Frankie looked over at her mother, at her profile. She looked her age, her hair was white, and yet the effect she made when animated was of a person undeniably, sexually, female. For as long as she could remember, Frankie had thought of womanhood as a territory her mother had staked a claim to. In order to be female herself, to be sexual, she'd felt that she needed to get away from Sylvia. Sometimes, when she'd been home awhile—too long—she thought that was the point of Africa for her.

"What world?" she asked her mother now. "I thought he'd retired from his world."

"Oh. That's just not going to happen, I don't think." Her mother shook her head, an almost-grim smile playing around her mouth. "He has *projects.*" Her voice put quote marks around this.

In Frankie's adult memory, her mother had always spoken of her father's professional life this way, with a tone of only-slightly-veiled contempt, or disdain. It was something Frankie didn't like in her mother, but she tried to resist that feeling now. It was too soon to give over to it. She said, "Well, good for him, I say."

"Mm," Sylvia said.

After a moment, Sylvia asked about the trip, and Frankie talked about it. Then about her work in south Sudan, where she had spent the last few months training and supervising the staff at the health centers her NGO was helping to set up. In turn, she asked her mother about the renovation of the farmhouse, which Sylvia explained in a depth of detail Frankie could tell she was enjoying. When they'd driven without speaking for a minute or two, Frankie said, "So, how does it feel, living here full-time?"

Sylvia tilted her head to one side. "I'm not sure. It's been raining off and on since we got here, so Alfie and I have been more or less trapped together in the house." She made a face. "No fun."

Frankie had a quick sinking sensation.

Sylvia spoke again. "But right now, it's paradise. As you see."

Frankie turned and looked out her window. It was paradise, she thought. The afternoon sun touched everything with gold, so that the grass, the fields, every tree, all seemed an invented green, not of this world naturally. Even the air seemed golden—the light itself was speckled and glittery where it was caught slantwise by dancing motes, by miniature insect life. She sat, silent. They were passing the old familiar landmarks—the hills, the wide fields with early corn in precise, lush rows. Intermittently she could see the black river rushing by below the road, and every now and then, around a corner or on a rise, there were the mountains off in the distance, bluish in the early evening's light haze.

They passed a tidy farmhouse and barn she remembered well. A mile or two after that, a familiar abandoned house that had gotten more derelict in the last few years. For the first time in a long time, she was relaxed, she realized. Her mother at the wheel, these old signposts. She felt herself drifting into sleep.

The road got bumpy, and Frankie opened her eyes. They'd turned off the asphalt village road onto dirt. Frankie sat up. They passed the

Louds' farm. There was a red tractor down in their fields, moving slowly through the tall grass, a bareheaded man, shirtless, driving it. Every rise and dip in the road were known to her now. Every house they passed had a name Frankie could attach to it, faces she could call up. They went right at the fork, and a minute or two later, there it was. Home.

She corrected herself mentally. Not home. It was no more her home than the Connecticut house had been.

They turned into the driveway. "Here we go," her mother said. She pulled up to the closed doors of the small sagging unpainted barn, attached to the house, which served as a garage in winter.

The air, when Frankie stepped out of the car, was cooler here. Was *better,* she thought, and remembered that she had always thought this, even as a child. It had been magic then, to arrive from wherever they were calling home that year. To feel the gift of some cleaner, finer life beginning. She breathed it in now. She stretched. Her mother had come around to the rear of the car and opened it, and together she and Frankie lifted the heavy bag out of the Volvo. Sylvia took the lighter bag, and Frankie followed behind her, pulling the heavy one over the resisting gravel and up the few steps to the little porch outside the kitchen.

"We're here!" Sylvia called as she stepped inside. She crossed the kitchen and disappeared into the dining room beyond. Frankie had just gotten the bag up over the threshold and into the kitchen when her father appeared in the doorway between it and the hallway.

"Francesca," he said with quiet satisfaction. He came forward and embraced Frankie, gently, less commandingly than her mother had. He stepped back, hands still on her shoulders, looking at her. "Frankie," he said.

"*C'est moi,*" she answered, stupidly.

Sylvia bustled back into the kitchen, and Frankie's father's hands dropped; he stepped away from her.

"We'll have just a little light supper," Sylvia was saying to Frankie, already moving on to the next step. "I know you're ready to collapse." And then: "Can you get that bag upstairs by yourself?" It was less a question than a directive, and Frankie felt it beginning, the irritation with her mother that was part of her life in her family.

Her father made protesting noises: "Oh no, I can do that," but Frankie said no, no, she would, and rolled the bag across the dining room. She could see that the table was already set for dinner. Her father trailed behind her and then stopped and turned back to where Sylvia was speaking to him from the kitchen. Alone, Frankie hauled the bag up the stairs, bouncing it heavily behind her on each one.

In her room upstairs, the room she'd had every summer since she was a child, she unpacked a few things from her carry-on bag and then went down the long, narrow hallway to the bathroom. Standing there, bent over the sink, she could feel her body automatically accommodating the slope of the bathroom floor, a sense memory that felt completely familiar to her—everything tilted in this old house.

She washed her face and brushed her teeth thoroughly at last. She looked at her watch: six-forty. She would try to stay awake until ten. Maybe nine-thirty. Back in her room, Frankie stripped off her airline clothes and put on the clean underwear, the slacks and shirt she'd packed at the bottom of her carry-on for just this moment.

She was thinking about her parents, about their retiring here. She was aware of being immediately grateful for their move—it was always easier to enter America here, in the country, than it was in the small city in Connecticut they had lived in before now. Once, when she had gone to the supermarket there to pick up a few groceries for her mother—she'd been back from Africa for only a day or two—she had suddenly felt so overwhelmed by the abundance, by her inability to choose anything in the face of it, that she left her cart in the aisle and walked out, her heart racing.

Here, everything was easier, simpler, more contained.

Though things were changing here, too, she reminded herself, with people like her parents coming to live here permanently, as well as, she knew, refugees from New York and Boston.

Refugees, she thought, and smiled ruefully. How different the meaning of the word in this context than in the world she'd just come from.

There were young people, too, moving up here. People like her sister, Liz, who was planning to live here full-time eventually. Her husband would work as a carpenter, a handyman, the same collection of odd jobs some of the townspeople did. Liz had said she wasn't sure what she would do.

In the old days, as Frankie was remembering them now, the lines had been more sharply drawn. There were the summer people, and then there were the townspeople. The summer people had work elsewhere, personal lives elsewhere, all of which were invisible when they were here; whereas the townspeople's lives and their work were visible to anyone who cared to look—especially when they were working in the summer for the summer people.

Now all those lines would be increasingly blurred. Frankie wondered how well that would work.

Dinner was simple, elegant, something Sylvia was good at. A Niçoise salad, crusty French bread—you could get that now at the supermarket, she said, supplied by an artisanal bakery that had sprung up in White- hall. There was a cheese shop, too, run by local cheese makers—they would have some tonight instead of dessert. She and Alfie had got into the habit, her mother said.

"Oh! and Frankie—Liz and Clark and the kids are coming up at the end of the weekend. They'll miss the tea, but apparently that can't be helped."

A quick series of images of her sister rose in Frankie's mind. Liz as an adolescent smiling wickedly at her in the backseat of someone's car across the summer boys seated between them. Liz's slender, naked body arced over the water on a night of skinny-dipping. Dark, pretty, sharp-tongued Liz, who'd surprised them all by marrying Clark, the posthippie hippie, as she called him. Gentle, easygoing, unflappable. Her opposite, it seemed.

And the tea! The Fourth of July Tea. Frankie had forgotten it, as she'd momentarily forgotten even that the Fourth would be a holiday. Now her mother started to reminisce, as she liked to do, about her girlhood here, about the teas then, when the men wore pale seersucker suits, when the women wore hats and dresses and white gloves and stockings. "Gir- dles, of course, were the downside of *that*," she said, and made a face.

Frankie was remembering it, too, then—the grown-ups dressed up in *church clothes,* as she thought of those costumes then. The kids were made to dress up, too, but once they got to the tea, the parents ignored them, busy greeting one another at this formal, start-of-summer event. The kids were free to run wildly around, to grab as many cookies as they could get away with, to lob moist green clots of newly mown grass at one another.

Later, in adolescence, the tea was more erotically charged. It was where you got your first glimpse of who was here this year, of the changes in the other summer kids. It was where you started the flirtations that shifted and shifted again over the following two months.

"These days," Sylvia was saying now, "the young people wear anything—blue jeans. Shorts, even."

Frankie had one glass of wine, two, and then realized she'd asked several times already if it was nine yet. At nine-thirty or so, after they'd done the dishes, after they'd settled in the living room and talked for a little while, she excused herself and went upstairs, stepped out of her clothes, and fell onto the bed. Only to wake, as she had, in the middle of the night. To start out on her long walk, thinking of everything she'd left behind. To turn back when she saw the car.

2

IT COULD HAVE BEEN SAID, it probably was said among certain of her friends, that Frankie was leaving Africa because of a love affair—but that was only part of the truth. The truth had to do with her work, her life generally. The truth was that it was that love affair on top of the other love affairs. The ones that ended because someone was transferred away, or chose to quit aid work, or just wanted to get away from Africa, or was married, or was, as with Philip, in some irrevocable way unavailable.

As Frankie knew she probably was, too, she'd gotten so used to the inevitable ending to things. And although she liked to think of herself as still open to experience—to love, she supposed—she was aware that the evidence was pretty compelling against it.

The work itself was part of what did it, of course. Ended things. But also began them. The extremity of it, the absorption in it, the fatigue, the high. The charge that passed among people laboring together in such hard circumstances, such challenging ones. The wish to take pleasure where you could, the sense that you needed it, that you had somehow earned it. Most of the people Frankie worked with felt this way. They joked about it, actually, they used it as a kind of aphrodisiac. They all had the feeling, living always so close to death, that they wanted somehow to affirm life. Sex was good for that.

Timing had been part of her coming together with Philip. He was closing out an emergency surgical stint in Sudan—there was at least a temporary peace in the area, so the crisis, which was what Philip's work was about, was just about over, for the time being anyway. Now a more normal, steady human misery was the problem. Malnutrition and hunger were a part of that everyday misery—and they constituted Frankie's work. She was arriving just as Philip left, then, arriving to supervise the feeding station, to set it up the way her NGO felt it worked best so that the local people could take it over. He would go, and Frankie would stay, at least until things were working satisfactorily. An assured ending before it even began.

Its beginning seemed foreordained, shut in together in the medical compound as they essentially were. This was what she told herself, anyway. What she always told herself, she realized. Later, when she asked herself, *Why him? Why not one of the others?* she didn't have an answer, not really. She knew how easily it could have been one of the others. But at the time, she chose to see it as inevitable. Him, him and no other, the lie she told herself, the lie she always told herself, the lie that turned her on.

It had started in more or less the usual way. They were sitting around talking after dinner, maybe seven or eight of them, all a little drunk. Several of them, Philip included, were smoking, and Frankie's eyes were stinging a bit in the thick air. Someone had put an old Leonard Cohen tape on the boom box, and the voices in conversation were all pitched loud in order to be heard over it. They were speaking of the events of the day for each of them. Philip and Rosemary had done an emergency Cesarean on a fifteen-year-old girl who'd been in labor and bleeding for three days. Her family had carried her for miles, and then she'd been picked up by an aid truck coming out from the little airstrip. The baby was all right, but they weren't sure if the mother would make it.

Another of the doctors was monitoring a young man who had been running an unexplainable high fever for days, and there was a girl who'd cut herself accidentally, whose wound was badly infected. There was dysentery, gangrene, tuberculosis. They shook their heads at these catastrophes, at the ruination, the endless crises, the odd, gonzo rescue of someone. They laughed. They actually laughed. What else were you to do?

Frankie's day had been hard enough, but less dramatic, so she wasn't talking as much as the others. Also, there was the fact that she'd arrived the day before and didn't really know anyone yet. Still, she was glad for the macho silliness all around her. Glad because it was familiar, it was the lingua franca of this work. Glad because it made all of them easy to meet, easy to know. It made her feel at home, even though she was having to learn, once again, the layout of the compound.

The room she was in was square, with a thatched ceiling and white-washed walls, a concrete floor. There was a bench along each side of the table. Kerosene lanterns were set on it, and a jumble of glasses and beer bottles and ashtrays was scattered over it. In the intervals between songs on the boom box, she could hear workers cleaning up in the open-air kitchen. Philip had gone after dinner to the building where the medical staff was housed to get a bottle of Scotch he'd bought on his last trip to Nairobi, and now he was moving around the table, pouring shots for everyone.

"*Frankie*," he said as he filled her glass. He stood back. Light from the kerosene lantern glinted in his glasses. "Such a very A*medd*ican name." He was a Brit, definitely ritzy. Frankie had gotten so she could hear the class differences when the English spoke, even when those differences were being mocked, as they were now.

"Francesca," she corrected. "Such a very Italian name."

"But you're not . . . ?" He frowned.

"No. I am, such an American. But in that American way, a bit of a mongrel."

"A *Mongol*?!" The music was very loud.

"Mon*grel*. Mutt."

He sat down next to her on the bench, his legs turned the opposite way from hers, his back to the table. "You don't look like a mutt. You look like . . . a setter. Irish. High-strung."

"Is this a game? Do I choose a dog for you now?"

"It could be. I could use a game, after my day."

Someone called to him from the other side of the table, and he twisted around. The other doctor, Alan, made some gesture, and Philip laughed loudly. Frankie wasn't sure if the gesture referred to her, but it irritated her anyway.

"A Newfoundland," she said.

"What, darling?" he asked, turning back to her.

"You know, one of those large, gentle bearlike dogs that leaves strings of slobber all over you."

"I would *never*," he said, grinning. "Though I'd love the opportunity."
That was it. That quick. That direct.

It was a little difficult to arrange, but they managed it over and over
in the next month. Frankie had had a brief affair with an African man
just before this, an affair that had ended because she wasn't interested
in marriage, wasn't interested in moving with him back to the United
States. He was angry about this. And then she'd been angry that this,
finally, was what he had wanted. Was really all he had wanted. Then he
was angry that she had the nerve to be angry at him. *Who did she imagine
she was?* And the contempt he had had for her as a woman all along—
a very African contempt—came pouring out.

So she felt some relief at starting things up with Philip, the relief of
being with someone who understood her life, whose own life was in
many ways similar. Neither of them, she assumed, had any long-term
expectations of the other. Still, during the month or so they were working next to each other, they conducted their affair with a hunger, a recklessness, that startled them both.

Once Philip had left, she assumed it would be over. She was surprised,
then, when he contacted her in Nairobi after she was back. He was staying on there for a while, for various work-related reasons. Just his voice
on the phone thrilled her, caused her to feel a heavy, dropping sensation
in her abdomen.

They saw each other four or five times a week for the next month or
so, mostly at her house, always at night; and then just before he left for
good, they took almost a week together in Lamu. When they climbed the
stone steps of the house they had rented, holding the lantern the stew-
ard had left out for them, its soft light moving up over the old, uneven
walls, making strange shadows, Frankie felt a weakness in her legs at the
thought of everything they would do with each other, to each other, at
the way in which their bodies belonged to each other. She realized over
those days that something had shifted for her. That without changing
any of her underlying assumptions, she had been imagining this *going
on*. Imagining a life together—though it wasn't located in any particular
place, though it consisted only of Philip and her. Though it was, in other
words, impossible.

But after he'd gone for good—there was, it turned out, a wife and children to "visit" in England—Frankie swung quickly back to her first understanding of things. She was sorrowful, she was pained, but within a few weeks, she was angry, mostly at herself—for her romanticism, for her sexual vulnerability.

And then slowly, over the next months, the months before she was to go home for her annual leave, she began to feel it was time to end this. Not just the kind of relationship she had with Philip, but her relationship, too, with Africa, with this whole way of living. They seemed connected somehow—the passionate affairs that ended, one after another, and the deep but temporary engagement she felt with her version of Africa's life. And it was always deep: the indelible memories of the children, of the mothers, the ones she'd failed as well as the ones she'd helped. The work that was so compelling.

And then was done. Finished. On to the next job.

All of this was what she was lost in thinking about on the dirt road in New Hampshire when the car appeared. When she stepped into the ditch at the side of the road. When she watched the car disappear, then rise over the next hill, dropping out of sight, rising again. She didn't give much thought to it then, or to the smell of smoke she'd been vaguely aware of for a while. She used both of them, though, as the signal to turn and head back.

The way home, all uphill, seemed longer. Seemed endless, actually, she was so tired.

The house was still, and she went upstairs and straight to bed. She thought she might sleep now. And only a few minutes after she'd lain down, she could feel the almost dizzy, falling sensation of complete exhaustion.

Later she woke again briefly. Something had pulled her out of her deep sleep, she didn't know what. Then she heard it—in the distance, a long, faraway, insistent sound, a honking. *Animal,* she thought for a moment.

It came again. Not animal: mechanical. But she didn't remember what it was or what it meant—she thought of it just as an odd, forgotten noise she would have to reaccustom herself to.

Her father was the only one home when she finally got up for the second time, around eleven. Hearing her clanking in the kitchen, he came in from the new wing, where he had his study now. He watched her heat milk for her coffee, and they talked of this and that—the trip home, how she had slept, a great blue heron he'd spotted down by the pond earlier this morning. Her mother, he told Frankie, had gone to town. Shopping. She remembered then the sound of the porch screen door smacking shut that had half waked her earlier. That, and the car starting up under her window.

As they were talking, Frankie noticed how stooped his shoulders seemed—the liability of being a scholar, she supposed. In the end, it gets you, hunched endlessly over all that recorded knowledge. He was wearing, as usual up here, a pair of brown cotton slacks—his UPS pants, she and Liz used to call them—and an old shirt, fraying at the collar. He had a little rounded potbelly, almost exactly bisected by his belt, and long, skinny legs. His face, too, was long and thin. His nose was beaky under his wildly curling eyebrows, half white now. There was a slightly simian aspect to the way he looked, mostly on account of the unusual distance between his nose and his upper lip, but he was attractive anyway, partly because of the gentle attentiveness he brought to bear on any conversation, any new person.

She looked like him, she supposed. Certainly more than she looked like her mother. She was almost as tall as he was, and as slender, and she had his long face; but, as he used to say to her from time to time, she'd invented her own coloring, different from anyone else's in the family. She had red hair, and her eyes were light—an oddly pale blue that could look washed out and empty when she was tired, as she was today. Liz was dark, like their mother.

Frankie had often thought that if she'd looked more like Liz, she would have had an easier time of it in Africa. As it was, her appearance had made people turn to stare at her in the street. Her skin itself, which was paper white, sprinkled everywhere with pale brown freckles, was part of that. The little children she worked with sometimes laughed at her "dots" and sometimes were terrified by them, as if they were the result of some spell, some curse called down upon her.

Today she was exposing a lot of those freckles in her shorts and tank top, in her bare feet, which made a light, whispering sound on the kitchen floor as she walked back and forth. She was aware suddenly of how happy she was to be dressed this way—happy to be barefoot, happy not to have to worry about giving offense with her body, as she would have in Africa with this much skin visible. It seemed to her an easy and very American happiness. The happiness of no rules.

She carried her coffee out to the porch, her father following her. They sat in the old Adirondack chairs facing the distant blue hills. The nearer hills were green. She was aware, suddenly, of birdsong everywhere and, somewhere off in the distance, a steady hum, a motor—someone haying or brush hogging. This was almost a constant here, she realized abruptly. The sound of someone else working—the background noise of summer life.

Her father was speaking now of some work *he* was doing. He had a project, apparently, just as her mother had said. Yes, he was reading for a prize, something to do with historical writing for a wider, lay audience. His face changed as he spoke of this, and she saw how proud he was of it, and remembered now that he'd spoken of it briefly last night, though she'd been too tired to ask about it, to really take it in. This would explain the books stacked everywhere, she thought, even out here on the porch. Though there had always been books stacked everywhere, wherever they went, whatever new house they moved into. Books that drove her mother mad: Why did he need so many? Where would they all *go*?

They chatted now about several he thought were strong contenders. He dug one out from the pile next to his chair, the chair he always sat in out here. He read a few paragraphs from it, looking up to see her reaction.

Frankie agreed, it was fascinating, and then a little silence fell between them. She was looking at him, thinking how unchanged he seemed. Always the same, with these shifting, fleeting enthusiasms to which he brought so much energy. She had a quick, surprised moment of sympathy for her mother's perspective, for her fatigue with Alfie's endless projects.

"Oh!" he said suddenly, as if just remembering something. "Did you hear the fire horn in the night?"

She had to think for a moment, but then she recalled the odd noise as she was drifting off after her walk. "Yes. Oh! *That* was it. Yes." And she imitated the sound, the long, distant honk she had at first thought was an animal. It was a good imitation, and her father made his quiet laughing noise, his head tilted slightly back, his face transformed in pleasure.

"It woke me actually," Frankie said. "Though I'd been up earlier. I'd been out walking around. Jet lag." The moon on the road, the cool night air. "I wondered what that was. That noise."

"That's what it was," he said.

She had some more coffee and set the cup down on the broad wooden arm of the chair. "Was there, in fact, a fire?" she asked.

He nodded. "The Kershaws. It's gutted, they say."

They, in this case as in most cases when *they* were quoted, referred to Sylvia, the one who went out into the world and heard the gossip and brought it home. Frankie's father almost invariably repeated it in this form, which she and Liz used to laugh at behind his back. Now she made herself respond as he clearly wanted her to: "My God! Are they okay?"

"Oh, no one was there. They're not up yet." Meaning they hadn't arrived from wherever else in the country they lived, almost certainly farther south—which was why to be here was to be *up*. Probably farther west, too.

"Well, that's good, I guess."

"Yes, they were lucky, in that sense. It's a terrible thing otherwise, of course."

"Of course. It would be." After a moment she said, "It's funny it should burn with no one there."

"Oh, these old houses." He shook his head, sighed. "They're tinder, basically. Anything could have caused it. They'd had the electricity turned on for the season, they say, so it could have been that—some old, worn-out wiring. Or someone told your mother that the painters were in over the spring. Who knows? Maybe rags, that kind of thing."

"I suppose it's possible." Though this had always seemed unlikely to Frankie. But then it occurred to her that she was probably confusing spontaneous generation with spontaneous combustion. One a fairy tale, one not. She thought.

"Eminently possible." They sat in silence for a moment or two. She wondered what he was thinking. His eyes, she noticed now, were empty in repose, staring out at the meadow, the hills.

"I sort of forget who the Kershaws were." She corrected herself. "Are."

He turned to her, looking almost startled. He cleared his throat, a tic she'd forgotten until just now. He said, "Well, she's the Olsens' daughter."

And he went on to bring her up-to-date with their history—how the elder Olsens were retired now and had moved to California, how they came up now only for a week each year and stayed with the Kershaws, who'd taken over the house. How "young Kershaw"—this was what her father called this man who must be fifty-five or so—was a lawyer for some white-shoe Boston firm and got up only for a week or two himself each summer.

Frankie wasn't listening to his words so much as she was hearing the shift from what had been his fleeting sorrow over the fire to eagerness about all this information; and she was struck again by the intense preoccupation he, as well as her mother, had with this little, closed-in world.

And then she checked herself. This wasn't fair, and she knew it. They read the *Times* every day, they watched the news. They could commiserate with her—they had commiserated—about the repressive and corrupt nature of the Moi government, about the violence in Sudan or Somalia or Kenya or Uganda, about clean-water issues in Africa generally, about the criminality of the banking system in Switzerland. They could speak of these things passionately. But always, Frankie felt, with a certain inherited vocabulary: *Tribal conflict. Numbered bank accounts. Globalization. Islamic radicalism.*

And when she spoke of her work, of the children—of the dying, or even of the rescued—they had trouble listening. "I don't know how you do it," they'd say, and Frankie thought she could hear in this the wish not to have to listen to any of the details, not to have to imagine it.

But after all, why should they? How much had she ever asked to understand what might be difficult in their lives?

She watched her father talking—now about the sale of a property down the road. She smiled at him, she sipped the dregs of her cold, bitter coffee. She thought about where she'd been the day before, about how far she'd come to be sitting here. How glad she was to be sitting here, and, yet, already a little bit restless, a little bit bored.

She heard the car in the driveway, and then the slamming of its door. The screen door banged shut, and there were footsteps, noises in the kitchen. Her mother's noises.

The steps came to the doorway out to the porch, and Frankie looked up.

Her mother looked from her to her father and back, and Frankie felt the sense she sometimes had as an adolescent, the sense of having laid some claim to him that her mother didn't like—or, at any rate, would try not to acknowledge.

Now she said brightly, "Well! Here you are, you two!"

3

SYLVIA HAD HAD TOO MUCH to drink, and that, plus her bad night vision, meant that Alfie insisted on driving them home.

She hadn't resisted. First, he was right. And second, she'd had a good time at the party.

She hadn't thought she would. She was feeling bad about Frankie, who, she had assumed, would come, too. She'd forgotten how jet-lagged Frankie would still be feeling, one day home. She couldn't possibly do it, she'd said to Sylvia. So they'd left her at home, alone, and Sylvia felt guilty about that. And then they'd been late arriving because they had to swing by Snell's for gas—Sylvia hadn't remembered to fill the tank when she went shopping earlier in the day. All this meant that she was short with Alfie, and they were silent and unhappy on the drive over to the party, both of them.

But once there, she had moved around, talking mostly to people she'd known for years, but also to a few strangers. She felt animated, attractive. Over the course of the evening, she began to have the sense that it could work, this business of retiring up here—something her first month in this new life, those long rainy days of early summer, had made her doubt.

They'd stayed too long, but so had many others. In the car, as they started home in the deep twilight, she'd leaned back and closed her eyes.

"Do you mind if I listen to the ball game?" Alfie asked. She looked over at him, startled. She'd been nodding off.

"No, that's fine." She sat up. "I'll do it." And she turned the radio on and fiddled with the buttons until she got a station carrying the game, already a little fizzy with static. It was the fourth inning, still no score. She tilted her seat back a little and looked up at the deepening indigo of the sky, listening to the slightly nasal, assured voice of Joe Castiglione. She liked that voice. She felt comforted by it. She closed her eyes again and imagined the things he was looking at—the brilliant green of the Fenway grass, the muted powdery green of the walls, the figures in white and gray at their stations, almost motionless until the ball was hit and they responded, moving wildly in different directions but in balletic synchrony.

She woke sometime later—suddenly, completely—to the dark outside the car's windows. The headlights made a bright tunnel ahead of them, the trees arching over it were caught at the edge of the light, falling away to join the blackness that surrounded them. The road was narrow, two lanes. She recognized nothing. There *was* nothing—no buildings, no milestones, just the black woods rushing past them. Her mouth was dry and tasted stale. The radio buzzed steadily.

She looked at Alfie. He was intent, focused on the road ahead, both hands gripping the wheel tightly.

She reached over and turned the radio off. "Where are we?" she said in the sudden silence.

He looked at her and then back at the road quickly. "I don't . . . *know*," he said. He sounded almost bemused by this fact, as if it had occurred to him just this minute that perhaps this was strange, that perhaps he ought to know.

She looked at the dashboard. It was past eleven. They should have been at the house now, getting ready for bed.

"How . . . what do you mean? How can you not know?" She felt a rising impatience that she tried to keep out of her voice, but she could hear herself, hear that she wasn't successful.

"I . . . I must have . . . taken a wrong turn somewhere, I suppose."

"But how long ago, do you think?" She'd gotten her voice under control. "How far back?"

He looked at her again, his mild, handsome face emptied out, blank. "I don't know."

Okay, she had thought then in the car. *This is it.* His failing, the thing they'd both been aware of in less critical moments, that they'd talked around, gingerly, over and over. The reason, after all, for him to be retiring, for their move—the negative student evaluations, the trouble sustaining his latest book. And for her, the increasing sense of an absence in him. Here, distilled, made pure and clear and undeniable.

Where the hell were they?

"I think you should pull over when you can," she said, as gently as she could. "Slow down." The car slowed, instantly. They crept along. Within a few miles she saw a spot ahead where the shoulder on the right widened a little. "There," she said. "Up there."

He slowed more and pulled over. Gravel crunched under their wheels. The headlights met an impenetrable wall of forest—trees, shrubs, undergrowth—all a surprising vivid green in this flat, harsh light.

"I'll drive," she said. "Put it in park." He obeyed her. She got out and came around behind the car. The air was cool and full of night noise. It smelled of pine, of earth. As she came to the driver's-side window, she looked down at him. He seemed frozen, his hands still on the wheel. When she opened the door, he looked up at her, a scared child, and then quickly turned away to fumble with his seat belt. He unsnapped it finally and got out.

"You go around to my side," she said. She hoped her voice was kind. That was what she intended, anyway.

He did as he was told, and they both got in and put their seat belts on. She slid the seat forward a few inches and put the car in drive. She swung it out onto the road again.

They'd keep going. It made as much sense as turning back. Sooner or later there would be something she'd recognize. Or a town, with road signs, arrows with mileage pointing to some place she knew. They had to be within an hour or so of Pomeroy in one direction or another. It would be all right. They'd get there, she told herself. She'd get Alfie to bed, and then she'd let herself think about this.

Six or seven miles later, the speed limit dropped to thirty, then twenty-five, and they were in the village of North Winslow, only forty minutes or so from the house. "*Here* we go," she said in relief. She looked at Alfie, but his face was as blank as before.

He had stayed that way even as they swung into the long driveway at the farm, even as she turned the engine off. She had to speak to him to get him to take his seat belt off, to open the car door.

When he'd used the bathroom and gotten into bed, she spoke to him as you would to a child—reassuringly, soothingly. She kissed him good night and said she'd be in herself in a little bit, she was just going to have a drink and unwind from the drive.

And now here she sat, on the porch, the night noises quietly riotous around her—the peepers' steady cheerful churning down by the pond, the odd owl hooting. She'd heard a distant cry as she sat down—an animal, caught, killed perhaps. The chair itself made little noises of dry protest when she moved in it.

He would be fine tomorrow, chances were. This was the worst it had ever been, but he had never not *bounced back,* as she thought of it. He would again, maybe commenting on the failure, as he sometimes did, "I completely lost my train of thought there," when he paused in the middle of a sentence he'd launched himself into, befuddled. Or "I forgot for a couple of minutes where I was going." And they would commiserate, though it was sometimes hard to keep the tone light—she was aware of the sharper note of real perplexity in him from time to time. But what had frightened her most tonight was that he wasn't perplexed at all—that he'd seemed so unconcerned with their being, essentially, lost.

At first, she had ignored the signs—he'd always been a little forgetful anyway, a little scattered. Years earlier, long before any of this had started, she had pinned a *New Yorker* cartoon to his study door—a bearded, anxious man in a tweed jacket, stopping a policeman: "I'm an academic. Where am I?"

Then, for a while, she was impatient, irritated. Well, she could still be impatient and irritated, if she were honest. But within the last year or so, she was mostly just worried. And as a result there was this—booze, which she used too often. The strained attempt not to notice, to be kind. The solitary assessing and reassessing. The managing of appearances. The covering up.

But it was he, after all, who had pushed them toward this move, to retirement. He who had faced that realistically. Who had brought them to this little town. To this house.

Which had been in her family since the town was settled, lived in from generation to generation. When it became her grandmother's, though, it had become a seasonal home, empty through most of the year. She'd used it as a summer retreat from visibility as a minister's wife—the place she could always come "to be as naughty as I care to be," she would say. It had become Sylvia's about twenty years ago because she was the oldest child of the only son, but mostly because she was also the only one in the family who wanted the managing of it.

And she might not have been interested either if it weren't for Alfie, who had loved it from the moment he saw it, and then for the girls, to whom it represented home in a way none of the other houses they lived in had—too many houses in too many towns as Alfie moved around in academia.

At first she had resisted the idea of retiring, of moving. What she had said to Alfie was that she wanted to keep on teaching. But as the fall semester dragged on, she realized that wasn't it, that there would be a kind of relief to stopping. That a part of her was tired of waxing enthusiastic about her students' halfhearted, mediocre essays, tired of hearing their excuses, the same disasters that had befallen students year after year and made it impossible for them to get their work done—parents divorcing, a sick grandmother, breaking up with a boyfriend or girlfriend. Sometimes they just forgot. No, although there were pleasures involved in her work—her colleagues, the occasional really gifted student, the sense sometimes of having won a class over to a writer she loved—there was also a lot she could easily leave behind.

No, her resistance was centered on Alfie. She didn't want to be alone with him, watching his old age happening to them both in slow motion. Being *in charge* of it.

Leaning back now in the old wicker chair, looking at the net of stars in the black sky above her, she thought of one minor episode after another. The time he didn't recognize his own coat and held it up for her to put on. The time he got lost on the way home from the campus and had to knock on a stranger's door, had to ask to use the phone to call her to come and get him. When Sylvia picked him up, she could tell that the woman who'd let him in was frightened of him. Sylvia had written her a note of thanks the next day, realizing even as she did it how self-serving it was, that she was trying to assert something about herself, to put some distance between herself and Alfie in the woman's mind. *He may be gaga, but I still know how to behave.*

They didn't make love anymore either. They hadn't for more than a year. She would become sexless, then—a sister, a daughter, a nurse. She would manage their lives in Pomeroy, as she'd managed getting up here this spring, as she'd managed their successful arrival home tonight.

She sat back in the creaking chair and looked through the window into the living room. She did love the house. In another life, she might have been glad to live her last years here. And it was in better shape now than it had been in a long time—the new bedroom wing on the ground floor, the new furnace, new storm windows. Insulation had been blown in, everything had been repainted.

All of this she'd been in charge of, too. And there would be other issues to deal with. There always were. Last winter the fancy new generator had gone on the fritz in a snowstorm. Who knew what else would come up? Algae in the pond, peeling paint, rot here and there. And all of these problems would fall to her to sort out, while Alfie worked on his book on Virgil's *Eclogues* or read or made notes for the Harper Prize.

The Harper Prize. He'd been so pleased to have been asked to be on the jury. She'd felt almost sick when he told her. She'd already been worried on his behalf, he was having so much difficulty with other intellectual tasks.

But it seemed cruel, given his pleasure, to remind him of any of that, so she'd said nothing. They'd gone out to dinner to celebrate, and in the subdued lighting of the only really elegant restaurant in Bowman, he had looked younger. And because he was so exuberant, so animated, he seemed younger, too. It made her think maybe he could do it, could call up in himself the sense of focus, the energy, to read carefully, to make an intelligent judgment.

And after all, it was a committee. If he weren't up to it, there would be the others to take over, to cover for him.

When she went into the bedroom, he was lying on his back, utterly still. She froze, unable to step closer. She had the sudden conviction that he was dead; but then he drew a shuddering, snorting breath through his nose and open mouth, and she felt herself relaxing.

She'd been holding her own breath, she realized abruptly, and because of that, perhaps, her heart was beating faster, a little irregularly.

As if she were excited.

No. That wasn't so. She'd been frightened, that was all.

She pulled off her clothes in the cool night air and put on her pajamas. In the bathroom, as she brushed her teeth, she watched herself in the mirror, ready to dislike what she saw there. But all that showed in her face was how tired she was, how old.

At six, she got up. In the night, she'd heard Frankie moving around in the living room, awake again, as she'd been last night. She'd thought briefly of getting up, of going in to talk with her, telling her about Alfie tonight, but decided not to. If it had been Liz, she might have, but Frankie . . . no. No need to worry her when she'd be leaving so soon.

She dressed in the living room so as not to disturb Alfie. In the kitchen, she got the coffee carafe out and set the kettle on to boil. When the coffee was done, she sat in the living room drinking it, looking out the window at the overgrown meadow down in front of the house. The grass on the lawn around the house was nearly as long—all the rain they'd had, and then the nonappearance of Adrian Snell, who was supposed to take care of the mowing as he took care of so much else for the summer people, though some of the newer ones used other, younger, handymen, too. But for Sylvia and Alfie and perhaps six or seven other old-timers, Adrian was the one who plowed, who mowed, who cut firewood.

She'd have to speak to him about the lawn. An image of him rose in her mind, the barrel-chested, self-assured man he'd turned into, completely at ease with himself in his own small world.

It was complicated, with Adrian, complicated because she'd grown up with him, seeing him every summer, and then coming to know him well in the one year she lived with her grandmother in high school—the year her parents were off doing research in Guatemala—which was when she'd been in love with him, and he with her.

In love, she thought now, and her face twisted. An infatuation, that was all.

This was how she'd taught herself to think about it afterward in order to go on seeing him year after year. To go on talking to him cordially while he filled the gas tank—though that didn't happen anymore, now that you paid with a card at the pump and filled the tank yourself. But she still talked to him about the summer tasks she asked him to perform. She talked to him while she wrote him a check.

She didn't like to think, and didn't often, of the few times they'd made love. It was not memorable sex, though at the time everything about it was powerful to her. But that mostly resided in her response to him, to the way he looked, the way he smelled. Sometimes just glancing over at his arms and hands as he drove a car excited her.

The lovemaking itself was awkward and usually uncomfortable. Only once had they done it in a bed, when her grandmother was away and he came to her late at night. That was near the end of her senior year, when she'd been accepted to college. Lying in the dark next to her when they were finished, he asked her not to go, to stay and marry him; and she understood, abruptly, what her grandmother had meant when she said at the tentative start of their high school affair, "I'd think about whether it's such a great *kindness* you're doing the boy, taking up with him before you go off to your real life." She'd been smiling, her voice was mild, as it usually was. Her eyes were unreadable behind her bifocals.

"This *is* my real life," Sylvia had said.

"Oh, *is* it, now?" her grandmother had asked. They were having dinner together, as they did most nights that year. Sylvia's parents had taken the two younger children with them, but they thought Sylvia should stay in the States for her senior year. It would be better for her college applications to have a normal year, to be able to take the required tests easily. So Sylvia and her grandmother learned to move around the old farmhouse companionably, to talk comfortably in the evenings over dinner; or, just as comfortably later in the evening, *not* talk, as Sylvia did her homework on the dining room table, and her grandmother read or wrote letters in the living room. "We're like monks, off to our cells," her grandmother said one night as they separated.

She'd wait to call Adrian until nine or so, she thought now, drinking her coffee. She'd have to remind him of their arrangement, of her expectations. This added a heightened sense of—what?—unpleasantness, she supposed, to the worries about the day.

———

But when Alfie got up, he was fine, he *had* bounced back, and she felt herself relaxing. She poured him coffee, and herself a second cup, and they went to sit outside on the screened porch together—it had warmed up enough by now to make this possible. He didn't mention getting lost the night before. They talked quietly, aware of Frankie, asleep upstairs. They talked about her, about how worn out she seemed, even taking the jet lag into account. They talked about the fire. They talked about Liz and Clark's arrival on Sunday.

After a while, she stood up to go to make breakfast. He followed her to the kitchen and poured himself another cup of coffee while she pulled out the equipment she'd need.

He went back to the living room while she got things ready. She could hear that he was listening to NPR on the radio, but she couldn't hear the words—the bacon frying made a kind of white noise. When she called him in and they sat down, he summarized what was happening in the world for her, mostly more on the Lewinsky scandal. She was tired of it already.

As they were finishing breakfast, she thought perhaps she'd try now, she'd ask him what had been going on the night before. But what did she want?

For him to acknowledge it, she supposed.

What he'd put her through? Was that it? Or—this would be more generous—what he was going through himself?

Maybe that.

She smiled at him. "So," she said. "What happened last night, do you think?"

"Oh, you were probably just tired, dear." His voice was reassuring. "It was so dark out, it's easy enough to make a mistake. I shouldn't have let you do it."

She was so disoriented by this that she didn't know what to say. What came out quickly, without really thinking, was, "But you drove, too." She couldn't help it, her voice was accusatory.

He looked at her with concern for a moment, frowning. Then he smiled, gently, kindly—his Alfie smile—and said, "Surely not."

She turned away, shocked. After a moment, without looking at him, she got up and started to clear the table.

Behind her, he seemed to be waiting for something. She ran the water over the first plate, watched the yellow paste of the egg yolk disappear. Should she argue with him? Should she insist he remember it as it had happened? Would that be punitive?

Or would it be condescending, punitive in a different way, to let it go, to assume he wouldn't be able to correct his error? And why was she so furious at him? Whatever it was, he couldn't help it, could he?

"Okay," she said finally.

And it seemed this was enough. At any rate, after a moment she heard him go out of the room.

As she finished loading the dishwasher, as she wiped the counters, scrubbing fiercely at the fine, faint sprays of grease from the bacon, she was fighting back tears.

It was in the midst of this confusion of feeling that Adrian's old blue pickup truck came up the driveway and parked by the barn. But it wasn't Adrian in it. She watched as a young man swung himself down from the cab, a skinny kid maybe twenty or so in a plaid shirt and blue jeans, orangey work boots. He opened up the back of the truck and pulled out two long boards, which he rested against the bed of the truck to make a kind of ramp. He walked up this and started to slowly back the riding mower down.

She wiped her hands. She blew her nose and went out to confront him. He looked up as she crossed the circular drive.

"I'm Sylvia Rowley," she said coldly, approaching him.

He looked at her for a few seconds before he said, flatly, "Hi."

"And you are?"

"Tink. Snell." He was a handsome boy, with dark curly hair that spilled over his forehead, that covered his ears. He had pale eyes, a greenish blue, with lashes so dark they looked mascaraed.

"I thought Adrian did our work," she said.

"Not no more," he said.

"Well, you're late, if you're in charge. This lawn is a disgrace." She swept her hand around grandly.

"Yes, *ma'am*," he said. A little smile. An assertion, she thought, that the *ma'am,* maybe even the *yes,* were meant ironically.

And then she was remembering. A scandal. Adrian's sister, much younger, always in trouble, pregnant in high school by somebody or other. This would be her boy.

"You're taking over for Adrian?"

"*Some* stuff. Just what he doesn't have time for no more." He reached into a red plastic milk crate full of tools and equipment in the back of the truck and extracted some bright yellow plastic ear protectors.

"I'm afraid I'm going to have to insist on Adrian unless you can do the work we have for you in a timely fashion." She waved around herself. "This is . . . unacceptable."

He smiled once more. "Ma'am? It's been raining." He spoke as though this was something everyone ought to know. "For about three weeks steady. And now it warms up overnight and everybody's getting here all at once and every one of um has got a list." He lifted his shoulders, his hands: *What can you do?*

Then: "If you want, you can talk to Adrian, but he's behind in his stuff, too. You can't do much about rain." They stood silently for a moment. "If you want, you can talk to Adrian," he said again.

"No. No, that's okay," she said. She was aware, suddenly, of how much she was taking out on this kid, of how unfair she'd been. Of her tone, which she hated.

And that word, *unacceptable.* Why that word? She detested it, that schoolmarmy word with its assertion of the hierarchical arrangement between them.

"Okay," he said. He put the ear mufflers around his neck and turned away, climbed onto the mower. She turned away, too, and went back to the house.

Inside, she sat for a while at the kitchen table, watching the mower make its slow circuit around the house, its noise sudden, unpleasantly loud through all the open windows.

He hadn't been rude, exactly, she thought—she'd been ruder to him than he was to her—but she felt injured, all the same. And she felt, reasonlessly, that the injury came from Adrian.

He'd wept when she told him she had to go to school, to college. That her family expected her to. She'd watched him, astonished that she could have such power over someone. Thrilled, really. It was like a balm to a wound she'd hadn't known she had. But as it went on, she was increasingly appalled—at how he looked, at the noises he made, crying. At the way he said, "Please. Please," his voice rising, weakened, on the second iteration of the word.

His weeping that night had made her imagine that her power over him was a permanent thing, something she could count on, something that belonged to her. She didn't think about how her own feelings for him had changed as she opened the acceptance letters one by one, as she spread them out on the kitchen table and allowed herself to imagine walking—solitary, unencumbered, beginning her real life—across the pathways of some campus or other. She didn't think of the way Adrian and his love for her had seemed suddenly irrelevant then. Or worse, a thick impediment, a hurdle to get over on her way there.

She didn't consider the possibility that his feelings could change, too, that he would seek a balm for the wound that she'd inflicted on him.

Summer came and, with it, the summer people, the summer kids her age—the ones she'd played with when she was small, the ones she'd gone swimming with or hiked with or danced with or had crushes on in summers past. She sank with easy delight back into all the old routines. It was as if she'd forgotten the intricacies and pleasures of that temporary, compelling world as she lived through this past year here, she thought. Now she was out almost all day, every day, and often at night, too.

She was glad Adrian had a job, that his time was taken up during the day. She did try to include him in whatever was going on at night, to include him as her boyfriend. It was sometimes complicated, a little awkward, but she did it, aware of her generosity, her sacrifice. Aware, too, that it would all be over at summer's end, that she would have her own life back, her new life.

He stopped by one Sunday with two of the summer boys. They wanted her to come swimming at Silsby Pond. They were going to pick up the Caulfield girls, too. Adrian was driving.

Adrian was often driving that summer, as he had the previous summer, too—though she'd thought of it differently then. Then, Adrian was just a town boy, just a town boy they sometimes used.

They used him, then and now, because Adrian was the only one of them with his own car. Most of the summer families had just one car in Pomeroy, though some probably had two at home. But most of them came up in one, and that meant it was complicated for the teenaged kids to get around as much as they would have liked—to go to the Dairy Queen in Somerset or the miniature golf course in Winslow or to Mount Epworth to pick blueberries or to Silsby Pond to swim in the potholes. But if you asked Adrian along, you had your means of travel.

She went inside to put on her swimsuit, to get a towel. Her bedroom was small and narrow. It sat apart from the other rooms on the second floor at the back of the house, just over the kitchen and its doorway. The sun was pouring in, and she stood for a moment in its warm light, naked, stirred sexually as she looked at herself in the mirror over her bureau. The window was open, and through the screen she could hear the voices below, talking. She heard someone say her name. She stepped over to the window, she pressed her face, her body, against the screen to look down at them, nearly directly below her. The soft, fresh air touched her everywhere.

The three of them were foreshortened from her vantage. Billy McMahon was sitting on one of the steps of the back stoop, his knees spread wide, his elbows resting on them, the disorder of his curly hair predominant from up here. Skinny Walter Eberhardt was standing on the bottom step, leaned against the handrail of the stairs. There was an apron of worn, packed dirt around the last step, and Adrian was standing in this, facing the other two. They were all laughing. They were laughing because Adrian had grabbed at his crotch for a moment and was moving his hand up and down, a pumping motion.

A joke. His joke. About her.

She stepped back quickly, covering herself with the clothes she held in her hand. After a long moment, she pulled on her bathing suit without looking again in the mirror. She pulled her dress on over it and bent to lace up her sneakers. She went into the bathroom and lifted the worn towel from its hook. She came down the stairs and across the dining room, the kitchen, and went outside to join them.

She might have had a sense then, if she'd been able to think about it clearly—which she wasn't for several more years—of how it would be as their lives took the forms they did, separately. Of how polite they would learn to be to each other. How carefully kind, in her case. How scrupulously accommodating, in his. Of the courteous, bland exchanges they will have in public. And then of how sometimes, as he offers her change through the open window of her car at the pump, as he turns away from her in the aisle of the low-ceilinged grocery store, she will catch the suggestion of a smile at the corners of his mouth, or a quick, rolling-sideways motion of his eyes for someone else's benefit—born of that same impulse, she guesses. The impulse to claim some ownership of their history, and also some salving distance from her.

But there was no reason for any of that to cause her pain or sorrow now. That was what she told herself as she set breakfast things out to be waiting for Frankie when she woke, as she moved around the house putting things away, cleaning up—always with the hard, nasal complaint of the mower following her, room to room to room.

4

Frankie sat in the backseat as they drove to the Fourth of July Tea in the old station wagon. Perched there, looking at her parents' heads from behind, she was suddenly remembering exactly how this had felt when she was young. Alfie and Sylvia were talking about which of the summer people had arrived, and as she listened to the familiar names, the quickly sketched updates, she could have been ten, or fourteen.

Though she was feeling fully her age, thinking about her father. She and he had walked together down to Liz and Clark's house this morning. It had been her mother's suggestion—that Alfie show Frankie the project, the house Clark and Liz would move into eventually—Clark had been building it himself piecemeal over the last two years.

She had the sense that her mother was *getting rid* of Alfie, and maybe of her, too, though she felt less sure of that. But either way, Sylvia seemed to want to be alone. She had clearly been upset about something from the time Frankie came downstairs.

She and Alfie had hiked down through the meadow instead of using the road, because Frankie wanted to look at the pond along the way.

The dock was still pulled up on the rocks. Several slats were missing. As they walked around the pond's edge, the frogs jumped from the bank into the water, a steady *plop, plop, plop* that preceded them. There were sweeps of algal growth visible under the water. Frankie saw a turtle's head break the pond's surface. A snapper? she wondered. Time would tell.

They mounted the hillock beyond the pond, stepping carefully through the low-growing wild blueberries and the thorny, arching blackberry canes. As they reached the top, the vista below opened up.

"There 'tis," Alfie said. In the meadow below was the small, simple house—a cottage, really—shingled in wood that still looked raw, a wide unscreened porch on the uphill side facing them.

They started down toward it. "It's almost done, isn't it?" Frankie asked.

"You'll see," Alfie said.

Frankie followed him through the overgrown meadow, holding her palms out on either side to brush her fingertips along the tops of the grasses and blossoms. Bees hung in some of them. The ground was uneven, and Frankie felt a jolt in her body with each step.

The area around the house was gravel and dirt. They crossed it and stepped together onto the porch. There was no door—a piece of plywood had been hammered into place where it would have been. Alfie stood back while Frankie peered in through a window, framing her face with her hands. Though it was dim inside, she could see that there were no finished interior walls, just the vertical studs announcing where they'd be. Foil-backed insulation lined the house's outer walls like silvery wallpaper, and some of the windows were in place. The openings for others, like the doorway, were boarded over. There was a table in what seemed to be the kitchen area, chairs set around it.

Frankie said something pleasant, noncommittal: *It looks like it'll be very nice.*

Alfie didn't answer, so she turned to look at him. He'd taken a step back off the porch onto the packed dirt. He was looking at the house, his eyes squinted, a slightly puzzled frown on his face.

"Don't you think, Dad?"

He turned to her. "This is . . . I believe this is Liz's house," he said, dubiously. And then, more certainly: "Yes. I think it is."

She had said yes, stunned. She wasn't sure what else to say to him. Was it a joke of some sort? Was she supposed to offer something witty in response? She had no idea.

But he turned then and started back up the rise. Frankie followed him, up the hill, down through the berry patch, and around the pond, then up again, across the meadow. She could see her mother on the porch, waiting.

They didn't speak until they got back home. As they opened the screen door, Alfie said to Sylvia, "We've had the house viewing. What's our next assignment?" and they both laughed, to Frankie's amazement.

Had she misunderstood his lapse at Liz's house? She thought she must have.

Now her parents' car was steadily mounting the hill behind the town, and at the last turn, the Mountain House Inn came into view, a looming white frame building that looked across the valley to the tallest of the local peaks, their tops rising bare and rocky above the tree line. This was where the tea was held every year.

They parked at the edge of the wide, semicircular driveway cut into the rising lawn, behind a long string of other parked cars. Frankie looked up at the hotel as they got out of the car. There was a deep porch across the entire front span of the ground floor. Above the porch roof, on the second floor, there was a row of evenly spaced windows with dark green shutters. Several of these had fallen off, and the ones that were left sagged at the sides of the windows. There was a third floor above that with a line of smaller dormer windows.

She and her parents started up the sloping lawn toward the porch, where, Frankie knew, there would be tables with punch and cookies and tea sandwiches set out. But within the first ten paces or so, they were ensnared in a conversation with Gregory Hinton and his wife. Dr. Hinton, as Frankie still thought of him, was some big mucky-muck at the National Institutes of Health, a hearty, white-haired man. His wife, Louise, was a good friend of Frankie's mother.

In Frankie's parents' generation up here there were many distinguished, important people. Poets, bishops, explorers of the human genome, presidents of this college or that. When Frankie was young, she had assumed that her father belonged in this company. She had realized only very slowly that he didn't, that his tenured position at what she finally understood was a third-rate college was not even in the same category of success. And in her own generation, almost no one had the kind of prominence some of the parents had. Hardly anyone even seemed to want it. They were all more self-invented, less allied with all those important institutions. Like her, she supposed.

Dr. Hinton and his wife were asking her about her life, her doings. *How amazing!* they said. *Still in Africa all by yourself! How fascinating that must be!* Frankie was aware of the pleasure she was taking in being thought of as a girl, a pretty young girl, again. They asked about Liz, and she got the treatment, too, in absentia—they couldn't believe she could have children as old as five and four and two.

After a few minutes, when the Hintons had turned their enthusiasm onto Alfie and Sylvia, Frankie extricated herself and went directly to the porch for a glass of punch, remembering on her way that Liz had often brought a little flask of rum in her purse to spike it with when they were in high school, when, for a while, Frankie had had the pleasure of thinking of herself as one of the wild Rowley girls.

The punch was pink, as ever, with circles of sliced oranges and lemons floating on its surface. Frankie served herself with the long, curved ladle and then went to the railing and drank. Standing there with her cup, she surveyed the scene. If you blurred your eyes, she thought, it could have been her childhood, an impressionistic Sunday-best gathering of parents and children on the grass—smears and dabs of color for the women, the men more drab. In her clear view, she couldn't immediately recognize anyone in the sixty or seventy people clustered on the lawn or standing on the porch near her.

She moved over to one of the tables covered with platters of cookies and little sandwiches. There was an old woman there, loading up a plate with at least one of each of the many kinds of cookies laid out—and there were at least a dozen. "An amazing spread," Frankie said.

"You know what I miss?" the woman said. She was short and plump, with an enormous drooping bosom that took up the entire space between her shoulders and her waist.

Frankie took a cookie herself. "What?" she said.

"Meringues. Ellen Babcock used to make meringues for the tea every year. Oh, how I loved them! Even if they did get gooey by the end of the day." She popped one of the smaller cookies into her mouth and ate it rapidly, her jaw swiveling. She made a little noise, swallowing, and then she said abruptly, "Now, who are you?"

Frankie told her.

"Oh, yes," the old woman said. She nodded and nodded. "I knew Sylvia quite well. She used to babysit for us when she was . . . well, I suppose, in high school. Is she here?"

Frankie pointed out Alfie and Sylvia, still on the lawn, standing in a circle with several others.

"Aha!" the woman said. "With that Rowley fella. Not quite as charming as he thinks he is, that one."

Frankie was startled speechless, this seemed so indiscreet. She picked up another cookie, just to give herself a few seconds, and then she excused herself, moving away from the old woman and down off the porch. She went to stand near a small group of people who seemed to be close to her in age. When they opened to let her into their circle, she said who she was, and, of course, she did know a couple of them, she recognized them as they said their names and introduced their spouses.

They talked for a while about which of them was staying up and for how long—*they must get together!*—about their parents, some of whom had died. When several of them broke away to greet other summer friends, Frankie moved on, too. She had a conversation with someone she used to like dancing with, Jay McMahon, a conversation about the music of that time, about her life in Africa, then about his work as an economist in London. He had that slightly *off* accent of someone who's lived abroad too long, faintly but definitively British. Frankie knew she, too, had a version of this, and that hers was undoubtedly British also, but the postcolonial version of British. Maybe posttribal, too—a little bit of that clipped, singsong African thing, sometimes she heard it herself.

When Jay moved off—to get some food, he said—Frankie talked for a while to a group of people her parents' age and found out more about their children than she would have from the children themselves, *Because their currency is their children,* she thought. How accomplished, how far flung. She wondered how her parents were explaining her, the spin they were putting on her own life. *Oh, Frankie's still in Africa, yes. She practically runs the East Africa office now.* Or maybe not. She could imagine another version, Sylvia, rolling her eyes, saying something like *God knows what she's up to over there.*

She was called upon to explain herself to this group of parents, and she did, not mentioning that she was on leave. That she wasn't sure when, or even whether, she was going back.

While they were standing there on the sloped lawn, she was suddenly aware that she'd been hearing the thumping of a bass, of drums, of rhythmic music, getting slowly louder. Hip-hop. And now much too loud. She turned. A long, low car was approaching in the circular drive, windows down, music thudding. There were four boys inside—young men, really—their faces turned to the lawn, to the milling summer people in their fancy clothes. Someone in the car must have said something, because they all laughed at once, throwing their heads back, one of them in the rear pounding the back of the driver's seat.

The music was deafening. Frankie saw that most of the people on the lawn had turned, too, turned to follow the slow cruise of the car along the driveway. It came to the end of the driveway and pulled out onto the dirt road, headed back the way it had come, and the music slowly faded, became mere thudding again, and was gone.

"Ah, youth!" one of the parents in her group said loudly, and several people within earshot laughed.

Just as Frankie was turning away from this group to move up to the porch, thinking that she'd get some more punch, she noticed a man standing a few feet away from her, with a camera. A camera trained on her.

Without thinking, she put her hand up to shield her face. In response, he instantly lowered the camera. He was about her age, with dark, curly hair, a blue work shirt, and jeans. She thought of her mother, of her being offended by those who wore jeans to the tea.

"Sorry," he said. Then, stepping closer, his voice lowered: "Are you a fugitive from justice?" He had an odd voice—hoarse, scratchy.

"I don't know why I did that," Frankie said. "I'm not. A fugitive from justice. Are you . . . a representative of justice?"

"Nope. I'm a loyal member of the fourth estate," he said.

"The fourth estate is not the clergy, I'm thinking."

He shook his head. "Press. Vile, scandalmongering, left wing, elitist, et cetera." He stepped even closer, his eyes steady on Frankie. "Bud," he said, holding his hand out.

"Bud is your name?"

"Yeah." Frankie shook hands with him. His grip was a little too firm. He was taller than she was. Quite a tall man, then. She was actually looking up at him, something she wasn't used to. His face, too, was big, almost doughy, with a pugilist's chin. His brown eyes were creased at the corners, amused-looking, and his hair, she saw now, was flecked with gray.

"Bud what?"

"Bud Jacobs."

"I'm Frankie."

"Frankie?"

"Short for Francesca. My father's mother was Italian. I'm named after her. Frankie Rowley," she said. "But I don't remember you. Are you new in town?"

No, actually, he explained, he'd been here for a couple of years. He'd bought the *Pomeroy Union*, the local weekly paper. "I'm embedded, as it were. Reporting back on the action"—he smiled—"as it *explodes* all around me."

Frankie looked around at the clusters of milling people, some already leaving, but other cars only now pulling up. There was a group of children running back and forth on the porch, screaming. "How would you write up this particular explosion?" she asked.

"Who came, of course. They all like to see their name in the paper. That's my bread and butter." He shrugged. "Who was visiting. And I always keep my eye out for the unforeseen event." He arched his eyebrows. "The spiked punch," he said dramatically in his whispery voice. "The marijuana-laced brownie. The lovers' quarrel." He paused. Then, dramatically: "The knife fight."

"Yeah, yeah," Frankie said, smiling at him.

"So, you? What shall I say about you?"

"'Visiting from Kenya, where she does all manner of noble stuff, was Frankie Rowley, the oldest child of Alfie and Sylvia Rowley,' ba-da, ba-da, ba-da."

"Kenya!" He was surprised.

But people usually were, and Frankie recognized the familiar pulse of pleasure she felt in his response, and then another quick pulse of something like embarrassment at feeling that yet again. *Grow up.*

She shrugged. "I'm an aid worker," she said.

"Aha. And how long have you been doing that?"

"About fifteen years now."

"Oh! A long time, then," he said. More surprise.

"Yeah," she said. "But it seems shorter. And then again, longer, too."

"Like so much of life," Bud said. There was a moment of silence, just long enough to make Frankie feel awkward. Then he said, "So. Duration of stay?" He held up an imaginary pad, a nonexistent pen.

"Unclear."

"Ah. Because?"

"Because . . . of burnout, let's say. Brownout, anyway."

He smiled. "By coincidence, the same reason I'm here."

"In your case, burnout with . . . ?"

"Oh, with real life, I suppose. At least as a newsperson encounters it."

Frankie looked around again. One of the parents, a mother, was dealing with the kids on the porch now. You could hear the sharp words springing out of her mouth as she bent toward them: "*Never . . . cannot . . . Right now!*" They stood silent, looking up at her, scared, resentful.

"Little risk of that with this crowd," Frankie said.

"Oh, I don't know," he said. "Anyway, I'm here to test that notion."

"And so far?"

"So far, real life knocks from time to time." He nodded. "Yes, even here."

"As in?"

"Births. Deaths. Illness." He shrugged again. He smiled at Frankie. "Zoning often does the trick. There's nothing like zoning for passion." He shook his head. "Zoning: *real life.*"

Frankie laughed.

"A big fire the other night," he offered. "That was pretty real."

"Oh, I heard about it." She thought again about the faraway, mechanical call, the smell of smoke in the dark. "Were you there?"

"Yeah, I went. I have a pager for the fire department calls. Fires, accidents, the proverbial cat in the proverbial tree, the dog fallen through the ice, et cetera. But I missed most of this one. We all did. It was pretty much over, I think, before a call even went in. All the guys could do was try to be sure it didn't jump to the trees."

"So, essentially, a bunch of men standing around watching a bonfire."

"Well, yes. And squirting their hoses on it." He nodded. "As men will." A little silence fell again. "It's sad though," he said. "It was a fine old house."

"So they can't rebuild it?"

"Have you *seen* it?"

"No." Frankie shook her head.

"There's just nothing there. Nothing much. The chimney. A stove. I'm going to head over there after this, to get some daylight photos. If you want to come along, you can take a look." He made a moue. "A look at what's *not* there."

"I am curious, I confess. I'd like to see it."

"Okay, it's a deal. I'll find you when I'm leaving." He turned, his hand on his camera again.

"But Bud . . ."

He stopped, looking back.

"I wonder, would you be willing to drop me off at home afterward?"

"Home," he said. "Your parents' home?"

"Yeah. Mine, too, for the moment."

"That's right there on Carson Road, too, isn't it?"

"Yeah."

"Easy enough, then. I'll be happy to, madam," he said, bowing his head, then moving away.

Frankie moved, too, back to one of the shifting groups.

By the time she saw Bud coming toward her again, the lawn was even more crowded with people and alive with conversation, and she was experiencing a sweeping sense of exhaustion—she would have gone with him no matter what, she thought, just because he was leaving before her parents were going to. She excused herself to Bud for a moment and went to find them. They were sitting up on the porch, along with several other couples, in the rockers. She bent over her mother's chair from behind, touching her shoulder, and told her that Bud, *this guy*—she waved behind herself vaguely—would take her home after they stopped to look at the fire at the Kershaws'. Her mother raised her eyebrows, and Frankie said, "I'm just a zombie at this point. I've got to get back as soon as I can."

"Fine, then," her mother said. "We'll be along in a while."

Frankie and Bud walked down the lawn together, and then along the row of parked cars, until they came to one he gestured at. "Here we are," he said. It was an old Saab, dented and rusty. He opened the door for her, and she got in, sinking gratefully into the passenger seat. It had an old-car smell. Not unpleasant, but funky. She noted that the fabric was worn away on the driver's seat and, when he swung himself in behind the wheel, she noted again how tall he was, how large. He started the engine. It made an almost comical amount of noise. She saw a few people at the edge of the lawn turned to watch them as they drove away.

"How did you do?" he said after a moment. She must have looked puzzled, because he explained: "The social whirl. Remembering people."

"Oh. Fine," she said. "They're all more or less *imprinted* on me. I probably couldn't forget them if I wanted to."

"So, what we learn from this is that you *can* go home again?"

"Well, this isn't quite home, of course."

"Africa is home." This was both a statement and a question.

"Mmmh," she said. "Also not quite." They were starting down the long, slow series of hills into the town. Bud had the car in low gear, and it whined steadily.

"Where is, then?" he asked.

She was quiet for a moment, feeling the emptiness of her fatigue, and, beyond that, a kind of general emptiness. "Damned if I know," she said. She looked at him. "Through no particular intention of my own, I seem to have succeeded at making myself a functionally homeless person."

"Hmm," he said. "I know that feeling, I think." The expression on his face seemed gently rueful to Frankie.

After a minute, she asked, "Don't you feel at home here? You've been here, what?"

"Three years now. I'm working on it." He laughed, quickly. "I'm discovering I feel more at home in the summer, in some ways, with the summer people. But I get what that's about. They're transient, and maybe I am, too. Or at least I'm seen that way."

"Wait a minute—*they* don't think of themselves as transient. The summer people. They are *permanent* summer people."

"Well, sure." He smiled over at her and then looked back at the road.

"But I think it's possible that the permanent *winter* people think of them as transient. In any case, they still think of me that way, I'm pretty sure."

"Well, if they think of me at all, they probably think of me that way, too." She lifted her hands. "Why not? I do."

"But where did you actually grow up?"

"Oh, all over the place. My father, Alfie . . ." She stopped and looked over at him. "Do you know my parents?"

"I've met them. Can't claim to know them, but I know who they are."

"Well, anyway, Alfie was making his way in the academic world all through my childhood." She smiled. "Mostly sideways, it must be said."

"So, how many places?"

"Five? Six? Something like that. He took a while to find his . . . niche, as it were."

"That must have been hard." When she didn't answer after a moment, he turned his head to look at her. "Or was it?"

"I don't know." And then she was remembering. "Actually, for a while, I think my sister and I thought it was a privilege, we thought it was exciting. Something other kids didn't get to do. All these fresh starts. Another chance to be a great success at . . . whatever."

"That's a nice spin to put on it. On . . . transience."

"Yeah. My mother's spin, I think. At *that* time." Frankie was thinking of her mother's irritation with her father later, of the sarcasm that had slowly taken over her tone. When had that happened? "At some point, it seems clear, it started to piss her off that he couldn't make a go of it anywhere. Until finally he sort of did. But early on I remember her—or I think I remember her—as insistent on his valor." She straightened up and made a fist. "His *value*. His *worth*."

"Hmm," he said.

After a moment, Frankie said, "Here's an example: Once I asked her what class we were. We must have been studying something about it in school. Or maybe I read the phrases somewhere. Upper class, middle class. Anyway, she said to me something like, 'Class has no relevance to our lives.'" And then Frankie changed her voice, made it fluty, definitely upper class. "'*Your father is an intellectual.*'"

Even as he laughed, lightly, hoarsely, Frankie felt a vague embarrassment. She had parlayed this anecdote widely in the African world she'd inhabited, where it was risible, fantasy, to imagine you could escape the insistence of history, economics, tribe, race, class. "Anyway," she said, "right now, I'd settle for anyplace with a bed, I'm so jet-lagged."

"Oh." He looked over again. "You *just* got here."

"Yeah. Two days ago, in fact."

"Do you want me just to take you home then? To your parents'?"

"No, I'm interested in this, actually. Curious, I guess."

"Okay. I'll be quick. I only need the one good shot. Then I'll take you home." He smiled at her. "Or whatever you call it."

She leaned back. There was a comfortable silence between them as they swung off the paved road onto dirt. At least she felt it as comfortable. She was watching the patchy sunlight moving through the thick trees they were passing as the car mounted the hill. Her window was open. The fresh air was blowing her hair back from her face. She shook her head and thought suddenly of the Muslim girls on the ferry from Lamu.

They had passed the turnoff to Liz and Clark's little house in the field and to her parents' house. About three-quarters of a mile beyond that, they turned in at the Kershaws' driveway. And then she smelled it. The fire. It was different from the kinder, more melancholic smell of two nights ago. It smelled scorched, and dampness was a part of the odor—something to do with all the water that had been poured on it, no doubt. The driveway was narrow and overhung. The trees on her side almost touched her arm, which rested on the open window's edge.

After about a hundred feet, they came out into a clearing, a lawn. In the middle of it stood what had been the house. There were a few partially burned trees keeping vigil around it, but it was what was left in the center that Frankie was looking at. Several structural timbers still stood in the sodden rectangle that was the house's footprint and, recognizably, a refrigerator, a blackened toilet, plus some other charred lumps of what could have been appliances or furniture. Aside from those, it seemed that all that was left was the fieldstone fireplace and the brick chimney above it, which rose straight up, pointing into the blue sky overhead.

They got out of the car. The smell was almost overpowering. Wisps of smoke still rose from the thick ash piled within the border of the stone foundation. The grass around the house was flattened, sodden— footprints visible everywhere.

Bud said, "I'll just be a few minutes." He started to move around the site with the camera held in front of his face, first horizontally, then vertically. He squatted, turning his head this way and that, then he stood up, trying for the best shot he could get of the chimney.

Frankie, to her surprise, was feeling almost tearful, swept by some sense of sorrow, of loss—though she couldn't remember ever having seen the house when it was whole; though it meant nothing to her personally.

What was it then? She supposed the complete obliteration of all that must have been richly personal here, the way in which the meaning of the house, whatever that was to the Kershaws, the Olsens, had been swallowed up in the fire. She thought of her parents' house, trying to imagine it destroyed in this way, burned up. She wondered if she would feel a sense of dislocation. She had actually been discomfited to some degree, she realized now, just by the little renovation they'd done—the blandness of the guest room they'd made out of their old bedroom upstairs, the startling, somehow naked newness of the fixtures in the enlarged bathroom off the kitchen hallway. She leaned back against the car and felt again a wave of physical exhaustion.

Bud was on the other side of the black hole now, still snapping away. Frankie watched him. It was like a dance, his quick movements, his whole long body turning now this way, now that.

Then suddenly she could tell that he was photographing her again from the other side of the blackened hole. In spite of the impulse she felt to cover her face this time, too, she didn't, she looked straight at him. After a few more snaps, he moved the camera away from his face, and they stood there for a long moment. Then he called across in his strange voice, "You've had enough?"

"I think so," she said, unsure of exactly what he meant. Enough of trying to stay awake? Of looking at the house? Of looking at him?

He stood still a moment more, and then he started back around the black pit toward her.

That night, after an improvised supper, Alfie went to bed first, which gave Frankie permission, too, or so she felt, even though there was still a lingering light outside. Upstairs, she lay in her bed in the darkening room, thinking again about what had seemed like Alfie's confusion down at Liz's house, and then the way he'd seemed utterly himself when they'd gotten back home only minutes later. She thought about the tea, about the carful of boys and the discomfort they'd brought. She thought of Bud Jacobs's face on the opposite side of the burned-out house and the quick sense of sexual possibility she'd felt. That was it, wasn't it, what had passed between them? Something exciting but too familiar. Apparently the only way she had to respond to a man she liked. *Time to learn a few new tricks.*

Then she was touching herself idly, thinking of Philip. In quick sequence, images of him in Africa flashed by. His narrow face, white with fatigue under the kerosene lamp over the dining table after a long, fruitless surgery to sew up a boy's machete wound. Waking in the dark next to him at the call to prayer on Lamu and silently making love. Afterward lying still, hearing the men's voices in the street below as they greeted one another on the way to the mosque. "Ah, the varieties of religious experience," Philip had whispered to her.

It seemed like a dream. He seemed like a dream, her time with him a thing she'd invented.

She fell asleep.

In the night, she woke suddenly. At first she thought it was the moon, which fell nearly as bright as a cold, colorless daylight into the room. She'd forgotten to close the curtains.

But then, lying there, she heard it again—the same faint, insistent noise that had waked her the night before. This time she knew instantly what it was.

5

BUD WAS IN THE CAR, on the way to the fire. His pager had pulled him awake from a deep sleep, so deep that he almost fell, getting up. He was standing next to the bed, listening to the dispatcher's voice giving the location before he felt fully conscious. It was the Ludlow house, she said, out on Pliny Road, number 7, almost to Pleasant Hill. He'd stopped only to take a piss, to splash some water on his face, to pull on his jeans and shoes and a shirt he hadn't bothered to button. He was already out the door, entering the cool dark of the night, when the fire horn blew, summoning the volunteers from wherever they were.

It wasn't until he was driving through the dark quiet of the village that he became aware of how hard his heart was beating, of his own audible breathlessness filling the car. He was excited. A part of him, he realized, was actually glad, even thrilled, at the prospect of a fire waiting. He shook his head and laughed quietly, quickly. *We are all boys,* he thought, *playing with matches.*

This was only the fourth fire he'd been summoned to in the three years he'd lived in Pomeroy. Most often the calls were for accidents—highway accidents, work accidents. Falls were big business. Some indoors: down the stairs, getting out of the tub. Some outside—through the ice in winter, off ladders, out of trees. Of the earlier fires before this recent twosome, neither had been truly worthy of the name. One was small, a chimney fire, and the other was a grease fire in a dirty kitchen. Both quickly put out.

Now, as he turned into the steep driveway, he could tell that this one was a bonfire, the same story as the Kershaw place. It was essentially over, the house long gone. Even in the car, he could hear the joyous roar of the flames.

He pulled in. There were cars everywhere, six or seven already on the lawn, in the driveway, angled oddly, some with their doors hanging open. Behind him as he killed the engine, he could see the cars whose headlights had followed him on the road and into the drive pulling up, parking, too.

He got out of his car and hiked up the driveway to the house. It looked like the setting for a mad party, every window brilliantly lighted. The flames jumping into the dark sky were yellow and full and happy. Sparks exploded high upward, lighting the air like small-town fireworks, then drifted away, dying, blinking out like fireflies into the black night.

There were men running all over. Some were hooking the pumper truck to a water tank. He saw that Dan Stark was the pipeman, that Kevin O'Hara was feeding the hose to him. Behind him he heard another car pull up, and Gavin Knox, one of the kids on the fire crew—there were three or four younger guys—ran past him in his turnout gear, and then, a few paces away, stopped, looking up, taking in the sheer scope of the thing, the fact that the house *was* the fire now. Was nothing else but fire. "Fuck!" he said in awe, making two syllables of it.

Bud saw Davey Swann, the chief, moving around at the side of the house, and followed Gavin over to him. He heard the kid yell, "Where do you want me?"

"What the hell difference does it make?" Davey yelled back. He sounded furious.

Tink Snell was suddenly there now with Gavin. He was wearing his gear, too. "Just watch out, watch for a jump," Davey yelled to both of them. "Get the bladders. What the hell else is there to do?" He started to walk away.

Bud followed. "Everybody's out of the house then?" he shouted, leaning toward Davey.

He shook his head. " 'Twasn't nobody there. Nobody home. Same as the Olsens'."

They stood, stupidly, for a few moments, watching the flames rise into the sky, watching the arc of water now rising uselessly into them. "Strange, isn't it," Bud said. "The two of them, so close together."

"More than fucking strange."

Bud looked sharply at him, and he looked back levelly, furious. "Don't you write that. Don't you write I said that."

Bud nodded, and then they both turned at a noise, the noise the outer wall at the side of the house made as it disappeared. It didn't quite fall—it was more that the wall had already been eaten, was just a lace of slender supports that now suddenly vanished into the frantic light. And then the roof sagged partially into the fire and began to be eaten, too.

There was the wail of a siren. Bud turned and watched another tanker rising up the steep drive and onto the lawn, probably from Winslow, the next town over. The chief left him, jogged over to it.

For an hour or so, as the house folded piece by piece in on itself, Bud walked the perimeter taking pictures of the fire, of the men working, the ones on the hoses and the ones with the bladders—backpacks of water—who were moving around watching for sparks that landed on the floor of pine needles here, in the dry leaves there. And all the while he was thinking about these two fires, starting in the middle of the night, in the middle of the summer. Both of them in empty houses.

What caused fires? Heating, in winter. You didn't have to be home, necessarily. Bad wiring anytime, sure, whether you were home or not. But mostly, most of the time, if you wanted a fire, you had to be home. Someone had to be home. Because mostly it was people who started fires. People using crappy space heaters. People cooking carelessly, or with defective stoves or equipment. People dumping not-quite-dead coals from grills in dumb places, or leaving a fireplace unattended or a cigarette smoldering at the edge of an ashtray. A cigarette that would burn slowly down on its own, tipping out when it got low enough, tipping onto paper or wood or fabric.

People.

This house was empty. The earlier fire had been in an empty house, too.

He'd talk to Davey again tomorrow. He'd get a quote he could use—by then surely he'd be willing to speculate on the record. Everyone else would be doing it.

He realized then both what he was thinking, and that he was excited by what he was thinking. It was arson. It had to be arson.

What a story. What a break. What a fucking lucky break.

And then, suddenly ashamed of himself, he said aloud, "Asshole."

Bud had read about the *Pomeroy Union* in an article in the *Washington Post*, a good long piece about the demise of small-town papers. The *Union* was one of three papers mentioned in the story, all barely holding on. It was run by one old guy and his wife with a small group of part-time, nonprofessional reporters. The printing was done forty miles away, the distributing by the owner and some kids he paid by the hour.

Bud was living in Washington at the time, writing on politics for the *Denver Post.* He was, he would have said, happy. He liked his job, he liked Washington as a city, he still thought that Bill Clinton might be a great president. But he was restless. Was it the sense of another political season coming on, with some of the same candidates getting ready to run and some of the same old clichés already being spouted? Maybe. Was it his personal life, more or less dead since his divorce just a bit more than a year earlier?

His second divorce, actually, which had been a killer.

As opposed to the first one, which had been from his college girlfriend. She and he had, it seemed, grown easily and slowly apart, into near-siblinglike, asexual companionship. From time to time, one or the other of them would suggest *working on it*—sex—and they would try. There was expensive underwear involved, and sex toys. On the last of these occasions, Bud hadn't been able to get hard. He had apologized. "My *prick* apologizes." When they had split up, the only acrimony was about who got certain books.

No, it was the second, disastrous marriage that had undone him. She was a political consultant working on Jerry Brown's campaign. It was not quite a rebound relationship, but close enough to it for him to be dazzled and endlessly gratified by his own reliable hard-on for her. Ha! Take *that,* you unbelievers! A hard-on connected to her beauty, to her intelligence, yes, of course, and to her apparent vulnerability. Later he would wonder how it was he hadn't noticed how unhappy she was. He didn't, he supposed, because he imagined he was the cure for that.

He was not the cure. In their sixth month of marriage, angry at him because he'd been out of town for two weeks covering the primaries, she had fucked several other men, one in a bathroom at a party, the other two in the apartment she shared with Bud, bringing one home from the bar where she'd met him, beckoning the other, an old married lover, from his own home.

He was crazy with jealousy when she told him. She blamed her loneliness, her despair, her sense that he'd drifted away from her—he hadn't called for a couple of nights in a row, he'd forgotten the anniversary of their meeting. She wept, he wept. They made up, they had great sex, he vowed his attentiveness, his love.

And that was how it went, over and over. It took him a while to see the crises as manufactured, as born of a need for crisis. It took him a while to understand the pitch she needed to live at, and to come to terms with the fact that he couldn't sustain that. It took him a while to see that part of that pitch was her near-constant feeling of having been wounded, betrayed, in ways that were unbearable for her. Which required apology, penance, on his side, a reshaping of habits if not personality. Ending it took months, in part, he slowly realized, because the ending itself was thrilling to her—the drama of it. There was even a gesture at suicide.

And finally he had to walk out. He couldn't negotiate his way out of it, he couldn't persuade her of the necessity of ending it, or of anything. He just walked away, overwhelmed with sorrow and relief.

So maybe all of that was part of his restlessness. He didn't know. All he knew was that there was something about the story of these small-town papers that caught his interest—perhaps because as a teenager in a small town in Colorado, he'd always been so aware of his local paper, of how important it was in his life, in his family's life. His grandmother liked the obituaries and the social column—who was entertaining whom, serving what for lunch, with what kind of party favors, every single stunningly boring detail. His mother clipped recipes and was passionate about local politics—she'd been deputy mayor of their small town for five or six years and was always active in local affairs. Bud himself liked to read about high school sports, which were covered exhaustively. And his father, and Bud as well, actually, followed the crime reports, usually someone driving drunk or kids overturning a car or nuisance complaints—animals running free and tearing up gardens, someone partying loudly and too late.

In any case, when he read about the *Union* again almost a year later in a piece that popped up on the Internet, when he saw that it was for sale, that the guy was giving up, he got in his car and drove north. He stopped in Concord. He'd concocted a story to pay his way, a story about politically active Republicans in New Hampshire and how they felt about the next crop of likely candidates who were already periodically visiting the city. He called on the three people he was going to use, did his interviews, and got back in the car.

It had been late spring when he left Washington, the magnolias almost gone by, their blossoms brown and unattractive now, the cherries just coming into bloom, the days sometimes hot—even too hot. The farther north he went, the more he moved backward in seasons. In Concord it was early spring. By the time he got to Pomeroy, everything was sere, brown, bare—Andrew Wyeth colors, except for the intense deep green of the pines and the white patches of lingering snow here and there in the woods. Late winter.

He didn't contact the paper's owner for the first few days. Instead he drove around, looking up at the looming mountains. He walked around the three little town centers, he hiked in the muddy woods, he fell into conversation with people he met. He stopped at the café for lunch, at Snell's Country Store for gas. Then he parked and went inside.

The store was a large, low-ceilinged room, with wide aisles of grayish, unfinished wood. The shelves were stacked with packaged food and household items. The space was dim, light falling in through the dirty windows at the front. The register was just off to the side of the door in a large, alcovelike space where there were also postcard and magazine racks, a collection of videos on display, and a few shelves of mostly cheap wine. A large fan, stilled for the winter, hung from the ceiling over the register.

The man at the register, Adrian Snell, said he owned the place. He seemed happy to answer Bud's questions between ringing up customers, most of whom he obviously knew. He was a stocky, strong-looking guy, big around the middle but not fat—just solid-looking. Even his head was solid and fleshy, the back of his neck permanently a reddish tan, his jaw square, his eyes oddly pale and pretty. He had a fair amount of white hair that he clearly took pride in—it was carefully combed into a pompadour. He wore a flannel shirt, his long-sleeved undershirt visible at the neck and at the rolled-up cuffs of his shirtsleeves. He was clearly a guy who liked to talk, a solid, satisfied man.

It was a friendly town, he said. "Course, you got your different groups. Farmers, a few left. Dairy mostly, and now some vegetable farms. Hunters. Fishermen. I'm both of those myself. Summer folks. Bunch of kids come up in the seventies or so and stayed, doing organic stuff and the like." He said Bud ought to read the bulletin boards around town. One here outside the store. One next door, at the post office. One at the town hall. "Give you a flavor of things." He pointed out a pamphlet for sale in the magazine rack that would tell him the history of the place.

On Saturday afternoon, Bud sat in on a book club meeting at the library. There was one man at the meeting besides himself, and maybe ten women. The book was by Updike, one Bud hadn't read. The man liked it. Most of the women didn't. The general consensus among them was that Updike didn't like women.

"How can you say that, 'He doesn't like women'? He *loves* women." This was Dan Stark, as Bud would later come to know.

"I didn't say he didn't *love* women," Mildred Early said. "I said he didn't *like* them."

"What's the difference?"

"Oh, if you don't know the difference . . ." She swatted at the air in front of her dismissively.

On Sunday, he went to the service at the Unitarian church. Safe enough for a Jew, he figured, and he was right—nary a mention of Christ. No sign of him either—no cross, and the church windows were clear, crazed glass, letting in the gently gray light of the overcast day outside. The minister was a woman, though Bud wasn't certain of that until she opened her mouth, and her voice—lovely and light—said, "Let us pray."

Afterward, he went to the coffee hour in the church basement. You entered through a door around the side of the church, descending three or four steps. Perhaps fifteen people were there in all, standing around on the shiny linoleum floor under the unkind fluorescent lights. Bud moved around, speaking to several of them.

The woman pouring coffee or tea introduced herself as Emily Gilroy. *Coffee,* Bud said, and picked up a doughnut. "Homemade," Emily said. And then, "So nice to see a new young face."

Bud said, "Young?" and turned to look behind him.

Emily laughed. Later he'd come to know her well. She was the clerk in the town hall, someone who heard a lot of gossip about everyone in town and was willing to share almost all of it. A resource, as Bud thought of her—seemingly incapable of keeping a secret. He liked the odd woman who couldn't keep a secret.

Sunday afternoon, he went to a Little League game in the field behind the white frame grammar school and stood leaning on a chain-link fence, shivering, with a half-dozen others as the Pomeroy team lost, 14–1, mostly on walks. By the end of the game, they had run through seven pitchers, the coach was so desperate to find anyone who might, perhaps, be able just to get the ball over the plate. Some of the boys were actually called in from the bases and the outfield to give it a try. Minutes before the mercy rule was invoked and the game declared over, a light wet snow began, disappearing as it fell onto the brownish grass. The woman next to him put her head in her hands and said to no one in particular, "Just take me out and shoot me now, why don't you?"

By the end of the weekend, he'd made up his mind. He'd read through the town's history, he'd talked to people he ran into. It all seemed yeasty to him, interesting, and he had an almost immediate sense that he could *get* it. He felt he could make a life here, professionally, personally.

On Monday, before he left to go back to Washington, he went to see the owner of the paper. They sat in his office, housed on the second floor of a brick building on the town green. The first floor was a real-estate office, its space mostly unoccupied in the winter, the paper's owner said. He was tall, skinny, hawk-nosed, in his early seventies. He wore a bow tie and a pilled, stained cardigan. Bud asked about the health of the paper.

It was doing okay, Pete said. That wasn't the problem. The problem was that he'd run it for almost fifty years with his wife. After she died, a year and a half earlier, it was too much work. But also, he said, and shrugged, "Not so much fun."

Bud remembered then the picture of them together in the article in the *Post*, standing outside this building in warm weather. Laughing, he thought. When he looked it up later, he saw he was right. She was stout and shapeless, a monolith, wearing a kind of dress he didn't think they even made anymore, sprigged with flowers. Pete was saying something to her, an eager, wicked grin on his face as he leaned in toward her, and she was laughing in response—her shoulders were lifted up toward her ears, her head was thrown back, her eyes were shut. Maybe that's what had made him notice the article, Bud thought. Fun indeed, embodied.

He wasn't sure if his offer would be accepted. Pete had been asking forty grand, and Bud only had twenty, his entire savings.

But two days later, back in Washington, he had a message on his telephone answering machine. "It's Pete. Two words. You're on." He called back, and they made the arrangements. Pete would stay on for six months to help him get going. Bud would get there as soon as he could.

He gave his notice at the paper, started packing in the evenings, throwing and giving things away. He contacted a real-estate broker in New Hampshire about rentals in the area and began to say good-bye to people.

Some of whom were incredulous that he could be sacrificing what seemed a great career to go to Palookaville, as one friend called it. Greg Maloney. They were sitting in a dark, noisy bar in Georgetown drinking tequila shots among all the handsome young people in charge of the nation.

"But didn't they used to keep the Jews out up there? Remember that Rehnquist thing?" Greg pointed at him. "A different kind of covenant *there*." He had a swallow and set his glass down, hard. "How can you be going to a place like that?"

"That was Vermont," Bud said. "Rehnquist was in Vermont."

"Vermont, New Hampshire: what's the difference?"

"Look, if you didn't go to places where they used to keep the Jews out, you wouldn't go anywhere."

Greg laughed. Then he said, "Seriously. What's this about?"

"It's who I am, man." Bud lifted his hands, then cradled the shot glass again. "Where I'm from, which is easy for someone like you to forget. I like it. Small-town stuff. I liked it way back then, anyway, except I felt obliged, in some way, to want more." Bud said this casually, but as he spoke, he realized how true it was. He remembered that he had wanted to stay, to go to the community college and marry his high school girl-friend, a basketball star with ash-blond hair who regularly beat him at arm wrestling. He remembered that it was the adults around him—his parents, his teachers, his coaches—who encouraged him to "get out," as they called it. And so he had, first to Colorado State, then to Denver, then to Washington.

He tried to explain this to Greg, who'd grown up in Manhattan and didn't need to get out of anywhere.

Greg conceded this. "It's weird to think of, actually, for me. Having that kind of divide in your life."

"Oh, it's not like it's something I've thought about much, up to now. But now that it's come up, I feel a kind of . . . I don't know. *Hunger,* I guess, for it. I'm *up* for it now," he said. "The weekly pace, and making what you can of what's right around you. Plus I'm forty-four. I'd like to slow down. Just live in one place. Look hard at what's around me. Try having a home. I've been floating along on top of that notion for a long time."

Greg made a face. "Home is overrated."

"You say that because you've got one." Greg did: a tiny former coach house in Georgetown, two kids, and a long-legged, funny wife with a busy career as a personal caterer.

Bud said, "I'd like the opportunity to decide that for myself."

"But what kind of stories will you be writing?" Greg asked. "Births, deaths, graduations? Town meetings? High school sports? That stuff gets old fast."

"Not as old as riding on a bus with a bunch of stale reporters and an aspiring candidate spouting every political cliché in the book: 'We need to move this country'"—he raised his hand and brought it down hard on the bar—"'Forward!' I'll take the local level."

"Okay, so take the local level for a while. Just don't burn your bridges, is all."

But that, Bud felt, driving north towing a U-Haul trailer behind his elderly car, was what he wanted. To burn bridges. To say *no* so he could say *yes*. Isn't this the American way? The fresh start? The new beginning?

Though it was also a lot like going home, he thought, as he crossed the state line into New Hampshire.

6

"Oh! Well, it has to be arson, don't you think?"

This was Liz, always so emphatic, so sure of her opinions. She was sitting with the rest of the adults, all but her husband, Clark, on the screened porch. Clark had gone down the hill to open the house in the meadow below, to drop off the duffel bags they'd arrived with, to turn the water on. The two older children, Daphne and Chas, were upstairs, exploring—you could hear their feet thudding on the floor overhead. The littlest, Gordie, was sitting on Liz's lap in the rocking chair. His head was leaned back against her breasts, and his bare feet dangled over his mother's knees, their soles a dusty gray. They danced a little with the chair's steady, slow motion back and forth.

"I mean, two in a *row*," Liz said. "Can there be any doubt?"

"Well, and they were empty houses, too," Sylvia offered. She and Alfie had their predinner martinis, Frankie had beer in a bottle, and Liz was drinking lemonade, since she was still nursing.

Liz waved her hand. "Say no more."

"Though it doesn't make any difference to label it, does it?" Frankie asked.

"But then they can start looking for clues," Liz said. And she went on to talk about a fire at the little prep school near Northampton where she worked as an admissions officer, a fire set, they discovered, by a student who was late with a paper and wanted an excuse not to have to turn it in. "It could be something as idiotic as that."

Sylvia's chair was turned to the view of the meadow, and now in her peripheral vision she saw a moving shape and focused on it. Clark, or a glimpse of Clark through the trees on the dirt road. As the conversation went on around her, she could see him making his slow progress back on foot, parts of his figure appearing and disappearing behind the maples and the clusters of birches that drooped over the road. She was fond of this son-in-law, the genetic donor of the children's coloring: they were all silver blonds, like him.

And here came the older two, back downstairs. They stood in the porch doorway looking around. Like Gordie, they were wearing shorts and no shirt. To someone else they might have been nearly indistinguishable, these three, a mass of beautiful pale flesh and curly white hair, but Sylvia had a keen, loving sense of the differences among them.

She had been surprised by her love for her grandchildren but, more than that, surprised by their love for her. She felt an almost absurd gratitude for it—for its sweet lack of complication, and for some sense of forgiveness she found in it, which she welcomed without really seeking to understand it. Now Daphne, the oldest at five, came to stand by Sylvia's chair. Sylvia touched her bare white shoulder, so warm and smooth. "Are you liking your school so much this year?" she asked, and listened as the little girl began to talk about her day care.

When she looked up a minute or two later, she met Frankie's concentrated gaze on her and Daphne. Frankie looked away quickly.

What was she thinking? Sylvia wondered. Perhaps the wish for children herself? The sense she'd missed that opportunity? They had spoken of it a few times. Once Sylvia had asked her outright if she'd ever considered it.

"Absent the man," Frankie had said, "I'm not interested."

"So?" Sylvia asked. "What about the man?"

"Long story short: what man?" Frankie had said, and laughed.

The screen door in the kitchen slapped shut: Clark arriving. In a minute or two he appeared on the porch, carrying a bottle of beer. Like Liz, he was wearing what Sylvia thought of as their uniform—jeans and a well-worn T-shirt. Both had on thick-soled sandals. His blond hair was caught back in a ponytail, something Sylvia found unattractive on any man, even Clark, who was otherwise quite beautiful. He and Liz made an odd couple—he so large and blond, she so small and quick and dark—though her hair, cut in a short cap around her head now, was touched with white everywhere.

He went over to where Frankie was sitting, pulling one of the chairs with a reed seat between her and Alfie. He sat down and turned to his sister-in-law. He started asking her about Africa, about her work. His attention was absolute, encompassing, and Frankie leaned forward into it, her face more lively than Sylvia had seen it since she'd been home. This was Clark's gift, this affectionate attentiveness.

Sylvia turned back to Daphne, who had started to sing her a song she'd learned in school about a man who washed his face in a frying pan. As the little girl started in on the second verse, Sylvia heard Clark say, "And when do you go back?"

This is what they were all used to: Frankie would come to the country for a few weeks, be back and forth to the office in New York for a few weeks after that, and then leave again. She couldn't hear Frankie's response.

"What?" Clark said sharply.

Sylvia looked over at them.

Frankie spoke more loudly. "I don't know, this time."

"Don't know *what*?" Sylvia said. Daphne stopped singing.

Frankie looked at her. Her mouth opened, then closed with a little noise. She lifted her hands and made a helpless, embarrassed face. She said, "When I'm going back. *If* I'm going back."

There was a beat of silence. Then Liz said, "Cool. You're going to *stay*." She was grinning at Frankie.

Sylvia was suddenly aware of Alfie, shifting forward in his chair. He was watching Frankie, frowning. He cleared his throat. "But you . . . you live in Africa, don't you?" He seemed alarmed.

"I have, until now," she said.

He nodded, then smiled. "Yes. That's just what I thought." He leaned back, the discussion over for him.

Sylvia looked quickly around at the others. Liz was watching Alfie sharply, appraisingly, but Clark and Frankie hadn't seemed to notice how odd this exchange was. He'd already started to ask her questions about her decision, and she was responding.

She was dismissive. Maybe she was just a little burned out, a little overwhelmed by the never-ending quality of the suffering, by the corruption. By the way in which aid work became complicit in all that.

"But what else would you do?" Clark asked.

Frankie shrugged. "New York is a possibility, I guess," she said. "Something administrative there. Either with Hunger Relief Action or with another NGO."

"New York!" Liz said. "But that's so expensive."

Frankie lifted her hands: *What can I do?*

"You'll end up in an incredibly small apartment in some marginal neighborhood," Liz said.

"Which sounds kind of romantic, actually," Frankie said.

"That'll wear off quickly," Sylvia said drily. She turned to the others. "Frankie had a house to herself in Nairobi. She had *servants*." Sylvia had visited her once for a week and stayed in Frankie's house. It was set in a garden with a lawn encircled by five other bungalows. The whole compound was surrounded by a wall overgrown with bougainvillea, the top set with glinting razor wire.

"I had a housemaid, Mother." Frankie's gaze across the porch was level.

They had had this conversation several times before. Sylvia had been uncomfortable with the colonial aspects of Frankie's life in Africa, with the privileged white world she inhabited when she wasn't at work, with her ease instructing the people who worked for her. She had been surprised at Frankie. Disappointed in her, in some way.

"And a gardener, as I recall it," she said now to Frankie. "And a *guard*."

"But those weren't just for me. They were for the compound." There were, in fact, two guards that manned the entry gate, one during the day, one at night. Both carried AK-47s, Sylvia had been shocked to see.

"You would have had those things, too, if you'd lived there," Frankie said. Her voice was cool, clipped. She sounded almost British, which Sylvia suspected was something she could turn off and on at will. Something that was, perhaps, useful to her.

Sylvia shook her head. "I don't think I could live with someone always in the kitchen or always cleaning up after me. Much less guarding me."

"You'd love a guard if the crime rate here shot up. If *people* were getting shot up."

"*Who*'s getting shot, Mama?" Chas asked. He had come out onto the porch, too. He was looking from Frankie to Sylvia.

Liz wrinkled her nose at him, shook her head rapidly. *This is adult stuff. Nothing for you to worry about.*

Frankie persisted. Her voice was harder, actually angry now. "And I can't imagine you and Daddy, say, brush hogging the pasture yourselves."

"Mumma, *who*?" Chas persisted.

"No one, hon. It's just a turn of phrase."

"That's something you won't need to worry about once we get up here," Clark said to Sylvia. She must have looked puzzled somehow, because he explained: "Brush hogging." He was smiling at her, eager to please her, eager, perhaps, to change the subject.

But Sylvia's irritation was immense now, general. She said, "Ah, but then I'll worry about your taking work away from the locals."

"Ah, but then I'll *be* a local."

A little silence fell. Liz said, "I think I'd ask a local about that."

"Yes, I think that's a club you might have to be asked to join," Frankie said.

"Bullshit," Clark answered genially.

Sylvia was thinking abruptly of a child she'd seen earlier today when she went to the village to get some stamps. Trailing his mother into the post office, he wore a T-shirt that said, FLATLANDERS GO HOME. She said, "I wouldn't take anything for granted, Clark."

Frankie laughed, abruptly.

"What?" Sylvia said.

"Oh, you're just so . . . *contrarian* tonight," Frankie said.

Clark was nodding, smiling at Frankie. Liz grinned.

Sylvia said, "I wasn't aware of that." A lie.

Suddenly Daphne bent forward and kissed the back of Sylvia's hand where it rested on her lap, a soft, light fairy touch. Sylvia, startled, looked at her, and she looked back, smiling, showing her small, scalloped teeth.

"That's a *magic* kiss," she said.

After a quick beat of silence, Sylvia said, "Thank you," washed with love for the little girl, and with shame.

"Hey, may I have one of those kisses?" Clark asked. He was grinning across at his daughter, his delight in her game—in her very being—visible in his face.

"Yes!" Daphne answered. She threaded through the chairs around to her father. He leaned over to receive the kiss on his cheek, but she said, "No. On your *hand*."

He held his hand out, and she bent over it quickly, and then stood straight.

"Magic!" he cried. "Did it change me?"

"Yes," she said gravely.

"Into a prince?" he said.

"No, Papa! It made you *happy*."

"Oh, yeah!" He nodded. "That's just what it did. I feel it."

"And now I'll kiss Mumma." And she went to her mother and kissed her hand, and then, more shyly, Frankie's, and finally Alfie's. He seemed not to notice, Sylvia thought.

"What about Gordie and Chas?" Liz said.

"Mumma!" she objected.

"What?"

"Kids don't need magic kisses. Only a*dults* are not happy."

Frankie laughed. "From the mouths of babes."

Now Liz turned to Clark and began to tell him about the fires, two in a row, the first one so close, the second only last night. She repeated the local news her mother and Frankie had offered her earlier—that this second fire was, like the first, in an unoccupied house, the Ludlows', and that, like the fire at the Kershaws', it had essentially destroyed the place.

While they talked about all this, Sylvia was remembering the night before. The fire horn had waked her this time, though Alfie slept through it. When Sylvia got up and went into the living room, she could hear that Frankie was awake upstairs, moving around. She'd called up to her, and Frankie had come down. They'd sat together for a while, speculating about the possibility of a second fire.

Afterward, lying in bed again next to Alfie's still form, Sylvia had realized how happy she had been for that hour or so, sitting with her daughter in her pajamas in the middle of the night, talking in low tones in the light falling into the room from the kitchen. It had taken her a long time to get back to sleep—some combination of that deep pleasure and then the disturbing notion of a second fire somewhere in the town.

Now Sylvia excused herself to go to the kitchen to put supper together.

A little while later, she was moving from the kitchen to the dining room with a stack of plates in her hands when she saw Alfie walking quickly down the hall to his study. And heard Liz's voice from the porch: "Oh, for Christ's sweet sake!"

What? she thought. She went to the doorway to the porch, the plates still in her hands. What had happened? They were frozen, Clark standing, Liz and Frankie looking up at him.

And then she saw what it was: Liz was nursing Gordie. The little boy was half lying across her lap, and her T-shirt was hoisted up on the side where he was suckling. A sliver of her white breast showed, but most of it was covered by Gordie's head.

"Mea culpa," Liz said to Sylvia. Her expression was of a tired amusement. "I just forgot how much it bothers him." She turned to Clark. "Forget it, sweetie."

"Oh. Yes, Clark," Sylvia said. "You know Alfie."

"Well, Jesus, though. It's just so . . . ridiculous." But he sat back down.

"Did he *say* anything?" Sylvia asked.

"No, just upped and left," Liz said.

"But you know he's always been that way. If it's any comfort, he didn't even like it when *I* was nursing. As a matter of fact, I think he usually left the room then, too. After Frankie, I didn't try again. Bottles for Liz, poor thing."

Liz grinned. "No doubt that's why I'm so much shorter than Frankie. But we're almost done anyway, aren't you, sweetie?" she said to Gordie's still form.

She looked back up at the adults. "You know what it is," she said. Her voice was full of mischief.

"What?" Clark said.

"He doesn't like that reminder that we're all animals." She made a rooting, piggish sound, then stopped. "Well, that *women* are anyway." She smiled meanly.

Frankie laughed.

"Well, he'll have forgotten about it already," Sylvia said quickly. "Why don't you all go in and sit down? Just about everything's on the table. I'll go get him."

Liz readjusted Gordie, lifting him to a sitting position and pulling her shirt down. He looked sleepy as he slid off her lap. Frankie and Clark were standing up, and now Liz got up, too.

"That's the good news," Liz was saying. "That he will have forgotten already. The bad news is, he'll have forgotten it already."

"Liz!" Frankie said, but she was smiling.

"So he's worse?" Clark asked, his voice lowered.

Sylvia went to fetch Alfie, leaving the room before she had to hear Liz's answer.

He was at his desk, in his study, looking out at the view, at the mountains. She spoke to him softly, and he turned to her. "Dinner's ready," she said.

"Ah," he said. "Delighted."

She turned away quickly and went back toward the noise of the rest of the family. She didn't want to look at Alfie, at his bland, empty face, so unaccountable for the feelings he'd stirred up on the porch.

Always so unaccountable, she thought.

An engagement photo of Alfie and Sylvia standing in a lost garden, blowsy, blurry roses growing over an arbor behind them. Standing at least a foot apart, each looking directly into the camera, as if unaware of the other. Both of them are squinting just a bit against the bright sun.

Oh, but they are aware of each other. Both are smiling, smiling in precisely the same way—shy, secretive, sexual. The picture is charged with the connection between them, and with their wish to hide it, to keep it invisible, for themselves only.

They met the year after Sylvia finished college, when, because it seemed to her that she could become anything in the world she wanted to be, she was working at a small bar and restaurant on the South Side of Chicago as a waitress. She had done this more or less in defiance of her parents, both well-known academics and intellectuals. She wanted to claim a life as different from theirs as she could, though, as it would turn out, the next year she would apply to graduate school in English, and through the years after that, while she began to raise her family—first Frankie, an accident, then Liz—she would struggle to complete her master's degree in order to have a version, anyway, of their life. A version that turned out to be different from theirs primarily in its lack of distinction—they had plenty of that—and its marginality.

Alfie was the part-time bartender at this restaurant, while he worked the rest of the time on the first of the three master's degrees he would eventually earn. The year was 1953. He was twenty-nine. She was twenty-two. They fell in love for all the usual reasons. They were both handsome and unattached. They were working together, the kind of work that requires a sense of almost dancelike physical partnership, particularly at the busiest times of the evening, and they had the sense of dancing well together. And they liked each other's stories, though later Alfie's story was the least important part of who he was for Sylvia.

But at the time, it was completely compelling to her—it was what did the trick. He told it to her over a series of late nights in the restaurant after they'd closed up and finished shutting things down. The other waitresses, the cook, and the dishwasher would all have left, slowly putting their coats on, sometimes having a drink or two before they went. Alfie and Sylvia would try not to seem as eager as they were for the others to go. When they were finally alone, they'd sit at a table out of sight of the front window, in case the manager came by to check on things—which happened every now and then—and talk.

Or Alfie would talk, and Sylvia, rapt, would listen.

This is what she learned: that he'd grown up in upstate New York, taken in at two months as a foster child by an older Italian couple after his mother abandoned him. There were other foster children in and out of the house, some of them troubled or delinquent, but none of them stayed for more than a year. Alfie was Francesca and Antonio's forever, they made this clear to him. He felt himself marked by this, he told Sylvia. Chosen. He believed in himself because they believed in him.

And they believed he was brilliant. He was bilingual—Italian was spoken at home. He could read at three. He was a math whiz. After his junior year at the regional high school, his teachers recommended he be sent away to boarding school—he needed more than they could give him to have a chance at a scholarship to a good college. And so he went to

Hotchkiss for two more years, his first time mingling with people from a world other than his own. It made him realize, he told Sylvia, how much of what was understood to be intelligence and good breeding in American life was simply a matter of money. Money, and luck. He had to scramble to catch up with the other boys, both in his classes and socially, but by the beginning of the second semester, he had mastered this world. Talking to him, you wouldn't have been able to guess his background. Only something a little wrong here and there—the ties he chose, his shoes, and then something odd, something slightly distanced or amused, in his stance toward the other boys. It took him a longer time, he said, to get in control of these details.

After two years at prep school, he went to Harvard, a full ride, where it was much the same story. Success on success, strength to strength.

Sylvia had felt her own life so completely ordinary next to his that she barely sketched it in. She didn't stop to consider until later, much later, that this had seemed ample information to him, that he didn't press her for details the way she had pressed him—though it was clear he was taken with the ease and privilege of her background. By the family roots in New England, the academic parents who traveled and had taken her and her brothers to various communities in South America; by her summer in France with the Experiment in International Living. Taken, too, by her recklessness and carelessness about all that. Certainly her story compelled him, but he was content with the outline, the bare bones.

No, it was her feeling for all of his story, his past, that allowed their life together to happen. Her curiosity about every detail. Her belief in him and in his own version of himself. Brilliant Alfie! Who'd given the Latin oration at his graduation from Harvard, who could freely quote from Donne and T. S. Eliot, Kierkegaard and Freud, Marx and Dante. Who was an enthusiast, in contrast to her own, regretted coolness. Who was passionate, exacting in his acquisition of each universe he set out to understand.

How could he do it? Keep straight the tics of various of Dickens's characters, argue the politics of the Gilded Age or the NAACP, explain the difference between the atomic and the hydrogen bomb, care so much about all of it.

When they went to hear Schubert, Liszt, Beethoven at Orchestra Hall, Alfie would get the scores beforehand and study them. While the music played, while Sylvia struggled just to listen, not to let her mind wander—to sex, to the question of whether they would marry, to money: how they would live if they did—Alfie's attention was absolute. His fingers stirred restlessly on his legs as if with the urge to be a part of the music: to conduct, perhaps, or to play an instrument.

They went to smoky bars on the South Side of Chicago and danced to Otis Rush, Little Walter, Muddy Waters. They went to the Near North Side to hear Max Roach, Dave Brubeck, Anita O'Day. They walked along the 57th Street Beach on a rainy day and came home to make love, their flesh chilled and damp. They went to street fairs, to jazz festivals, to little art galleries, to lectures at the university, to concerts downtown, to the Compass Players at Jimmy's bar. There was nothing that Alfie didn't want to know about, to talk about—politics, poetry, comedy, music, race relations, science.

By the time Sylvia finally finished her master's degree in English, with time off to have Frankie, Alfie was well into his own second master's degree, in world religions this time. The first had been in economics. They moved to New Haven for his third master's—in history—and Sylvia started the part-time teaching that would constitute her career, working as an adjunct in various small public and private colleges.

Liz was in second grade by the time Alfie got his doctoral degree and, finally, his first full-time teaching job, at a little college in Iowa. By now Sylvia had come to understand that the restiveness, the eclecticism, of Alfie's intelligence were going to be liabilities in the academic world he wanted to inhabit. More, she saw the wide-ranging quality of his many interests as, finally, self-absorption, a sort of armor against any deep human involvement. She had come to understand how distractible he was, which she hadn't noticed at first. How he was always hurrying to the next universe to read about, to master, but never quite deeply enough. She was like her own one-person, skeptical tenure committee. What she wondered now when he launched himself into something new was *What on earth will* this *lead to? What is the* point?

He was denied tenure in Iowa, and at four other colleges he taught in for various lengths of time. But finally, after his book on Jacob Burckhardt was published by a university press, they went to the small, not very distinguished school in Connecticut, Wadsworth College, where he was granted tenure and where they lived until his retirement.

Through all this, his relations with the girls were another source of Sylvia's disappointment and anger at him. While they were small, he was delighted by them in the odd moments his attention happened to light on one or the other, but he wasn't really interested in them in any steady way—though, of course, being Alfie, he read Piaget, Erikson, Ariès, Winnicott. And he certainly wasn't interested in any of the physical labor involved in their care. He had never changed a diaper, only rarely prepared a meal for them or helped feed them. Sylvia held herself partly to blame for this. They had had Frankie while she was still in his thrall, and she had felt then that his time, his work, were too important for him to assume any of these duties. By the time Liz came along, this had been established as their division of labor, and it seemed too late to ask for anything different.

When the children began to have interests in the wider world, though, they commanded his focused attention, and each of them flowered under it. Sylvia could watch it, feel it happen—their turn away from her to him. She, who'd been overwhelmed by the work and responsibility of raising them on their erratic income while she also tried to have a work life of her own, she who'd managed all their moving around, she who'd changed their diapers, bathed them, fed them, read to them, sat up with them at night when they were ill or frightened, helped them with times tables, phonetics, costumes for school plays, who'd gone to field-hockey games, soccer matches, swim meets, theatrical productions, recitals—she began to fade into mere backdrop in their lives. While Alfie—brilliant Alfie!—stepped forward, center stage, to engage and dazzle them, as he'd once dazzled her.

She understood the way she seemed next to Alfie: fretful, rigid, concerned with things they thought were of no real importance—money, deadlines, laundry, their SAT scores, their grades, groceries, getting things fixed around the house—who would choose these for preoccupations? Certainly Sylvia hadn't. But they were things that had to be attended to, that someone needed to be responsible for.

She was bitter about all this, she knew that. Jealous in some way, she supposed—an easy, hateful emotion she struggled with. She tried not to let it creep into her daily life, into her interactions with all of them, but she could hear herself sometimes—impatient and demanding, occasionally contemptuous—and she felt a dislike for herself more intense than anything she sometimes felt for Alfie.

It was in these years that she thought of leaving him. It was beginning to happen all around them—in Alfie's department, in their church: the separations, the divorces, the messy rearrangements of the marriages and friendships of couples their age. Even on their street in Connecticut there were two couples who had, in essence, swapped spouses. It took Sylvia several months to get straight which new couple was living in which house, with which children.

She wasn't sure whether she ever would have done it—left Alfie—and it didn't matter in the end, because at about that time Sylvia's mother died, of cancer. Her father had died several years earlier, so now a modest inheritance came to Sylvia and, more important, the house in New Hampshire, a house she loved, as she'd loved her grandparents, who had seemed, more than her parents ever had, to own it—and also, more than her parents had, to love her. Sometimes even now when she looked around, when she touched things, she felt their presence, particularly her grandmother's.

But mostly the house arrived in her life as a place where she could be alone, free of Alfie and whatever his current distraction or passion was. And it seemed this solitude was what she had needed all along. She'd go up and stay by herself for a weekend, occasionally a week, and return feeling glad to see him, ready for his energy to rescue her again, as it had when she was younger and unsure of her own direction. More occasionally Alfie used it as a scholarly retreat, a place to work, which left her alone. And this was enough, this and her work and her friendships, to restore her to a sense of herself.

After a noisy dinner, dominated by the children's conversation, by Alfie's discussion of various books he was reading and his explanation of the

Harper Prize, Frankie started to shoo everyone out of the kitchen so she could do the dishes. Clark said Liz should stay up for a while to visit with Frankie—he'd unpack at their house and get the children ready for bed. Sylvia persuaded Alfie to join her in walking down the hill with him and the children.

She and Daphne walked slowly behind the others. Clark and Alfie were talking up ahead. Clark had Gordie on his shoulders, and Chas was running in circles around them, exploring things on one side of the road or the other.

Down below, they looked at the state of the house, and Clark explained what he planned to do while he was here this time. As he began to run a bath for the children, they said good night and started up the road together.

They were silent as they walked. Sylvia was thinking back over the events of the evening—feeling again her joy in her grandchildren, her private pleasure in her own children. Remembering, with a pinch of shame, how things had played out with them tonight, her tiresome public resistance to them. Yes: her contrariness. For this, too, she knew, she somehow held Alfie accountable, fair or not: surely she wouldn't be as she was if he had not been as he was, would she?

Now, as they walked slowly back up the hill, she was remembering the walks she and Alfie and the girls had taken many summer nights after dinner, before the evening activities started—those mild summer vacation activities: reading or doing a puzzle or playing a board game.

On the walks, Liz usually ran ahead, as Chas had tonight, but Frankie would often lag behind to walk with Sylvia and Alfie and sometimes try to join in their conversation. Thinking about it now, Sylvia felt sad at how irritated she had often been with Frankie—with her clinginess, her wish to please, particularly her wish to please Alfie.

She looked over at him now, frowning in concentration, as if he saw something that commanded his attention on the dirt in front of him. Or perhaps he, too, was thinking of all that had happened this evening.

More likely something he'd read, or whatever he'd been talking about with Clark on the walk down.

In the old days, Alfie wouldn't have allowed the silence that had fallen between them. Neither of them had spoken since they left Clark's house, and more and more now this was how they lived—side by side, silently.

She could feel the low sun warm on her back. Their long shadows moved ahead of them on the dusty brown road.

And then she noticed that he was walking oddly, jerking his leg and arm on almost every step. She watched him. Was it some sort of little seizure, perhaps? Should she say anything?

"What are you kicking at, Alfie?"

"The dog." He sounded angry.

"What dog?"

"The goddamn dog." He kicked, swatted out with his hand, and his shadow moved convulsively.

She was without a response, confused. By what?

Everything.

His tone! When had Alfie ever used that tone? She watched him, she watched his shadow's convulsive movements.

And then she understood, abruptly, that that was what he was irritated at—his shadow. His shadow: the imaginary dog. Who leaped away every time he threatened.

She was so shocked she didn't know what to say.

They walked on, Alfie lurching, grunting, Sylvia stunned to silence, until finally they arrived at the shadow of the stand of white birches at the end of the driveway and their own shadows were swallowed by the larger one of the trees. Alfie calmed down almost instantly. She could feel herself relax, and she realized she'd been holding herself in horrified attention.

They turned into the driveway together, and when they emerged from under the trees, they were almost facing the sun as it was about to disappear behind the ridgeline below the meadow. This meant that their shadows were behind them and to their right, invisible to Alfie. He walked calmly the rest of the way home, his face seemed at peace.

I should have said something, Sylvia was thinking. *I should have* helped *him*. But part of what she was feeling was that she hadn't *wanted* to help him. She didn't know how to, for one thing. But also she didn't want to assume responsibility for him yet again. She was tired of being responsible.

Wasn't that it?

When they came in, Liz and Frankie were sitting together in the living room. They hadn't yet turned the lights on, and the room was bled of color. There was some odd tension in the air. Liz looked up brightly at them, and said, as if warning Frankie of something, "*Here* are Daddy and Mother." There was a pause, all of them looking at one another.

"And not a moment too soon, apparently," Alfie said. Sylvia turned to stare at him. *Back,* it would seem. Back from wherever he'd been only moments before.

"I'm off to bed now, my girls," Alfie said. A faint smile played over his face. A mischievous smile. "So you can talk about me all you wish."

"Oh, Daddy," Liz said. But she was smiling.

"It's true. Feel free." He turned into the kitchen, passing Sylvia without looking at her.

She heard him say, "Why is it so goddamn *dark*?" and the light behind her came on.

Sylvia turned and went into the kitchen, too. Alfie was gone, down the hallway to his study, or maybe, as he said, to bed. She was aware of not caring which, of relief just to have him away, somewhere else, beyond her purview.

She got a glass from the cupboard. In the pantry she poured it half full of gin and took a long swallow. She went back into the kitchen and got a tray of ice from the refrigerator. As she noisily popped three or four cubes out of it, she called out to the living room, "Do you girls want wine? Anything?"

"No, nothing for me," Liz said.

"I'd have a beer," Frankie called back. "If there are any left."

Sylvia poured herself a little more gin, enough to cover the ice cubes, and got a beer out of the refrigerator for Frankie.

When she came back into the living room, Liz stood up, as if she'd been waiting for Sylvia's return. "I'm going to head down," she said. "Clark has his hands full. Plus I'm tired. Too much excitement around here for me." She came over to Sylvia, embraced her quickly, a kiss on the cheek. She turned to Frankie. "See you in the a.m.," she said.

When Liz was gone, Frankie asked Sylvia if she wanted to sit on the porch. "The sunset looks to be one of those cinematic jobs," she said.

"Yes, lovely," Sylvia said, distractedly.

And it was cinematic. The very word. Almost garish. It went on and on, the moving cumulus clouds first golden, then a flaring orange, then slowly more pink. She and Frankie were talking through all this, but peacefully, lazily. They discussed the children. Frankie thought they were beautiful, and part of that, for her, was how *fat* they were—that was the word she used. How healthy, "in that lovely American way." Her voice sounded sad, and Sylvia thought of the children Frankie worked with then, how the images of them must come to her here from time to time.

They talked about Clark's ponytail—Frankie agreed with her, voted a resounding no, which gratified Sylvia. The pink of the sky had become a fading lilac by now. As they talked on, the scattered low clouds slowly grayed, until all the heat was out of them and you suddenly noticed the sky behind them, a clean blue again, almost turquoise at the horizon, rising to a darker overhead vastness, pierced and made familiar by the stars.

Sylvia thought she was looking at the Big Dipper, but she didn't mention it. None of them but Alfie was good at identifying the constellations, and her primary weakness in this regard was her capacity to see the Big Dipper everywhere. They had fallen silent, surrounded by the night noises and the creaking of one chair or the other, the lazy clinking of ice cubes in Sylvia's glass as she lifted it or set it down. She had the impulse to apologize to Frankie, but she wasn't sure she could have named the thing she was sorry for.

But then Frankie got up to go to bed anyway. She was exhausted, she said. "Maybe by tomorrow I'll finally be in your time zone."

Sylvia sat on alone in the dark. Finally she got up. She went down the hallway into the unfresh warmth of her bedroom. As she was undressing, she had a sudden memory of an evening like this with her grandmother, during that period of real trouble with Alfie, the time when she had thought divorce might be the answer.

She had come up to New Hampshire without him. It must have been near the end of the summer, because the evening was chilly. She and her grandmother had both put jackets on to sit outside. Sylvia had had a drink then, too, one of several she'd put away over the evening. Her grandmother had noted that and had asked about it, about why she was drinking so much.

"Is it so much?" Sylvia had asked. "It feels like not *quite* enough."

"Sylvie." A gentle reproach. It was dark out by then. There was a lamp on in the far corner of the living room, but its light barely reached them on the porch.

"Oh, I just . . . can't stand myself, Gram. I'm so mean. I'm so unpleasant."

"To whom? Not to me."

"No. Not to you."

"To whom, then?"

"I suppose to the children, mostly."

"Not to Alfie?"

"No, there's no point in being unpleasant to Alfie. He's impervious." She laughed quickly, bitterly. "His *gift*."

They had sat in silence for a while, the easy silence she had with her grandmother. Maybe she'd come up just for this, Sylvia thought. To be at ease, finally.

"That's not a gift," her grandmother said at last in the dark. "It's a great failing."

"Yes," Sylvia had answered, and this suddenly seemed the truth to her. The explanation for everything.

"Do you still love him?" her grandmother asked.

Sylvia felt a wide gulf open under her. A blackness. "Yes," she said, as if she could save herself with a lie.

After a while her grandmother said, "Well, it'll be all right, then."

And Sylvia had chosen to believe her.

7

Two house fires in Pomeroy within the span of a week have raised the fears of local residents. Both occurred in the unoccupied summer residences of families who hadn't yet arrived for the season. They started in the early hours of the morning, when they were unlikely to be noticed until they'd almost totally destroyed the houses. In each case, by the time firefighters arrived, according to Pomeroy fire chief Davey Swann, there was nothing to be done but try to prevent sparks from starting fires in nearby brush or trees.

The first fire, which destroyed the summer residence of the Kershaw and Olsen families, was called in by Emily Gilroy early in the morning on July 3. The Gilroy home is a quarter mile up Carson Road from the Olsen house, in the direction of Green Pond. At about four o'clock, Emily Gilroy said, she was wakened by the smell of smoke. She got up and looked out her window. Down the hill from her house, she could see what she described as "a flickering glow" in the area where she knew the Olsen house to be. The men on duty were summoned, to no avail.

The second fire occurred in the early morning hours of July 5. This time Alice Dyer, awake in the night to tend to her newborn daughter, happened to look out a window that had a distant view of Mt. Epworth. She saw a large fire partway up the road where the Ludlow house is. Again the call went in, and again firemen arrived with little to do but try to prevent the fire's spread beyond the already engulfed house.

Fire Chief Davey Swann has called a meeting at the Town Hall for Thursday night at 7 p.m. to discuss these fires and what residents can do to prevent others. All are encouraged to attend.

———

There was none of that desultory, trickling-in stuff. When Bud drove past the town hall about ten minutes before seven, he could see that the place was already full. The double doors were flung open, and there were people still standing on the steps, moving forward slowly into the dimly lighted interior. He had to drive a long way past the low building to park—he was almost to Snell's when he found a spot in the row of cars. He walked back slowly, relishing the feel of the warm night air and the pinkish light on the hills that banked the town.

On the steps, he waited behind Ed Carter to file in. Ed was a summer resident. He had met Bud often, but he still nodded in a purely obligatory way each time he saw him, as though there could be no reason for him to want to talk to Bud, or even to remember him. He was a geezer—white haired, skinny. But an expensive geezer, with a deep tan, wearing what Bud thought of as the high-WASP uniform: green pants, loafers with no socks, a yellow Izod shirt that exposed his skinny brown arms.

Once Bud got inside, he saw that it was pretty much standing room only, the rows of folding chairs already nearly full and so many people still milling at the back that there was a kind of wall of heat and amplified voices competing with one another that you had to push your way into. He moved forward slowly through the crowd. He greeted Annie Flowers, an elderly summer person who was friendly to everyone. She was tall and boney, with yellowish teeth—a smoker, though you rarely caught her at it. "Apparently it's a form of homicide," she'd told Bud once. "So it's really not possible to practice it publicly anymore."

"Our town crier!" she said now, enthusiastically. "Look at what you've created," gesturing as expansively as she could in the crowd.

"It'd be nice to think I had that much power," he said.

"But you do! It's the power of the press."

He smiled at her. He waved to several others who'd raised their hands here and there in greeting to him—Emily Gilroy, Charley March, Shelley Edmonds. As he did, he was conscious of thinking how at home he was here, aware of taking a certain pride in it—*Look how many friends I have*—and then quickly feeling a bit foolish on account of that. He stopped to talk for a moment to Harlan Early, who was on the fire crew and said he'd give a lot for a good night's sleep. There had been another fire the night before, the third in six days. Bud had gone to watch it and had spent half the morning writing it up. Now he and Harlan speculated, as Bud had heard others doing throughout the day—at Snell's, at the café, where he'd stopped midafternoon for coffee—about the possibility of more. Of a kind of reign of arsonous terror that might be upon them.

"I don't think we're anywhere near equipped for *that*," Harlan said. "I mean, we're all just volunteers. We got day jobs we have to do."

Bud agreed and commiserated—he was tired, too—and then moved on to find a seat, making his way to the side of the hall where the windows were open onto the thick shrubs pressing against the building outside. He found a spot next to a couple of teenagers and half sat, half leaned, on the sill, surveying the noisy room. He spotted six or seven guys from the fire squad, including several of the younger ones who didn't usually come to town meetings—Gavin Knox, Tink Snell, Peter Babcock.

Many of the summer people seemed to be here. They were recognizable— the women, anyway—by a kind of gesture at stylishness in their dress. But the crowd was about evenly divided, summer, year-round. He saw two of the three farmers left in town sitting down near the front, notable in part for what wasn't stylish in their attire. One was actually wearing overalls.

Adrian and Lucy Snell were in the front row—Adrian was turned around to talk to someone in the row behind them, and Bud could hear his assertive voice over the rumble of the crowd, something about the Enrights, about the fire last night at their house. Those who knew were eager to tell. Bud suspected that half the conversations in the room involved the Enrights' fire and the implicit assertion of being *in the know* that was part of passing the news along.

Ah! Now he saw Frankie Rowley sitting with her parents near the back. Her hair was redder than he remembered, and she had pinned it up. Good luck with that—loops of it had escaped and were draped against her neck. Draped prettily, he noted. He watched her, hoping she might look his way, hoping he could catch her eye and wave. Something. Anything. He'd thought of her several times in the last week but had done nothing about it. He wasn't sure if he would. It hadn't sounded as if she'd be around very long. Though that had its attractions, too.

A guy her age was next to her, a long-haired guy in a T-shirt. A boyfriend? Somehow this didn't seem likely—a vibe he'd gotten from her—though now they leaned together talking, smiling at each other. Maybe that vibe had been imaginary, Buddie boy. Projection.

At five past the hour, Davey Swann got up from the first row and went to the lectern at the front of the low stage. Bud felt a pang for him. He knew Davey wasn't comfortable with public speaking. Even with a small group, like one of the monthly meetings of the firefighters that Bud had attended a few times, he always seemed embarrassed, no matter how routine the agenda was. Tonight he had apparently made notes: he set a little sheaf of paper down on the lectern in front of him. He'd dressed up a bit, too—a white shirt, a tie—and it gave him an undertaker's air. He had a long, thin face, a wispy mustache. He looked small and over-whelmed. He introduced himself and then announced quickly in his gentle, high-pitched voice what Bud and probably two-thirds of the others sitting there already knew—that there'd been another fire beyond the two reported in the town paper.

There was a collective gasp among the few who hadn't heard this news yet, and then a low buzz of conversation here and there as they took it in, as they, too, speculated on what it meant. It quieted as Davey went on to explain it: the Enrights' place. Pretty much totaled, like the others. He said that in any case three fires were three too many. Someone in back yelled, "Louder!"

Davey cleared his throat, raised his voice. "We're . . . concerned, I guess you could say, about this. We've asked for the state arson investigators to come in and have a good look around."

There was another stir in the room—at someone's saying the word *arson* in an official capacity, Bud assumed—and Davey looked up. His eyes moved around the room quickly. "Don't anybody get worked up about this though. This is . . . precautionary, just to be sure."

He drew a deep breath. "Meantime—" he started, but someone in the crowd called out, "Why's the state coming in? Why don't *you* guys have a look around?"

Davey was stopped, momentarily. He nodded a few times, as if to say, *Okay, that's fair.* Then he said, "Well, the thing is, we don't one of us volunteers know a thing about arson. Our job is just to fight fires, to put them out. These state guys, they know what signs to look for. How to say where it started, for instance. If there were accelerants used, that type of thing. That's something you need training for, and our training is just to be firefighters, EMTs, that kind of thing." He made an apologetic gesture, a lifting of his hands. Then he cleared his throat again. "But what I want to suggest in the meantime is that you think about alarm systems, all of you, the kind that get tied into your smoke detectors. That way, the way it works, as soon as anything starts up, the smoke detectors trigger the alarm, and the alarm would go in to the alarm company, and then they'd call us. Just precautionary, but, for instance, in these three fires, if we coulda had that kind of heads-up, we coulda put them out before they did all the damage they did."

Someone's hand was up.

"Samuel," Davey said.

Samuel Weed stood up, tall, tweedy, a great mop of white hair. Distinguished. A fine poet, or so they said. "Speaking of this alarm system," he rumbled now. "How much would such a thing cost?"

"I wouldn't know."

"Meaning, you don't have one," Samuel said. He seemed amused by this as he sat down.

Davey sighed. "I live in town, Samuel. It's different when you're out a way like you are. If I was you, I'd get one. I'm just saying that if these three houses had had such a system, they might still be standing. Or partially standing." His mouth tightened. "More of them than is now, anyway."

Annie Flowers rose slowly, more or less *unfolding* herself to her full height. In her gentle, cultivated voice, she asked, "But why would *anyone* be deliberately burning houses? It makes no sense." She looked around for an answer.

After a few seconds, when no one else had responded, Davey said, "Well, I guess you could say arson makes no sense. Unless there's some motive like insurance?"

"Well," Annie said.

"Are you suggesting the Olsens or the Ludlows set their own houses on fire?" This was Ed Carter.

"I'm not in the business of suggesting anything," Davey said. "I'm saying it's a common motivation." He gestured. "Bob," he said.

Bob Bigelow stood in the third row and turned sideways so that the largest possible number of people could hear him. "Not to say I'm an expert or anything, but I believe there are pathologies that result in arsonous behavior. Theoretically anyway. That it's not necessarily something that does make sense to other people. My understanding is that it's a compulsion, the expression of deep-seated psychological disturbances."

Adrian Snell had turned to see Bob behind him. Now, without standing, he said, "Okay, there's that explanation." His voice boomed. "But there's insurance, too. I bet half of arson fires are insurance fires."

Davey said that it hadn't been established that any of the fires were arson.

There was a silence. No one else stood up.

"So that's what we're doing," Davey said. You could hear the relief in his voice, Bud thought—it was almost over, his stint. "We're calling in the state arson squad. Plus, we're going to have us a kind of skeleton crew at the fire station twenty-four-seven until we're clear what this is. And Bob, Bob Bigelow"—he gestured—"is organizing a rotating night watch, with a group of men who've volunteered. Three men a night, just driving around in a couple of shifts. Since he's putting this together, we'll let him talk."

Talk he did, for more than ten minutes, ignoring the various hands that had gone up almost immediately. *There are people who love a meeting,* Bud thought, and Bob was one. Though he was a kind man, Bud knew. And he sometimes wrote a thoroughly researched piece for the paper, usually a discussion of local flora or fauna—bird sightings, the location of certain rare mushrooms. Now he explained in detail how he and several others had come up with this proposal, and asked for volunteers to sign up after the meeting.

Others followed him. Louise Hinton was starting a list of rental possibilities for those whose homes had burned, so they wouldn't miss the summer up here. Jay McMahon needed volunteers to clear the burn sites once the arson squad was done—haul away the debris and charred timber. The town was making the garbage truck available for free, and there was a call for more volunteers.

There was an overelaborated discussion of timing and logistics for these efforts. Someone objected to the private use of the garbage truck, and there was a prolonged discussion of that and how it might affect the town budget.

Bud had been taking notes throughout all this—he was planning to use them for an article that would appear in next week's paper—but at some point, he stopped. He looked around slowly. What was going on here? He was struck by the imbalance: the people talking, the people taking over the meeting, were summer people. It was true that a couple of the year-round residents had called out a question or two, but the others who'd stood, who'd asked questions or volunteered opinions or had their own agendas, were all summer folk or people who'd been summer folk and then retired here.

Sitting there, he thought that it was likely he hadn't seen this dynamic before because he hadn't seen this mix of the town's population before. At the town meetings, especially the big ones in March, it was only the year-round people who came, who voted. And in the summer, the events were always organized by the summer residents, for the summer residents.

This was interesting to him, this meeting, because of the kind of *deference,* he supposed you'd have to say, that the year-round people were showing to the summer people and their projects.

As he was thinking about this, he realized that his gaze had settled on Frankie. Her head was tilted to the side, she was apparently listening to Bob, who was speaking again. But then, as if she felt Bud's eyes on her, her head swung slowly in his direction and she met his gaze, still frowning in concentration, her mouth slightly open.

He raised his hand as inconspicuously as possible in greeting. Her mouth closed, she nodded and turned away. He watched as a deep redhead's blush rose from her neck and flooded her cheeks.

Davey Swann was standing up again. "No one else?" he asked, looking around. "Okay, then," he said. "I'm going to turn things over now to the police chief, Loren Spader."

Spader got up from the third or fourth row, a large man, his belly slung like a bulging sack over his low belt. He came slowly up the center aisle, giving everyone ample time to view his backside. His uniform pants were wide and low, bagging off his butt. His bald spot was clearly visible. He came to the front and looked around thoroughly, nodding at a few people, palpably more comfortable than Davey. He had no notes. He stood to the side of the lectern, resting one hand on it.

"Okay, folks," he said. "What we have here is maybe nothing. A coincidence. Or maybe just some kids, you know, a coupla pranks that got out of hand. Or maybe some kind of firebug thing that we need to be thinking about proactively. And maybe the state arson squad can answer some of these questions. But for now, here's what I think all of you should be doing. First . . ." He paused, milking the moment for all he could get from it, Bud thought. "Stay in touch with your neighbors, and be watchful for your neighbors. If you're going out for the evening, or you're going to be away, okay?" He raised his eyebrows, looked around. "Let. A. Neighbor. Know. And let these guys on the fire watch know, so they can swing by your place maybe more often. That would mean calling Bob. Right? Bob?"

Bob stood again. Yes. Yes, he'd take those calls. He supposed that the procedure would be that he'd relay this information. He gave out his phone number—various people in the audience wrote it down—and said he'd pass along any relevant information he received to the appropriate patrollers.

Loren went on. Bud was watching him, taking in what he said, but he was fixed on Frankie, his thoughts were of her, even while he was recording what Loren was saying—asking them now to leave lights on, day and night. He talked about installing floodlights with sensors outside, about leaving a car parked conspicuously, even when you weren't home.

"And here's another thing. Lock. Things. Up." He hit the lectern with his fist on each word. "At night, for example, before you go to bed, lock your doors. Lock your windows. When you go out, lock all the windows on the first floor. Lock the doors, okay? Let's take this seriously. Let's be proactive. Those are easy things to do, and you should all be doing them."

Annie Flowers stood up again. "But I have never in my *life* locked my doors, Loren. Not once, all these years, all summer."

Leonard Cott followed. "I hate to tell you, Loren, but we don't even have a lock. We just padlock the doors when we leave in the fall, and then unpadlock them when we come back in June. So there's our situation." A self-satisfied smile moved quickly over his face, and he sat down.

Summer people again, Bud thought, making notes of their comments.

The smile on Loren's face had changed in its nature, its warm condescension losing all heat. He was silent a moment, looking around with a half smile. Then he said, "Maybe you all need to make the acquaintance of a locksmith."

Someone called out, a woman's voice, "This is *not* why we come here." There was something threatening in this tonally, inflectively, as if to say, *If you can't manage this better, we* won't *come here anymore.*

Everyone heard it. The room was quiet. Loren Spader's smile had gone icy now. "This is life," he said, nodding rapidly. "Get some locks." He walked back to his seat.

After a long moment of surprised silence, Davey got up again. "Well!" he said brightly. "I guess we should adjourn, unless there's anything else." He looked around, clearly hoping there wouldn't be. And it seemed there was enough discomfort at the way the woman had spoken to Loren, and surprise at Loren's rudeness in return, that no one wanted to prolong things further. "Okay, then," Davey said. "Bob will be waiting to collect names for a night watch." He waved behind him at the table. "And Louise, too, if you've got a house you could let someone stay in for a bit. And Jay, to help with the cleanup, right?" He nodded in agreement with himself several times. "All right, then, we're adjourned."

Bud sat for a moment in the window as his neighbors filed past, talking to one another, occasionally one of them greeting him in passing. Some moved forward, to sign up with one of the organizers, but most were headed for the open double doors. The night was twilit beyond them.

As he slid from the windowsill he'd been perched on, Bud could see Frankie's head above the crowd, and her swan's neck, but he was pinned in place by the crowd moving into the open aisle between the rows of seats and the windows.

And now here was Loren coming out of his row, moving toward Bud. People were giving him space, undoubtedly because he'd startled them with his rudeness. Bud fell in next to him. "That was an interesting thing to watch," he said.

"Fucking flatlanders," Loren answered, not bothering to lower his voice very much.

"Hey," Bud said. "Watch who you're confiding your deepest feelings to."

Loren raised a hand, part apology, part dismissal. "It is what it is. Still, I didn't hear you complaining about having to lock your door."

"Well, the thing is, I'll have to find my *key* first," Bud said. "I know it's in there somewhere."

Loren barked a kind of laugh. "Yeah, yeah," he said. "And good luck with those civilian patrols. We got fifty square miles of country in this town, and half the houses up some long, hilly driveway?" He shook his head. "No way they're catching anyone."

They were almost at the open doorway. Bud could feel the cool evening air.

They stepped outside. Loren raised his hand in a kind of farewell without looking at Bud again and walked away, down the steps and along the edge of the road. Bud watched him moving quickly up the road, past the clusters of chatting townspeople, to his cruiser, the only car parked on the grass of the town green. He didn't stop to speak to anyone.

Now Bud looked around for Frankie. Gone. Probably just as well. He wasn't sure what he would have said to her. He was afraid that whatever his opening, he'd come across as what he was—a guy on the prowl.

The light from the building fell on the last few groups of people still talking below him. Someone laughed loudly, and one of the groups broke up, people ambling off into the near dark in different directions, calling their echoing good-nights to one another.

Bud stood there alone for a minute or two. The air felt soft, fresh. The darkening sky was still a pale almost lilac blue at the western horizon. Behind him in the town hall, Bud could hear the clatter of people folding the chairs up, stacking them against the wall.

He should go back into the hot room and help. This was how he had come to know people in Pomeroy, how he had made himself at home here—hanging out with people, joining a reading group, attending meetings of the historical society, of the school committee, of the Pomeroy Thespian Troupe. And volunteering, first at the school, where he helped with the student paper, then at the library, where he taught a tiny journalism class in the winter months.

He had conscientiously worked at it. He had wanted it—a home. But the conversation in the town hall tonight had made that seem suddenly a contentious issue to him, as though the fires were somehow framing a question he needed to answer for himself about whose home Pomeroy was, whose experience defined it—the chatty, self-assured summer people or the observant, perhaps resentful, year-round folks. A question about who owned the town and who merely used it. Wasn't that what had been under discussion tonight in some way? Didn't it have some connection to the way the meeting had evolved?

Something along those lines anyway—he wasn't quite sure. A question that had arisen for him before, but vaguely. Not like tonight, when it seemed to have sprung so pointedly to life.

He'd have to think about it. He'd have to figure out how to come at it.

For now, he turned and went back in among his neighbors to help.

8

COMING HOME IN HER parents' car from the town meeting, Frankie was only half listening as Clark and her mother talked about the idea of arson and about which of the suggested precautions they might take. She was distracted because she had suddenly started to think of her walk on the dark road the night of the first fire. Of the car she'd seen, and the smell of smoke. Of the possible connection between the two.

Clark was talking about the riskiness of leaving their house empty, unprotected, when he and Liz went back to Massachusetts. He was so clearly worried that, on an impulse, Frankie offered to move down to their place after they were gone. She was offering for his sake and Liz's, but even as she was speaking the words, she realized how much she wanted the move, the change, for herself.

Why?

She supposed because she was feeling aimless and oppressed at her parents' house. Her indecisiveness about her life was open for comment there in a way it hadn't been before Clark's question had forced her to talk about it, and Sylvia had started to offer suggestions about her choices, clearly impatient for Frankie to make a decision one way or the other. Which was just what she had wanted the time not to have to do.

But she was feeling oppressed, too, oppressed and saddened, by the situation between her parents—her father's strange failing, something she'd seen clearly from time to time in her days living with them, and her mother's often irritated, sometimes seemingly almost frightened, monitoring of that. It made Frankie feel sorry for them both, but it wore on her, too, and a part of her simply wanted to flee.

"You're sure about this?" Clark had asked in the car.

They were in the backseat, her parents in front. Frankie had to make a conscious effort to keep the eagerness out of her voice. "Yup, it's okay. I'll do it."

"It's not exactly the Ritz, the shape it's in."

"I'm happy to. Don't worry about it."

So by the time they got home, back to her parents' house, it was decided, though over the next few days, the last days of Liz and Clark's weeklong stay, she wavered more than once, flooded with guilt about what she thought of as *leaving* Sylvia and Alfie.

Liz didn't help with this.

Frankie had had a long talk with her the night before she and Clark left. They'd had dinner together down at her house. Clark had gotten the Sheetrock up, and what had been one huge room was now three—two smaller bedrooms and the large room with the kitchen at one end and a sitting area at the other. They had eaten at the big table in the kitchen area, and afterward, Clark had offered to bathe the children so she and Liz could have some time alone.

They went outside onto the porch and sat in the butterfly chairs, inherited from Alfie and Sylvia. They could see the quick flitting of the bats in the twilight. Frankie had been waiting for this moment. For the first time she spoke directly with Liz about what she'd noticed of Alfie's odd moments of failing.

Liz was ready. She had multiple anecdotes of his earlier lapses she'd stored up. She relayed them to Frankie now, embellishing them with her dark sense of humor. She described her attempts to discuss them with Alfie himself—impossible—and with Sylvia, who was more reasonable but unwilling, or perhaps too frightened, to acknowledge that they might be really serious.

"Do you think we should be doing something?" Frankie asked.

Liz didn't know what they could do, really, but she was so glad Frankie had brought it up. "The minute you said that thing about not going back to Africa, I thought, *Yessssss!*" She made a fist and yanked it downward. *"She's staying! I won't have to do all this alone anymore."* She'd often felt overwhelmed, she told Frankie now, by the sense she had of being responsible for their parents. She said that one of the reasons for her reluctance to move to Pomeroy was that she didn't want to be Sylvia's "crutch." She was frightened of getting sucked in, she said. "But if you're here . . ."

"Well, I won't be *here*," Frankie said.

"But I mean just in the country, just in this neck of the woods. *Visiting*, for God's sake. I'll take a *visit*."

After a moment's silence, Frankie said, "Well, I don't know how much help I could ever be with Sylvia and Alfie. I mean, you know the difficulties Sylvia and I have with each other."

"Oh, you just have to learn not to take her so seriously," Liz said. "Just make her laugh at herself. She enjoys it."

"I wish I could, but that's your MO, Liz. Not mine."

A little while later, the children came out wearing T-shirts for bed, their skin pinked from their bath. They wanted Liz to come in and read to them.

Frankie got up, and they all said their good-nights. Before she left, she promised Liz she'd talk to Sylvia about all this, she'd try to get a sense of what Sylvia was thinking about Alfie, what she might be planning. When she turned at the road to look back, she saw Liz moving into the lighted doorway with the three children around her and felt an odd mixture of something like envy, something like remorse.

For much of her youth, Frankie had been jealous of Liz, who was outgoing and lively, surrounded always by a group of friends, even when they were new in a place, as they so often were. Frankie was the loner, the awkward older sister, though she usually had one friend, almost always someone as studious, as shy, as she was. Her real focus, though, was on the adults in her world—teachers, yes, but even more than that her parents, whose attention she was always in hopes of receiving and whose preoccupation with everything but her was painful.

Later she could understand this in a way she didn't at the time. After all, why should they have paid attention to someone doing so well in school? Someone so orderly, so careful? Someone who didn't complain or get in trouble? Why should they not have been more engaged with

Liz, temperamental and lively, sometimes wildly emotional, occasionally in trouble academically. Of course it would seem to a parent that Liz needed more, that Frankie needed less. The very goodness she cultivated—surely they would notice it and turn to her and praise her and conspicuously love her!—was the thing that set them free to turn to Liz. But not just to Liz, of course. Also to their work, and their colleagues and everything else that took up all their energy.

In midadolescence, though, a kind of miracle happened in Frankie's life: from one day to the next, it seemed to her, Liz became her friend—perhaps because Liz was entering her freshman year in the high school where Frankie was a senior and knew the routines. Knew, also, older boys. In any case, suddenly Frankie felt as though she belonged somewhere, in a way she hadn't before. As she and Liz drew closer over that year, she felt a sense of deep relaxation, of comfort. She was happy to put herself in her younger sister's hands, to share in the kinds of adventures Liz invented. She was aware of counting on Liz to structure their lives, which Liz was glad to do. For a short while, then, Frankie was one of the high-spirited Rowley girls, and she liked how that felt.

But then she left, she went off to college. And when she came back after her first year away, she was aware of a certain distance from the role she was playing with Liz. She saw it as a role. But she did play it again for the few weeks in May and June that she was home and, yes, enjoyed it again, even while understanding, this time around, how much more Liz enjoyed it.

By the time Frankie came back again, at the end of that summer, the summer between her freshman and sophomore years of college, her family had moved for the last time—away from Chicago to Bowman, the little city in Connecticut where they would stay for the next twenty-five years or so. Liz was sixteen, with two more years to go in high school. She would have time to grow used to this new place, to think of it as home, as Frankie's parents would. But there would be this further separation for Frankie—that she would never live there for more than a few months at a time.

She had a sense of displacement, then, from all of them and their concerns as they moved around in their new lives. Liz especially. Suddenly the kinds of adventures Liz was inventing—sneaking out, getting stoned, meeting boys at the quarry—seemed to her, in some way that was freeing, irrelevant.

Because that summer—the summer between her freshman and sophomore years of college—she had gone to Kenya for the first time, a student with a program that offered American college kids the opportunity to live in developing countries. And in Kenya, she'd felt something like a sense of *ease,* though that was not how she could have explained it then. What she said when she got back was that it had been interesting, which it was. That the people had been warm and gracious, which they were. That the terrain was the most beautiful she'd ever seen. And all of that was true. But what she didn't say, or didn't really understand until much later, was that she felt at peace there. The rules, the codes for life, that had seemed so elusive to her, even within her own family, simply didn't matter anymore. Frankie was free. Or that's what she felt.

All this had lingered uncomfortably in her relations with Liz over the years, especially as their lives turned in such different directions—Liz, with her marriage to Clark, with the children, with her surprising gift for motherhood, domesticity; Frankie to a life away, to a commitment to her work above all, to her series of lovers. Over the years, Frankie often had the feeling that Liz, as well as her parents, was waiting for her *real* life to begin—the return home, the man, the marriage, the house, the children.

Perhaps, Frankie thought, Liz saw her tentative decision not to go back as the beginning of all this. Perhaps she imagined a kind of sisterhood—*daughterhood*—they could share if Frankie stayed. If she stayed in this neck of the woods.

The next morning, Clark made a trip up in the truck to get Frankie and her bags. Sylvia came out of the house to see him off—she'd said goodbye to Liz and the children earlier. Frankie turned around to look at her as they rumbled down the driveway. She was standing alone by the back porch, looking after the truck, her hand on the knob of the door, her body turned to go back into the house, where Alfie waited for her. Her face looked as stricken as it usually did when Frankie left for Africa at the end of a home stay.

At Clark and Liz's house, they unloaded Frankie's possessions. Then Clark slung the two old duffel bags he and Liz had arrived with up into the truck bed. The kids had come out when they heard the truck return, and now they clambered up into the wide front seat and the jumper seat behind it. After hugging Frankie, Liz pulled herself up, too, and they drove off, yelling, waving. Frankie waved back until the truck turned onto the road. She stood there on the porch until she couldn't hear the noise of the engine anymore.

In the silence, the very air felt stilled, quieted. She went into the house. Inside it was cool and dim—the grayish tone of the Sheetrock Clark had put up absorbed the light. The heads of the screws and the seams between the panels were still exposed. This was going to be her project, covering them. She had insisted on this, to pay them back, she'd said, for letting her stay. A little bit each day, she told herself now, and maybe by fall—would she still be here in the fall?—it would be done. She stood there in the kitchen, momentarily immobilized. And relieved, she realized. Relieved to be alone. Relieved to have a place of her own—for a while, anyway.

The secondhand refrigerator made a low gurgle and rattled, a bit like someone clearing his throat, then turned itself off. The propane for it and for the stove hung on an outside wall. Clark had told her that he'd gotten the tank at Snell's, that she'd have to take it in and exchange it when it was empty.

She started to move around slowly, looking at things, touching things. Six old chairs were arranged unevenly around the big dining table, whose top was round and scarred and streaked with Magic Marker colors. In the middle of the table was a bird's nest. It had a worn piece of blue ribbon woven into it. When Frankie touched it, a bit of dirt crumbled out onto the table.

At the other end of the long main room, two wicker chairs sat companionably by the woodstove, their faded blue cushions flattened by long use. There was a worn trunk set between them, and on this were little heaps of other things the children must have found and held dear: a pile of acorns, some drying flowers, a greenish glass bottle, a heap of smooth, white stones. The whole place smelled of the lumber Clark had built it with, a smell both fresh and slightly chemical.

Frankie rolled her big suitcase into Liz and Clark's room. The only furniture in here was a mattress on the floor and a cast-off bureau from Alfie and Sylvia's house, repainted now a bright, pale turquoise. Frankie saw that Liz had left a set of sheets and a faded quilt on the bed. Crawling around on top of it awkwardly, she made it up for herself. Then she unpacked her suitcase for the second time in this visit home, putting her summer clothes away in the drawers Liz had cleared out for her in the dresser, leaving the few cold-weather things at the bottom of the suitcase and rolling it into the closet.

When she was done, she went outside with a pair of scissors to cut some meadow flowers—purplish joe-pye weed, blue cornflowers, the flat, delicate fretwork of Queen Anne's lace. A hawk circled high above in the cloudless blue sky, tilting now this way, now that, riding the currents of air, watching the field for a motion smaller than hers. She had a sense of timelessness then, something like déjà vu. She *belonged* here, she felt suddenly, moving in this familiar field, cutting the flowers that had grown here, wild, for a century.

The sun was hot on her head and shoulders as she walked through the tall grasses, snipping. She was glad to come back into the cool of the house once she had a sizable bouquet. She ran some tap water into one of Liz's clear-glass Mason jars and arranged the flowers in it. She set the jar and its drooping bouquet on the trunk by the chairs. She went into the bedroom and got the book she'd borrowed from her parents' shelves—*The Portrait of a Lady*. She sat in one of the chairs and started to read. She heard the refrigerator grumble back on, she heard the sawing of the crickets in the heat outside. Slowly she lost herself in the words about another kind of countryside—tamed, green, shadowy. About another kind of expatriate.

The next day dawned sunny and bright again. Frankie woke on the mattress on the floor with the light streaming in. The window was open, and the manic early-morning energy of the birds was startlingly loud. She lay there for a while, taking pleasure in looking at the room from this angle—the expanses of gray Sheetrock, the old bureau, immense from down here. The world she could see outside the windows from her vantage—treetops, sky—was blue, green, white. Finally she rolled over and stood up to begin the day, her first day alone in America.

She made some coffee and scrounged a breakfast from what Liz and Clark had left—granola and an apple, the last one left in a bowl Liz had kept on the counter in the kitchen. She would have to go to town for supplies today, which would mean borrowing her parents' car. She sat in the shade of the porch to eat.

When she was through, she went inside and surveyed the shelves and the refrigerator to get an idea of what she'd need. She made a list. She'd go to Snell's, she decided. She knew everything cost more there, but she wasn't sure she was ready for the supermarket. Snell's was small, familiar, manageable—a baby step. And then she'd go to the library. There were no books at Liz's house except a few for the children, and there was no television. If she was to be solitary, she would need a regular supply of books.

She got herself ready for town. Then she took the meadow route up to her parents' house, circling the pond slowly, watching the frogs jumping in. The ripples lapped outward from their entry points, lifting the algal smell into the warm, still air. She'd been swimming regularly this past week, sometimes with Clark and Liz and the children. They'd all worked on the algae with the big net, but it seemed a never-ending task.

Her mother came to the kitchen door, alone. She was dressed, wearing one of her men's shirts and blue jeans, but her white hair was still disorderly, and her face was drawn, her eyes deeply shadowed. Alfie was still asleep, she said in a low, whispery voice. And yes, it was all right to borrow the car—she had nothing particular planned for the day.

Suddenly Frankie was imagining her mother's day, the void, the *nothing particular*. Except, for Alfie, the very particular Alfie. She felt a surge of sympathy for Sylvia.

Her mother had turned away and sat down at the kitchen table. She was writing a list of a few things she wanted Frankie to pick up for her.

"Can you read this?" she said, handing her list to Frankie, her large, clear, almost-printed writing.

"Yes," Frankie said. Sylvia gestured at the keys, on a hook by the door, and Frankie lifted them on her way out.

She drove down the long, swooping hills, coasting much of the way to Snell's. At the last minute, though, she decided she'd go to the farm stand first.

It was about fifteen miles away, some on the two-lane, some back on a dirt road for a stretch. There were only two other cars parked outside the stand—it was still early. The double doors to the shedlike structure were thrown open. Pastel phlox and bright daylilies stood in galvanized buckets in a row by the door. Inside, the vegetables and fruits were set out in mismatched baskets on the counters and tables. The place smelled wonderfully of dirt and basil and the sweetness of the pies the owners baked and sold.

The only tomatoes they had were hothouse, hard as apples, so Frankie chose cherry tomatoes. She put garlic into her basket, too, and lettuce, and onions and potatoes. She brought all this to the table with the cash register, and the weather-worn youngish woman with lean, ropy arms emerging from her T-shirt helped her unpack it. She rang things up and put them into a brown paper bag. Her skin was almost the same shade of brown as the bag, Frankie noted—walnut-colored and deeply creased. Frankie guessed she was about her own age. There was dirt under her fingernails. She thought about how it would be to live such a life. Gardening, running a farm stand.

This was a game she had seemed to be unable to resist playing over the last week and a half. Practically everyone she'd encountered since she arrived had raised another possibility for her. On the drive back to Pomeroy with the produce in the backseat, she considered some of the alternatives she'd briefly entertained. Could she run the town library? Could she tend gardens for the summer people? Could she teach in the local school? Work for the little publishing house Jack Churchill ran? Each had seemed briefly inviting, until the next one came along.

At Snell's she got Sylvia's items and then her own—milk, bread, more granola, coffee. She was third in line at the register, which was being run by Mrs. Snell. The woman whose groceries she was ringing up was more vaguely familiar—a summer resident, Frankie was pretty sure, judging by her clothes. Jeans, but *money* jeans, with a tailored linen blouse over them and small pearl earrings Frankie suspected were the real thing. She was buying three bottles of wine. "I thought I had wine," she said to the couple next to her, also familiar to Frankie, but not familiar enough for her to remember their names. Year-round Pomeroy people, at any rate. "And then I looked on the shelf and realized that that was in Connecticut, that I had absolutely not a drop here!" She rolled her eyes and shook her head at her own foolishness, and they and Mrs. Snell laughed with her.

But as soon as she was out the door and the waiting couple started setting out their groceries to be rung up, the woman said to Mrs. Snell with heavy sarcasm, "That must be just so awful, having *two* houses to have to keep track of."

"Lord knows *I*'ve got trouble enough with just the one," Mrs. Snell said, her hand in constant motion.

This was a nice neutrality, Frankie thought. And then she considered the Snells briefly, how neutrality was probably a necessity for them here. They would always be called on to straddle the worlds, to have allies, and probably even friends, in both camps.

When it came time to ring Frankie up, Mrs. Snell was cordial. "Now, you're Frankie, I think," she said. She was a lean, handsome woman with gray hair and dark, nearly black eyes that were so alert they almost seemed to be snapping.

Frankie said yes.

She shook her head. "It about kills me that I can remember you when you were so little." And without a break in the rhythm of sliding the groceries down the slick wooden counter with one hand and ringing them up with the other, she said, "You tell Sylvia I said hello, will you?"

By the time Frankie got back to Liz's, after picking up some library books and returning her parents' car, the day had changed, had become cloudy and cheerless. A good day to work.

She had a quick lunch, and then she changed into her oldest blue jeans and a T-shirt. She got the equipment out of the closet off the kitchen and started on her project. First she cut off a strip of the mesh Sheetrock tape. She pressed the strip down smoothly in place over one of the open seams in the living room. Clark had showed her how to do this—this and applying the joint compound.

She repeated the process with the tape over and over. When she was finished, she stood in the middle of the room and looked around at the gray walls, now striped regularly with the tape's lighter color. The effect was of some strange, muted wallpaper.

She went out to the porch and pried open one of the five-gallon buckets of joint compound sitting there. She dug into it with a putty knife, scooped up a large glop, and dropped it onto the hawk Clark had bought for this job. She liked the wet, muddy smell of the compound. Back inside the house, she began to spread the goop over the mesh and over the heads of the sunken Sheetrock screws. There was a pleasant rhythm to this, she discovered—the slapping of the goop onto the hawk she held in her left hand, the slow, careful smoothing of it onto the walls, feathering it out into nothingness with the wider taping knife.

She let her mind wander while she worked. Liz and Clark. The fires, and the question of arson. Her parents. Memories of Africa. The light-struck grasses of the savanna, with its occasional acacia tree. The hustle of Nairobi. The smell of diesel and cookstoves in the air. She thought of the little African girl who'd also been waiting in the Nairobi airport for the plane to Amsterdam ten days ago. She'd been dancing in the waiting area as though in front of an audience—well, Frankie was her audience, and the little girl knew that: she kept smiling shyly at Frankie. Her dancing was both sexual and not. That is, it would have been sexual if a sexual person were doing it, but since she wasn't, it wasn't. It seemed, simply, joyous. It made Frankie both happy and somehow sad to watch her.

Frankie had seen her again briefly in the Amsterdam airport, and she was transformed. Her skin actually seemed paler. She looked, along with her parents, tired and frightened—robbed of some aspect of herself that had been alive, had been *dancing,* in Africa. Which was, Frankie realized now, the way she felt, too. Diminished. Flattened. White.

Late in the afternoon, she stopped. Her hands and arms were aching. On the porch, she scraped the leftover compound off the hawk back into the bucket—half empty now—and then went around to the side of the house to wash off the tools under the spigot there. She felt a few drops of rain land on her bare arms and looked up. The sky was a uniform grayish white, with shreds of a darker gray wisping fast across it.

She went back in to clean herself up. She had just finished washing the little crusts of dried goop from her face and hands and arms in the bathroom when she heard slow, hesitant footsteps on the porch.

She froze. It felt as though her heart shifted in her chest. She willed her breathing to be even as she hung her towel carefully on the hook next to the sink, as she stepped into the big room. A man stood at the open door, a dark shape behind the screen. Even as she drew her breath sharply in, she recognized the shadowy outline: her father.

"Daddy!" she said, her relief caught in her voice. She stepped across the kitchen and opened the screen door to let him in. But when she stood facing him, the opened screen door at her side, he was unmoving, looking at her in what seemed like puzzlement. His appearance was a bit derelict. His shirt was unironed, and he'd missed a few spots shaving.

"Come in, come into my parlor, said the spider to the fly." She gestured theatrically. This didn't help, apparently: he did step in, but he stopped just inside the door, looking around as though he were unfamiliar with the place.

And then she thought that probably, in a sense, he was. The last time he'd seen it was before Clark got the Sheetrock up, she was pretty sure. It looked so different now that it might be confusing to him.

In any case, she kept talking, she would have said anything to keep the sense of friendly chatter going, to give him time.

Time for what?

To remember her? It was the first time this idea had occurred to her, that he might not recognize her, and it struck her how far she'd come in her thinking about her father since her arrival. The many small things she'd noticed and talked about with Liz: his absenteeism in any group larger than two, which was to say any group. His repetitive returning to the few things that compelled him—the prize he was reading for, the fires, the situation of each of his children. His confusion, his occasional *lostness*. Most of all, the way he looked a good deal of the time, the frequent deadness behind his eyes.

She got him inside, seated at the table. She got him to consent to tea. While she set the kettle on the stove, while she struck a match and lit the burner, while she lifted down the glass jar of tea bags from the open shelf, she kept up a running stream of talk. Jabber, really—just anything that came to her. What she'd been doing all day, pointing out the whitish patches of drying joint compound. The news she'd heard on the radio. The possibility of rain. He was watching her cautiously throughout, nodding sometimes.

When she came to sit with him to wait for the water to boil, there was a little silence. He was frowning at her, as though something about her was confusing or disturbing to him. He leaned forward, almost squinting. He said, "Did you . . . make me come here?"

This seemed so absurd that she couldn't help laughing. "With my magical powers, you mean?"

His eyes widened. "Do you . . . ? Are you . . . ?"

"No, no, no. I'm just teasing, Dad. I don't have any *powers*. None." He didn't look reassured, and she made her voice gentle. "Maybe you just wanted to see me," she said. "Maybe you came just for a visit."

His face relaxed. "Yes. That must have been it." He looked up at her, smiling. "Maybe I thought I'd like some tea."

"Well, let me take care of that. Easily done." She stood and busied herself setting up a little tray, poking around on the shelves and in the lower cupboards, assembling cups, saucers, milk, sugar. Two spoons, two old, faded cloth napkins from a wicker basket on one of the shelves. The teakettle whistled, and she poured water over the bags, then carried the tray to the table. Ceremoniously she set things out for him, for herself. She poured the tea and sat down. As she added the purling milk into her cup, she noted that he was putting spoonful after spoonful of sugar into his. She decided not to say anything.

As one, they raised their cups, they sipped. *Too hot*, she thought. *Goldilocks.* He set his down, too, and sat back and looked around again. Then he smiled at her. He said, "Sometimes I get . . . confused. You may have noticed."

Frankie took a deep breath, she was so surprised, so unready for this admission. But she wanted to be steady for him. She said, "I have, Dad. Yes."

"I think it's something to do with my . . . memory."

"Probably it's not quite as good as it used to be."

"Well, whose is?" He said this jauntily, cheerfully.

"So true," she said.

They were silent for a minute. She felt the air stir and looked out the windows at the dark sky over the rising meadow.

He cleared his throat, as if to call her back. "But mine is getting rapidly worse," he said.

"Yes, I think that is true." She looked back at him. In spite of his appearance, he was *there,* she could see it in his eyes.

"I think it's likely I have Alzheimer's disease," he said. "You know what that is, don't you?"

"I do."

"It was a fascinating story. I read it." He was almost smiling.

"What story?"

"Oh, one of the books. The books for the . . . the prize. The prize I'm working on."

"The Harper Prize."

"That's right. A fine book, explaining it, how the brain is slowly more or less strangled. It would seem."

She didn't know what to say. In some ways, he sounded so much like himself, interested in this new subject he wanted to master.

He had some more tea and set his cup down. "Fascinating, too, in a way, to be on the receiving end of it."

"Oh, Dad."

"No, no," he said. "No pity. You know the Larkin poem."

"I don't."

He laughed, his sudden, gentle apology of a laugh that tilted his head slightly back. "I don't either anymore, but for a few lines. 'What do they imagine, the old fools?'" He smiled. "That's me," he said. "An old fool. Larkin describes the way one thinks as one descends, the way the past and the present become confused. And dreams, in the mix. It's quite . . . true, I think." He sat for a moment, looking at nothing—the table, the teacup: the blank look returned to his face. And then he seemed to gather himself. "The last line answers the question," he said to her.

"What question?"

"'What do they imagine?'" He raised his finger, as he often did, she thought—a gesture she would remember later. "'We shall know.'"

She didn't say anything.

"Your mother and I, we can't really talk about it. But I want you to know this, that I do understand it. I know what's happening to me."

"All right."

"Sylvia and I . . ." He trailed off, and shook his head.

He looked up, out the window, where the trees were bending sideways under the sudden audible lashing of the wind. He said softly, "Odd way. To disappear."

"You're *not* disappearing."

"Oh." He raised his eyes to her. "Yes. I am. When your brain changes, you become . . . another. There's a story, in the book, about a man with a brain injury. A trauma. A sweet man, gentle. Who becomes profane. *Lewd.* This will happen more slowly to me, and doubtless in a different way. But like him, I will disappear. The consciousness I've cultivated with . . . well, with so much *vanity,* I suppose"—he lifted his chin and laughed once, lightly—"will go." He sat, looking at his hands holding his teacup.

After a moment, he said, "It raises the question, doesn't it: when a person is changing, as I am, at what point are they no longer who they were? The person . . . the person is partly the structure of the brain, it seems. So, I will be . . . someone else. I will cross a line. At some point."

"It will be a long time, Dad. You have lots of time still to be you." Her voice was flat, defiant.

"I think you're trying to make me feel better, Frankie." He smiled and looked utterly like himself. Alfie. Her father.

"Well, why wouldn't I?" she said.

"Don't." His voice was gentle.

After a moment, she said, "All right."

"What I'm trying to say to you is that it won't be me it's happening to anymore. It simply won't matter, not to me. Not to who . . . I've been, before this, all my life. And that, my dear, is a comfort to me."

"Cold comfort." She could hear the anger in her voice.

"But comfort," he said.

She reached across the table and put her hand on his. He turned his up, underneath hers, and held it. They sat that way for a moment.

Then he released her hand and sat back. They were quiet a minute more. The refrigerator kicked on with its intestinal rumble.

She felt a need to keep him talking, to turn the conversation to any-thing else, really—but to keep it going. "How is the rest of your reading? Reading for the prize?"

"Ah!" he said. And with pleasure visible in his face and audible in his voice, he launched himself. He spoke of another book he thought might be put forward and the reasons why.

When she had asked the right number of questions, when they'd fallen into a silence she was more comfortable with, she said, "Shall we walk back up together?"

"What a nice offer," he said.

"I'll just be a minute." She went into the bathroom and quickly brushed her hair, which had curled wildly in the humid air. She put on lipstick. Then she went into the bedroom to change out of her work clothes, splattered here and there with dried joint compound. She was quick: she was aware of him, waiting in the kitchen, she worried that he'd get up and leave without her. Which would be fine, except that he'd agreed to wait. And she wasn't sure he'd remember that.

But he was still sitting at the table when she emerged from the bed-room. *My sweet father,* she thought, thinking of his bravery in talking to her about his illness, of his elegance in turning then so easily—for her sake, really—back to the prize. She chose not to think, for the moment, of the various ways he'd creeped her out over the last few weeks.

He looked up at her. "I meant to tell you," he said. "There was a fire."

"I know, Dad."

"No, there was another fire. *That's* what I came here for—to tell you that."

She stood there, momentarily speechless. This had moved too quickly for her—his shift from being so present to this, now, which she assumed was old news about one of the fires she already knew of.

But then it occurred to her that there *could* have been another fire. A fourth fire. Or would it be the fifth? But there was no good way to ascertain that with him, was there? No question that would make it clear.

"That's just awful news, isn't it?" she said, hoping she sounded con-cerned enough.

"Yes, it is," he said. And got up.

Together they walked slowly up the road to the old farmhouse, chatting about the weather, about Liz's children, about the first of the wild blueberries, just ripening. A perfectly reasonable conversation. The rain started, lightly, just as they got to the back porch.

Sylvia looked up from her desk in the corner of the living room as they came in from the kitchen. Her eyes tightened, and moved quickly from one of them to the other. "Well, this is an unexpected pleasure." She set down her pen.

"I would have called, except . . ." Frankie held her hands up. "No phone."

"Was Alfie down with you?" Sylvia turned to him. "You went down to visit?" There was something sharp in her tone.

"Yes." Alfie and Frankie said it together.

Sylvia's lips pursed. "I wish you'd told me," she said, after a second or two. She looked at her watch. "Well, may I offer you a drink?" she said to Frankie. She stood up. "It's almost five. This would be on the up and up."

"I will if you'll join me."

"I certainly will. Alfie? A drink?"

"No, no. I'm going to read for a bit, I think."

"As you wish."

Frankie followed her mother into the kitchen and sat down at the small white table. She looked out at the rain, falling gently but steadily now.

Her mother got an ice tray out of the refrigerator and stood at the sink, noisily whacking the cubes out. She fixed each of them a gin and tonic with a wedge of lime. She set out a plate and put crackers on it, and a thick slice of hard cheese. She brought this over to the table and sat down opposite Frankie. She turned on the light hanging on the wall over the table. Harsh lines leaped to her face. "What a gray, unpleasant day it's turned into," she said, looking out the window. "Clark and Liz got out just in time."

Frankie thought what an odd verb choice that was: *got out.*

"What have *you* been doing all day?" Sylvia asked.

"Oh, Sheetrocking and rolling." And then, to her quizzical face, "Applying joint compound to all the Sheetrock seams and the exposed screw heads at Liz's house."

"Ah!" she said. "That doesn't sound like much fun."

"It's something to do. It makes me feel helpful, which I'm grateful for."

"Yes, I can certainly understand *that*."

"Can you?"

"Alfie's not the only one who retired, you know."

"Of course. I do know that." Though she hadn't given it much thought, her mother's work. What it might have meant to her to give it up. Somehow they'd all always seen her work as primarily utilitarian, a matter of finances—they needed the money. It was Alfie's work they talked about at the dinner table, Alfie's work that led them from one home to another. Alfie's work that was *important*. "So what do you imagine for yourself, in your retirement?" she asked.

"I suppose I can't say, really. But something. Something that will let me find a way to feel . . . at home, here."

This startled Frankie further, this turn of phrase. "But don't you feel at home? I mean, it's been your summer home for so long. And your family's."

"That's so. Of course that's so. But summer has always been vacation time. Time *away* from home. No, the only time it was really home was when I lived here through the year, with my grandmother."

"That's the time your parents were in South America, right?"

"Yes. They'd taken my brothers, but left me here." She stopped for a moment, looking out the window as if seeing something there. Then she looked back at Frankie. "But I think in the end what that year made me see was how much it wasn't my home."

"What do you mean?"

"Oh . . ." She shook her head, screwed up her face. "I don't know. I was itchy to get out, that's all. Everyone's itchy to get out at that age. You certainly were."

"And I did, didn't I?"

"Very thoroughly, I would say." She sipped at her drink and set it down. "No, the person who feels at home here is Alfie. He loved it from the get-go."

Sylvia cut herself a slice of cheese and pushed the plate over toward Frankie. Without looking at her daughter, she said, "He just meandered down?"

"Yes. I'm not sure he knew why, exactly." This was the first time Frankie had acknowledged aloud to her mother that she knew there was something wrong with Alfie.

"Thank you for bringing him back."

"I'm happy to." They were quiet a moment.

"I should have kept an eye on him, but I . . . I just didn't." Sylvia sighed.

"Is it Alzheimer's disease, do you think?" There. She'd said the words, too.

And Sylvia didn't flinch. "I don't know," she said. "He has an appointment in a couple of weeks to see a new doctor here for some tests. I've talked to this one ahead of time about my concerns. That was impossible in Bowman because the doctor there had been Alfie's for so long that he wasn't willing to discuss Alfie with me behind his back. This time we're starting out that way—behind his back." There was a kind of fury in her voice, but Frankie thought it was anger at the situation, at what she was being forced to do, rather than anger at Alfie, so she didn't respond to it.

Instead she said to her mother, "He thinks it is. Alzheimer's."

"What do you mean? *Alfie* thinks it is?" She sounded incredulous.

"Yes. He's read about it—well, haven't we all? But he's got a book about it, a prize book. Anyway, he was very articulate about it just now. He knows he's . . ." She made a face. "*Disappearing* is the word he used."

"He said that to you?"

There was something so sharp in her tone that Frankie thought she'd made a mistake—that she shouldn't have started to talk about this with Sylvia. But she'd launched herself, she couldn't retreat now. "Yes. I thought he was very brave."

Sylvia was smiling. A bitter smile. "No doubt." She had a long swallow of her gin and looked out the window again. "He wouldn't dream of discussing it with me."

Frankie was silent for a long moment. Then she said, "I'm sorry, Mother."

"Oh, God, Frankie, don't be sorry. It's just the way it is, isn't it? You're his confidante"—she pronounced it in a very French way—"and I'm his warden. And he's my prisoner." She laughed quickly. "Unless it's the other way around: that I'm *his* prisoner." She smiled at Frankie, a grim smile. "Either way, it's no fun, standing guard. Asking him where he's going every time he leaves."

Frankie didn't know what to say. Finally, she offered, "We're all standing guard, these days." She shrugged. "It reminds me of Africa, actually. We're not quite at the razor-wire stage, but one or two more fires and maybe we'll get there." She sipped at her drink. Then thought of a change of subject: "Oh, Dad told me there was another fire?"

"There was. The Averys' place. They came home from a party, I guess, and the house was just about gone. The firemen got there with not much to do."

"Oh! So they were *living* there."

"Yes. They'd been up about a week."

"Jesus."

"What?"

"Well, this is different, don't you think? I mean, this is really different."

"What do you mean?"

"Just that before, the other houses that burned were empty. Really empty. No one was living in them. It wasn't only that they were . . . unoccupied for the evening, like this one. They were still closed up for the season. So this seems scarier. As if he's no longer being so . . . *careful,* I guess you'd have to say. It makes you think that someone might actually be at home next time. Someone could get hurt."

"'Next time,'" Sylvia said, looking out the window and then back at Frankie. "I suppose it *will* just go on. After all, why stop now?"

After a moment, Frankie said, "I suppose the other possibility is that he'll be scared off by how defensive everyone is getting, by the alarm systems and the locks and whatnot."

"Maybe," Sylvia said. "Are you at all frightened, down at Liz's, all alone?"

"No," Frankie said. And then she remembered. "Well, that's not quite true. I had a little moment of panic when I heard Daddy on the porch, actually. And even for a few seconds when I saw him. Before I recognized him."

"Nothing like in Africa, though."

"No." And it was—nothing like. Still, she had the impulse to defend

Africa, to say, *I wasn't truly scared there.* But she knew how much being white, being privileged, being an expat, had kept her from needing to feel fear.

They sat in silence for a moment or two. Frankie was aware of the sound of the rain outside in the trees, and of its soft drumming on the roof.

"So," Sylvia said, "you're not sure if you're going back." Her eyes were suddenly keen on Frankie.

"No."

"No, you're not going?"

"No, I'm not sure."

"Are you just, what?" She lifted her hand. "Tired of it? Worn out?"

"I am tired. Yes. Not so much of it, but tired. Really, really tired." She had another swig of the gin.

"Was there someone? Someone you were involved with? There?"

"Why do you ask?"

"You seem . . ." Sylvia frowned. "Sad, in some deep way, I suppose. Not just tired. Sad."

"I *am* sad." Frankie tried smiling at her.

"Then it's over? Whatever? This other person?"

"Oh, it was over before it began."

"Oh!" She sounded startled. "Was he . . . is he, married?"

"No. Or he is, but he and his wife don't live together. They haven't, for a long time. She's in England, anyway. But that's not the point."

"Are there children?"

"They're grown. More or less. He doesn't see them often."

"So, he is available, after a fashion."

"No." Frankie laughed quickly. "No, he's not. Available is exactly what he's not. Or I couldn't have him, anyway. He wouldn't . . ." She drew her breath in sharply. She found herself unable to breathe normally. She realized she was afraid of weeping in front of her mother. But not for Philip, she knew that. For all of it, for everything she couldn't have in Africa.

Once, in her last days supervising a clinic in Sudan, she had been reviewing the protocols with the staff. There was one nurse whose skills she was sure of, a woman in her twenties she had deputized, though she knew this was disrespectful of the older women. "Esther will remind you of all this when I leave," she had said to the group.

One of the older women had spoken then, her voice flat and bitter with anger. "When you go, you will be *gone*."

And she had felt it then, again, the way she was forever a *mzungu*, the way she lived in a different element from them, the way she was always—to them, to herself—*going*. Because nothing there was hers, it couldn't be hers.

"He wouldn't . . . ?" Her mother's voice was gentle, and it called her back.

He had wept, she was remembering. Philip. He had come and knelt by her chair on the rooftop terrace in Lamu and leaned his head against her bare arm. His breathing had thickened unevenly. She felt his tears on her flesh, and she was startled, unsure of where his sorrow came from, what it meant. She was aware of some sense of obligation to him in that moment, and the simultaneous realization that she might actually be relieved when he was gone. She felt that as a possibility even as she turned to him, reached for him: along with the sadness came the eagerness for solitude.

Now, with her mother, she expelled her breath sharply. "Just, he *wouldn't*, I guess. Nor, in fact, would I." She smiled, what she supposed was a bitter smile. Tired, yes, her mother was right. But as much tired of herself as of anything else. "There was, I guess you'd call it, a built-in impossibility. Neither of us was . . . *home*, after all. Neither could, really, beckon the other, into his life, in any sense. 'What life?' might have been the operative question. Though I suppose even that wouldn't have mattered if we'd felt something . . . Oh, I don't know."

"It's always a mystery, isn't it?" Sylvia was looking out the window. She'd sat back away from the light, and her face was wistful, Frankie would have said. Almost beautiful.

Frankie was too surprised to speak for a moment. A gift, from her mother. An invitation. "What is?" she said.

"Oh, how anyone musters the will, or the courage, or the foolhardiness, to imagine a lasting thing. And then why that turns out so well for

some people and so badly for others." She shrugged. Outside, the rain
was suddenly heavier.

"A refill?" she said. She held up her glass, empty but for the ice cubes
and the shredded lime wedge.

"I guess not," Frankie said. She held up hers, still half full.

"Ah, I should start supper anyway," said her mother. "You'll stay?"

And not even thinking about whether she was hungry, she said yes.

Alfie had napped instead of reading, and he seemed refreshed at dinner.
They talked about Clinton and Monica Lewinsky, about marital fidelity,
about the hypocrisy in Washington. They talked about the raging success
of the movie about the *Titanic,* and then about the event itself, the actual
sinking. Alfie, not surprisingly, knew a good deal about it.

It was almost dark when Frankie left. The rain had stopped for the time
being. Her mother had loaned her a flashlight, and she walked home on
the dirt road, jolting on each step down the hill, the little circle of light
skittering and dancing on the wet gravel ahead of her. She thought once
more of her walk in the dark her first night home. It seemed, yes, a real
possibility that she'd seen the arsonist. His car, anyway. She'd need to
decide what to do about that, if there was anything to do.

When she turned off into Clark and Liz's driveway, the house loomed,
a dark shape in the field. Then she saw it: a light flickering inside. She
stopped short, her heart suddenly pounding. She stood there for perhaps
ten seconds, remembering that she hadn't locked the door when she left,
the first time this had occurred to her.

The light in the house had vanished when she froze, and now, as she
moved again, the light moved, too—and she realized, with a kind of
ecstasy of relief, that she was seeing the reflection of her own flashlight
in the dark panes of glass. She moved the light beam back and forth, and
the light in the house moved, too, from window to window. She drew a
deep, sighing breath.

Even so, she approached the house nervously. She opened the door
and waited on the threshold for a moment or two before she entered
the kitchen, listening to the stillness, running the flashlight around the

room. The sudden groan of the refrigerator coming on startled her. She switched the flashlight off.

She came in and shut the door behind her, turned to slide the bolt into place. She looked up and was startled for a half second to see a movement in front of her, a shift—before she recalled that there was a small mirror on the wall next to the door, a mirror that had a little shelf for keys below it. She leaned forward to look more closely at the face—her own face, transformed by the dark: the glint of her eyes, evil-looking in the surrounding blackness, her grim mouth. A stranger. She was remembering suddenly that she had done this as a child sometimes, looked at her reflection in a mirror in the dark, perhaps to scare herself with her transformation. Or maybe not so much to scare herself as to wonder at it, at the sense of herself as an *other* in the world, the sense of seeing herself unfamiliarly, as perhaps others saw her.

Her hand found the light switch and she flicked it up.

And there she was. The same face she'd seen thousands and thousands of times, looking back at her, not a stranger, not frightening or *other*. So familiar that she couldn't really know how she looked.

She thought of her father. She wondered if he saw himself as a stranger sometimes when he looked into a mirror. As an intruder in the house. She'd read about that as a symptom of Alzheimer's, and there was some fancy, Oliver Sacks–y name for it, the failure to recognize yourself in a mirror, in life. This must be the kind of thing that was beginning to happen to him, this misunderstanding of reality. Like seeing a fire when it wasn't there, when it was just a reflection of light in a glass pane; like seeing a stranger when you looked at yourself in a mirror. But he wouldn't have the ability she had to figure things out, to correct himself, to reassure himself.

When she was finished in the bathroom, she went into the bedroom and undressed in the dark there. The sheets were cold against her naked flesh, and she huddled into herself. Slowly the room began to emerge as her eyes adjusted to the darkness and to the shades of black contained within it—the two slightly paler rectangles where the windows were, the darker darkness that signaled the bureau, the different tones in the different planes of the walls. She was aware of the stillness of the world around her and, slowly, as with the blackness, the emerging variety of quiet noises within that stillness: the air stirring, the leaves responding, the drops shaking from them as though it were raining anew.

Then she was in Kenya, hearing the feral dogs howling, the music and faint shouting of some distant, celebrating neighbors, the conversation of the guard with someone walking by, the creak of her wooden bed when she shifted in it. In this complicated stillness and darkness of memory and the present, she lay and waited for sleep.

9

WHAT LUCK! HERE SHE WAS, the Pre-Raphaelite, parking outside Snell's just as he was setting the groceries he'd bought into the passenger seat of his car, having to awkwardly slide a bunch of crap—papers, wrappers, tapes—onto the floor with his elbow as he did this.

"Hey," he called over, straightening up, turning in her direction.

"Hey, yourself." She came around the car that was parked between them. She was smiling, wearing baggy shorts and a man's denim shirt with the sleeves rolled up above the elbows. There were freckles decorating all those long white limbs.

He leaned back against his car, facing her. He was aware of this as a way he might hold her here for a minute or two. Or longer. "How are you doing, in our regrettably exciting new world?" he asked.

"You're speaking of the fires."

"The *arson,* we suspect. Don't you read the paper? And if not, why not?"

She smiled. Another thing he liked about her, the gap between her two front teeth.

She raised her finger. "Actually, this reminds me that I wanted to get the paper. Subscribe, that is."

"Very easily done."

"But here's my problem: I don't have a mailbox."

"But I can just put two of them into your parents'."

"No. The thing is, I'm living at my sister's house now. Just down the road from my parents."

"Ah, the new house in the field."

"That's it."

"I've watched it go up. It looks nice. Better than nice."

"It is. But it doesn't have a mailbox yet. I suppose it won't until they move up here, and God knows when that will be."

"Then I'll bring it to your door." He made a foppishly elegant gesture, a half bow.

"Oh, do *you* deliver the papers?"

"About a third of them. I've got a kid who does it around the green. The urban route. And someone else who does Route Seventy-Two. But I do the outliers on the other side of town. Like you."

"I had no idea you were so . . . multifarious."

"Some say *talented*. I wish you would too. *Multifarious* sounds kind of utilitarian."

"Talented, then. But what *is* the news?"

"You probably know better than I do. I feel as though I'm always bringing up the rear, marching along well behind the gossip. You must hear it all, with your parents around."

"Not so much now. Since I moved out I don't get the news. So"—she gestured, her hands opening at her sides—"I need you."

"How nice, to be needed." She looked away quickly, and Bud felt embarrassed. Felt he'd pushed something. "You heard about yesterday's fire," he said quickly.

"I did. You mean, the one at the Frenches' place." He nodded. "Yes, my mother had heard, so I got the story when I borrowed the car." She gestured behind herself at an old station wagon. "I guess I do still get some of the gossip." She frowned. "But they put that one out, right?"

"Yeah, the Frenches happened to come home pretty soon after it was set, apparently. They called it in themselves and had started to run their hose on it while they waited for the fire department."

Bud had gotten the page and gone again to the fire, but by the time he got there, it was out. There was a kind of childish giddiness among the guys, and no rush to pack up. It was still light out, for one thing, and more important, they'd beat this one. The kitchen cabinets along the wall by the door were partially burned and the ceiling scorched, but not much more was damaged. The Frenches had made a celebratory pitcher of martinis and were serving those and beer to anyone interested. Many were.

"So I heard correctly," Frankie said now.

"You did. But have you heard this?" he asked. *"Guys for rent."*

"'Guys for rent'?" She wrinkled her nose. "What does that mean?"

"Guys will come to your house and stay awake for you. Sit on your porch. Armed."

"Shades of Africa," she said. "Who is this?"

"Oh, a couple of local guys. Kids, really. Peter Babcock. Gavin Knox. They've got signs up in a couple of places with that frill of tags at the bottom with their phone numbers. Quite a few takers, it looks like."

"How entrepreneurial."

"I guess. But this is just a by-product of the fire news."

"Everything is now, isn't it. A by-product of the fire news. Every conversation I have starts with that."

"Every conversation everyone has."

"Speaking of which, I've been thinking about something." Her face was suddenly very serious. "I was realizing it only last week, after the town meeting where we first heard the dread word."

"Arson."

"Yeah. Because I think I might have seen the arsonist."

"What do you mean?"

"Well, his car anyway." And she told him a story about taking a walk in the middle of the night—the first night she was home, she said, jet-lagged. About the smell of smoke. And about a car coming over the hill from the Olsens' direction at that unlikely hour.

"God, it might really *be* something," he said. "So, what else do you have? The make? The color, the license plate?"

She shook her head.

"Nothing else?"

"No. I mean, that's why I didn't think of it earlier, I suppose. It didn't really . . . register at that time. Maybe it was grayish. It was so dark out. It was a beater, I think—do they still call them that? It seemed, maybe, older. It had slanty-eyed taillights."

"Ah, ah. None of that racist stuff."

She smiled. "Sorry, but that's the only thing I remember clearly. The slant, and then watching them go away. The eyes. Kind of disappearing behind a rise in the road, and then appearing again lower down."

Her hand made a wavy gesture. "So," she said. "Who do I report this to?"

"You probably need to talk to Loren Spader, sad to say. It's not much, but it could help, looking for those Asian eyes."

"Why 'sad to say'?"

"Just, he's kind of a local jerk."

"He's the fat guy, right? The police chief?"

"Yes. The chief, and then, as it happens, also the entire department. Do you want me to set it up for you?" He'd go along with her, he was thinking. It might be of interest. And then there was his interest in her.

"Would you?" she said. "It'd make it quicker, I suppose. Otherwise, I'd have to track him down."

"I will. I'll let you know."

She was frowning. "But you know, I'm not sure how well I remember them. The taillights. If he wanted me to pick them out, somehow. You know, if there were five of them backed up to me . . ."

"A kind of vehicular lineup."

"Precisely. I'm not sure I'd get the exact lights. I was really, really tired. And distracted."

"By what?"

She was silent for a few seconds. Then she shrugged. "Just . . . by jet lag, I guess."

"Ah, yes." Another silence. It occurred to him that she might be shy, and this touched him, somehow. They stood there. And then, stupidly, he asked, "You're shopping?"

"Yes. Dinner. I'm going to go in and buy pasta and a cheap bottle of wine. And cereal. And bread."

"Carbs galore."

"I've been to the farm stand already." She gestured toward her car. "Fruits galore."

"Ah, then you're excused."

She started to turn away.

"It was . . . it was nice to run into you. And come Tuesday? You'll find a paper waiting for you."

"Where will I find it?"

"On the porch. There's a porch, right? I'll try to hit it from the car. Always a challenge."

"You'll drive in with it?"

"For you, of course."

"That's so nice of you. And what will I owe you?"

"Depends how long you want it. There's a summer rate, and then a different rate if you're staying on. Are you?" He said this as though announcing to himself that this was an impossibility, he heard that in his own voice.

"Not . . . really. Not past, maybe, early fall."

"So, you're going back?"

"I don't know."

"Why not?"

"Why not what?"

"Why don't you know?"

"Oh, just . . . It's complicated."

"Try me."

She drew a deep breath. "Because, I guess, I've come to feel—in Africa—that I'm . . ." She looked at the ground, then up, at him. "Temporizing, I guess you could say. With my life."

"More." He made a beckoning gesture.

She seemed embarrassed, suddenly. She said, "Just . . . in work. In love." She shrugged. "Or in sex, anyway." She made a short laughing noise.

He was startled, maybe even a little shocked. He was about to try to ask her about this—he couldn't quite imagine how—when she said, "I think what I'm going to do is explore some other possibilities in the States." Her eyes moved around. "I couldn't live *here,* though. I don't think."

"Many do."

"Yeah, but that's not the kind of work I do. It's not . . . transportable to a place like this. I mean, I could be in New *York.* I could do something connected to it there." She shook her head, and her hair swayed thickly. "Not here."

"What is your work exactly? AIDS work?" Hadn't she said that?

"No. It's hunger. *Aid* work. Malnutrition. For me, it's African work. I know it could be lots of other places, but Africa is the place I . . . Well, I was going to say the place I live, but I guess I can't."

"The place you might or might not be going back to."

"Right. But there is, there's lots of other stuff I could do here, in the States. I mean, the program I work for is actually run out of here."

"Here, meaning New York."

"Yes."

"But that's not *here*—New York. That's *there*. Way over there. I locate myself"—he pointed to the ground at his feet with both forefingers—"here."

She looked at him and smiled. "Are you scolding me?" she asked. "For not planning on staying here?"

"No. No, no. How could I? Not ever. I just *got* here."

She tilted her head. "Okay, then." She started to turn away.

"Okay, then. I'll be in touch about Loren."

She stopped. "I don't have a phone," she said.

"Ah. Well. I'll leave you a note."

"Okay," she said.

"Are there days, or times, better for you than others?"

She grinned at him. *Mind the gap.* "All times, all days, are utterly the same for me at the moment."

"Nice work if you can get it," he said.

"You think so," she said. She started to walk away again.

And he turned away, too, went around his car to get in on the driver's side, carefully not looking at her as she disappeared into the store.

Bud was up in the night on Saturday at a fire that destroyed most of the house belonging to the Coolidge family. No martinis served there. They'd been home, in bed, and had barely gotten out. They stood watching their house burn in their nightclothes, the parents and three kids, preteens. Someone had given the children blankets to wrap up in. Natalie Coolidge kept saying—to Bud, to anyone else who spoke to her—that all that mattered was that they'd gotten out, that no one was hurt.

He wrote this up when he came home, and then, after sleeping fitfully, half waking from time to time with the smell of fire on his skin, in his hair, he went to pick up Frankie.

She was quiet on the way to meet Loren. Bud couldn't stop looking over at her as he drove. She'd dressed up a little. This would be wasted on Loren. She wore sandals and bright red toenail polish, thank you very much. Her hair was loose again today, the curls swarming her shoulders.

Her profile was unmoving, remote.

"You couldn't be nervous." She didn't answer. "Are you?" he asked.

She drew in a long breath, looked at him. "What if the car had nothing to do with it? With the fire. I don't want to get some innocent . . . adulterer, sneaking home in the dead of the night, in trouble."

He smiled. "I like your sense of sin."

"Me and Bill Clinton."

"Now there's a guy who's given adulterers a lot to be grateful for."

"Mmm." She turned away again.

"I wouldn't worry about it. This would just be something to start with. They'd need other evidence before they arrested anyone."

She was quiet for a while. Then she said, "What kind of other evidence do you mean?"

"Well, motive would usually be a possibility, wouldn't it? But in this case, I guess maybe not—this seems so almost without any possible motive to me. Or with a motive so . . . perverse as to seem uninformative. But I suppose they'd be looking for the weapon."

"The rope, the knife, the candlestick."

"Yeah. Or maybe a can that smelled of kerosene, or whatever the accelerant was. Or maybe fingerprints. Or footprints."

"Tire tracks."

"Yeah. That kind of thing."

She shifted her long body slightly, turning it to him, and he was aware of a sudden sexual *thrum* in himself. "So, do they have any of that?" she asked.

"They're not talking, if they do. No comment, no comment, no comment." This was true for the arson squad and the state police. Bud had been in touch with them both. Loren, on the other hand, was full of hints. He'd suggested they did know what the accelerant was. "Oh, we got a good idea about that, all right."

This was outside the post office. Loren was sitting in his car, parked close to the side of the building, hidden enough so he could catch people who didn't come to a complete stop at the intersection, the only one in town.

Bud was leaning over Loren's open window, looking down at him. There were food wrappers scattered over the floor and seat of the passenger side of the car. "Could you share this good idea?" he had asked.

"I could not," Loren had replied, with deep satisfaction, grinning up at Bud.

Now he and Frankie turned off the road at the redbrick building a few doors down from Snell's.

"But isn't this *your* office?" Frankie asked.

"Yeah. Loren's meeting us here because he doesn't have an office. Or his office is his car, mostly. You're dealing with small-town stuff here, Frankie." He pulled into the three-car parking area and turned the engine off. He got out and started around to open her door, but she had opened it already and stepped out on her own, so that he was just in time to awkwardly more or less help her close it.

She smiled at him, charmingly, noticing his ridiculousness, he was sure. "Thanks," she said. She followed him up the walk to the door and then in through the cluttered real-estate office on the ground floor. "It's up here," he said, gesturing to the stairs that led to the rooms above, the rooms that housed the paper. She went ahead of him. He followed her, watching the sway of the red skirt moving up the stairs, the white of her legs.

Upstairs, she turned slowly around in the big open space. There wasn't much here. Bud's desk, a couple of chairs, a long table, shelves, and file cabinets. "But where's the printing press?" she asked. "Where are your cub reporters?"

"Ah. Well, the press is in Whitehall, a guy who runs it off every week, along with the Winslow paper and a couple of others. As well as a lot of other stuff—the brochure for your next concert, let's say, should you be planning one. And the cub reporters . . ." He shrugged. "Well, they're not cubs anymore. Three out of four are actually a bit geriatric. And they're all part-timers, anyway—four or five people who regularly write the odd article. For free, I might add."

"So what you're saying is you basically do the whole thing more or less alone."

"Yep."

"Isn't it lonely?"

"No. Not at all. Half the time I'm out and about, talking to people, going to things. And when I'm here, I'm on the phone most of the time. So, no. Now: would you like some coffee?"

She would. Bud had a cheap coffee machine on the long table against the wall. There was a half refrigerator under this table for milk, among other things. While he fixed the coffee, he explained the decor, how he'd inherited the setup from Pete when he bought the paper. "The only thing I changed was to throw away a couch so sprung you could feel the floor when you sat on it."

She remembered Pete, vaguely. "I think he had a nice wife, too. Sort of . . . plump?"

"She died a while back," Bud said. "But that's what I hear, that she was nice." The machine made its gurgling noises as the coffee dropped into the glass pot, and Bud told her the story of buying the paper. Just as they sat and were drinking their first sips, Bud at his desk chair, Frankie in the one worn armchair, they heard the door downstairs bang shut. A woman's voice called out, "Hellooooo!"

"Hi, Barb," Bud called back, getting up. "It's the real-estate broker," he said to Frankie. "Barbara Simms. Do you know her?"

Frankie shook her head.

"I'm just here for a bit!" Barb called up. "I have an appointment at four."

Bud went out to the top of the stairs. Barb was standing at the bottom, her face lifted to look at him. She was fiftyish and attractive in her carefully made up and constructed way. He had once told her that she was the last person he knew who still teased her hair. "And I was the first, honey," she had said, grinning. "You don't mess with a good thing."

"We're not here long, either," he said to her now. "But we're expecting the chief of police any minute."

"Oh, God!" She stuck her tongue out. "That windbag. What for?"

"Oh, I just wanted to go over some stuff about the fires."

"Okay. Well, forewarned is forearmed. I'll send him up." She moved away from the foot of the stairs, out of sight. After a second, just as he was turning back in, she called up, "You know, it's like I'm your god-damned receptionist."

"And don't think I don't appreciate it." He came back and sat at his desk again. They started to talk about the fire the night before. He told Frankie it had gutted the house so thoroughly that it left no evidence.

"No evidence except for the complete impossibility of six fires . . . six?" she asked. He nodded. "Six fires in the same tiny town in the span of a couple of weeks."

"The unlikelihood, in any case."

"Yes." After a moment, she said, "That's why I'm at my sister's house, actually. The idea being that as long as someone's living there, the arsonist will be less likely to strike."

"That would have seemed reasonable until the last three, I guess."

"Which were in houses where people were living."

"Exactly. It's as if there's been a kind of gradual upping of the ante. Davey Swann and the arson guys now think that the brushfires earlier in the summer—there were three of those, I think—were probably set, too. So you had those first. And then you had some unoccupied places. And now, some occupied ones."

"Which is pretty scary."

"And people are pretty scared."

"Are they? Do you hear a lot about it?"

"First- and secondhand." He nodded, and suddenly, somehow, they were looking at each other in a way that felt charged to him.

She looked away. "Thus your friends, I guess."

"What friends?"

"Renting themselves out."

"Oh, those guys. Yeah, they're playing on that. Or counting on it, anyway."

They each had some coffee. Bud was watching her. "Are you?"

"Scared?"

"Yes."

She shrugged. "It comes and goes," she said. "If I hear something, some animal or something, or even if I let myself *think* about it too hard, I can get scared." She looked into her cup. "I lock the door when I leave now, for all the good it would do. And at night, ditto." Her face lifted to him. "Do you?" she asked.

"I haven't yet taken to locking things. But a couple of times I've gotten up in the night, thinking I heard someone. And then slept downstairs. So, yeah. I suppose I'm scared, too, in some sense or other."

She started to say something else when they both heard Loren downstairs—his voice, speaking to Barb.

"Voilà," Bud said. They both fell silent and turned to the opened doorway, listening as Loren slowly and noisily ascended the stairs. He stepped in, breathing hard, wearing his uniform, holding his hat pressed against his chest.

Frankie had got up, and now she crossed to him, extending her hand. She was taller than he was by several inches. "I'm Frankie Rowley," she said. "We've probably met before, but, anyway, I'm glad to meet you again, if that's what it is." She laughed, a single, quick exhalation. She *was* shy, Bud thought.

"Loren Spader." He was nodding slowly, steadily. "Good to meet you."

Bud gestured to Loren to sit in the desk chair, and he moved over to perch on the long table next to the coffee machine. Frankie sat down in her chair. Bud asked Loren if he wanted coffee.

"Nope," he said. "Thanks. It just makes trouble when you spend your day driving around in a car."

"I can see that would be true," Bud said.

"It is true," Loren said. They talked for a minute or two about the fire at the Coolidges', agreeing about their good luck. Then Loren turned to Frankie. "So, Bud here tells me you saw something."

"Maybe. I think so. It's just, I was out walking in the dead of the night—I'd flown in from Africa—I live in Africa and I'd flown in that day. And I had jet lag, so I was up."

Loren nodded, several times. "This was what night?"

"The night of the first fire. The one up beyond my parents' house on Carson Road? The Kershaws'." She sounded nervous.

"Okay."

"So I'd gotten up, got dressed, left the house"—she took a deep breath—"and I was walking toward town, away from the Kershaws." She went on, telling him the same story she'd told Bud. The car, stepping off the road out of its path, noticing the slightly slanted horizontal taillights go down the hill.

"*Okay*," he said again, and this time his hand made a circle: *And*?

"Well, that's it," she said nervously, apologetically. "It's not much, I know. But Bud thought . . ." She looked at him, then quickly back at Loren. "*I* thought it was possible, not until later actually, but I thought it might be the arsonist. Maybe not, but maybe. And that the taillights might be a kind of . . ." She sighed. "Identifier, I guess."

He asked about the make of the car, the color, and she came up as blank as she had earlier with Bud.

"So that's it, then?" He sounded disbelieving.

"Yes. I'm sorry not to be more helpful."

He shook his head, as if correcting himself. "Oh, no, this is helpful, this is helpful." He started to get up, making a little grunt of effort as he lifted himself out of the chair. "I can do something with this." He picked up his hat, which he'd set on Bud's desk. "I might ask you to look at some photographs in a few days," he said.

"Photographs of . . . ?"

"Taillights. Car taillights. I'll just drive around and look. See what I spot and take some pictures."

"I was afraid of that. Because, uhm . . ." Her hand rose to her hair and pushed it back. "I'm not absolutely sure I'd be able to pick them out. Particularly if there were several varieties of the same lights."

He sighed. "Okay, fair enough." They were all standing now. "I have to say, though, what is it with women and cars?"

"What about women and cars?" she asked.

"They never notice them!"

"But, what is it with men and cars? Why are they always so interested in something so fundamentally uninteresting?"

Loren looked at her, and then he grinned, suddenly. "There you have it," he said, and then he turned to go.

"I *am* sorry I can't tell you more," she said quickly.

He stopped at the doorway to the stairs. "Well, I'm sorry, too, but this is something. Something to start with, anyway. Thanks for this, Bud." He gestured at Bud with his hat. "Miz Rowley."

Bud said, "Anytime," at the same moment Frankie said, "You're welcome."

They could hear him descending the stairs, then speaking to Barbara. They were looking at each other. When they heard Loren let himself out, Frankie grinned suddenly. Big grin. Big, he would say, *sexy* grin. She blew out, noisily. "*That*'s over."

"Or maybe not."

"But the hard part."

"It didn't seem hard. You did good."

She nodded. "Thanks."

"I'll take you home? You done with the coffee?"

She nodded. Bud carried the cups to the deep sink—an old laundry sink Pete must have installed himself. Frankie slung her purse on her shoulder, and they headed downstairs.

Barb was at her desk, looking at some photographs laid out there. Frankie introduced herself, and they talked for a minute. Barbara asked about her parents: their retirement here and how that was going.

"I think it's a big adjustment for them," Frankie said.

"But it is *such* a gorgeous property," Barb answered, as if relevantly.

"I never think of it that way," Frankie said. "As *property*, I mean."

"Well, if you ever do, think of me the next *second*," Barb said, and laughed.

"You're a little like a vulture, Barb, you know that, don't you?" Bud said. He opened the door and held it for Frankie.

"I take pride in it."

They were quiet in the car. It went on too long. Bud said, "What else have you been up to today? Church?"

"No. No, I don't do that."

"Ah. Lapsed?"

She nodded.

"Lapsed . . . what?"

"Protestant. My mother's religion. Actually, my grandparents' religion. My grandfather was a preacher. Presbyterian. And we used to go to church regularly, especially when we were up here. So I was a churchgoer. But not ever a believer, even in my memory. Were you?"

"No. No, my parents are really secular Jews. More or less socialists. Religion was so over for them. If I'd even started talking *belief* around the house, that would have been cut off pretty quickly. So I was deliberately raised a nonbeliever—that was their intention for me." He looked over at her. The wind was having its way with her hair—half her face was covered. "Sounds like not, for you."

"No, I think they would have had me believe. We did the whole thing early on. Sunday school. Confirmation class." She swept her hair back with one hand. "But I was a gimlet-eyed kid. I saw hypocrisy everywhere around me among the grown-ups, who were always *on* about honesty and kindness, not hitting, et cetera, and yet were so much not up to the job themselves." After a pause, she said, "And then there was God—such an unattractive character! Why be so jealous, so small, with the whole universe your own? And why call on us to be so good—so giving, so forgiving, so open and sweet, when you hardly model that for us."

"Yeah, a noticeably vengeful guy."

"Exactly." The car was mounting a hill in the shadow of overhanging trees. They were silent for a minute. Then she said, abruptly, "Even so, I so much wanted to be good. The *ideas* in Christianity, I have to say, moved me. The notion that you're called on to do something about human suffering." She'd been turned away, looking out her window when she said this, but now she turned back to him and smiled. "Plus, I just plain wanted to please the grown-ups—I was a bit of a suck-up."

After a moment he said, "Do you think that has anything to do with the kind of work you do? That religious . . . training. If not belief. Did that get you to aid work?"

"Maybe. I suppose humanitarianism is its own religion in a way." She made an odd face. "Or maybe it's just another kind of colonial power. Who knows?" She shrugged. "At the start, though, it was just a way to go to Africa. To justify going to Africa. I had to do *something* there. Something . . . useful. But the selfish impulse, the impulse just to be

there—that came first of all. Then came the reasons. And all the training." Both hands rose now and gathered her hair into a ponytail at her
neck. Her breasts rose, too, under the sweater. She looked over at him.
"And you?" she said. "How about you, with journalism?"

"Oh, I pretty much backed into it. I wanted to be a photographer—
wars, natural disasters, the great romance of that—and I was mostly
thinking about that, though I took a couple of journalism classes in college. But I started just by sending pictures in everywhere I could think of,
and got so I was a stringer for the *Denver Post.* And then they asked me
to cover a couple of campaign visits out there, and I wrote some stuff to
go along with the pictures, to explain them, really, and pretty soon that
was mostly what I was doing—writing. First as a stringer, just sending
stuff in. And then as a hire. And then I went to Washington, and then—a
long, long then—I was tired of that and I came here."

"Are you ever sorry you left?"

"I suppose. From time to time. But you choose, don't you? And it was
my choice." He looked over at her. She was listening intently, her eyes
steady on him. "I made my bed," he said.

"Still, it must sometimes feel so far away from the action."

"Yeah, but a lot of the action that makes the news in Washington is
pretty silly. Inconsequential, finally. Or so it seems to me."

"Oh, I agree. I've been listening to the radio on and off while I've been
working on the house, a lot of news on NPR, and I'm struck that I don't
think I've heard Africa discussed even once since I've been here. It's so
strange for me. I mean, not that Africa has to be in the news, but . . ."
She turned away, looking out her window. Then she said, "You know, it's
always hard, coming back. Bridging the worlds. But this time around,
it's so pointed, the sense of disconnection. It feels, completely this time,
either/or."

"Whereas at other times?"

"Well, it didn't, not so much. Somehow—maybe it's just being up
here, not in a city—but America seems so insular now. More than before,
yes. And the Clinton stuff, which is so ridiculous, really, is part of that for
me. I mean, how can *this* be what Americans are talking about—Monica
Lewinsky?—when there's so much . . . horror in the world."

"And I suppose the fires add to that feeling for you. That everyone here is so taken up with them."

"I hadn't thought of that, but I suppose it's true. But I can forgive that more easily."

"Good. We need your forgiveness." He had meant to make a joke, but as he looked over, he saw it hadn't worked. She looked stricken. She turned her face away to look out the window.

When she turned back to him, her eyes seemed immense. She said, "I'm sorry. I'm sorry. You must think I'm so . . . holier than thou. And that's not what I mean."

"I don't think that." She didn't respond. "But on the other hand, maybe you should mean it. Compared to what you've done in your life, what I've done is . . . self-indulgent."

"Don't, Bud. You're embarrassing me."

"Why? I'm being serious."

"But you shouldn't be. I told you, my motivations were, they *are,* really complicated. For everything I did, there were all kinds of . . . satisfactions." They rode in silence for several minutes. They had turned onto the dirt road that led up to her parents' house, her sister's house. Bud was aware of the noise of the tires. "Here's an example," she said, turning to him. "When I met you at the tea and you asked me where I was from, and I said, 'Africa,' you were impressed: '*Africa!*'" Her voice was amazed, imitating his surprise. "I got to dazzle you with how cool I am, that sneaky pleasure."

"Yes, indeed."

"But, *enjoying* that."

"Yeah. Unforgivably sinful."

She looked at him for a long moment. Then she said in a low voice, "Give me something here, Bud."

"Okay. Sure. I get it. I get how much fun it is being cool. Amazing people. Sure. But I don't see what's so evil about finding some pleasure in that."

"Well," she said.

"We're coming at this from different places," he answered.

"I'll say."

"All right, I'll make my confession, then."

"Speaking of churchgoing."

"Yes. And speaking of secret, shameful pleasures."

She sat up. "Okay, what?"

"When I first realized that the fires were likely arson, I was happy."

"*Happy!*"

"Right."

"Happy, why?"

"Why not? I yam what I yam, a newspaper guy, and it's a good story. I've had other papers picking it up from the AP, the stuff I'm doing right now, and the worse it gets, the longer it lasts, the more that kind of stuff will happen. Christ, if it gets really bad, some prize committee may sit up and take notice."

"And that's what you want?"

"Of course that's what I want. That's the game." He looked over and thought he saw a pinch of disapproval around her mouth. "Okay, and then I don't want it, too." He turned his smiling face back to the road. "But there *is* a sneaky pleasure in all that. That's all I'm saying."

She sat, looking at him, her hair dancing. "Well," she said.

"Yes, well."

"Here's to sneaky pleasures, then. I guess we both indulge."

They were pulling into the driveway. "Guilty, as charged," he said.

10

~~~

SYLVIA WAS AWAKE—she had heard something, some small noise. The red numerals on the clock glowed 4:37. Light was seeping in around the edges of the dark shades. Alfie was lying next to her, deeply asleep. She lay still and listened, hard, to all the noises of the world outside as they greeted the day. She could hear birdsong. The air itself began to stir, and the trees, responding, made a gentle sibilance as they shook their leaves, like a long exhaled breath. There was nothing beyond that.

Alfie muttered something in his sleep.

What was it she'd heard? Footfall?

Oh, come on. Not likely.

Probably a shift in the old house or the tiny stir of a mouse.

Nothing, in other words.

She was getting as bad as everyone else.

Everyone but Alfie. She looked over at him. More and more since they'd moved up here, he had been having sleep disturbances, but they were sui generis. He'd go to bed at eight or nine, exhausted, but then he'd get up, sometimes for several hours, in the middle of the night. It made him slow to wake in the morning. Often he had a nap in the afternoon, too, and she found she looked forward to that as much as she'd looked forward to the children's naps when they were small.

She remembered those nap times now: she had smoked then, and she could call up with pleasure the expansive feeling of luxury as she lit the first cigarette in the house's afternoon stillness and turned, at last, to her own work. To rereading whatever story or novel she was teaching in her class or to the papers she needed to mark up and grade—even that was a chore she welcomed as a retreat from the mindlessness of her daily rounds with the girls.

Here, it was in the mornings, the mornings she woke before Alfie, when she had that same feeling, that feeling of letting go of an obligation, a duty. The feeling of claiming herself again. She'd been aware of it especially since the girls had left, Liz back to her life in Massachusetts with Clark, Frankie down to Liz's to house-sit.

She'd been thinking a good deal about the girls the last week or so. It was shocking to her, but it always was true, how ready she was for them to be gone, after being so impatient to see them beforehand. And now that they *were* gone, how much she missed them again.

She got up. She picked up her robe from the foot of the bed and crossed to the door. Just as she reached to shut it behind her as quietly as she could, Alfie stirred. "Without that," he said.

She pulled the door to. She went into the bathroom and stood for a moment, taking it in. Every time she entered this transformed room, she found satisfaction in its design. *Simple, plain,* was what she had asked the builder for, and that's what she'd gotten. The floor was painted wood, and there was wood wainscoting. She'd found an old claw-foot tub at the salvage place in Whitehall, and Al—the builder—had gotten a pedestal sink for her.

As she brushed her teeth, the cool air blew in on her from the open window next to the sink. Too cool. It had been so warm when they went to bed that she'd left the windows open, feeling a little nervous but also vaguely defiant as she remembered Loren Spader's suggestions about closing the house up at night. Now she shut her lips around the stem of the toothbrush and turned to lower the window—stopping as she did, her hands on the frame, to look at the light of the sun touching the tops of the trees at the bottom of the meadow, changing the tone of their green with its golden, warm light. The sky beyond the hills was a deep, cloudless azure. Something stirred on the ground in the meadow, brown and quick. A marten, most likely. She imagined its mean little face.

And then she remembered: today was the day of Alfie's appointment with Dr. Thibodeau. She rinsed her mouth and went into the kitchen.

It was still deep in shadow, but Sylvia didn't turn the lights on. She liked the natural light, the underwater quality to it. If Alfie had been awake, the old Alfie, he'd be complaining. "It's as dark as a coal mine in here." He'd flick the switch, without asking her: "Let there be light!"

She shut the window over the sink now, too, and filled the kettle with water, put it down gently, quietly, on the stove to heat. While she set up the clear glass carafe with its filter and scooped in the darkly fragrant granules of coffee, she was thinking of her own visit to Dr. Thibodeau the first week up here. The younger woman had been soft-spoken, sympathetic, and Sylvia had been instantly drawn to her.

Alfie wouldn't like it, she knew—the idea of his doctor being a woman. Sylvia had discovered only slowly over the years how deep the feeling ran in him that women were inferior to men in most ways. It didn't hold for any of the women he actually knew—her, his daughters, his students—but it came up at odd moments as an underlying belief, which the particular women he knew were the clear exceptions to. So he would be irritated at her choice.

Too bad, she thought. *I'm the one who counts now, the one who needs to be able to talk to the doctor, to feel understood, and as though I understand.*

What Alfie would like, on the other hand, was that Dr. Thibodeau was pretty, pretty in a slightly plump, slightly unkempt way—short and brunette and slow-moving, but with hazel-brown eyes that seemed intensely focused on you as you spoke, that seemed part of the way she listened. They could do some simple tests, she had said to Sylvia, looking at her earnestly with those soft eyes, tests that would tell a lot about his cognitive functioning. They wouldn't be definitive, though—Sylvia understood that?

Oh, yes, she said. She'd read all about it, books she'd hidden from Alfie, though he noticed less and less what she was doing unless it got in the way of some plan or project of his. She knew the tests were always provisional, that they couldn't really tell, in the absence of other symptoms, what was causing the dementia. For that, they needed to look at the brain; and to look at the brain, the patient needed to be dead.

They had scheduled the appointment, though Sylvia hadn't bothered to tell Alfie about it, since he'd only forget and she'd have to tell him again. And yet again, probably. No, she'd tell him when he got up today, after he'd had his coffee. Soon enough.

She had disliked Alfie's doctor in Bowman—a chilly, pompous Freud look-alike, down to the goatee and the rimless glasses. The one time she'd approached him on her own to express her concern about Alfie—she'd called to try to make an appointment to see him—he'd refused to talk to her about anything on the phone or even to see her without Alfie present. *Alfie* was his patient. If he, Alfie, was willing to have her come in *with* him, fine. Otherwise, no. "I'm sure you understand," he'd said in his forbidding, professional voice.

"Yes," she'd said politely, though she'd been furious. But she'd turned much of that anger on herself. How stupid of her to have sought any understanding from this martinet, this doctor-puppet. She'd decided she'd put the whole issue off until they came up here and then start over with a new doctor. Someone who would talk to her. Someone she liked.

Sylvia took her coffee into the living room and sat down on the couch, swinging her legs up and tucking her cold feet under her robe. From here she could see the top of Liz's chimney rising behind the knoll at the bottom of the meadow. She wondered how Frankie was doing, alone down there.

Frankie. Who looked suddenly older this time around. Not sadder-but-wiser older, though that too, but *older* older. Physically. But maybe it was the sadder-but-wiser stuff—this man she'd been involved with—that was aging her. Or maybe it was just the passage of time. She was, after all, forty-three now.

Frankie. Sylvia had a sudden clear memory of her as a child. Remembered holding her head between her own hands and tilting it down degree by degree as she kissed first Frankie's chin, then her lips, then her nose, then her eyes and forehead, and then the top of her silky head—Frankie's mouth open in delight, laughing. Where was that? She was so little, it must have been in Chicago still, in the basement apartment on Fifty-Sixth Street, before Liz was born. She remembered Frankie's warm hands on her own face as she woke one morning, the little girl having climbed into bed with them in the middle of the night. Frankie's eyes, so light, were already open, waiting for Sylvia's to open, too, and when they did, in response to the warm, dough-smelling touch of Frankie's hands, Frankie said, "Mumma," her breath warm on Sylvia's face, her neat little wide-spaced teeth exposed in a delighted smile.

It was that she missed, she thought—the sense of owning, being owned, by their flesh. Now, much as she loved her daughters most of the time, they were really just people she knew. And it was not really them that she missed when they were gone, she thought suddenly. It was the children of her imagination, those small children who had so much *belonged* to her. Not the adults, with their work, with their busy lives.

Sylvia had visited Frankie in Africa for the first time only a few years earlier. It had surprised her, the version of Frankie she saw there, so competent, so comfortable and relaxed. But perhaps this is always the way it is with your children, she had thought, when you see them whole, in their own worlds, where they seem so different from the partial versions that arrive for a visit, that reenter the family and take up again at least some aspects of their old roles, their old family status.

She had asked to see Frankie's work—she wanted to understand what compelled her to stay in Africa. Frankie took her along to a feeding station for refugees, one she'd helped to set up months earlier, now being run by locals under the supervision of a nurse from her NGO. They went by plane the first leg of the way, a small prop plane that held six people. It flew low over the open terrain, the grassland and the strangely shaped trees below. They were buffeted dangerously, it seemed to Sylvia, by every breeze. But the others on the plane, the pilots and Frankie's two colleagues, seemed not to notice—they kept talking, yelling to one another to be heard, laughing—so Sylvia tried to ignore her own fears.

They landed near a village of mostly mud huts with conical, thickly thatched roofs—though there were also a few shops of rusty corrugated metal along the dirt road. These shops were open, with produce and what looked like secondhand goods laid out on the counters.

Two cars awaited them, and they drove for what seemed like hours. The roads were so deeply pitted that their driver often had to turn the car almost sideways to avoid getting stuck. Sylvia's back ached from their jolting progress.

The station was a series of mud buildings with thatched roofs, some whitewashed, some not. The refugees were mostly Somalis, those beautiful women and their children, their slender faces now grotesquely thin in many cases. A few were doing well, but many of the newly arrived children were lethargic, too weak or numbed even to cry, their eyes sunken and old, world-weary in their skull-like faces, their bellies distended, their hair an odd reddish color. Two that Sylvia noticed seemed far gone. They lay motionless on pallets on the floor, their mothers lying next to them, cradling them—their arms and legs just sticks, bone and claw. They wouldn't survive, Frankie said later. They'd come in too sick.

Frankie moved easily among the children and their mothers, speaking a language that Sylvia couldn't guess the meaning of except for Frankie's tone: concerned, full of sympathy, but always also pointed, cool, efficient. As she watched Frankie touch a mother's shoulder, a child's forehead or belly, Sylvia realized she had never noticed her daughter's hands before now, how graceful, how white. How quick, while also seeming slow, infinitely careful.

There was an argument with the nurse before they left. She was impatient with Frankie about the arrival of supplies, equipment, food. Frankie was solicitous and accommodating, but firm. There were difficulties, but the NGO was trying to correct them. It would get better. She must be patient.

It was hard, Frankie told Sylvia later. Convoys carrying medications and food had been intercepted, robbed.

"But medications and food for *children*?" Sylvia had asked.

"Everyone needs food," Frankie had said flatly.

They drove back over the potholed roads they'd come in on, Frankie silent now. And then they had the flight back to Nairobi. They took a taxi home, and from its windows as they drove, Sylvia saw skinny cattle grazing imperturbably in the scrubby grass on the median strips of the busy road while traffic whizzed by in either direction. They were herded by tall, unsmiling natives in bright robes. Drought, Frankie said when Sylvia asked about it. The Masai grasslands were brown, so they drove the cattle to any place where there might be forage.

As they approached and entered Nairobi itself, Sylvia took in anew the life of the place, the buses and *matatu,* the streets crowded with people walking—walking in suits, carrying briefcases; walking in cheerful patterned dresses, carrying enormous bundles on their heads. They passed shopping centers and the dusty central park. They passed all the entrepreneurial improvisations—juice stands, fruit stands, clothing stands, their goods sometimes spread out all over the sidewalk, people milling around, looking, buying, bargaining. The smell of cooking fires, of disinfectant, hung in the air.

And then they were suddenly back at the peace and order of Frankie's compound, driving through the squealing metal gates opened by the guard, the air around them scented with mimosa, with frangipani. Inside, Alice, the maid, had left dinner under dampened towels on the kitchen counter. The sun sank, and dark encircled them as Sylvia and Frankie sat eating outside on the patio overlooking the trimmed green lawn and the tropical garden, which teemed with colorful plants Sylvia had always thought of as annuals—lantana, impatiens, bougainvillea. Dinner was a cold spicy Swahili dish, a bit like curry, and they each had several glasses of a chilled South African wine. It all seemed criminally luxurious in contrast to where they'd been.

But when they brought their dishes in to clean up, there was no water at the taps. They went to bed without washing the dishes, without showering, without flushing the toilet. Before she dropped off, Sylvia heard Frankie shutting the rape gate, heard its clatter and then the sharp click of the padlock.

Sitting in a corner of Dr. Thibodeau's office, watching the back of Alfie's head as he bent over a task the doctor had assigned him, Sylvia was thinking how vulnerable he looked from this angle, as hunched and concentrated as a second grader, even his white hair tufted up awkwardly, like a child's. Dr. Thibodeau was sitting next to him, leaning over to watch what he was drawing. She had asked him to perform a number of tasks—to count backward by sevens, to copy a design. Now he was supposed to be drawing a clock face, showing the time as ten past eleven. He had started off confidently enough, though he'd protested the nature of the task.

"Oh, I know, it does seem silly," Dr. Thibodeau had agreed. "But just as another kind of doctor might want to test for something you'd likely have no sense of at all—something in your blood, let's say—just like that, this exercise may show me things you wouldn't take notice of, or even care about. But to me it'll be quite . . . *useful!*" Her voice was always warm, deferential. *Silly me, to be interested in this foolish information.*

Now he was faltering. He stopped and turned to her. "Well, of course," he said, "with Roman numerals, the two is like the eleven. So it's hard to . . . separate them out."

"That is so true. Maybe we should just stick to Arabic numbering."

He seemed to freeze. "Arabic?" he asked, after a few seconds.

"Yes, you know, the figures we usually make for a one or a two or a three."

He hunched over the table a little longer. Dr. Thibodeau was encouraging, though Sylvia could see that the pencil was moving only slightly, only occasionally. "Very good," she said.

After another few minutes, he sat back. "That's it," he said. And after a long silence, contemptuously: "You know, digital clocks have made this . . . stupid."

"I know," she said. "Even my watch is digital now." She held her wrist up for him to see. Then she said, as if only idly curious, "I wonder if you could tell me now the three words I asked you to memorize earlier."

"I have no memory of that," Alfie said. His voice was dismissive.

"Oh, yes," Dr. Thibodeau said cheerfully. "There were three nouns I named, and you repeated them for me? I just want to go over them one more time. *If* you would be so kind." She curtsied her head slightly, smiling warmly at him.

There was a pause, a long pause. Sylvia was aware of her own tension, of her wish that he do it, that he triumph, and of the quickly dawning, shamefully gratified knowledge that he couldn't. That she was right: that it was real, his failure.

Alfie finally said softly, "No."

"All right," said Dr. Thibodeau. "Let's move on. That part's not so important anyway."

He had a few more tasks to perform. And then Dr. Thibodeau thanked him, as warmly as ever, told him she thought he'd done fantastically, that she was so grateful to him for enduring these assignments, but that they were useful in her thinking about cognitive function. She stood, and he did, too, more slowly. And took the hand she extended to him. "You've been so patient with all this," she said.

"Oh, no," he said. "It was fine. I won't say the most *interesting* interview I've ever had, but I didn't mind."

Dr. Thibodeau laughed. Her hand moved to his back, and she was gently guiding him, moving with him, to the door. "I'm just going to chat with Sylvia a few minutes about the same tests, so if you can just wait in the aptly named waiting room. I think there's a *Newsweek* there. *People* magazine, too, but I don't imagine that's quite your cup of tea."

He exhaled, a quick, amused sound. No, he said. No.

The door was open now, and Dr. Thibodeau said to the nurse, "Dr. Rowley will wait here for his wife, Liddy. We'll be a few minutes."

Just as he turned to go, Alfie raised his finger and smiled triumphantly at her: *"Pencil!"* he announced.

She laughed. "That's it! The word was *pencil.* Right you are. *Horse, rose, pencil.* Good for you!"

When the door shut, Dr. Thibodeau came and sat in the same chair she'd been in, next to Alfie's. She swiveled in it to face Sylvia. "You can probably tell that we had pretty mixed results there." Her face was sober.

"I'm not surprised," Sylvia said. "But you know, I'm relieved. I'm ashamed to say that, but the thing is, I thought he might just breeze through all this, and I'd be left thinking I was just imagining things. Or exaggerating anyway."

"No, there's clearly some real loss. You're right." She tilted her head and smiled sadly at Sylvia. "And that feeling you have, of confirmation, really? That happens often. It's a great relief to people to have some clarity finally. So don't be ashamed. Not in the least." Her tone was as warm, as reassuring, as it had been with Alfie, and Sylvia wondered for a fleeting moment whether she ever let go of this, whether she made ironic remarks, jokes, about a patient occasionally—maybe to Liddy. Or at home, to her husband, if she had one.

"So what comes next?"

"More tests, I'm afraid. But these will seem *medical* to him, and therefore probably be less distressing in some ways. Easier to deal with, to explain to yourself. Blood work, an MRI, some things like that. Liddy will set it all up for you at the hospital."

"And then what?"

"Well, then comes the hard part. Because there just isn't a lot we can do. We have a few drugs that can slow things down—slow the progress of the disease. So it's good you brought him in now. The earlier the better. But as you probably know, the trajectory is set, and the prognosis is not good if it's Alzheimer's. It *is* a terminal disease, after all."

They talked awhile about the way it usually went, about the timing of the various stages, about how long it would be before the test results would come. Sylvia was growing tense about the notion of Alfie, waiting outside, but she asked, "Why is it so much worse since we moved up here?"

"I'm sorry, I know you told me, but when did you move, again?"

"In May. When Alfie retired."

"Well, sometimes the kind of changes he's just gone through, both in his routine and then also in his physical surroundings, can be a trigger for a . . . *lurch* forward, I guess you could call it." She was frowning. Her face was earnest. "Any change, really, is challenging. So this one, well, it might have been a sort of double whammy, sad to say, with the actual move and then the retirement on top of that."

"But it's really marked. And he seems so much more . . . remote now. Very quickly. And he's had what I guess I'll have to call hallucinations."

"Oh, really?"

"Yes."

"Tell me about those."

Sylvia did. The shadow he mistook for a dog. The idea he had—Sylvia thought it might be left over from a dream—that their daughter had been kidnapped by terrorists. "This, even though we'd had her over for dinner the night before."

Dr. Thibodeau said all this raised some other possibilities. She herself had noticed a stiffness in his gait, and also that he still had a good command of language.

"Most of the time," Sylvia said.

"Yes. And some of these symptoms are a bit different from Alzheimer's. So it's possible it's a disease called Lewy body disease."

"Is that better? Is it curable?"

"No. No, not really. It presents differently, but the course is similarly downhill. It's just, if it's Lewy body, he'll have days when he seems better suddenly. Or even quick switches in and out in a short period of time. But ultimately a slow decline, just like Alzheimer's."

They sat silently for a moment. "I'm so sorry," Dr. Thibodeau said.

"Yes," Sylvia said, getting up.

As she left the room, her eye fell on the drawing, Alfie's drawing of the clock face. It was a rough circle, more an oval, actually, with an uneven, almost deckled edge. Only the top-right quarter of the oval was filled in, an X at 12 and a Roman numeral I about where the 3 would have been. There was a wavering arrow on the left-hand side, somewhere between where the 9 and the 10 might have been. It looked as though a three-year-old had drawn it. Her shock was almost physical.

In the car, Alfie seemed both relaxed and tired, suddenly, and Sylvia decided she wouldn't go shopping at the supermarket, which was what she had planned. There was enough stuff in the house. She could just stop at Snell's for what she'd need to tide them over for a day or two. She was mentally reviewing the contents of the pantry and the refrigerator for possible meals when Alfie spoke.

"That young woman," he said. "What is it that she's studying?"

"Something about memory."

"I'm afraid I wasn't of much help to her," he said.

"Oh, I think you were, some."

"I'm surprised you didn't tell her that's not my field."

She ignored his tone. "I don't think that mattered very much. She said she'd be able to make use of some of it, anyway."

"Well." He settled back again. "Good."

By the time they got to Snell's, he was asleep, his head dropped forward, his hands resting on his thighs, palms turned up. As she turned off the engine, she wondered what to do about him. She didn't want to take him in with her, newly awakened, bewildered, and have him traipsing behind her in that state for all to see. But would he be confused if he woke out here on his own? Wonder where he was? Leave the car? After a moment she decided it was better to leave him and trust—hope—that if he woke, he'd recognize Snell's and know that he should wait for her.

She got out of the car slowly—*sneakily,* she said to herself—and shut the door as quietly as she could behind her, latching it only partially. She mounted the broad, scuffed wooden steps and went inside, the bell attached to the door announcing her.

There were four or five people moving around inside the store. Adrian was working the cash register, and she felt the slight sense of unease she always had at the idea of an encounter with him. He was standing, arms folded across his chest, talking to Loren Spader. They both turned and nodded at her as she came in. She raised her hand in response, and they returned to their conversation. Spader's loud voice could be heard again as she moved to the back of the store to get milk. He was expounding on his theories about arson, the unavoidable topic everywhere in town. "Just you wait," he said. "He'll do his own house eventually, that's what this is all heading toward, and then who's going to suspect anything? He'll be just one of the crowd of victims collecting damages."

Adrian murmured something, and they both laughed. Then she heard Loren calling good-bye to Harlan Early, who was shelving things close to where she was standing. Harlan called back. The bell on the door jangled again as it shut behind Loren.

Sylvia collected coffee, milk, bananas, oatmeal, and went to the register. Adrian bowed his head once to her. "Sylvia," he said, and started to reach for her groceries as she set them down.

His hands moved quickly, smoothly, touching the items, punching in numbers. Without looking at her, he said, "Alfie got himself a gun yet?" There was something mocking in his tone, making fun of the notion of Alfie, the city boy, being able to use a weapon.

It annoyed Sylvia on Alfie's behalf. "Why would he get a gun?" she said. "He's not going to shoot anyone."

"*I'm* planning to." There was a satisfied smirk on his face. "I've got one right by my bed. The guy gets *near* my house, the sensor lights go on, and *boom!* he's dead."

"Hmm. Remind me not to come calling on you at night."

His hand stilled. There was a long pause. Adrian was looking at Sylvia, looking at her as he hadn't in perhaps fifty years—directly, honestly. His eyes were the same, the pretty, gentle bluish gray, and she remembered her feelings for him then, all of them.

When he spoke again, his voice was lowered, soft. "I don't need to remind you of that, Sylvie," he said.

And then he turned back to the cash register, his hands moved again, he pushed her groceries past him, and rang up what she owed him.

11

THE SEVENTH FIRE BEGAN on the front porch of the Froelichs' house. It consumed the rug that sat just outside the door for people to wipe their feet on, and then a rag rug that sat just inside, redundantly—both of them soaked with the lighter fluid that had been squirted around on the porch and through the gap underneath the door. Inside, the fire hesitated a bit, licking the drops that had sprayed out beyond the doormat, and then it leaped over to the larger straw rug that sat under the living room furniture. It ate this slowly and then began hesitantly on the couch, producing mostly just a slowly thickening, dark, roiling smoke.

There was a second fire at work in the dining room, started soon after the first. It flared up at the windows, where the fluid had been splashed in through the screens—the Froelichs had forgotten to close those windows in their rush to get to a dinner party they were late for. She had been angry at him because he'd come home messy and well past the hour he'd promised to return, wanting to show her the fish he'd caught; so the windows were, as she explained later, the last thing on her mind. She'd done well to remember to shut the dog into the little study under the stairs where he stayed when they were out—though she came to regret that deeply, since that was where he suffocated.

The fire rode the sheer dining room curtains to the ceiling, where it turned, flattened against the plaster surface, and made its way sideways, searching out the oxygen at the open stairwell, beckoning the living room fire to follow it. It rushed up the stairs, lighting the curtains at the staggered windows in the stairwell that looked out over the Froelichs' driveway to the dirt road in front of the house.

Where Franklin Goodyear, known to the teenagers in town as the

Goodyear Blimp, was driving by on his rounds as a volunteer patrolman and saw it. He stopped his car, got out, and walked up toward the house and the flames flickering in the stairwell windows. He stood there stupidly for some seconds—he'd never seen a house burning before, and it had, he thought, a certain beauty—and then turned and ran back, drove fast to the next house down the road, the Edmondses'. He drove directly across their lawn to the back door and banged on it. Margaret Edmonds heard him, though Shelley did not, something that confirmed for her again that he was going deaf. She stopped briefly at the hall mirror to pat her hair in place and went to the door. When she opened it, Franklin Goodyear gestured wildly. "Your phone, your phone, your phone. Where is it? There's another fire!"

The first firemen arrived within fifteen minutes, and though the damage was considerable, the house wasn't destroyed. It lived to tell the tale, as Davey Swann said. The state arson squad was able to say with assurance that yes, this one had been set.

But Bud had barely written that story when the eighth fire occurred, this one in Marjorie Griffith's tiny writing studio, up a long driveway in the woods, its slow burning invisible until it was nothing but a charred pit in the ground. "I think he decided the seventh one was too close to the road, too easy to spot," Davey said. This, too, was in the July 18 issue of the *Pomeroy Union*.

"All eight of these fires are now presumed to be arson by local police and state arson officials, as are the earlier brushfires of the spring," Bud had written. "According to Fire Chief Davey Swann there's a distinct pattern that's emerged over time. Most of the fires seem to be carefully planned for maximum property damage and minimal loss of life, the fire at the Coolidge house being the major exception. 'In almost every one of these fires there was no one home at the time and we're grateful for that,' Swann says. 'But that also means there's no one there to report it and so we've got us less of a chance to put it out.'

"Last, all these fires have occurred in summer homes, the homes of people who don't live in Pomeroy year-round. Whether this is because there's a greater chance of no one's being home in one of the houses of a part-time resident or because the summer residents are being singled out is something Swann doesn't care to speculate on. 'Someone lots smarter than me's going to have to figure that one out,' he says modestly. 'All I know is, I'd get up here fast if I lived somewhere else, and I'd stay put for the rest of the summer.'"

What he'd actually said was "I'd get my goddamn summer ass up here fast," but Bud didn't feel obliged to quote him entirely.

"The state police are more willing to speculate," Bud had written. "A source there who wishes to remain anonymous told your reporter that the divide between year-round and summer residents could offer a possible motivation for what otherwise seems a series of motiveless crimes. 'It could be that there's some kind of resentment at the heart of this. Class resentment.'"

Bud had gone on to write up the officer's other theories, too. Insurance was one, "though we're getting kind of beyond the pale for that with the numbers of fires you got here." Some sort of land grab was another possibility. The trooper also mentioned his personal theory about the widespread pyromania of volunteer firefighters. "Half of them are nuts. It's a well-known fact."

Bud had mentioned this notion to Davey Swann to get his response. Davey said he was certain that his firefighters would be willing, "to a man," he said, to take lie-detector tests. Bud quoted this in the article, too.

"I'm here to drop off the paper," he said. He'd been parked in his car outside her house—her sister's house—for about twenty minutes, passing the time by reading the *New York Times*. He'd told himself he could stay for half an hour, and here she was, with time to spare. He got out when he saw her coming down the hill, walking slowly through the long grass. The sun was in her face, so he wasn't sure she saw him until she stopped partway down the hill, as if startled, and then, apparently recognizing him, started down again, a smile altering her face.

"That's very kind of you," she said now. Her hair was wet, in ringlets. She was wearing jeans and a big shirt, unbuttoned. It flapped open to reveal a black bathing suit. She carried a towel draped over one shoulder. "But I thought the deal was I was going to find the paper waiting on the porch."

"Well, I tossed it, but I missed the porch."

She grinned. "But I'd never have known that if you just got out and *put* it on the porch."

"Then I thought I'd say hello," he said. "You've been swimming?"

"My parents' pond." She gestured behind her. "I'm the only one who uses it, now that my sister and her kids are gone."

They stood a moment. There was a pleasant, slightly algal smell coming from her. He said, "I wanted to ask if you'd seen Loren again, among other things."

"I have. I should have told you." She said he'd stopped by only two days before with a series of photographs, clearly taken by Loren himself with a not-very-good camera—shots of cars parked in a variety of situations. One, she said, was in a yard full of discarded junk and startled-looking dogs. One was in a driveway. One, slightly blurry, was taken on a road, the top of Loren's dashboard visible in the foreground.

"I was not helpful, I'm afraid. Any one of them could have been the car I saw. I mean, they all had a *version* of the slant I sort of remember. I couldn't really distinguish between them. Among them. There was only one I knew for sure *wasn't* the right car."

"Well, maybe it gave him something to start on."

A little silence fell between them, and he was suddenly aware of the noises in the air—the faint stirring of the trees, distant birds calling. Abruptly she asked him if he wanted to come in.

"Sure. I confess I've been curious about this house, watching it go up."

She led the way onto the open porch. She opened the door and indicated that he should precede her. He stepped directly into a large, open room, partially finished, the walls striped and dotted with dried white joint compound. The furniture was clearly secondhand, but somehow charming to him in its improvisational quality. A floppy bouquet sat in the middle of the table in a glass jar, small blue and white flowers. "This is pretty much it," she said. "Two bedrooms there." She pointed to a little hallway, an opening off the big room. There was a bathroom straight ahead, the door open to reveal an old sink suspended from the wall. He could also see partway into one of the bedrooms, just the Sheetrock wall lit by sunlight.

"I like it," he said. "I can't imagine living here with kids, but I like it."

"I like it, too. It's been a retreat for me. And a project, as you see."

"*You're* putting the walls up?"

"Oh, no, my brother-in-law did that. I just did the goop, as my sister calls it. I've actually enjoyed it. I'm tediously perfectionistic, so it's the ideal job for me."

"You are. Perfectionistic." He was asking.

"I am." She draped the towel on the back of one of the chairs set around the table, and went over to the old refrigerator and opened the door.

"Aid work must have been tough, then."

She looked back at him. "It was. I had to let go of a lot of perfectionism. But what was left served me well. It's always served me well." She smiled. "I like being perfectionistic most of the time."

"And here it's serving your brother-in-law well. Lucky fellow."

She shrugged. "I'm the one who gets to live here right now. So it's serving me well, I'd say. Would you like a beer? Some wine? I have no hard stuff."

"I'd love a beer. I can celebrate paper day being over."

"Paper day?"

"Yeah, yesterday and this morning. Kind of the most useless day of the week." He sat down at the table while she moved around getting glasses and an opener. "I drop off the pasteup, then I go back late in the day and pick up the papers, bring them back here, and spend some hours in the evening putting advertising inserts in with the help of my part-timers, and then we divide them up for delivery. And today, we deliver. It's work any idiot could do, and I always feel I'm wasting my time doing it. But I sort of like it, on the other hand." Frankie set a glass down in front of him and sat down at the table, too. "A sign of stupidity on my part, I suppose."

"That's exactly how I feel about this." She gestured around herself. "Stupid work is sometimes good. Work that leaves your mind free to meander."

"Ah. And what has your mind been meandering to while you did your stupid work?"

"Oh, free-floating stuff," she said. "Africa. My parents." She looked up at him. "Of course, the fires from time to time. That can occasionally stop me in my tracks, imagining I've heard the arsonist rustling around on the porch or something. I just hate it."

"Don't we all," he said. Sitting this close to her, he could see she had no makeup on at all. She looked about twelve years old.

She poured some beer from her bottle into her glass. "So, what's in the news? Same old, same old?"

"You heard about Harlan Early."

"I did not."

"Ah. He shot himself."

Frankie looked stunned. "He *killed* himself?"

"No. No, no, no, no." He smiled. "But he shot his *toe* off. He's on crutches now."

She said, "This wasn't intentional?"

"No. An accident. He thought he heard a noise in the night, and he had a gun by the bed, a hunting rifle. I can't quite imagine how it happened, but apparently he was more or less picking it up and swinging himself out of bed at the same time, and *ka-boom!* That was it."

"Yikes," she said.

"Exactly—yikes. His wife was asleep next to him, so she woke up in absolute terror. And then she was furious at him, she said. And the toe"—he shook his head—"gonzo."

"I bet that really hurt," she said. And then, "But it's kind of funny, too."

"So he says. That it hurt like hell. But he's mostly embarrassed." He had some beer. It was Sam Adams, one of his favorites. "I also bring you reports on the two latest fires. They're finally willing to say that at least one of them is, in fact, arson, so that's new. News," he corrected himself. "This was the Froelichs'. The one where the dog died."

"Oh, God, yes. I heard about that. That was awful."

"It was, poor guy. I hate thinking about *that*," Bud said. "He was known to me, actually."

"You knew the *dog*?"

"Yeah. In the sense that he liked to chase the car when I dropped the paper off. He'd come out, greet me, we'd have a perfectly reasonable conversation. Then, as soon as I pulled away from the mailbox, I was his archenemy. His nemesis." He shook his head. "He was a golden, going white from the bottom up. A nice old guy." He had been momentarily almost tearful when he heard about it.

"That's really changed things, hasn't it?" Her face was sober. "I mean, the fires were bad enough before, the houses being lost, but to kill an animal . . ."

"Yeah, suddenly it's not just real estate." They raised their glasses simultaneously and drank.

She set her glass down and turned it slowly. When she looked up, she was smiling again. "Though Marjorie Griffith's studio was not just real estate, either. A genuine community loss, that one," she said.

"In what sense?"

"Oh, it was famous with the teenagers in town. I assume it still is."

"Famous for . . . ?"

"Being left open, basically. And having a bed in it. And being far away from anyone else's house. You sneaked up past her house, and once you were on the path through the woods, you were home free. I'll say no more."

"You need not." He was thinking of Frankie, moving into a dark cabin, moving to a bed inside it. Lying down. "Did you avail yourself of the facilities?"

"Along with about a thousand others."

"It must have gotten crowded from time to time."

She laughed. "It didn't. Who knows why not? Maybe the guys had a way of *reserving* it."

They were silent a few seconds.

"The thing is," he said, "I'm here to ask you on a date."

Her face stilled for just a few seconds, and then she smiled and said, "I'm honored. Amazed and honored. I can't remember the last time anyone asked me out on a date. What did you have in mind?"

"The fire-station dance. Friday." It had been announced only over the weekend, with posters at Snell's and at the post office. All the ministers in town had been charged with announcing it from their pulpits on Sunday, and Bud had written it up for the paper. They'd run out of money, the fire department, on account of the extraordinary number of fires they'd been called to, and a committee had been formed to plan several events to raise funds. There was this dance, and the following week, there was to be a bake sale on the green.

"Oh, I saw that. I was thinking about going. It's a barn dance, right?"

"It's *in* a barn, but the Churches' barn is not your grandfather's barn. It's more like . . . a pavilion, let's say. So it's a regular dance. That's my sense."

"A *pavilion*?" She made her voice snooty. "Why, it's been years since I went to a dance in a pavilion."

A dry wind pushed into the room, and the screen door jumped and then slapped back into its frame. They both looked at it and then at each other. They both looked away.

After a moment he said, "So? Will you?"

She smiled, revealing the gap he so admired. She bowed her head quickly. "I will. I'm pleased as punch."

The next night when Bud opened the door to leave the office, he almost cried out at the sight of the figure crouched there on the front stoop.

And then saw it was Ed Carter, straightening up, seemingly as startled by Bud as Bud was by him. "Oh! Bud," he said, further surprising Bud, who would have doubted Ed knew his name. "I didn't realize you were in."

"The paper lives up on the second floor, Ed. I was hiding out up there. But can I help you?"

"I was just dropping off a letter for you. Trying to slide it under the door, in point of fact."

"There's a slot for mail," Bud said, and pointed to it.

"Ah, I didn't see it through the screen."

"Well, now I can take it in my bare hands anyway, if you like." He opened the screen door, which meant Ed had to step back slightly. "What's it about?"

"It's more or less a response to your last column."

"Ah," Bud said. "Interesting. Come on in, why don't you? I'll read it now."

"Oh, no need for that."

"A clue, then," Bud said, "as to its nature."

"It's from a group of us."

"Yeah?"

"Yes. We're concerned, I guess you'd say, about certain . . . *element*s in your reporting."

"Now you do have to come in." Bud hoped he was managing to keep his tone friendly.

"The letter speaks for itself," Ed said, and smiled his chilly smile.

"Let's talk about it," Bud said. He held his open hand out as he stepped back, and slowly, clearly reluctantly, Ed put the letter into it.

And came in, though Bud hadn't been sure he would.

He flicked the light switch by the door and gestured Ed over toward the chairs Barb kept for clients. Standing next to them, he opened the letter.

Fancy stationery, Ed's address at the top. Two pages, single spaced, maybe five paragraphs. It was signed on the second page by fifteen or twenty people. They seemed, at a quick glance, to be all summer people. As Bud began to read, he saw why that was the case. They were "concerned," they said, about the possibility that his reporting would heighten tensions between year-round and summer people.

This had to be a response to the idea of the state trooper he'd quoted—his notion that class resentment might be a motivation for the fires.

The writers wondered if Bud was fully aware of the years of effort that had gone into creating a community here, one that rose above the class boundaries he'd pointed to. Those efforts were described in several paragraphs he skimmed quickly.

In the final paragraph, they called upon him to publish a paper that supported, rather than undermined, the good relations among *all*—underlined three times in ink—the groups in town. There was no need for a small, weekly country newspaper to be disturbing to its readers.

Then the signatures, some large, some small, in the aggregate rather like the Declaration of Independence, he thought.

Bud looked up. Like him, Ed was still standing. He'd moved to the side of Barb's desk, as if to put it between him and Bud.

"I'll certainly take this into consideration, Ed." He tried a smile. "Thank you," he said. "Thank you for bringing it by."

"I think you'd do well to consider it. At least that."

"I have to say, though, that in return I'd ask your friends to reconsider their notion of what news is. Which, by the way, it is my *job* to report."

Ed lifted his narrow shoulders. "The news is what you make it."

Bud shook his head. He was trying to keep his face benign, pleasant. "I disagree. I think there's a kind of integrity to it," he said. "Necessarily, I'd say."

"Oh, come on, Bud," Ed said, unable any longer to keep the contempt out of his voice. "This is not the Pentagon Papers. And you are not the *New York Times.*"

"Don't I know it," Bud said.

They stood, looking at each other. "So the issue is joined, apparently," Ed said.

"Well, if you put it that way, I'm afraid so," Bud said. "But look, thank you for letting me know your response. Thank your group, please, for its opinions, for being so open and frank. I'll reread it carefully. What more can I say?" He raised his hands, smiling.

When the screen door had shut behind Ed, Bud sat down in Barb's desk chair and read the letter again, and then the names. The signers included Annie Flowers, the Cotts, the Caulfields. Frieda McMahon, whom he'd always liked. Walter Eberhardt.

They weren't the town, he reminded himself. They were maybe twenty summer residents. They didn't even vote here, most of them.

But many of them were people he'd thought of as friends, and Bud felt wounded. Ganged up on and, almost childishly, hurt.

He needed a grown-up to talk to.

Pete came into the hall with a book in his hand, his finger inserted in its middle. He was wearing his half-glasses for reading, which made him look like a scold. He was dressed exactly as he always dressed at work—the khaki pants, the cardigan. Only the bow tie was missing.

He lowered his chin and looked sternly at Bud as he held the screen door open for him.

"Sorry to interrupt," Bud said.

"Are you?" His eyebrows went up. "Interrupting?"

"I'd like to. If you'll let me."

"When you put it that way, I more or less have to, wouldn't you say?"

"Politeness would dictate."

"And I am nothing if not polite." He led Bud into the small, low-ceilinged living room. Nothing had changed at Pete's house since Bud had first known him, except for a slight *embrowning*. A light grime, around the wall switches, for example. The worn look of the lace or tatted headrests and armrests on the chairs—the general sense of a bachelor carelessness about the exact definition of clean. Though everything was always tidy, picked up, arranged, down to the folded newspaper, set atop several other folded newspapers on the coffee table.

"I see you're keeping up," Bud said, gesturing at the pile.

"Lots to keep up with," Pete answered. "You want coffee? A beer?"

"I want to talk."

"I'm having a beer, then," Pete said.

"Fine. I'll have one, too."

"One, two, buckle my shoe," Pete said, leaving the room. He came back in a minute with two beers in bottles, no glasses. He handed one to Bud and sat on the couch with his own. Bud had sat down in one of the two old-fashioned armchairs, both with those worn-looking lace circles.

"I had a letter tonight," Bud said, after he'd had a swallow.

"Oh?"

"From a group of summer folk. Delivered by hand by Ed Carter, no less, so I heard his take on it as well. They're worried about my reporting."

"Your reporting of . . ."

"The fires, of course. Worried about, let's see . . . 'Exacerbating tensions,' I think the phrase was."

"Uh-oh."

"Yeah." They both had some beer and were silent for a long moment. Bud had learned Pete's pace when they were working together—the long pauses, the slow responses.

"These would be tensions between year-round folks and them?" Pete said, finally. "The summer folks?"

"Yeah."

"You plead innocent?"

"I said I was simply reporting the facts, ma'am. The usual shuck and jive."

Pete smiled. He had another swig of beer.

Bud did, too. He rested his bottle on the doily on the arm of his chair. "What I wondered was whether there was ever any such issue for you. And, if so, how you handled it."

"Oh, lots of issues. Not that one, but others."

"Such as."

Pete thought. "Creeping socialism," he announced. "This accusation coming from year-round folks who tend to Republicanism. Probably a letter a week saying that." He sat for a minute more. "Too much national news, though I always tried to bring it around to home, don't you know. How this or that policy would live out here. But still, found objectionable from time to time."

"But not this town-gown stuff. Or summer-winter, I guess you'd say in this case."

"Not that, no." He shook his head. "But that's newer anyway."

"Newer how?"

"Well, that expectation that we'll all *get along*—that didn't used to matter so much."

"Because?"

"Because there was no such expectation. There was no social mixing." They sat quietly for a minute or so. "Look," he said. "My mother worked as a maid at the Mountain House, so I speak with some authority on this."

"When was this?"

"Before she married my father. Maybe, let's say maybe 1920 or so. Chambermaid. Changing sheets. Cleaning up after folks. Messes. Bathrooms. That kind of stuff. And then when all that changed—this was after they were married and had us—she still cooked and cleaned for summer people. And sometimes there'd be some party, end of season, where the help got invited—you know, the field guys, the gardeners, the like. And my parents would go, and we children, too. This would be in the thirties, I guess. Into the forties. But this would be a special event, you understand. Noblesse oblige. The exception to the rule. There was never the expectation that my parents would be invited, say, to a dinner party or anything like that. We knew our place. Our places." He tapped the opening of his bottle. "I suppose it was the sixties that changed things, to some extent."

"How so?"

Pete thought for a moment. "It gave people the idea that class differences weren't right, somehow. As a matter of social equity. Of morality, let's say. Partly it was that so many new folks undertook to do the kinda work my parents did—farming, work with their hands. Carpentry. And these new folks were college educated, they were solidly middle class in their backgrounds, so they saw themselves differently." He laughed quickly. "They did *not* know their place. And then there were some fairly utopian notions, I guess, that could get played out here more easily than they would have had a chance to in a city, let's say."

Bud had rarely heard Pete so expansive. "And how did you fit into all that?"

He shifted on the couch. "Well, the paper had changed everything for me by then. Starting it up. Before then, I didn't know if I could stay on here. But the paper, it made a kind of place for me that was everywhere and nowhere socially, all at once. And that was what I wanted when I came back."

"Came back from . . . ?"

"From the war. From college, the GI Bill."

This was news to Bud. He'd heard no war stories from Pete, no college stories.

"And then I married Iris. She'd grown up here, like me. She was partly what I came back for. She was a teacher, in Winslow, the high school. English. She'd gone to Plymouth State—it was a normal school then. But she was ready for something new when we married, and she came on board at the paper. Ran everything at the business end. So we had each other. We made a kind of . . . universe, I guess you could say. A two-occupant universe. We liked it that way.

"So I didn't have to concern myself with what you're talking about.

And my feeling is, most of the year-round folks don't. They just don't. I may be wrong. But worrying about those issues—well, let's just say that I see why it was summer folks writing your letter." He set his bottle down on the table.

"Any suggestions for me, then?" Bud asked.

Pete shook his head. "Just, same as always."

"Which is?"

"Enjoy yourself. No point to any of it otherwise."

They sat in silence for a while. Bud finished his beer. He said, "You're my guru. You know that, Pete?"

"If I'm your guru, my friend, you have more problems than worrying about class issues in Pomeroy, New Hampshire."

"Well, I do have more problems than that, but I'm not discussing those with you."

"Ah. Because . . . ?"

"Because they're women problems. Woman. And not really problems. Just . . ." He lifted his hand.

Pete grunted sympathetically. "Just don't let it mess up your day job, is all I'll say about that."

"So far, so good."

They sat. Pete seemed completely relaxed in their silence.

"What were you reading before I so rudely interrupted you?" Bud asked.

Pete made a dismissive motion with his hand. "Just stuff I've read before. That's the good news about getting old. At my age, I can just reread all the stuff I've read before, and it comes at me fresh. Even when I remember it, it comes at me fresh."

"So what is it you're reading?"

"*Lord Jim.*"

"Ah," Bud said. "I remember it only vaguely. I haven't read it since college, I don't think."

"I do Conrad every four or five years," Pete said.

"You're an inspiration, Pete."

He snorted.

After a few moments: "I have a question for you."

"Shoot," Pete said.

"Who do *you* think is setting the fires?"

"I don't have any idea. But he's in our midst, that's all. And that, my friend, will make for an interesting summer."

"If he goes on."

"Oh, he'll go on. Till he's caught, don't you think? And maybe, somehow, that's the point."

"He wants to be caught?"

"Yes."

"Then why would he set them at night?"

"Well, there has to be the game. If he set them in front of us, where's the fun?"

"You're not arguing that this is conscious."

"No, not that. But it is a curious crime, isn't it? You know, a public crime. We're supposed to notice it, after all. That's really the point. You're supposed to write about it."

"But he can't want to get caught."

"Maybe not. But it teeters right there. He's saying to you, *Make me famous*. And when he reads you, he thinks, *I am famous*. But then I can't stop. I have to stay famous. And that brings me closer and closer to getting caught. Maybe I even up the ante. Maybe I *do* do it in the day."

"Pete, you're making me think that you're the arsonist."

"I don't have the energy, my friend. But just keep writing him up. Make him happy. Make yourself happy. Forget class relations. It ain't your beat." He shifted forward on the couch, as if to stand, and in response Bud got up, setting his beer bottle on the coffee table next to Pete's.

"Thanks, Pete."

"Anytime." They started out of the room.

"I may take you up on that."

Bud sat in his car at the edge of the town green for a few minutes, watching Pete moving around his house, alone. It was dark out now, the green was empty. Pete went back to the kitchen, presumably with their beer bottles. Then the windows there went black, and a moment later he appeared again in the living room. He was carrying his book, the sad story of a young man trying to redeem himself. He sat down at the end of the couch, next to the lamp, and raised the book, bent his head toward it. Bud found himself unexpectedly affected by the sight.

And then he was imagining himself at Pete's age, living here, alone. Running the paper, rereading old books.

Pete wore it well. Bud suspected he wouldn't.

He started his noisy engine and watched as Pete's head lifted up, as he looked out to where Bud turned his headlights on and put the car in gear to start home.

12

~

ON THE POSTER IN THE LIBRARY, the dance had been called a sock hop. And sure enough, people were heeling their shoes off and setting them in a line by the door, though that left a number of them, like Frankie, barefoot rather than sock-footed. The floor was cement, buffed and gleaming, cool under her feet.

The vast open space of the barn was busy with people. It *was* a sort of pavilion, Frankie saw. There were wide doors slid open on three sides, so you had the sense of the outside everywhere around you, an outside that was groomed and manicured. "Now this is a *lawn*," she'd said as they drove up.

"Told you so," Bud said.

The music was loud and scratchy, someone's old tape or burned CD of Chuck Berry doing "Brown-Eyed Handsome Man." She felt Bud's hand—warm, authoritative—on her back, moving her into the crowd. It was the first time he'd touched her, and her body registered this, a kind of thrill along her spine that moved downward. She had the impulse to turn to him, to touch him back, but she kept walking, kept moving where he directed her, her breath just a little uneven.

At the same time, she was looking around, taking things in. The assembled group, she saw, was more inclusive than the tea had been, which made sense: the tea was launching the summer season, such as it was, and that was of import mostly to the summer people.

This event had nothing to do with the season, unless you thought of this summer as the arson season. Everyone was here. Several hundred, probably. She saw Marie Pelletier, who cleaned and did household errands for her mother, and Adrian Snell. Harlan Early was hunched

over a pair of crutches, deep in conversation with Annie Flowers. Lucy
Snell was talking to someone Frankie didn't know, but there were others she recognized—the Goodyears among them, and the Arderys, Jay
McMahon and his wife, whom she'd met at the tea. There were a lot
of kids, both teenagers and some young-adult types—some in couples,
paired off, some hanging out in groups with others of the same sex.
Some beautiful young women, she noted, and remembered, with a sudden pang, what it had been like to be young here in the summer, a place
where she had felt freer and more comfortable than in any of the other
places she had lived with her family.

There were a few strays her own age and Bud's. As they moved toward
the bar, on the other side of the huge space, she wondered how they
would have been described, she and Bud. When she had told her mother
who she was going to the dance with, Sylvia had said, "Bud Jacobs. Well,
that makes sense, I suppose—I hear he's a bit of a womanizer." Which
meant, Frankie assumed, that he'd been seen at town events and elsewhere with other women.

"Well, Mother dear," she had said, "in that universe, I would definitely
be a manizer. Which is why I don't live in that universe."

"You think not," her mother said.

Now she and Bud pushed up to the table. It was a cash bar—beer
and wine for those of age, Coke and punch for those not. Loren was
stationed there checking IDs, but he didn't seem to see them, and she
moved quickly to the other end of the table.

The music had stopped, and now it started again, some doo-wop
group. Bud had to shout to get their beers from the guy behind the table.
Frankie recognized him as the fire chief, who'd been so awkward at the
town meeting. Bud shouted an introduction. Yes, Davey Swann. And the
other man—the guy who was serving them—was Gavin Knox.

"Oh," she yelled. "You're for rent." Wasn't he one of the men Bud had
mentioned?

"Me and some others." He grinned. "Interested?" There was definitely
something flirty about him.

"I seem to be managing on my own, thanks."

Bud turned to her, holding two large plastic cups of beer. She took hers, and they threaded their way out of the crowd. As they walked, the beer sloshing in the cups, Bud leaned over to speak to her, and she was aware of him physically, suddenly—his solidity, his large head, his pleasant, soapy smell, which encircled them. He was saying he'd take his pictures now and get it over with. Then maybe do just a few more if something fantastic presented itself. He'd warned her about this on the way over—that he was at least partly on duty tonight—and when they'd gotten out of the car, he'd opened the back door to take his camera out. It hung around his neck now.

The music stopped again, and he straightened up. That thing happened again, Frankie noted, wherein they were looking at each other with what seemed to her, anyway, a consciousness of finding the other attractive, of being found attractive. They were both smiling with the pleasant sense of it, the unspoken thing. Simultaneously, they raised their plastic glasses—womanizer, manizer—and drank. Some further rock and roll started.

"Okay," she said. "I'll see you in a bit." He set his beer down on one of the small, high tables scattered here and there in the big space. He stepped a few paces away from her, then turned, raised his camera, and took her picture. Or pretended to. Maybe he didn't, maybe it was just a way of reminding her of the day they'd met. In return she raised one hand to cover her face momentarily. She saw that he was grinning in response before he moved away.

For a while she was on her own, then, and she moved around, talking to people. She took note of the fact that she felt entirely comfortable in a way she hadn't at the tea. Perhaps it was because of Bud, because she was *with somebody* in some sense. She saw him now and then as she chatted with one person or another, and each time was startled by how much she liked to look at him, this tall, rangy guy in jeans and his work shirt, with his slightly-too-long graying hair.

But maybe she felt her sense of comfort because she knew people in Pomeroy now. She had said hello once or twice a week to many of the people in the room. She'd had the odd conversation with them—about the fires, of course, but also about the weather, about something in the news. And in fact, she'd had a kind of social life, limited but pleasurable. Two of the people she'd talked to at the tea had found her through Sylvia, and she'd gone to a few wine-and-cheese gatherings—the specialty of the summer people—and to one dinner party, stunning to her in its organization: they'd been assigned places at the table with little hand-written cards and, afterward, played charades.

What's more, it turned out, as she moved from conversation to conversation, that there were many people here solo tonight—maybe that, too, made things friendlier. Solo, because someone needed to stay home to guard the house. "Yeah," Julie Hess said to her. "I'm supposed to head home at ten-thirty, so Dean can come and dance."

"I guess it would be a perfect night for an arsonist, wouldn't it? *Take your pick, they're all out at the ball.*"

"That's what we're afraid of," Julie said. "I mean, we've got the kids at home, but that's even more reason for one of us to be there."

"Of course," Frankie said.

She had the same conversation several times over, so much so that she began to worry a bit about Liz's house, though she'd locked it up carefully before she left, even the windows.

And then Bud was there. "Dance, miss?" he said.

"First, I need to unload this." She pointed to her half-full cup. They moved together to the edge of the barn, where she set it down on one of the open horizontal structural pieces.

They moved back toward the center of the large room. Bud was a good dancer in the gangly, quasi-autistic mode of her youth. Around them, a few people who seemed to be of her parents' generation were actually jitterbugging. The teenagers or those a little older were moving against each other suggestively—pumping against each other, in fact. Frankie and Bud were the most free-form, it seemed. Certainly the least intimate as they moved around separately. But Frankie, anyway, was intensely aware of Bud's rhythm, was trying to form some kind of response to that with her own body. They kept it up for four or five fast songs.

When a slow number came on, Bud moved in easily to hold her. It wasn't exactly comfortable—they were both sweaty and pulsing with heat—but she liked his size, she liked the power of his arms holding her, turning her. She liked looking at his face, so close to hers, smiling, inches from a kiss. At the end he did a nifty twirl, with just the suggestion of a dip, which made her squeal.

After a couple more dances, they fetched their beers and went to stand in one of the open doorways to cool off. There were several others clustered there in groups, out of the noise, talking. Someone asked Bud about the *Boston Globe*—there was a rumor that one of their reporters was coming to town. They had been talking for only a few minutes when Loren appeared behind Bud, smiling in what Frankie thought of as a hungry way.

"Bud, Frankie," he said, by way of greeting. And then, with barely a return greeting from either of them, he launched into his news. "Looks like we got us a suspect or two, thanks to you."

"Oh, *no*," Frankie said.

"Is this on the record?" Bud asked.

"Now, I don't know about *that*."

"Yes or no?" Bud asked. She was struck by his voice. It was still friendly, but it had toughened, somehow. *Professional Bud.*

"You could say some leads have opened up. More'n that, you'll have to talk to the state troopers. I just wanted to thank Frankie here for coming forward."

"You're welcome," she said. "I guess."

"Is it just a matter of the taillights?" Bud asked.

Loren turned to him, sly again, that killer half smile at work. "We got a bit more. We got a bit more. We're working on it."

"What does that mean, 'working on it'?"

"I'm not at liberty to say more than that. Just, we're talking to people of interest."

"On the basis of the taillights, or additional information?"

"Oh, we got more than the taillights, at this point in time." He nodded and nodded.

"But you can't say what."

"I wouldn't like to, nope."

"You're going to make me talk to the state police."

"You got that right." His face was smug. Delighted, really. He nodded to her and then walked away.

She had some more beer. "This is just what I was afraid of," she said. She shook her head.

"What? You didn't think it would actually help when you talked to Loren?"

"Do you think it really *is*? Helping?"

"It is hard to tell, with Loren." He smiled. "He's certainly a guy who likes his job."

"Doesn't it all sound . . . bogus, though? A little bogus?"

"*He* sounds bogus. But he always does. It's likely there's something behind it, but you just can't ever tell with him."

"So *are* you going to talk to the state police?"

"I am. Yes. There's a trooper who lives in Winslow who's been working on the fires, too. The only state trooper I really know. He's been willing to talk and talk. He's the anonymous source in this week's paper."

"All I want to know is that they're not harassing everyone with slanted taillights just because of what I said."

"Well, that is *certainly* the most important aspect of all of this, and I'll try to ascertain that for you."

"I'd be grateful."

"That's what I'm hoping."

She smiled at him, trying to think of a quick response, when suddenly, inside, "Sgt. Pepper's Lonely Hearts Club Band" came on. "Ah, they're getting closer to my era," Bud said. They'd both finished their beers. "Dance?"

They went back in. They danced, and as they danced, Frankie was remembering dancing in Africa. The beer, the heat in the barn, the out-of-date music, all these reminded her of so many nights at various medical stations or field hospitals or feeding centers. The staff, the doctors, the supervisors, all done for the day, all a little drunk, sweaty, a mass moving in the lantern light—laughing, eager not just for the dancing, but for what came next for some. Tonight, with whom? That open, random, sexual charge, the eyes meeting, searching out someone else, meeting again.

And now, with Bud, she felt that same sexual heaviness in her abdomen, between her legs. Did she want this, again, when she'd be leaving soon? Shouldn't she be more careful here, where her parents lived? Shouldn't she be more careful of Bud?

God, shouldn't she be more *inventive*?

And yet she was so attracted to him.

It was about eleven when they left the dance. Most of the people still out on the dance floor were teenagers, it seemed. There were plenty of older people staying on, too, but they were mostly standing around the tables, or in the doorways, holding glasses of beer or wine, talking.

People called to Bud, not to her, and he turned to wave, to call back. His hand rested on her back again as they walked, and she was aware of its light finger touch, then the warm flat of his palm moving down to her waist. It felt like a claim of sorts, and she was pleased, almost in spite of herself.

They walked in silence to his car. The night had gotten cool, and Frankie shuddered and hugged herself. Her damp hair was clammy on her neck.

"Cold?" Bud asked. He was opening the door for her.

"I am, a little. I should have remembered to bring a jacket. I always forget how cold it can get at night, even in summer." She slid inside.

"Reach around back and see what you find. I think I've got a couple of sweaters back there."

Frankie turned and got up on her knees. The backseat was a mess. There were stacks of papers, shoes, wrappers, several unidentifiable shapeless garments. She felt around. Yes! A sweater. She sat back with it, turning it to get ready to pull it on. Bud got in on his side. "But what about you?" she asked him, the sweater still in her lap. "Aren't you cold?"

"I'm not, honestly. Go ahead."

She pulled the sweater over her head and wiggled into it. It was big, and it had Bud's pleasant smell. The sleeves were so long they covered her hands entirely.

He started the car and it made its preposterous noise as they drove away. "In a couple of minutes, the engine should be warm enough to turn the heat on."

"I'm okay now."

They drove down to the town, talking about whom they'd seen, what they'd heard. They'd just started back uphill in the direction of Liz's and her parents' houses when he said, "Oh my God!" He swerved suddenly, and they were on the shoulder, stopping, tilted almost into the ditch.

"What! What is it?" *A fire,* she was thinking, looking around for it on her side.

"Come on, come on," he said quickly. He got out. She opened her door and he was there, holding his hand out to her.

"What?"

"Come."

She took his hand and stood up. He put his arm around her, turning her around to face north across the Louds' field, and she saw it. The night sky was shimmering slowly, green changing to pink, long shining passages of light, like immense, slowly moving colored flames.

"The northern lights!" she whispered.

"Aurora borealis," he said. "I've never seen them."

"I did. Once. Here. As a child." Alfie had waked them, and they all went out and sat in the meadow. Now the long pale flames shifted slowly, mysteriously to blue. "Oh!" she cried.

With his arm around her, they walked forward, into the field. She stumbled over the uneven ground, almost dizzy, and his arm pulled her closer against him.

"Let's sit," he said. They did, awkwardly. After a minute or so, almost as one, they lay down on their backs. Bud's arm was under her neck and head, and she turned slightly into him.

They watched. The sky to the north kept shifting, kept changing color, sometimes throbbing close to the horizon, sometimes radiating so far across the heavens that the colors fingered almost overhead.

In between and around the light show, they talked, their voices made whispery by what seemed so vast above them. About the lights, about what caused them—Bud knew, and he explained them to her. About the last fire, at the Cotts' house. For the first time, Bud hadn't responded to the page. "I feel like I've seen the fire. And I wanted to sleep, more than anything."

After a silence, she said, "Did you know you had a reputation in this town?"

"I did not. A reputation for what?"

"My mother told me you were—and I believe I am quoting directly— 'a bit of a womanizer.'"

There was silence for a moment. "Just a *bit*?"

"This is what they say, apparently."

"And it's not going to help, showing up with you tonight. Yet another woman."

"So you plead guilty?"

"I plead guilty to living in a small town, mostly. And being an unmarried, and therefore pretty visible, male."

"It would work that way, wouldn't it?"

"You wait."

"I probably won't."

"Won't wait?"

"Yes."

"Meaning, won't wait around to see?"

It felt as though they'd come around to this point in their conversations before, that she'd told him this before—that she didn't think she was staying. She said that to him. There was a long silence.

"I suppose it's something I'd like to know for sure, one way or another, before I . . . what? Decide to put my womanizer's moves on you."

"A true womanizer would need no such assurances."

"There you have it."

"Have what?"

"Proof that I am not a true womanizer." His body shifted next to hers. "Should you need it."

"Though you got me horizontal pretty easily."

"But arranging the aurora borealis—that took a long time."

"Thank you, then. It's really spectacular."

They lay still for a while. Occasionally one of them raised a pointing hand to be sure the other saw some changing aspect of it—the flickering motion of one licking light, the abrupt change in color of another, green to pink, pink to blue.

He leaned over her and kissed her. Her whole body seemed to soften inside, and she moved her face, her mouth, against his. He made a noise, and she pulled back, just slightly. Enough so that, after a moment, he did, too. She felt torn, wanting him, not wanting to start another unfinishable thing.

They lay silent for a while.

"Why did you leave Africa, anyway?" he whispered.

"I told you. I don't know where to be. Where I want to be."

"Was there a guy?"

Frankie smiled in the dark. "I must be transparent. My mother asked me that, too."

"And what did you tell your mother?"

"There was, yes. But he mattered less than, I guess, the nature of our relationship."

"Which was?"

"Temporary. Impermanent. All the people I met—I guess I mean men, but women, too, actually—were impermanent. Fugitives. From divorces or boring careers or too much sorrow. Or themselves, maybe. I had one affair after another with people essentially in transit. And I was in transit."

He didn't say anything.

After a minute, she said, "And my work life was the same. You fix one thing over here, and then there's another one over there, and while you're in the second place, bad stuff happens and the first place falls apart again." Bud shifted next to her, rose up on his elbow. She could barely see his face in the dark, but she felt his breath, his presence, warm over her. "Sometimes I felt . . . complicit in that. And sometimes we were. We *were* complicit. If you flood a place with free food, for instance, farmers don't bother to plant. What would be the point? So you perpetuate hunger, in a way, by trying to alleviate it. And sometimes you end up feeding fighters. Prolonging conflict. Or they prolong the conflict because they see it as a means of access."

"Access to?"

"Aid: Food. Money. Medicine. Sometimes, and I only slowly understood this, they used hunger, they used starvation, as a way to *get* aid, to position themselves. Famine as a weapon." She took an audible breath, then shook her head. "But that's only part of it.

"Oh!" she said, and pointed. He turned. A kind of low, warm incandescence spread out across the horizon, as if some new, brilliant, midnight sun were about to rise.

When it shifted, she spoke again. "Philip, the man I was involved with, used to say that it was better to know your role, to know your place. You get in, you get out. He didn't pretend he was changing things. I think it made it easier for him in some ways."

What Philip had said to her was *Whatever I've learned from doing this work—and I'm not sure what I've learned—I don't delude myself. Exactly the opposite. It's instruction in how fucking useless I am, in any larger sense. As you are also, my darling.*

Now Bud said, "So did that make it easier for him than it was for you? That . . . that attitude? What was his name?"

"Philip." She said, "In some way, yes, I think it did. In the short run, I know what kept me there. The people. The children, especially. Seeing them get better. It was like a transformation. In the mothers, too. Saving lives, after all.

"But in the long run, less and less did. And I suppose I'd begun to notice the long run. He helped me with that. Both his . . . philosophy, I suppose you could call it, and then, actually, the very nature of our relationship. Because it seemed like more of the same."

"A metaphor for your dilemma."

"You might say so. I felt I was temporizing, as I've told you. With my life."

"Yes," he said.

Frankie was ashamed, suddenly. She felt she'd talked too much. She'd complained, when she had no right to.

After a long silence, she said, "And you?"

"And me what?"

"And you. Your history. Work. Women. Are *you* temporizing?"

He seemed to be pondering it. Finally he said, "No. I don't feel I am. I have a kind of stake in things, I guess you'd say. Literally, having bought the paper. Actually, I think that was my answer to that notion."

"The notion of temporizing."

"Yes. Coming here. Making it my home. Writing about it, so making it my work, too." Bud lay down, flat on his back again. "You know Pete, the guy who owned the paper before me?"

"Mmm." She was glad he was talking, glad to be hearing about him.

"He said an interesting thing to me. That he couldn't have stayed here without the paper. That it gave him a way to be here, a way to be at home here—without, maybe, buying into everything involved. So, maybe like your friend . . ."

"Philip?"

"Yeah. Old Philip. A way to be in and out at the same time."

After a moment, she said, "And women?"

"What about women?"

"Don't be coy. I told *you.*"

"In a general way you told me."

"I ask no more from you. Just, generally, you've had girlfriends here before."

"Girlfriends here, yes. Though I've slowed way down. And wives before."

"Wives? Multiple wives?" This startled Frankie. Though why should it?

"Two. One that doesn't count. The starter marriage. Isn't that what Margaret Mead called it? We're allowed that, right?"

"I guess."

"And then one serious mistake."

After a long moment, she said, "But I thought the point of the starter marriage was that you didn't need to make the big mistake."

"Ah, I think I wanted the big mistake, somehow. The drama. But in the end it wore me out. And then it was over."

Frankie wanted to ask more about it, but she wasn't sure she should. And the lights were leaving the sky anyway. They might have been lying in the field for an hour by this time. The sky was turning black and starlit again. Bud was shivering, and she'd curled against him to try to help him stay warm. "You're cold now," she whispered.

"It's okay," he said.

"This was . . . so astonishing."

"All of it."

"We should go," she said.

"Should we?"

"You're cold."

"It's okay."

"*I'm* cold."

"Ah."

He rolled against her; he kissed her. For a moment her whole body moved, rejoiced, in response to the length of him, the size of him against her. Her mouth answered the warmth of his.

And then she checked herself, she pulled just slightly back and smiled at where his face was. "I should go."

"I don't want you to."

"But the show is over."

"Is it? It is. I guess."

"I should go. I'm actually worried about Liz's place."

"Okay."

She sat up, and he did, too, and then they stood. He put his arm around her again, and she leaned against him as they walked slowly, bumping oddly over the rough ground, back to the car.

They drove up the dark hills without talking. He pulled in at Liz and Clark's, where the porch light was on. He turned to her. "Thank you for this evening. For being my date."

"I liked being your date. Thanks for being *my* date."

"I think the date is the one who got asked. Not the asker, I don't think."

"Well, what are you then, to me?"

He grinned in the half-light of the porch light, a slow, widening grin. "We shall see, shan't we?"

Frankie didn't have an answer. After a moment, though, she leaned over and kissed him. Just their faces touching. His flesh was cool, but his mouth, opening, was warm, and tasted sweet. He made a noise, a sigh.

She sat back and turned to open her door. She got out of the car. The night was cold. At the door to Liz's house, she turned under the light to wave, but he was already in gear, just starting to drive away.

Some part of her was disappointed, ridiculously.

13

THE RIDING MOWER had been sitting in the middle of the overgrown lawn for three hours now. The pickup truck with its ramps set out was smack in the middle of the driveway. If she'd wanted to go somewhere, Sylvia would have had to drive over the unmown grass to get out. Not that she wanted to go anywhere, but it was the idea. The principle.

The boy—the young man—Tink, had driven up at about eleven, and with what seemed to Sylvia his usual deliberated, elaborate slowness, set the planks out, backed the mower down, donned ear protectors and goggles and started the engine up.

Alfie had been having a bad day anyway today, and this clearly tipped the balance. He'd come almost immediately into the kitchen, where Sylvia stood at the door watching Tink.

"Tell that . . ." He pointed out the window. "Tell him to go away."

Sylvia turned to him. His face was working, agitated, his jaw moving up and down, his head almost palsied.

"It's just the mower, Alfie. He's doing the lawn."

"No! That machine."

"Yes, the machine that mows the lawn. The mower. He comes every week, to cut the grass."

"It's too loud."

"Well, I agree with you." She stepped over to him, touched his elbow. "But come, let's shut the windows in your study. Come on. That will help." And perhaps it would. They were new windows, double-glazed, tight. She took Alfie down the hall, matching her gait to his unsteady one. As she shut and locked the last of the windows, the noise was suddenly domesticated. It was as though someone were mowing off in the distance—an almost pleasant sound. She shut the curtains, too, so Alfie wouldn't see the machine as it passed around the house again and again, and she turned the desk lamp on over Alfie's work. Her eye fell on the papers scattered around, filled with Alfie's vertical handwriting, almost completely illegible now.

"There!" she said. "Cozy and quiet. Perfect for working." She hated herself—this tone, this condescension. Next she'd be using the nurse's first person plural: *Now we're going to sit down and we'll just get at it.*

May I die first.

"But I don't know where my books are," Alfie protested. He sounded like a child.

"They're right here." Sylvia gestured at the stacks he'd placed on his desk, four or five of them, sloppy towers of different heights lurching this way and that.

"No, I mean the other books."

"These?" She pointed to the bookcases lining the three walls of the room where there were no windows. They held the several hundred books Alfie had culled from his libraries at the college and the house in Connecticut.

"No, no." He was angry at her now. "The *others.*" You idiot.

"I'll tell you what," she said, willing herself to patience, to cheerfulness. "You sit down and do your work, and I'll go get the other books."

He looked dubious.

"Okay?" she said. "Okay," she answered herself. And she was grateful to see, as she walked to the doorway, that he was complying, that he had sat down and was pulling in, to do his "work."

She shut his door behind her. She was thinking that this would give her a chance to get all the piles of books that were now messily stashed around the house into his study, at least for a little while. She started to gather them onto the kitchen table, beginning with the two piles from the porch, thickened with damp. She had just bent to pick up the pile on the floor by his living room chair when a motion outside flickered at the edge of her vision. She stood up and went to the window.

It was the police car, the big green star taking up the whole driver's-side door. It had driven right across the lawn to Tink's mower and stopped in front of him. Now the mower stopped, too, and Tink dismounted, though he didn't turn the motor off.

Loren stayed in his car. She could hear their voices, yelling, though not what they said. She assumed he was asking about her—he'd come to her house, after all—but it didn't make sense to her. Why hadn't he just parked his car and come to the back door?

Ah. Perhaps because that would have been difficult with the truck taking up so much of the driveway. She felt a helpless irritability rise in her. She wanted to slam Alfie's books down. She wanted the noise of the mower to stop.

She crossed to the porch door and stepped outside. She walked through the lanky grass to Loren's car and greeted him and Tink. She had to shout to be heard, and she could barely hear Loren's shouted greeting in return. She wasn't sure whether Tink said anything at all. His face stayed impassive. Dull. It *was* dull, she thought. Dull and sullen and pretty. She stepped toward him and shouted, "Could you please turn *off* your mower." She gestured at it.

It seemed to her he paused just a beat too long before he turned back to the mower. A beat meant to tell her he could goddamn well choose or not choose to do as she asked.

The silence that fell when the mower went off seemed shocking. Embarrassing, really. Loren was grinning up at her.

"Hope you're well, Sylvia," he said.

"I'm fine," she said, ignoring Tink, who was coming back to stand by the car. And then she saw that there was someone in the backseat. She lowered herself a little to look in. His head, too, was ducked, to see her. "Gavin!" she said.

"Hi, Miz Rowley."

"Are you boys in trouble? What is this, Loren?" She had stood back up and was looking at Loren levelly.

"I was looking to borrow your yardman for a bit."

"But he's in the middle of things here, as you see."

"Yes, I do. And I apologize for that. But we won't be too long. Just a few things to talk over."

"But what's so important? Why can't it wait?"

"If you insist, Sylvie, I'll wait. We could wait, couldn't we, Gavin?" His tone was jovial.

"I can wait, for sure," Gavin said.

"It's just, I'd rather not," Loren said, looking directly at her.

"Well, I suppose it's none of my business . . ."

"It's town business, Sylvie. You don't need to concern yourself with it." His tone had cooled.

"Oh, for God's sake, Loren," she said in exasperation. "Go ahead." She stepped back from the car. "It's inconvenient, to say the least. But I suppose that's it, isn't it? The law speaks, and that's that." She turned to Tink. "Go ahead, then," she said.

Without looking at her, the young man went around the car to the passenger side and got in.

Now Loren smiled up at her again. As he started to turn the car around, he raised his hand in a regal salute. The king, riding off in his carriage.

"Please don't be too long," she called. She thought his smile deepened, but she couldn't tell for sure. She was sorry she'd fed his vanity, or whatever it was. She turned and went back into the house, where Alfie's books waited for her.

At about two-thirty, she called Adrian. He wasn't at home, so she tried the store. Tink had been called away, she said, and the mower and truck had been sitting all over her yard for hours now. Her voice, she thought, was conciliatory. She was always careful of her tone with Adrian.

"What do you mean 'called away'?"

"Loren Spader stopped by and picked him up."

There was a few seconds' silence. "Loren," he said.

"Yes."

"On official business?"

"It seemed so. He was in the police car. He had Gavin Knox in the backseat."

"Gavin?"

"Yes."

Another pause. Then: "I wonder what those boys got up to." His voice had relaxed, it sounded slightly amused. Gavin's involvement must have been reassuring to him, she thought.

"Well, whatever it was, it's taking a while to resolve it. And meanwhile, I'd either like my lawn mowed or for this equipment to go away."

"I s'pose I could get up there in, maybe, half an hour or so."

"That would be perfect."

It was less than half an hour, though, when she heard his car in the driveway. She stood up from her desk to watch him park behind the truck. He started across the yard toward the back door, and she quickly went to the kitchen so he wouldn't have to knock, so he wouldn't disturb Alfie, who was taking his afternoon nap.

He started when she opened the door—clearly he hadn't expected it—and his face seemed unguarded, open, in a way she rarely saw it.

"I'm sorry about this, Sylvie," he said, gesturing behind him at the truck.

"Oh, it's okay," she said. "Just, can you get them out of the way?"

"No, I'm going to finish up mowing now. I'm not sure when Tink's coming back."

"Are he and Gavin in some kind of trouble?" she asked.

"Sounds like maybe. Anyway, Loren took them over to Black Mountain, to the state police. Fran"—this was Loren's wife—"wasn't sure when they'd be back."

"Is it about the fires, do you think?"

"I wouldn't think so. Both of those boys're on the fire squad, don't you know."

"No, I didn't realize that."

"Yep," he said. "No, Fran said it was something about a car, maybe one of theirs. What I'm hoping is that it's not some hit-and-run kinda thing."

"Oh. Yes. That would be terrible."

"But we don't know."

They stood for a moment. It was, Sylvia thought, the longest exchange they'd had in years.

"Well, I'd better get on it," he said. "I won't do the trimming today. Just the mowing. Then I can get that out of here anyhow."

"Fine. I'm grateful for anything."

He turned and went around the corner of the house. Sylvia went back inside. She'd make tea for Alfie. The mower would surely wake him.

So she was in the kitchen when the mower started up again, and between the noise outside and her own noise inside—the running water, the kettle clashing on the stove as she set it down—she didn't hear Alfie. She didn't hear the porch door slam shut after him, she didn't hear him shouting at Adrian. She didn't see him, either, trying to pull Adrian off the mower. Just suddenly the motor was off.

And then she did hear him, his terrified voice, shouting senselessly something about the house being his. "You're *not* going to wreck it!" and she was across the living room, across the porch, the door was slamming behind her as she stepped outside.

Adrian was holding Alfie, easily. Alfie was frantically swinging his body back and forth and shouting, and underneath that, she could hear Adrian's voice, steady, reassuring, saying Alfie's name, saying *Calm down, calm down*. She stood, aghast, some paces away, and then Alfie saw her.

"They're coming again," he said, piteously.

She went to him. "Alfie," she said. "Alfie." She held him, too. She and Adrian were holding him between them, trapped like some child in a game, *Take the keys and lock him up*.

Sylvia was looking into Alfie's face as she spoke her words now, the same kinds of words Adrian had been saying—Alfie's name, and then that it was all right, it was all right. She could feel Adrian's hands on her arms, gripping them. Holding her.

Holding Alfie.

Alfie calmed, slowly. His mouth opened and shut again and again, fishlike. She relaxed her embrace experimentally. She could feel Adrian doing the same, releasing her, and then, when Alfie stayed unresisting, trembling, he let his arms drop, he stepped back, away from her and Alfie.

She could see that his face was stricken, full of pity—for Alfie or for her? He met her glance, and for a moment she had a sense of who he might have been to her if their history hadn't been what it was.

She turned away then, to Alfie. "I put some tea on," she said to him. "Come inside. Come with me. It's all right." And speaking gently to him, her arm around his shoulders, she moved him, stumbling, toward the house. "It's all right."

She led Alfie to his study, where the curtains were still drawn, the windows shut. She hoped it would feel hermetic, safe. She got him to sit at his desk, she showed him his books.

Once he seemed calm, or quiescent, anyway, she went back to the kitchen. The kettle was boiling vigorously, its metal top chattering. Adrian was standing in the open doorway. She turned the heat off and took a step toward him. "I guess it would be better if you just didn't try to mow right now." She was almost whispering.

"Yes." He turned his hat slowly in his hands. He looked at her. They stood perhaps three feet apart. "I didn't know, Sylvie."

"He's . . . not well."

"Yes. Well, I moved the truck out of your way till Tink can get it. The mower . . . I'll leave it there. Maybe when you're not going to be home? You could call? Tink or I could come up and mow quick and get it out of your way."

"Thank you."

"He's . . . ?"

"It may be his medication. He seems . . . worse, suddenly."

"Ah."

They were quiet for a moment that grew into a question. "We think he has Alzheimer's," she said. And even as she said it, even as his face shifted in sympathy, she knew she was announcing it to the town, that he would tell. His gentleness with Alfie today, their strange intimacy, the way he'd looked at her and whatever that meant, these wouldn't have much weight in the balance. He would tell, because such information was his currency, as surely as the cash in his register.

"I'm sorry for that," he said. He *was* sorry, she could hear it. "He was a fine man. Such an intelligent man. It just seems . . . wrong, doesn't it?"

She nodded. "Well, life isn't fair."

"Aah, we know that."

She moved to the Hoosier cabinet to get the tea for Alfie. "Thank you, Adrian," she said. "For everything."

"That's okay, then," he said. He put his hat on his head and turned and left.

The rest of the day had seemed endless, though Alfie was quiet. Silent, actually. He seemed utterly spent. Each time Sylvia passed his study door, he was sitting in his rocker, staring off at nothing. Either that, or dozing.

For dinner, she warmed up some soup. Alfie barely ate any, though he had two pieces of pie afterward. She had two martinis and wanted a third, but stopped herself.

By eight-thirty, Alfie was in bed, sound asleep. Sylvia tried her novel, one Frankie had recommended, but whether she'd had too much to drink or was just too agitated by the events of the day—Tink and Loren. Alfie. Adrian—she couldn't settle into it. She moved restlessly around the house, sitting briefly in the kitchen, then at the dining room table. The windows were black. Alfie's snoring was oppressive. She needed to get out, to talk to someone, if only for fifteen minutes.

She'd try Frankie, she decided. Drive down. If Frankie wasn't home, she'd be back up within five minutes. If she was home, she'd stay no longer than half an hour at the most. That was all she needed. A human voice.

She pulled on a sweater she'd left draped over the back of a dining room chair and picked up her keys on the way through the kitchen.

The night air was chilly, and the darkness was absolute—no moon, no stars. Adrian had moved the truck partway down the driveway, she saw, and pulled it off to one side. She drove past it to the road and turned right, downhill.

The lights were on at Frankie's. Sylvia's relief was so great she was, for a moment, tearful. It took her a few seconds to notice that there was a car pulled up at the side of the house, an old car. Who could that be?

And then she remembered. Of course—Bud Jacobs.

She hesitated for a moment, but then she thought, *This might be better.* This would keep her from unloading all her sorrows onto Frankie. Half an hour of polite chitchat, then, with Bud or whoever this visitor was, chitchat that would probably be distracting enough, pleasant enough, to lift her spirits, to send her home ready to manage another day with Alfie. And perhaps tomorrow would be better. It often worked that way—after a really horrible episode, he would seem suddenly himself again for a few days.

And then it occurred to her: there might be something romantic, something sexual, going on between Bud and Frankie.

But no, here was the door opening, and Frankie standing in the light, looking out. She'd seen the headlights, no doubt. Sylvia turned off the engine.

"I thought it might be you," Frankie called. As Sylvia got out of the car and walked across the yard, she stepped back. "Come in," she said. "What a nice surprise." She gestured behind her to where, yes, Bud Jacobs was standing up at the big table. "You know Bud, I think. He knows who you are, at any rate."

"Yes," Sylvia said, crossing the room to shake Bud's hand. "We've met a few times, town gatherings of one sort or another."

They talked briefly about these events. Then he asked after Alfie, and Sylvia reported he was sleeping.

"Sit. Sit down, both of you," Frankie said. "What would you like? Coffee? I have decaf, too. Or wine? That's what we're having. Bud brought some over." She was at the refrigerator.

Sylvia said she'd have a glass of wine.

Frankie brought her a jelly jar and set it down. While she was pouring wine for all of them, Sylvia turned to Bud and said, "Well, there's no dearth of news for you this summer, anyway."

"No," he said, smiling. "It's kept me jumping. And probably neglecting stuff people would much rather read about."

"Oh, I think everyone wants to read about the fires. I think we *need* to read about them."

"Well, I'd agree. And I have to say, it's a high for me to know how widely the paper's being read right now." His long fingers turned his glass slowly on the scarred tabletop. "But why do you say people *need* to read about it?"

"Oh, I think . . . to be prepared, in part. And then, it's interesting, the question of arson, and arsonists. Why they do it. How they do it. Wouldn't you always read an article about arson?"

"Especially if it's close by," Frankie said.

And they went on talking about it, passing around the things they knew, the things they'd heard. Then they talked for a while about the debate in town over whether to put up a cell-phone tower in the town woods. Bud was always attentive, his face alert, noticing. Sylvia was aware of her impulse to respond to his focus, his interest. She said to him, "Here's something else entirely, but interesting, I think. Loren Spader came by today to pick up Tink. Tink Snell, who was *supposed* to mow my lawn. He had Gavin Knox with him, too—Loren did."

"What do you mean, he had him?" Something had shifted in Bud's tone.

"Well, in the backseat. And he took Tink also. Adrian came by later and said they'd gone off to the state police, but that's all he knew."

Frankie was looking at Bud. "Because of the fires?" he asked.

"No, no," Sylvia said. "Because of something to do with a car."

"Oh, God, I knew it!" Frankie said. She leaned her head back, shut her eyes. "Unh," she groaned. "It's because of the taillights, I'm sure of it."

"Oh, probably not, Frankie," Bud said. He was trying to be reassuring, Sylvia could tell. And she could also tell he didn't really believe what he was saying.

She asked then what Frankie was talking about, and Frankie and Bud explained Frankie's having seen what might have been the arsonist's car, her reporting that to Loren. Loren's coming by with photos of car taillights he'd taken here and there around town.

They talked about what they knew of Tink, of Gavin. Of how unlikely it was that either of them could be the arsonist. Sylvia was thinking about Tink, about the way in which she felt insulted by every encounter with him, but she didn't mention this. After all, she was at least partially responsible for what seemed like his contempt for her, or his dislike, anyway—she'd behaved so badly when she first met him. And she couldn't believe that any of that was connected to the arsons.

Bud knew them both a little. He thought Gavin was "a nice kid" and that Tink was maybe of marginal intelligence. At any rate, incapable of this long, planned-out terrorism. "Plus, they're both on the fire crew," he said.

"Oh!" Frankie said. "Well! Doesn't that make it even more likely?"

Sylvia watched him smiling at Frankie. "You'll explain this theory?" he said.

"Oh, *you* know this theory," Frankie said. "You wrote about it, the trooper talked to you about it." She turned to include Sylvia. "They sign up because they're fascinated with fires. They like to put them out, they like to start them. They just plain like *fire*. Something about it is . . . thrilling, I guess."

"Yeah, well, I find them interesting, too," Bud said. "I always like to go when there's a call. But that doesn't mean I'd start one."

"Nor have you joined the fire department."

Bud made an acceding motion, a lift of his shoulders.

Throughout this exchange, Sylvia continued to watch them, their attentiveness to each other, the pleasure apparent in their looking at each other. The pitch of Frankie's voice. Were they sleeping together? There was clearly something going on between them, some spark.

They talked about the fires, then, how they differed from one another, how bad each was. Sylvia knew the older Cotts well, and she talked about their house, which had burned the week before, how it had been built in the twenties or thirties by the town's master builder and had a number of his trademark elements, among them wooden wainscoting throughout.

"All of it nice, dry wood by now," Bud said.

"Yes, kindling essentially."

"I heard it made an amazing bonfire."

At one point, Sylvia said she should get back up to her house, she was worried about Alfie. But Frankie poured her another glass of wine, pointed out how deeply he slept now, hadn't Sylvia said so?

"Until about midnight or so," Sylvia said. "Then he seems to think he needs to get up. I can hear him moving around. But as long as I can hear him, I figure it's all right, and I try to soldier on in my quest for the requisite eight hours." They laughed. She had thought quickly about telling Frankie about Alfie's confusion today—his panic, really. But then she knew she wouldn't, couldn't, with Bud there. Bad enough that Adrian had seen it.

Though bad wasn't what she had felt about that in the moment it happened. What she had felt, she thought now, was a strange kind of pleasure when they were holding Alfie, when they were almost holding each other. And this too might have been part of why she didn't speak of it to Frankie.

But she and Bud had moved on, anyway. They were talking animatedly about fires as a childhood fascination. The wonderful sulfuric smell of matches. They both argued for the superiority of wooden to cardboard matches. Bud remembered the technique of lighting matches with a flick of a thumbnail, with a quick slide across a metal zipper. It made Sylvia recall the bonfires of her youth, and she talked about them—the leaves of the Chicago street raked together into an enormous pile and set alight on a dark fall night, the hangers bent into sticks for marshmallows, the marshmallows burning, dangling down, the faces of the children in the firelight, rapt, naughty.

They spoke of other pleasures of childhood. Making yourself dizzy by spinning around. The amazement of numbing a leg or a hand by lying on it oddly for a while. Breaking through the surface of an ice-covered puddle in winter, lifting up an entire magical sheet of the clear, cold, wet stuff.

Suddenly there was noise in the room, a buzzing. "Uh-oh," Bud said, standing up. He took something out of his pocket—a pager—and pushed a button on it. A woman's voice, distorted, hard to understand, spoke from it. "Call for a fire," she said in a squawking, fuzzy voice.

"Ah, *fuck*!" Bud said. And then turned quickly to Sylvia. "Sorry," he said.

"Repeat, call for a fire," the voice was saying. "Address, Carson Road, number nineteen."

"Nineteen, on this road?" he said, looking up at them, his face questioning.

"Alfie!" Sylvia cried. She was already standing up. She saw him, sleeping, smoke around him, or waking to fire, confused and helpless as a child. She was in motion, picking up her keys, her sweater, stepping quickly to the door. He would have died while she sat there drinking wine, talking. She pushed under another thought, a momentary glimpse of release for herself in this, whatever was happening.

She ran across the dirt to her car and fumbled with its door. Frankie was running out of the house, getting in on the other side. At first, Sylvia couldn't find the key on her ring in the dark, and then she finally had it, had it in the ignition, and the car started and she pulled forward. She was about to turn out into the road when she heard the siren approaching and stopped. After a few moments, the town fire truck went by, headed uphill, siren wailing. There were two cars following it, driving fast, and then Sylvia swung out and joined the caravan.

She followed them up the hill and into the long driveway. There were three or four cars already parked in the driveway and on the grass—and men running all over. But the flames, she saw with relief, were rising only from the barn, just the barn. She got out and had started toward the house when the door to the porch off the kitchen opened and Alfie came out between two men in fire gear. Each was holding one of his arms. He was in his pajamas, looking around, amazed and frightened at the chaos, the yelling.

Then she was there, she had him. She put her hands on his face and turned it to her own, she spoke to him, and he seemed to see her. Later, she couldn't remember what she said. The meaningless words you say to a child: *It's all right, it will be all right, shh, shh, come with me.*

Frankie was beside her, she saw. One of the firemen asked if anyone else was home, and she heard Frankie tell him no.

Together she and Frankie led Alfie back to the car. She noticed a faint but pungent smell centered on him, and she wondered how long it had been since he'd bathed, feeling a pang of guilt, of shallow embarrassment, for that, for Frankie's surely noticing it, or the firemen, one or the other of them perhaps thinking that she hadn't been taking good care of him in this way, either. And somewhere under all of that—she was only momentarily aware of it—a pulse of rage: this, too, she'd have to be in charge of, apparently.

By the time they got him settled in the backseat, Sylvia next to him, Frankie in front, Sylvia looked up and saw that the flames were already quieting under the arc of water rising over the barn.

Alfie asked, "But what *is* this . . . event?" in a perplexed, irritated tone.

Frankie laughed in relief, and Sylvia started to try to explain it, feeling a complicated relaxation engulfing her as she did. *A fire,* she said, *set by someone. The barn saved—you see?* "And you, you were in the house, and they rescued you."

"But who were they?"

"Yes, Mother," Frankie said. "Who were those masked men?" and it was Sylvia's turn to laugh, as much in relief as anything else.

After Alfie had gone back to bed, she and Frankie sat together for a while. Bud had stayed, too, but not long, just long enough to be sure Alfie was safely settled and to tell them what he'd learned about the fire from Davey Swann.

Tink Snell had called it in.

Loren had dropped him off here a little while ago to pick up the truck after their day in Black Mountain—Adrian had called Loren on his car phone to tell him he wanted Tink to get it moved tonight.

Tink had told Davey that as he was turning the truck around, he had seen something—a flickering—moving inside the barn, at the back. He'd gotten out, gone around behind the barn, and discovered the corner farthest from the house engulfed in flame. He'd tried the door on the house and found it unlocked, found the telephone in the kitchen, and called the fire station. Then he'd gone outside again to find a hose. There was one, attached to a spigot coming off the porch. It didn't stretch far enough to reach the fire, but he began at least to wet down the side of the house connected to the barn. He was still doing this when the first firemen and then the fire truck arrived.

"Well, thank God he was here," Sylvia said. The three of them were in the kitchen, at the table.

"Yeah, quite the coincidence," Bud said.

"I guess it would be, wouldn't it?" Frankie said.

"Sure would," Bud answered.

"Do you not believe him, then?" Sylvia asked. "But why would he lie?"

"He'd lie if he'd set it."

"But why would he set it and then call it in?" Frankie asked.

"It makes him a hero, doesn't it?" Bud said. "I mean, he's under suspicion, clearly—he and Gavin—and this would make him a hero." After a second or two, he shook his head. "Ahh! I don't know. I don't know enough about it. About the fire, or the timing of Loren's dropping him off—all that stuff. To be discussed."

"Well, I'm just grateful it wasn't the house," Sylvia said.

"Of course. I am, too," he said, and then Frankie went out on the porch with him to say good night.

When she came back, she sat down, facing Sylvia. They didn't say anything for a moment, and then Frankie said, "You're okay? You want me to spend the night?"

"No, no, you don't have to do that. No one's going to come and set another fire here tonight, of that I'm certain."

"That's not why I'm asking."

"I know."

After a moment, Frankie said, "*Are* you? All right?"

Sylvia laughed quickly. "Of course not, darling. I'm a mess."

"I know I would be, in your shoes."

"Oh, it's not because of the fire. The fire." She lifted her shoulders. "Well. That's easy."

"'Easy'?"

"It's just . . . I'm not sure I can *do* this." She heard the wobble in her own voice and took a deep breath.

"Mother."

"I will. I will do it. But it seems like . . . too much."

Frankie leaned forward in her chair, her face earnest, concerned. "What can I do? How could I help?"

"Ah, Frankie. I don't want you to do any of this. This is, really, the least I can do for Alfie now."

"What do you mean?"

"I mean. I suppose. That I don't love him."

"Mother. He's not . . . himself. So naturally . . ." She trailed off, looking steadily, sadly, at Sylvia.

"No, that's not it. It doesn't have to do with his illness. I haven't loved Alfie for a long time. And I should love him."

Frankie sat back, her mouth opened slightly.

"I should have loved him," Sylvia corrected herself. "If I'd loved him, imagine! I could do this gladly now for the sake of that. I would take care of him now for the sake of having loved him before. So I . . . I will take care of him. And hope that no one thinks I'm brave or noble or anything like that. I'm doing it, I will do it, so I can feel . . . decent, at least. Just barely decent."

"I'm sorry," Frankie said.

"I know," Sylvia answered.

Frankie's voice changed. "Surely there are programs. Visiting nurses, or some kind of day care . . ."

"I don't know. I don't know anything beyond what I've talked about so far with the doctor."

"Well, maybe I can find out. I could research this for you. Find out what's out there."

"This isn't the city, you know."

"I know. But there must be programs for people, somewhere. It will make me feel better to do this. To check it out. And maybe there really will be something."

"All right, Frankie. I don't mean to be difficult. Yes. Thank you. Maybe there's something. I'd be grateful."

The old house made a noise. Sylvia looked over at Frankie. Her face was open in a kind of yearning compassion. In an impulse responding to that answering warmth, Sylvia said, "You know, for half a second, when I heard it was our house, when Bud said *nineteen,* I thought Alfie would be dead. I thought I'd be free." Her voice was almost a whisper. "I thought it was done, I'd be free."

"Mom." *Don't,* Frankie's face said.

"And then. And then I wanted to get him, to find him, to rescue him, or whatever I could do."

"Of course. That's what you wanted."

"Mmmh," Sylvia said.

Frankie looked away. Then her hand rose quickly to her own face, as though she'd just thought of something. After a moment, she seemed to sigh. She'd pulled back somehow, Sylvia could tell.

She shouldn't have told her any of this. She had no right to tell her.

She looked over at Frankie. "I'm sorry, dear," she said.

Her daughter's pale eyes met her own again. "I know," Frankie answered.

14

AN AUGUST HEAT WAVE. Even at night it didn't cool down, though that might have been partly because the sloped roof above Bud's bedroom wasn't insulated. He'd been awake several times, once because he heard something and thought immediately of the arsonist, though he realized, after he'd gone outside and walked around the house, that it was just a raccoon trying to get into the garbage can—it was tipped over, the bungee cords that held the lid on still attached.

He woke the other times because that had made him nervous.

But mostly, he woke because it was hot.

He got up just before five, after lying there for almost an hour in the heat, listening to the birds asserting their ownership of the day. The sky was light, though the sun hadn't risen yet. He didn't stop for coffee. He just went outside, got in the car, and drove through the quiet town. There was one other sleepless soul out, a woman, walking with her dog by the green. He drove out of town and turned onto Silsby Pond Road.

It was a short hike in from where he pulled the car off the road to the massive rocks that constituted the streambed, and to the series of potholes cut into them by the same glacier that had heaped them up here. Only one of these, the largest pothole, had a flat lip that you could rest on—this one was technically Silsby Pond. But there were other, smaller bowls above it—a series of descending holes with slick, mossy slides between them. The teenagers in town climbed up barefoot and probably sometimes naked to the top of this series and slid down the sloping rock face from one to another.

Bud left his clothes on the open rock by the large hole and dove in. The water, even now in August, was bitingly, painfully cold, and he swam fast across the surface, turned, and swam back. He did this perhaps twenty times, and then he climbed out and lay down on the rock in the noise of the rushing water.

The sun was up now, and the rock underneath him was warm. His penis had shrunk almost shockingly in the cold water. He rested his hand on it as he lay in the sun. *Come back, my friend.* And then he was thinking, predictably, of Frankie Rowley.

A womanizer, she had called him.

He supposed he'd earned the title in those early days in Pomeroy. He'd met probably every eligible female in town by the end of the first month after his arrival—there had been a series of parties in his honor then, to welcome him, to introduce him to the community, to thank him for taking over the paper: clearly people had worried it might fold.

By the end of the second month, he'd begun and finished a quickly tempestuous and almost as quickly contentious relationship with a woman, Patty Babcock, who ran a small pottery in North Pomeroy. The last episode between them had involved her coming to his house in the middle of the night. He had told her a week or so earlier that he needed to cool things down a bit, that he didn't want to—that he couldn't—spend as much time with her as he had been. He was feeling guilty at that point about not taking over fast enough from Pete, who clearly wanted to be relieved of as much responsibility as possible as soon as Bud could manage that. "There are some interesting fish I hear calling to me in the distance," Pete had said. But more than that, Bud felt he hadn't had time to settle into his rented home, to explore the town. To get to know people on his own, without Patty.

"There's someone else," she said. Her face, whose charm was dependent on animation, had fallen, and looked flat, dull.

There wasn't, he assured her. How could there have been time enough, let alone the energy, for anyone else? It had to do with his need for more work time, and for time alone.

Evidently she didn't believe this explanation. And perhaps she was in some ways right not to—Bud was certainly aware of the ebbing of the infatuation that had driven him for a few weeks. At any rate, she had begun to call him, to call him at odd hours of the evening or the night, to hold him on the phone as long as she could, clearly suspicious that he had someone else in his house or in his bed. Finally he stopped answering the phone after ten, even though there was always the possibility that someone was calling about some event that he might want to know about—a fire, an accident, or a birth or death.

Finally one night at about eleven, she'd come over, uninvited. And in the middle of the argument that ensued, he had agreed—yes, no—he didn't want to see her anymore.

"I knew it." She shook her head, her mouth tight and mean. "Because there's someone else."

"No, because of this, because of this, because of this," he said, smacking the kitchen counter over and over. They were standing by the back door. Bud was trying not to let her any farther in. "This *behavior,* this jealousy." He tried to pull himself in, to speak calmly. "This behavior."

"How dare you use that word, *behavior*? You're not my parent."

He looked at her, feeling an enormous distance. "You know, the problem is I don't even like you anymore, Patty. You made me not like you." And then this struck him as funny, the whole crazy argument struck him as funny, and he started to sing, "'You *made* me not like you, I didn't wanna do it, I didn't wanna do it . . .'"

This didn't go over well. Things got noisier, and Bud asked her to leave. She wouldn't. So he did. He went to the office and slept on the couch there. When Pete came in and woke him up, he said nothing to Bud about this unprecedented event, and Bud told him nothing. He told him nothing, either, of the state he found his house in when he went home that evening, which had shocked him: books and papers strewn about, the bed ripped up, clothes lifted from the bureau and thrown onto the floor. And he told him nothing of the threats that ensued, the broken window one night.

But by the middle of the third month, when Bud had taken a different woman out to dinner in Winslow, Pete said casually to him at work one day, "You can't be doing what you're doing, Bud, my friend." They were standing at the big work table, figuring out the layout for that week's front page.

"Which is what?"

"You know what." Pete moved a few things around and stepped back to look again. After a few moments he said, "You have to watch your . . . spacing, with women. These are all people you're going to be seeing over and over again. Maybe you're going to need to talk to them for a story. For information." He moved to the coffee machine and poured himself another cup. He added sugar and tasted it. He said, "You can't be embarrassing people. Hurting them. Even if they should know better than to be hurt."

Bud didn't say anything. They stood side by side, looking at their work.

"It's not the city," Pete said. "You're not anonymous. Everyone knows your business, sooner or later. And it matters, what they think of your business."

And then his tone changed. "It was easier for me, being married like I was. And having the wife I had—everyone liked her way better'n they liked me. People put up with me on account of her. You're gonna have to be more . . . judicious, let's say."

Bud didn't answer. He felt the weight of his decision to move here, the carelessness, as he suddenly thought of it, of the way he'd reached it.

"I speak as your friend," Pete said, still without looking at him.

"I know you do, Pete," he'd answered.

After that, he had been judicious. He let weeks pass between dates with the new woman, a teacher in the Pomeroy grammar school. And when things ended between them—ended with what he felt was agonizing slowness and elaborate, polite care on his part—he waited for months before turning to another woman, a summer resident, one he'd been attracted to the year before. Things were easier with her because she was going to leave, she expected things to end when the summer ended.

And after that, for the most part he kept his pecker in his pants, as his high school football coach used to say. Brandishing it only occasionally when he felt a sort of ease, a lack of intensity, in a woman's reaction to him.

Frankie was different, he thought now, lying in the warming sun, hearing only the rush of the water. There was a focused responsiveness in her, a kind of susceptibility, he felt, which both drew him and made him cautious. He felt cautious, too, about her uncertainty. He had the sense that she could matter to him in some deep way, and he didn't want to start something with her if she was about to leave. She was mobile, he was not. He had made that choice, and he was clear about it. Clearer about it now than he had been when he made it.

He slept then, for what he thought was ten minutes or so. When he woke, his flesh had dried. He stood up and pulled his clothes back on.

On the walk back to the car, he was thinking again about Frankie—just about the way she looked, the timbre of her voice. Then about the fire at her parents' house.

His mind went to Tink Snell, and he was remembering—how did he know this?—that he lived on this road, somewhere up higher, it must be.

He'd look, he thought. Why not? He must be close.

As he drove up the worn-out dirt road, steering carefully around the exposed boulders in the roadbed, he wondered about how many other corners of this town he'd never cast his eyes on. Early in his life here, he'd tried to drive or walk everywhere. He'd explored the five cemeteries, one of them so overgrown that he wasn't sure at first he was in the right place. He'd swum in all the ponds in town—Hurd's and Green Pond, and the man-made one by the inn that had been torn down years before, and the one up here, Silsby. But sometimes, as now, driving somewhere, he'd realize he was seeing a road or a house or a vista that he'd never encountered before.

It made him think about how impossible it was for the fire-watch guys to keep an eye on everything, as Loren had said.

The road kept rising, and then suddenly it opened out to a clearing. To a hilly meadow, he saw, with a dirt track running up it. He stopped where he was, still partly in the woods at the field's lower edge. At the top of the meadow, he could see a trailer perched on cinder blocks, a car parked next to it.

And a man—Tink—moving from the trailer to the car, loading something into the trunk, then bending over, rearranging things. He was wearing only jeans and work boots. Bud watched him until he stood straight, slammed the trunk closed, and went back inside the trailer.

He sat there, waiting, but Tink didn't reappear. After a minute or two, he eased the car into neutral and let it roll silently back down the hill. Within a hundred yards or so, he spotted an area big enough to turn around in, and backed into it.

At home again, while he made coffee, while he sliced a piece of bread to put in the toaster, he decided he'd stop by to see Frankie today. Yes. He'd ask her out for dinner. He hadn't really taken her out yet. He'd gone with her to the dance, yes, but that was different. Civic. Work related—he'd had to take the pictures, after all. Even if they had ended up later lying next to each other in a field, talking, kissing.

He stood at the sink drinking his coffee and looking out the window at the mountains beyond the river, at the road that cut horizontally between them. A lumber truck went by on it, a miniature from here, the logs so many twigs stacked up on its trailer. The mountain peaks were still in shadow. The only radio station you could get here was from Vermont, and the long-winded guy there was discussing the subtleties of weather in his self-satisfied way.

What were his intentions with Frankie? Sex. Well, yes. He'd thought about it, her, numerous times in ways that were at once all too generic—legs opening, et cetera—and very specific. Her face, her smile, the paper white of her skin, her tumbling hair. He liked her physically. He liked looking at her, he liked the way she smelled. He'd liked touching her the other night in the field. He could have made love to her there, then, if she'd responded to him with any answering passion. But she'd seemed hesitant. Not in a way that made him think it couldn't or wouldn't happen. In a way, instead, that seemed to him to spring from all that was unclear and unresolved and troubling to her in her life—and that seemed to be just about everything.

On the other hand, they were both freezing their asses off at that point.

The toast popped up noisily. Sometimes it flung itself out so enthusiastically that it landed on the counter, and he always felt cheered when this happened. Not today. "Wuss," he said to this slice, nicely browned. He buttered it and sat down at the table, chewing contemplatively.

He regarded this bread, from a bakery in Whitehall, flecked with seeds and grains and oats and flavored slightly with molasses, as one of the reasons for living where he did—though he would have been embarrassed to offer it as an argument to any of the friends he'd left behind in Washington.

The toast, and also the view from his house. When he was living in Washington, he'd watched television in the morning, the chatty news shows. Here he listened to the radio and looked up at the hills.

The angle out onto the hills was part of why he'd chosen the house. In itself, it wasn't much. A small former summer cottage, awkwardly winterized. Its first-floor windows, which he imagined as charmingly multipaned in their previous life, were now huge, fixed, double-glazed picture windows. The ones upstairs had simply been replaced with cheap versions of themselves, but the double glazing up there had leaked at some point long before he had moved in, and the views upstairs were therefore all befogged—when you woke and looked out, the day always seemed grayish and unpromising.

He was watching the light shift in the room and half listening to the news while he ate. And then suddenly he was paying attention—they were talking about Kenya. Kenya and also Tanzania: bombings. He stopped chewing, hurriedly set his toast and coffee down, and crossed the room to the radio. He knocked his chair over in his haste, and it went scudding backward over the uneven floor. He turned the volume up.

The NPR correspondent in Kenya was talking about numbers killed. Large numbers. Thousands wounded. It was at the U.S. embassy. Not inside the embassy, they hadn't gotten inside, but right in front. The other bombing, the one in Tanzania, was clearly coordinated with it—they had happened within minutes of each other.

He was thinking of Frankie. She might not know this yet, and it would be important to her. She might know people who worked at the embassy or someplace close to it. They said many nearby were wounded or dead. People just walking past, people in the building opposite.

He'd go to her place now, he thought. He'd let her know, if she didn't already. He could stop by again later, he could ask her out then. He was already upstairs, getting a sweater, brushing his teeth. He didn't bother to shave.

The sun was just entering the valley as he drove across it. He had the car radio on, in case there was more detail, but the hosts had moved on now—they were discussing the Lewinsky stuff again. He turned it off and drove in the relative silence of his car's engine noise, wondering what this would mean to Frankie, how she'd receive it.

She came to the door in a bathrobe, her hair in a single braid draped over her shoulder. No makeup. White. Very white.

"*This* is early," she said, with the gap-tooth smile that made Bud happy every time he saw it, no matter what else was going on.

"Yeah. For a reason," he said.

"Come in, then. Tell me." She had stepped back, and he came in. A low morning light streamed into the room through the windows over the sink. There was a book open, facedown, on the kitchen table, a paperback. A coffee mug sat next to it. Her robe was a pale blue, draped, clingy. He watched her hips under it as she walked back to the table and sat down.

He went to stand closer to her, by the table. "I just wondered, did you hear about the African bombings?"

"Oh, *no!*" she cried. She was looking up at him. He could see most of one breast, a minimal, graceful weight to its curve, very white, too. But now, as if in response to his news, her hand rose, and she pulled her robe together at her neck. "What *hap*pened?"

He explained what he knew, what he'd heard. He sat down next to her as he talked, watching her face, the anguish he could read there in response to what he was reporting to her.

When he was done, she was silent for a moment. "And they think it was terrorists?" she asked finally.

"Yes. They said some Islamic sect, I think."

She shook her head. "Ah," she whispered, frowning. Then, after a few seconds, her light eyes on him: "So, it was just the embassy?"

"I don't know, Frankie." He shook his head. "Damage to more than one building, I think they said. But I think it was just collateral damage. The embassy was the target, they seemed pretty sure. And then there's the other bomb in Tanzania. But I don't know, actually."

"There are people I should call," she said. She stood up abruptly, then stopped. "Ahm." She was still frowning. "It's what? Early afternoon there." She bit her lip. She wasn't really talking to him. "Maybe I should go up to my parents.'" She turned away from him. "Yeah, that's what I'll do." She went toward the bedroom doorway.

"You could use my phone," he said, watching her. "I'll be out for a while. I've got an appointment." He didn't, but he could invent something to give her some privacy.

She looked back at him. "You know, that would be great. Just . . . so much less complicated."

"Good. I'm glad."

She went into the bedroom. He could hear her moving around, drawers being opened and closed, the rustle of clothing. He tried not to think of her taking her robe off, dressing, but was unsuccessful and, in spite of himself, turned on. When she emerged, she was wearing blue jeans and a long-sleeved white T-shirt. She carried a green sweater. "I'll just wash my face," she said.

"Fine. I can wait."

She was in the bathroom for several minutes. When she came out, she'd loosed her hair from her braid—it fanned out over her shoulders. She'd put on eye makeup, and lipstick, too. He felt pleased, imagining this was for his benefit.

She took her cup to the sink and rinsed it. She picked up her book from the table. "I better take this," she said. She tucked it into the big straw bag she used for a purse. "Sometimes you wait a long time for a connection. And then it disconnects, and you have to start all over."

On the way back to town in Bud's car, he turned the radio on. At seven, the top of the hour, the bombings were discussed again, but again, the hosts moved on quickly to the domestic news. He turned it off.

"I think I'm going to take you to my house," he said. "Not the office."

"Okay." There was a question in the word.

"Yeah, it's just that the office line will ring off and on, and people will be leaving messages. My line at home is more private, less of a hassle."

"Okay," she said again.

"You think you might know someone . . . ?"

"I don't know. But the wife of a friend—a colleague, really—works at the embassy, or she did. And who knows? Any one of a lot of my friends might have been there for something or other. I'd just like to check." There was a silence. "I might call New York first, to see what they know."

"Okay." They came to the paved road, and Bud turned left.

"I'll keep track of the charges," Frankie said.

"Don't worry about it."

"And Bud?"

He looked over at her. *What?*

"Once I've done all that stuff, do you mind if I call around locally a bit?"

"No."

"I told my mother I'd research care options for my father. She . . . was having a hard time the other night, after the fire."

"I'm sorry."

There was a long silence. "Clearly, I should get a phone."

"If you're going to stay," he said.

"Even if not. Too much going on." She had turned away and was looking out the window. They were passing the town green. There were two large dogs, one white, one yellowish, wrestling. She turned back to him. "Who'd have thought it?" she said. "I come home—back to the States—for downtime. A sabbatical. A retreat in the country, to think things over. And all hell breaks loose here, and now all hell breaks loose there. What does it mean, you think?"

"That there's no such thing in life as a sabbatical?"

She smiled, a quick sad smile.

At his office, after he'd dropped Frankie off, after he'd shown her how the coffee machine worked, he started his workday. He had a message on his voice mail from Georgie Morrell saying that Paul Ardery had been taken to the hospital with what they thought was a heart attack. He'd have to follow up on that. And Matt Reinhart had called, the guy from the *Boston Globe* who'd started to follow the fires after the piece of Bud's that AP had printed. He was just checking in, wanting to know about any new developments. Bud called him back and left a message about Frankie's parents' fire. Then he wrote up his own account of that one for the paper, mentioning that Tink Snell had phoned it in.

When he was done, he made himself a fresh pot of coffee. As it was dripping through, he heard Barb come in downstairs, and he called down and offered her a cup.

She came up, and they talked, as they sometimes did. She had heard about Loren driving Tink and Gavin down to the state police barracks the day of the Rowleys' fire. "But just to talk, they say. And you know what I say to that? Enough already. Just arrest someone."

"Yeah," he said. "The hell with evidence and witnesses. Let's get this *over* with."

"I'm at that point, man."

"What, you're scared?"

"Scared shitless. But I've got, like, three suitcases right by the door," she said. "If he lights my house up, I already know what I'm taking out."

"What?"

"Oh, mostly sentimental crap. Photos of my kid when she was little, and letters, and some of my favorite clothes." She smiled. "That's a problem. I have to keep opening up the damn suitcases to find something I want to wear."

After a moment, Bud said, "I'm going to use this."

"For what?"

"As an example of how people are dealing with the arson, natch."

She snorted. "Or *not,*" she said.

When he opened the door, he could hear Frankie in the living room, still talking on the phone. He stood there for a few seconds in the doorway. She was saying, yes, she would be interested to look around. It sounded as if she'd moved on from the events in Africa to whatever the local stuff was that she'd wanted to explore.

He shut the door, deliberately making enough noise in the kitchen to announce himself. He went around the corner to the living room. She was on the couch, her long legs curled beneath her, the phone propped on her shoulder. Her paperback was open on her lap. She was writing on the endpapers, notes in ink. He took her in, the wide swell of her buttock and thigh in her jeans, the long white foot tucked beneath that swell, the messy hair, the glasses, the freckles—there was nothing he didn't like. She raised her hand in response to his appearance in the doorway, and he went back into the kitchen.

Just as he'd finished making himself a sandwich—leftover chicken, chutney, cucumber slices, and the bread he was so fond of—she came into the kitchen in her bare feet.

"Want some of this?" he asked.

"Sure," she answered. She seemed subdued.

He got out a serrated knife and sliced the sandwich in half, holding it flat with his hand. He put each half on a plate and carried the plates into the dining area. He came back to the kitchen for glasses and paper napkins. She was standing, looking out the window. "What do you want to drink?" he asked her.

She looked over at him. "I'll get it," she said, taking the glasses from him. "Water's fine for me. What do you want?"

Bud said water, too. She put ice in the glasses and filled them. In the dining room, they sat down opposite each other. She picked up the sandwich and took a bite, and Bud felt a pang, a yearning, for exactly this unremarkable domesticity.

"What's the news?" he asked.

Her mouth was full, her jaw working. She raised a finger: Wait. Finally she swallowed and said, "Everyone I know is okay. The person I most worried about, the one who actually worked there, is fine. But it's just awful, they say. So many people hurt, and people just flooding the hospitals. Thousands. It's . . . they can't take care of them all. All these windows blew out, so there was glass everywhere. Horrible injuries just from that. And it was mostly, of course, Africans who got killed and hurt."

"I heard a couple of Americans died, too." He'd had the radio on again, driving back from the office.

"Oh, I know. And I don't mean I wish they all *had* been Americans. But just, it all seems so misplaced. Poor Africa."

They sat silently for a moment, and then lifted their sandwiches again. After another minute, she said, "Everyone's really worried now, too. The aid agencies, I mean. Especially the American ones and the church ones. They're worried about who will be next. But for now . . ." She lifted her shoulders.

They were quiet. Then he said, "I'm sorry."

"Oh, I am, too." She rubbed her face. "But thanks."

"Do you wish you were there?"

"Part of me does, I suppose. But I wouldn't be any more helpful than the average bystander."

"Because it's medical?"

"Oh, I don't know." She gave a light, quick, mirthless laugh. "I'm not sure I was ever any use in Africa."

"Hey." He reached over and touched her hand lightly. "That's not true. You're just . . . this is just, overwhelming, I suppose."

"Probably," she said. And then, in a minute, "You know, once, this past spring, I was working in Sudan, in a village—I was going from village to village, actually, working with local people, with the Ministry of Health. We were trying to help them set up programs in health facilities to deal with malnutrition. You know, training people, supervising systems. I was doing a lot of the care myself. Feeding tubes, that kind of thing." She paused and looked over at him. She said, "But these weren't health facilities as you and I know them. Really, they were huts. What you should imagine is people lined up outside huts."

"Okay," Bud said.

"*Quietly* lined up. That was something that always saddened me. How quiet they were. Their acceptance of . . . life, I suppose. And of our rules for them. It was . . . I found it almost unbearable sometimes."

Bud nodded.

"Anyway, this was in an area that was safe," she went on. "Or it was supposed to be safe. We wouldn't have been there otherwise. And if we hadn't been there, they wouldn't have come. But we were there, and so they did come. They came from miles and miles around. They walked, mostly. Women and children and babies. Some fathers."

She had been looking down, remembering this. Now her eyes snapped to Bud. "But it wasn't safe. We were in the midst of things when an elder from the village came to tell us that an armed group was maybe a few hours away, approaching. That we had to go, we had to get out, right away. He told everyone, the people waiting, too.

"So *we*, we packed up all our fancy stuff, our radios, our computers, our medical equipment, and left. Trucks, you know, took us to the airstrip so we could get out. And we could see the villagers leaving, too, carrying *their* stuff, possessions bundled in cloths on their heads or their backs. Carrying their babies—some of them the babies we were supposed to be treating. Heading off into the bush to hide, to wait it out."

She sat still. She was playing with her napkin, tearing it into strips. "We left. We left, and they stayed." She made a funny noise, an exhalation. "That was always our option," she said. "To go. Our great *privilege*." She was sarcastic, angry.

"But if you'd stayed, you would have been killed, I assume."

"Killed, or raped." She shrugged. "Or maybe not. Not all of them were. We heard it wasn't too bad." She laughed, once. "But you see my point."

"I don't, really."

"Oh, I don't know. Just . . . I had a way out. I always had a way out. And it marked a terrible . . . divide, I guess you'd say. I wasn't *African*. I couldn't be *African*."

"And that's what you wanted?"

After a pause, she said, "I wish I could explain it. I just . . . I felt so . . . allied with them, but when we were up against it—when *they* were up against it—I couldn't be their ally." Her hair swayed as she shook her head. "And this, this bombing . . . why should they be chosen to suffer again, when the bombers wanted to punish America, clearly?"

"Because the bombers were very, very stupid."

After a moment, she nodded.

"Or very, very callous," he said. "Or both."

They sat without speaking for a long moment. They were finished eating, though she'd left part of her sandwich.

"Do you want anything else?" he asked.

"Food?" she said.

"Yes."

She gestured at her plate. "No."

"Shall I take you home then?"

"Oh, you don't have to do that. I can call my mother, if it's not convenient."

"No, I want to do it. I just meant, are you finished with everything you need to get done on the phone."

"I am. For now." She pushed back from the table. "I've got a healthcare place I'll want to go look at in Whitehall, and one in Black Mountain. They've got an Alzheimer's day-care program and a visiting-nurse association in the Whitehall center, and a hospice attached to an Alzheimer's program in Black Mountain. I think something might work out for my mother—for my father, really. But I want to check it out first."

"You've been busy," he said.

"I got a lot of calling done, yes."

"Will you need a car when you go?"

"Bud." She made a stern face. "I'm not going to ask you to drive me to Whitehall."

"No, I didn't mean that. Just . . . you could use my car."

"I'm not going to *borrow* your car, either."

"No? Why not?"

"Because you need it. You're like Loren. It's your office."

He laughed. "Now there's a nightmare vision."

"What?"

"Becoming like Loren."

"Well, that's not going to happen. Never fear."

"If only you could guarantee that to me."

"Mmm," she said. Her face shifted somehow. "I guess there are no guarantees."

Her voice was cooler, and he realized that it had come around again, that he had pushed it—there was something in what he had said that seemed to be asking for something from her.

Now she got up with their plates and went back to the kitchen. And then to the living room, to get her purse, her book. He was silent. He rinsed the plates in the kitchen and put them into the dishwasher.

In the car, more than halfway to her house—her sister's house—she spoke first. "Thank you," she said.

"For?"

"For letting me use your home. For listening to me. For coming to tell me about the bombings. That was . . . kind."

"Shucks," he said. She looked over at him and, after a moment, grinned. He was happy, suddenly.

"For showing me the aurora borealis," she said, still smiling.

"Come on: for *arranging* for the aurora borealis."

"Well, that too. *That* was kind."

"That was *work*."

After a minute, she said quietly, "It was wonderful."

When they parked in front of her sister's house, Bud wasn't sure what to say. He wasn't sure even if he should turn the engine off.

"I think you'd better come in," she said. She was facing forward, as if they were still driving, as if there were something to look at in the road ahead.

Something happened in his body, and he felt himself getting hard. "Because . . . ?" he said.

"Because I have so much . . ." She turned to him, not smiling now. "So much to thank you for."

15

A Letter from the Editor

Here's what an arsonist on the loose does to a small town. First, of course, everyone is afraid. That could happen anywhere, but in a small town, the person you're afraid of is bound to be someone you know, someone you probably see regularly in the store, at church, at the post office. The sense of community that is the bedrock of small-town life is broken, suddenly. People look at one another with suspicion and fear, friend to friend, father to son, wife to husband.

Everyone is on edge. In our town, the fires have almost always been set at night, so people don't sleep well, listening for the footstep outside on the porch, the splash of kerosene or gasoline or charcoal starter at the doors or windows. Families take turns. Tonight I get to sleep and you stay awake to watch; tomorrow night you'll sleep and I'll stay up. Everyone is exhausted. The men in the volunteer fire department are exhausted, too. They've risen again and again from their beds and driven across town to try to put out fires that were set with the confounding intention of causing maximum damage.

People have armed themselves. We're a community of many hunters, so that wasn't a difficult step, but it was a radical one, getting the guns out before hunting season, having them always loaded and close at hand. It's resulted in at least one accident, fortunately not fatal. But more important, it's brought the fear of one another to that extreme a possibility: If he comes here, I will shoot him. Or worse: Let him come here. I want to shoot him.

There are plenty of business opportunities that present themselves, and there are those ready to step in and seize them. Would you like a handgun, or an alarm system, or someone standing guard at your door all night? Could you use extra locks, or motion-detector lights? These have all been *made available for purchase, and many of us have bought at least one of them.*

This is to say nothing of the loss of housing stock in the community. Thirteen structures have so far been totally lost, and two more will require substantial rebuilding. Some of the losses are of houses that had survived from the town's founding in 1785. Some were built by a local master builder of summer cottages in the twenties and thirties, Hall Moody. All were vested with memories, with history, both personal and civic, and all are mourned, not just by the families that owned them, but by the whole community.

By now the wider world has begun to notice what's going on here. It wasn't surprising when the Winslow and Whitehall papers sent reporters to talk to townspeople about the fires. But after the fifth fire, the wire services began to reproduce parts of local articles, and that has happened more frequently with each additional fire. Your editor has been contacted by the Boston Globe *and the* New York Times, *and we've had several visits from the* Globe *reporter. At this point, our town's story is national news.*

There are other visitors, too. We've gotten used to the state police cruising the roads, parked at Snell's or the café. Most of us drive or walk daily past the office the arson squad has opened behind the post office in Pomeroy Center. And we welcome the work the state police and the arson squad are doing to try to help us. But their presence, too, marks a change in our lives here, and we'll be glad when we no longer have need of them.

The local and state police report that they have several persons of interest they are speaking to. For the sake of everything we hold dear in our town, we hope they can make an arrest soon and end the state of siege our citizens feel they've been living under these past weeks.

Bud was still covering all the local news, all the usual stories. The weather, the deaths, weddings, illnesses, the meeting of the North Pomeroy Social Club—"All the Usual Refreshments Served"—the interminable repair of the bridge over Silsby Brook.

All of these, though, were just the thrumming background music to what was really happening, the fires, and he'd written about them from every angle he could think of by now.

He had covered each fire as it came along, of course. He had talked to the victims, including those who'd been in their houses when the fires started—there were three of these families by the end of August. He had written stories about how the fires had changed the owners' lives. He had written about how they changed the lives of people in town. He did a story on the one person who'd been hospitalized as a result of the fires—Dan Stark, treated for smoke inhalation.

He had done a piece on the first town meeting on the fires, and another later when the head of the arson squad spoke to the residents and tried to explain to them how difficult investigating arson usually was.

As a result of that meeting, he had written an article on arson itself, full of statistics, statistics that amazed Bud as he uncovered them: That arson accounted for almost half of New Hampshire's fires—probably more when you considered that the local fire chiefs didn't report them all as they were supposed to. That suspects were rarely identified—named in only 17 percent of the reported fires. That a minuscule percentage of those suspects ended up in prison, because of lack of evidence or lack of witnesses. Because of not enough law enforcement in small towns or not enough trained arson experts in New Hampshire. Because of the difficult burden of proof. It made it seem more understandable to Bud, less perplexing, that the officials still seemed so much in the dark about the Pomeroy fires.

When Harlan Early shot himself, Bud wrote about that. When, after the sixteenth fire, reporters from both the *Boston Globe* and the *New York Times* had come to town to do stories—*the picturesque small town where no one used to lock their doors, turned into an armed camp*—he wrote that up.

He'd ridden along with the members of the fire watch one night and wrote about it. He did an article on the difficulties some of the victims were having collecting on their insurance policies because of the questions raised by the likelihood of arson.

Fire had upended him.

Fire, and Frankie Rowley.

———

He felt as if these two things had arrived at almost the same time in his life to act as weight and counterweight. One or the other by itself might have thrown him off balance. Instead, they sat side by side in his thoughts

Sometimes, actually, fire and Frankie merged, crazily, so that he could be writing something up about the latest fire, his mind full of images of all of the bright, noisy fires he'd seen, burning in the dark. He'd lift his head for a moment to think of what should come next, only to have a sudden vision of Frankie rise in his mind, Frankie, her endless white legs splayed out under him in the moonlight, calling out the way she did when they made love, a kind of breathless crooning sound he found sexy beyond words. And he'd bend to his writing again with a hard-on that would linger through the next sentence and feed also the next image that rose. And the next.

That first afternoon, the day of the bombings in Kenya, she had seemed fragile to him, once or twice tearful as they were making love—some combination, as she explained it to him afterward, of being with him for the first time and thinking of the awful things that had just happened in her world.

She'd corrected herself. *In what had been her world, until a few weeks ago.*

He had undressed her slowly that day, standing on the mattress on the floor in her bedroom. They knelt together then, and lay down with each other. Her flesh felt cool, her hair smelled of something spicy as he pressed his face into it where it lay, spread out in a tangle, on her pillow. He had been almost tremulous himself, moved by her tears, by her white body. They were tender with each other, and he was thrilled by the length of her, by the deep muscles around her spine, by her wide bottom in his hands, by the way her flesh warmed slowly. She had sighed, perhaps gasped, when he came into her, so easily, and he had held her close, moved slowly inside her. Afterward they lay side by side, facing each other, and he held her face, ran his thumbs gently over her cheeks, her lips.

They had slept. When they woke, the sun had moved from the room, and it was cooler. She was turned away from him on the mattress. He could watch her slow breathing, watch the curve of her wide hip. He moved closer to her, angled his body against her back, a perfect match. He grew hard again against her buttocks. "Ah," she had whispered, waking, and turned, smiling, to face him.

That was three weeks ago. Five fires ago. Perhaps twenty times making love ago, Bud hadn't kept count. They'd been wild for each other, crazy, the way you are when you're coming to know the other, to know the other's body, everything you can do to it, that it can do to you. He sometimes felt her going into what he came to call *overdrive,* something he associated with what she'd told him of her life in Africa, her sexual life there; he'd actually occasionally tried to slow her down, a first for him. Though even so, sometimes they ended up finishing in inventive positions on the mattress on the floor, or in a chair at the kitchen table, or standing up, pushed against the wall.

They didn't spend the night together, though; Frankie didn't want to do that, and he agreed, aware of how visible her life—their lives—were. Better, then, to have his car parked outside his own house when people start getting up in the morning and looking out their windows or taking walks or driving to Snell's or to work. Better for Frankie to have no car parked at her sister's house. And better for both of them, they also agreed, not to leave their houses empty overnight, after all.

And this was helpful to him, this enforced separation—along with how busy he was with work. He was trying not to grab at her. He knew this was his habit with women, he knew how much trouble it had gotten him into before. He was trying to curb it with Frankie, trying not to push her. He reminded himself that he'd met her only two months ago, but each time he thought of that, it made him remember the way she'd looked, standing alone on the lawn on the Fourth of July at the Mountain House Inn. Fragile, he'd thought at the time, though some of that could have been just her white, white skin. Or jet lag. And then the surprise of her gap-toothed smile. Of how much he'd liked talking to her.

And the amazement of her tearfulness that day at the burned-out house. He still had that photo, in a drawer at the office. Frankie, her butt resting on his car, her hands behind her making a cushion for it, her red skirt, her white skin, her wild hair blowing, partially obscuring her anguished face.

They learned about each other lying in bed, talking. He told her about coming here, about buying the paper from Pete, about what it meant to him, what he wanted it to mean. She talked about her sense of helplessness sometimes in her work in Africa—how no matter what she did, what systems she set up, mothers were still watching their children die from illness and malnutrition, most of the time because of things she couldn't change or make better. Things like lack of infrastructure and resources. Like the effects of civil war. Like corruption and lousy governance.

She told him about the difficulties in her parents' marriage, about Alfie's apparent decline. About all the different places she'd lived as a kid, about her sense of alienation from her family's life. He talked about the feeling he'd had growing up that his parents loved him too much, that they thought he was better, smarter, than he really was, and the sense of inadequacy this bred in him.

She told him she loved his voice. He told her he talked the way he did, almost in a whisper, because of a high school football injury to his larynx. He told her how much he had loved football then because he'd loved to hit.

"But isn't that the same as *being* hit?" she asked. "I mean, *smack*! And you're both in pain, no?"

"That didn't occur to me until much later."

When they were done talking or making love, his life went on much as usual, almost unbelievably to him. He'd take the pasteup to Whitehall, pick up the copies, deliver them. He'd go to his office and talk on the phone to someone, he'd go out in the town and poke around, he'd go to meetings or interviews or town events or to another fire, and another fire.

And then he'd come back and bring her the news of all this. He intended it as a kind of gift, he supposed—his way of looking at Pomeroy, of understanding it. Though what he only slowly became aware of was how his way of looking at it was changing. Afterward he would think of this period—this period of the fires and his new love for Frankie—as the time when he came to feel a part of Pomeroy. When it truly became his home.

He'd stopped in at Snell's one night about two weeks or so after they started to make love. He still wasn't sure they'd be together that evening—it wasn't a given. Some nights she had dinner with someone she'd known in her youth and had remet. Some nights she went up to spend the evening with her parents. But he thought he'd get wine, just in case, and then maybe he'd drive by and see if she was home.

Or not, he told himself. Maybe he'd wait to hear from her. One day she'd stopped in at the office to invite him over and, one other time, left a note in his door. Unexpected gifts that made him happier than they should have, probably.

Either way, he thought now, wine would be nice, so he pulled in at Snell's on his way home and parked alongside the other cars.

It was the end of the day, and the store was moderately busy. Adrian was ringing up customers, so Bud just waved to him as he walked in, and to Loren, who was last in line at the register, behind a couple of other people. He greeted Harlan, who was stocking shelves, and they talked for a while about his recovery—he was off the crutches now. "But I'll be longer living it down than my foot will be healing," he said.

Bud went to the back to get some milk for coffee, to look around in case he saw something else he needed, and while he was there, he heard voices rising from the front of the store—Adrian's voice, and Loren's. Adrian was saying something to him about Tink.

They spoke more quietly, back and forth, as Bud moved down the dog-food and bread aisle to get a little closer. He could hear Loren say, in his self-satisfied tone, "I don't know why you'd object to my talking to him. We're just driving around, having a normal conversation."

"I'll tell you why. Because you're taking him away from his work," Adrian said. "And I need him at his work."

"Well, *I* need to talk to him."

"What about?"

"Oh, this and that."

"You've talked enough by now. He's told you everything he's got to say. I want you to leave him alone."

Loren said something back, smoothly, quietly.

"And I'm telling you, you can't talk to him anymore unless you're going to charge him with something," Adrian said angrily. "And you've got nothing to charge him with."

"If he's worried, he can always ask for a lawyer," Loren said.

"The boy doesn't have a lawyer. And he would never ask for one."

"Well, we told him he could if he wanted to."

"How many times did you tell him that?"

"I only have to tell him the one time, Adrian."

"There's some people you need to tell more times than that."

Loren chuckled. "You're gonna have to get someone to rewrite the fucking Constitution then," he said. "What I'm saying is he could get one, anytime he wants."

"Charge him, and he will. You're not charging him because you don't have any reason to."

"I can't discuss that with you, Adrian." Loren sounded amused.

Sarah Chick turned into Bud's aisle, pushing a cart with a few groceries in it. Bud moved away, back around by the refrigerators, then forward again in the next aisle over. Loren said, "All I'm saying is he's an adult, and I'll treat him like one."

"And what I'm saying is you're not. You're treating him like a kid you're trying to take advantage of."

Bud moved away again, but he could hear them as he went back for the milk. Back and forth they went, Loren silky, Adrian furious. It ended only when Sarah came up to the register behind Loren with her cart, which meant Loren had to pay for his two Ding Dongs and move on.

When Bud saw Frankie that night, he reported all this to her, too. "I would have stood there by the soups for as long as they were talking, pretending to decide between low-sodium and regular chicken broth, but it was over at that point."

"Poor Bud."

"I am a nosy bastard. All to have something to talk about with you."

"God knows we've got nothing else to do," she said, moving on top of him.

He decided he'd talk to Gavin and Tink about being under suspicion—maybe there'd be a story in it. At worst, he could offer it to Frankie.

He found Gavin at his work helping to build a big glass house up on Pleasant Hill, a house whose visibility and obvious expensiveness was an issue for a lot of people in town. He asked the contractor, Kevin O'Hara, if he could borrow his guy for a while. Ten minutes, O'Hara said, so he and Gavin walked a little distance away on the packed dirt of the construction site and stood looking back at the house.

Gavin was basically amused by the whole thing. Yeah, he'd gone with Loren and Tink to Black Mountain, and then Loren had come by again, to Gavin's house this time, on a weekend, and they'd driven around and had some coffee together at the café. But when he came a third time, at work again, Gavin just said no, that he didn't have time. "I mean, it's not like there's a law that says you've got to do everything Loren tells you to do. And he's just trolling, just trying for anything he can get, it seems to me. Hoping you'll make a mistake and let something slip." He laughed. "I mean, here's a guy who had nothing better to do when I was in high school but try to catch kids making out. Coming up outside your car parked somewhere and shining his flashlight on you hoping to catch you with your ass in the air and your pants around your knees. Fuck him." He laughed again. "I told Tink that, too. That he just has to tell him he's too fuckin' busy to talk all the time. But that's not something Tink can do, I guess." He shrugged. "Maybe he likes the attention."

Later that day, Bud spotted Tink on a tractor in the Louds' field. He pulled his car to the side of the road and walked out over the stubble to where he was. Tink turned the motor off as he approached, but he didn't get down, so Bud found himself looking up at the kid, the sun in his eyes, Tink's face in shadow.

He hadn't had anything longer than a quick exchange with Tink in the past, so now he introduced himself, he explained he was writing a piece for the paper on the way the investigation of the fires was proceeding, and he understood Tink and Gavin had been asked some questions.

"Yea-up," he said. He was looking off at the tree line.

"Do you think Spader suspects you?"

He shrugged. "I suppose."

"Does he tell you why?"

"Not really."

"But you've spent a lot of time together."

"Well, that's just, you know, spendin' time." He shrugged again. "Don't mean much."

After a few seconds, Bud said, "So you're not guilty."

"Nope."

"Have you told Spader that?"

"He didn't ask that."

"He didn't ask if you'd set the fires?"

"He asked that, and I said no. He didn't ask if I was guilty."

"I see," Bud said. "Well, do you expect he'll have more questions for you?"

"He don't ask so many questions."

"So you, what? Just drive around together?"

"That. We get coffee. Went fishing once. Went once to the Castle." This was a small amusement park between Whitehall and Winslow.

"So you enjoy these . . . drives?"

"They're okay."

"It doesn't bother you that they interrupt your work?"

He smiled, for the first time. "It bothers my *uncle,* that's for sure."

"But not you."

"Nope. Just, I don't like to fail Adrian."

"He was about as opaque as anyone could be," Bud told Frankie.

"Do you think it's just that he's stupid?" she asked.

"I have no way of knowing. It could be a brilliant strategy, for all I can tell." They were lying on the mattress, huddled close to each other under the quilt. The night was suddenly chilly, perhaps even down in the forties. "Our friend Loren is going to royally fuck this thing up with all his coziness," Bud said.

"How so?"

"It's coercive. It's like beating someone up until he confesses, only different. Loving him until he confesses. It's illegal pressure."

"Do you know that's what he's doing?"

"I don't. But it's seems pretty clear. They make a very odd couple otherwise. And their great friendship didn't begin until after Tink fell under suspicion."

"Until I picked his car out."

"This is true."

Frankie moaned. "I should have kept my big mouth shut."

"Let's talk about that," he said. "Your mouth. Open. Shut."

16

ॐ

IT WAS LIKE COMING AWAKE, Frankie thought later about the weeks after she began to sleep with Bud. Sometimes a bit painfully, the way your limbs felt when they'd been numbed for a while and were tingling back to life. But mostly it was like opening her eyes on new day after new day. Very different from her affair with Philip—or with other lovers in Africa.

Even physically it seemed so. Everything was slower and more private, somehow. It occurred to her at one point over those early days with Bud that at least some of the excitement of her love affairs in Africa had been that they were public. That they were *observed* in the close quarters everyone inhabited. She remembered Rosemary, the South African nurse, who'd been involved with Philip in the months before Frankie arrived on the scene, saying to her one night in the room they shared, "You'll find, I think, that he gives excellent head." A way of signaling many things to Frankie, among them, that everyone knew that Frankie and Philip were sleeping together, and that Rosemary had had him first.

Frankie had said, "That's just *so* good to know, Rosemary," and continued dressing.

"A bit like high school," Bud said when she told him this story.

"I suppose. For me, more like Pomeroy used to be in the summers of my youth—the pool of boyfriend candidates was so small, and the moves anyone made were so visible."

Bud made a noise. "Like Pomeroy *now*."

"No. That's my point. This is different. It's . . . private."

"You imagine it's private. I can guarantee you that at this moment, there's someone, somewhere in this town, talking about how often my car has been parked outside your house."

"But that's not part of anything between us. It doesn't feed us, it doesn't matter to what's going on right here that they're doing that."

"And somehow, in Africa, it did."

"Oh, yes. I think so." She was thinking of the parties they had sometimes after work, the way your eyes met someone's and the sexy thrill of that. But it was that, yes, in connection with the sense of others watching your eyes meet, of others being part of that connection. Once, she and a doctor whose name she could no longer remember had moved to the screen door from opposite sides of the room and gone into a darkened kitchen off the porch, where everyone else was still dancing, and fucked, pushed up against a table there. Frankie hadn't climaxed. It was all too hurried, too awkward. But she had been turned on, wet. And when they came back and began to dance once more—moving quickly away from each other, becoming once again part of the gyrating mass—everything sexual in the room had seemed amped up. Everyone there seemed to be part of it. To have been part of it.

She and Bud were, as usual, on the mattress on the floor when they had this conversation. It was early afternoon, a warm sunny day. Bud had stopped by just before he went off to Whitehall to drop the paper off to be printed. Frankie had been painting the walls, wearing just some cutoff shorts and an old bathing-suit top as she wielded the roller, when he arrived. Dots of the white paint speckled her arms and legs, even her belly.

Bud had said, "Hey," at the screen door and opened it. She went to turn down the radio, the roller still in her hand. When she turned to him, he was grinning at her. "Aren't *you* something?" he said, in his whispery voice.

Her mouth opened. She went quickly to get some aluminum foil to wrap the roller and brush in. She shoved them into the freezer, and then, with Bud almost carrying her, they had danced their way into the bedroom and knelt together on the bed, pulling at each other's clothes. He'd turned her to get her shorts off and then turned her again, and she was thrilled at that, at his strength, lifting her body, pulling her hips up to him as he knelt behind her. His whispering was urgent. "This way. This way."

Now they were side by side, talking. Frankie could feel the sweat on her chest, the warm wetness on her thighs, between her legs. The sweet, soapy odor of sperm was in the air.

"Yeah, the sex was fun there," she said. "But somehow . . . I don't know. It also wasn't real. It was like being on a playground in grammar school. Everything had to do with the *group*." Her hand moved over her wet chest, stroking it. "It wasn't real," she repeated. She couldn't quite explain it to him.

"And this is."

"Well, it's real*er*."

He laughed, lightly. "Nice to hear."

She was thinking, too, about how sex in Africa was connected with alcohol. She didn't talk about this with Bud—she wouldn't have liked him to know how much alcohol had fueled her nonwork life there. But this part of things was different with Bud, too. In fact, they often met utterly sober in the evening after he'd been to some meeting or social function he was covering for the paper, or in the day, during a break in Bud's work. And this, too, made it different, the acute alertness Frankie brought to it, the physical intensity this made possible. Several times she'd wept after she came, and Bud had held her and stroked her arms, her face.

There were other, more practical ways in which Frankie seemed suddenly to have come alive. She got a telephone, after first consulting Liz, who agreed with her that it made sense. What she said was "I suppose if someone did start a fire, or you saw something or heard something, you'd have to hike all the way up to Mother and Dad's to call it in."

"Which is useless," Frankie said. She was standing in Sylvia's kitchen, where she'd come to use the telephone. "Though I have to admit that up to now I've sort of enjoyed being unreachable by the world."

"That's wearing off, I bet."

Frankie was thinking of Bud, of how it might change things between them to have him able to call her, to have her able to call him. "I think so, yeah. At any rate, I'm ready to give it a try, the old twentieth century."

Liz seemed to have consulted Sylvia about it. At least Frankie was pretty sure it must have been Sylvia who made the money available to have the line brought in from the road. In any case, Sylvia came down a day or two later and said Liz had asked her to give Frankie the go-ahead.

So Frankie called the phone company, and a few days after that the phone guy came. He was in his fifties, she would have said, stout and bearded. He was outside for most of the time, bringing the wire in from the road.

But then he was in the house, breathing noisily and heavily as he went about his work. He'd heard about the arsons, but in his opinion the phone was useless as a means of defense. "If you're here, he's not gonna do it. If you're not here, what's the difference?" He thought the answer was to move into town. "You're just asking for it, living way the hell out here with no reason to be living out here."

"Are you speaking of me personally?" Frankie asked. She had been trying to read while he went about his work, but he kept interrupting her.

"*All* of you. All of you. You think you're having some sorta back-to-the-land experience and whatnot, but these things just wouldn't be happening if you lived in town."

Frankie said she was sure he was right, she thanked him for his concern. While he was there, she stayed carefully polite, but she was almost weepily glad to be alone when he'd left.

Her first call, of course, was to Bud.

On a sunny August afternoon, Frankie and Sylvia were sitting in the living room together, having a drink. Frankie had dropped in as she returned her parents' car—she'd been to the town library and the grocery store. Alfie was resting, as he so frequently seemed to be. The door to the screened porch and all the windows were open, the smell of the new-mown grass worth commenting on, Frankie thought. So she did.

"Ah, yes," Sylvia said. "Tink Snell was up today, mowing." Sylvia, she noticed, had refilled her martini glass once already, topping off the ice cubes, the twist of lemon, with straight gin.

"Well, it's pretty fabulous." She sipped her drink. "So, you're still having him come?" She thought of him, that gorgeous boy. She thought of the night he'd called in the fire up here, before she'd slept with Bud. It seemed a world ago.

"Why not?" Sylvia said.

"I guess the idea that he might have started the fire here. Or others, too."

"He can't start a fire while he's mowing. And I'm a wreck no matter what."

"So you're wakeful?"

"Of course I am."

"Really? Alfie, too?"

She laughed. "God, no. Alfie seems incapable of sustaining anxiety at this point in his life."

They were silent for a moment or two. Then Frankie went ahead and asked: "Any results from the tests?"

"She says it's clear there's loss. And they can see what look like dead areas in his brain."

"God! What a horrible thing to think of."

Sylvia nodded, and drank. After a moment, she said, "But she says it might be something else, though. She said it might be something called Lewy body disease."

"Which is? Not as bad, I hope."

"Well, it is as bad, really. Just different. So it hardly matters."

"Different how?"

"Oh, it has a slightly Parkinsonian element to it—you've noticed he moves a bit stiffly, I'm sure. And then there's the business of going in and out of it—you know, sometimes he seems pretty good. And then, even minutes later, he'll seem really bad."

"Yes," she said.

"That's more typical of Lewy body. As are the hallucinations."

This was news. "What hallucinations?"

"Oh, sometimes mistaking one thing for another. Or imagining things. Visits from people. That he's in his room at his parents' house. Or he thought you had been kidnapped once."

Frankie was thinking of the Larkin poem her father had mentioned to her. She'd gotten the book out of the library, *High Windows,* and thought she'd rarely read a darker vision of life than the collection proposed. But "The Old Fools," the poem Alfie had mentioned, seemed remarkable to her in its description of how the old people thought. And it seemed recognizable to her in what her mother was saying now.

They were silent again. Frankie wondered what Sylvia was thinking, and then her mother said, "Well, maybe we'll end up hiring someone eventually."

"Hiring someone?"

"To guard the house."

"Shades of Africa," Frankie said, trying to make her voice light, teasing.

"I suppose."

But Sylvia didn't seem to be thinking about the argument they'd had the night Liz and Clark arrived, the argument about Frankie's dependence on servants in Africa, including the guards at the gate.

"Aren't you nervous down at Liz's?" Sylvia asked now.

"No more than usual. Which is to say a little bit all the time. I'm up in the night, too. But it seems pretty clear this guy at least *tries* to set them when no one's at home."

"But it looks like no one's at home all the time at Liz's, since you have no car."

"I suppose."

"Maybe you could just rent someone's car, instead of renting a guard."

"Maybe I should *get* a car. I can't go on borrowing from you forever."

"Well, that's up to you." And after a moment, "Though if you went to New York, a car would just be a burden. You'd end up selling it."

Here it comes, Frankie thought.

"Is that still a possibility?" Sylvia asked.

Frankie smiled at her. "Almost anything in this world is still a possibility for me. I'm all potential. Everything is possible. Until I go to New York and actually talk to someone about what there might be for me to do."

"Hmm," Sylvia said. She had some more gin.

And a little bit later, Frankie excused herself and left.

By the time she got down to Liz's, she had decided that she would do it, she would rent a car. Later it would occur to her that she had avoided for a while longer thinking about her mother's question about the future, about New York; but at the moment, the more important question for her was the one having to do with mobility. A little later in the evening, she called Bud and arranged to go with him next Monday afternoon on his weekly trip to the printer in Whitehall to pick up the papers.

Where he dropped her at the rental-car office, and where, in spite of the laborious attempts of the guy running the office to upgrade her, she rented the smallest, least-powerful compact available.

It was six by the time she drove away. She was hungry. On an impulse, she stopped in Winslow at a restaurant whose name struck her as familiar—she thought she remembered it as a place people in Pomeroy used to go to for a slightly upscale meal when the need arose. And yes, when she went inside, she recognized it—the big plate-glass windows looking out on Winslow's Main Street, the white-paper table covers, the open kitchen behind a long counter.

She sat at a table by herself and had some wine, and then a half portion of pasta. There was music playing in the background, nothing she recognized, and the clink and tinkle of silver and glassware all around her. She found herself eavesdropping on the conversation next to her, a couple discussing what kind of refrigerator to buy. And suddenly, absurdly, she felt happy. She supposed having the freedom the car provided was part of it. But there was more. Some way in which she was excited by being alone in a public place, being alone and mobile. She felt reminded of a part of herself she seemed to have left behind when she came to stay with her parents.

She wasn't sure whether it was a result of that feeling or a corrective to it that later that evening she got dressed up in a skirt and low-cut top and drove to Bud's office. She waited until the cars in the lot were gone, the cars belonging to the little group of volunteers who helped him with the papers on Mondays, and then she pulled in and parked.

He must have heard her come in, because his silhouette appeared in the doorway at the top of the dark stairs just as she started up, and he was halfway down to her before she was halfway up, unbuttoning her shirt, sliding his hands into her underpants, into her, pushing her down onto the stairs, saying her name over and over, his face in the shadows stamped with the intense focus that had become so familiar to her, so exciting, when they made love.

When they were done, sitting next to each other on a step in the darkened stairwell, he asked her if she wanted a drink. Frankie was breathless, her blouse unbuttoned, her skirt up around her waist. "I think I *need* a drink," she said. They got up and went into the office, and he poured each of them some bourbon in mismatched glasses. She set the underpants she was carrying down on the table and clinked her glass against his.

They talked for a while, and then Bud washed their glasses and they went downstairs and out to their cars. And though they had said good night standing in the little parking area, when Frankie turned right off Main Road, where Bud should have kept going straight, she saw that he had turned also, to follow her. The sight of his headlights behind her, the steady distance he kept from her in the black night, all this made her nearly breathless as she drove. At Liz's house they stumbled across the yard and into the dark house, into the bedroom, where they made love again without turning on any lights.

Frankie loved having a car. For a few days, she spent most of her time driving around, much as she had when she was an adolescent in Pomeroy. She drove to North Conway and went to the outlet shops. She went swimming a few warm afternoons at Silsby Pond, once with Bud. She drove to the Dairy Queen outside Somerset and had a frappe, sitting at a sticky wooden picnic table with various initials and messages carved into it.

And then finally she called the places she'd found in the yellow pages and talked to earlier, the ones that she thought might work for Alfie, might offer some relief to Sylvia. She made appointments at both.

But walking through these places, watching the residents in groups doing activities that Alfie would have no interest in—sing-alongs, exercises, movies, cooking, reminiscing, or else just watching television— Frankie was remembering her father's open contempt for Sylvia's occasional preoccupation with the Sunday *Times* crossword, his lack of interest in the board games she and Liz, and sometimes Sylvia, played in the summer evenings. She recalled the time when, after sitting through an hour or so of Monopoly with the two of them and a friend, he had divided his properties evenly between them and left. She'd heard him say to Sylvia on his way through the kitchen, "They certainly don't call them bored games for nothing, do they?"

No, Alfie would need a topic, maybe a book, as a prop. He would be bored, and he would probably bore others. Alfie was a loner, she saw, looking at these other old people, who were not. It might not always be the case—he might change—but the fact was that if he ever became capable of the kinds of activities she was looking at, it would be a mark of his greater disintegration.

In the end, she suggested to Sylvia that they might do best to see if Marie Pelletier could come in and stay with Alfie a couple of times a week. Maybe, she suggested, Marie could busy herself with other chores Sylvia could set out for her so that Alfie wouldn't be aware that she was monitoring him. "If she could do that maybe twice a week, I could come in maybe one afternoon. That would give you three afternoons to go out and just . . . be alone, I guess. Or call on someone. Or . . ."

"Two would be ample, Frankie. I'm not going to ask you to help."

Frankie lifted her shoulders. "Okay. But I could be your backup." Sylvia started to shake her head. "If you *needed* it. Only if something came up. You know. What if Louise wanted to go out for dinner, just the two of you? Something like that."

And so they agreed.

Marie, it turned out, agreed, too. But she couldn't, right away. Until the summer folks were gone, she could only do one afternoon—she had too much cleaning and catering to do.

Then Sylvia started to worry about money. She wasn't sure she could really afford Marie. It seemed extravagant, since she didn't really *need* her. It made Frankie realize, she told Bud, how little she knew of their financial situation. "I can't tell if it's just the same old penny-pinching impulse she seems to have been born with, or something real."

They were at Bud's house, which was a new venue for them since Frankie had rented the car. They were upstairs, in his bedroom. Frankie had been touched by the order of the house, by the care with which Bud had furnished it. She liked this bedroom, in spite of its strange cloudy windows. She liked the little painting on the wall, a stucco farmhouse in a green field, impressionistic. She liked the clean white sheets, mussed now, and damp with sweat and their juices. She liked the plaid coverlet on the bed, which they'd pulled up to their waists in the fall air coming through the windows.

It was only the first hint of fall, the steady cool of these evenings, but everyone felt it. Now, in addition to the conversations about the fires, people talked about the change in the weather, about a maple flaring fuchsia here or there, about the quickly melting snow seen high on a mountain one morning.

"There's no family money, then," Bud said to her now.

"No money at all," she said to him. "Just the farmhouse and the land."

"Well, shit. I thought I was latching on to some serious bucks."

"Nope."

After a silent moment he said, "You know, your mother may be thinking about the long haul with him, and then what'll be left for her own old age. It's not cheap, Alzheimer's care."

"But what about the government? What about Medicare?"

"I don't think so, Frankie. I think they don't pay for that long-term, not-purely-medical stuff. So she might feel like she's staring down a long, dark expensive tunnel she can't see the end of."

After a minute, Frankie said, "Poor Sylvia."

"Yeah. It's a tough one."

"Well, not just that. She doesn't even love him, that's the problem."

"How do you know that?"

"She said so. To me. That night their barn was set on fire. After you left, we were talking for a while, and she told me."

"Okay, but come on. She was just being honest, in a way. He's so compromised."

"Yeah, but that wasn't it. She said she hadn't loved him for a long time. That there was no . . . *store,* I guess you'd say, of loving goodwill, based on the way she'd felt for him earlier. Based on who he'd been, ever."

After a moment, he said, "That is sad. God."

They lay still for a while, and then Bud turned to her and began to move against her. She could feel that he was hard again. It seemed funny, suddenly. "This is so odd to me," she said.

"What? This?" He pushed his cock against her hip.

"No, not that. I meant talking the way we do, in between." He rose up as if to move on top of her, but she put her hand against his chest.

"Stop. Stop for a minute."

"That's asking an awful lot, Frankie."

"I'm asking it."

He lay down again, on his side, propping his head on one hand.

"This is new, Bud. I've never . . . *chatted* . . ." She laughed. "I've never talked like this with anyone about these . . . teensy events, in my life."

"Oh, well. That's my specialty. Teensy events, and the chatting thereabout."

"Be serious."

"You be serious. What are you saying?"

"I feel so companionable with you."

He made a gagging sound. "Eros, please."

"Well, there's that, too. Plenty. But I'm just not used to this other. This kind of talking."

He was quiet for a long minute. "You're used to talking about grander things," he said. "Larger things."

"Moment by moment, I suppose not. The people I worked with, we talked a lot about . . . practicalities. How to do things. Or *get* things. A lot. About politics, some. But these personal issues, this kind of daily-life stuff—no."

"So it seems like . . . small talk."

"I guess so."

He had stopped, completely, and lain back, his forearm lifted to rest on his forehead.

She felt he was hurt. She hadn't meant to hurt him. "I'm sure you know what I mean," she said. She ran her hand over the flesh of his shoulder. "I'm always aware of it, coming back to the States. That the *scale* of things, of people's preoccupations, seems small. You must feel that. I mean, you used to write about national politics."

"Ah. Well. You want to know about *small,* then yeah, let's talk about national politics. It's all strategic. None of it's big."

They didn't speak for a minute. She let her hand fall.

Then he said, "Look. Frankie. I get it. You were doing work that felt important to you."

"If sometimes futile."

"If sometimes futile. And you were with people who weren't fretting about house fires or signs of memory loss in their fathers. Or whether they had enough money to pay the mortgage. And I'm sure that did feel more like asking the big questions." He nodded several times. "Yes. Living large, morally, philosophically. *What then must we do?*" he said in his hoarse voice. "And my God, I admire that. I wish I'd lived that way, ever."

After a long moment, he said, "Although I might have felt some of that the first couple of years in Washington," he said. "But I'm at peace with what I'm doing now. And I even think, deluded as I may be, that I get to ask the odd big question."

He turned on his side again and propped his head up once more. "And I don't mean to suggest that asking those questions is a privilege, exactly, but let me just say that someone, somewhere, is always worrying about the small stuff. The children's grades, the Alzheimer's symptoms, what's for dinner. The *money,* for God's sake, in a strictly small-town way.

"But chatting with you." He shook his head. "Chatting with you here, that's got nothing to do with that. I'm chatting with you because I fucking care about you." He reached over and brushed his fingers lightly across her breasts. She could feel her nipples tighten.

"You know how you said nothing was permanent for you there?" he asked.

"Yes. That I was temporizing."

"Okay. Just . . . I'm saying I'm interested in permanence. I mean, with you, whatever that means. I want exactly this. Sex. Chatting. Every now and then maybe the consideration of something really immense. Whatever *that* means."

"Are you angry, Bud? I didn't mean to make you angry."

"I'm not." He was quiet for a moment. "Not really. I'm mostly just . . . perplexed. About how to get to you."

"You've already gotten to me."

"That's not what I mean, you know that. It's just, we keep coming around to this, as you've pointed out to me more than once. The question of what's going on between us. What it is, I guess. So I'm just saying it now. I won't say it again." He lay back down. "Over to you, Frankie," he said, gently. "You figure it out. And when you do, let me know."

She was quiet a long time. "That's a big responsibility."

"Oh." He shook his head on the pillow, and then he grinned suddenly. "Teensy."

~

17

"What do you mean, he's gone?"

Her mother said, "Just, if he's not down there with you, I've no idea where he is."

Frankie was standing in the kitchen, still half asleep; her mother's call had waked her, her mother's question—*Is Alfie down there with you?*—had made no sense, and this made no sense, either. "Well. What do you mean? He wasn't there when you got up?"

"Yes, exactly. So where is he? Where can he be?" There was a frantic note in her mother's voice.

Frankie tried to make her own voice reassuring. "He can't be far." The floor was cold under her feet. "The car is there, right?"

"Yes."

"So maybe he got up and just went for a walk."

Sylvia said nothing.

"He's gone for a walk by himself before." Frankie sat down and pulled her feet up on the chair. "Hasn't he?"

Sylvia made an odd noise, a sigh, a strange, pained expelling of air. "Well, the thing is," she said finally, "I think he might have left in the night."

"What do you mean?" She wanted coffee.

"Well, he got up in the night, as he often does, and, I just . . . slept through. I heard him, but then I went back to sleep and I didn't wake again. Usually I do, but I didn't. I just didn't this time." She sounded near tears, suddenly.

Frankie said, "That doesn't mean he's been out all that time, Mother. He probably waited until dawn, until it was light, and then went out.

He wouldn't go in the dark, would he?" Though it was actually still not fully light now. At least not in Liz's house, which sat in a little gully. The kitchen was deeply shadowed. "How long have you been up?"

"About an hour. I thought . . . well, I hoped, pretty much that, what you said. So I waited, thinking, *Okay, he'll be back.* And then I thought, well, maybe he'd gone down to see you, and I called."

"Okay. Look. I'll get dressed and I'll be right up. I'll come up by the field, in case he's somewhere between us, in case he came that way and fell or something. And you stay there, in case he comes home."

"He's not coming home."

"He might. I'll be right there."

Frankie had been lying in bed when the phone rang, lying there running through the strange, disjointed series of images, yearnings, that had constituted her life for the last several weeks. Now she moved quickly, pulling on jeans, a turtleneck, and a heavy sweater, warm socks, her hiking sneakers. She brushed her hair, her teeth.

When she stepped outside, she realized the air still held the night's chill, so she went back quickly and got her jacket.

Her breath plumed as she hiked up the rise into the weak sunlight and then walked quickly back down through the blackberry canes, slowing as she came to the pond. Alfie wasn't there, wasn't drowned, and it was only as she felt the relief of this that she understood how much she'd been pushing away the imagining of it—his face, his form, under the still, clear, brownish water.

Now she started to call his name across the field, turning one way and then another as she walked: "Aal-fie! Aaal-fie!" And hearing back only birdsong, the brushing of dying, dry grasses against her legs.

Her mother was on the porch, waiting for her; Frankie could see her from halfway up the meadow, her arms tightly crossed, her shoulders hunched against the cold. As Frankie came up the porch steps, her mother stepped forward and held the screen door open for her. Her face was set, haggard. "So," she said.

"Yeah," Frankie answered. Together they went into the house. The heat was on—Frankie could hear the new furnace in the basement, and the air inside smelled of it, and felt dry.

"Do you want coffee?" Sylvia asked. "I was going to make some. I hadn't got around to it yet." Sylvia was bundled up in an oversize sweater. She had large, puffy slippers on her feet that made a sliding noise as she walked around.

"Yes, let's have coffee. And then we should figure out what we ought to be doing." Frankie followed her into the kitchen and sat at the table. As Sylvia moved from the sink to the stove to the cupboard, setting things up, Frankie had her go over again, in closer detail, the events of the night.

Nothing had been unusual. He got up about midnight, which was typical. He moved around the bedroom for a bit—dressing, Sylvia thought, or gathering his clothes to dress out in the kitchen.

A light had gone on somewhere down the hall. It was very faint at the bedroom door, just a slight lifting of the blackness there, so she assumed he was in the living room, reading, and she relaxed. "Usually when he reads, that's a good thing," she said. "He's up for a few hours and then he comes back to bed. It's when he's agitated, when he keeps moving around, that I worry. Sometimes then I get up. Or just lie there, more or less monitoring him." She was at the stove, pouring the water into the glass carafe.

"But you went back to sleep this time," Frankie said.

"Yes, I thought everything was okay." She poured more water in, waited, poured again. They were both quiet, and the only sound for a minute or two was the dribble of the coffee into the lower part of the carafe. When it slowed, then stopped, Sylvia poured the coffee into their cups and brought them over to the table, then went back for the little china milk pitcher. They sat opposite each other.

The sunlight had climbed over the hill behind the house and reached into the room by now, lying in warming squares over the table, the refinished floor. Frankie put her hand into the light on the tabletop, feeling the slow warmth on her skin. She was thinking of Bud, she realized. She was thinking of calling him, telling him about her father, and there was part of her that was aware of the pleasure this thought brought her, the thought of his being *in* this with her—in the midst of all this worry!—a thought that contained momentarily all of her sexual feelings for him, her yearning. How strange.

She must have made a little noise, because Sylvia set her cup down and said, "What?"

"Oh," Frankie said. "Just, I think we should give him, maybe, an hour."

"You think we should wait that long?" Sylvia's face was lit harshly by the horizontal sunlight.

"Well, if he went to the beaver dam, or around Hurd's Pond, for instance, it would take him that long to get back."

"But I'm not sure he's capable of getting back."

"But those are all paths he hikes a couple of times a week."

She shook her head. "Not this summer," she said firmly. "He hasn't wanted to go anywhere this summer. We went to the beaver dam with the children once or twice, and down to Liz and Clark's two or three times. And there was that one time he came down alone to see you. But that's it."

They sat for a long moment. Then Frankie said, "Okay, I'll go out and look."

"But where will you go?"

"I'll go to those places. Hurd's Pond and the beaver dam. That'll put me on the road for a bit of it, too."

Sylvia was silent.

Frankie said, "And why don't you call around to the neighbors up and down the road and see if anyone's seen him?"

"But it's so *early*," Sylvia said.

"It's an emergency," Frankie said firmly. "Call."

While her mother was looking for the phone book, Frankie finished her coffee. Then she headed out, about a half mile up the road first, to where the path to the beaver dam turned off. She moved back and forth from sun to shade along the road, grateful always for the warmth when it was the sun's turn. She was calling intermittently, her voice a lonely sound amid the cheerful morning noises of the birds.

The path through the woods to the beaver dam was shady, and the widening pond they'd made was in deep shade, the backed-up water black and still. There was no sign of Alfie, though Frankie couldn't imagine what a sign would be. She stood by the pond turning around slowly, calling his name in every direction, and then she started back.

As she drew near the house, she had a sense of the futility of what she was doing. He could be anywhere. He could be frightened of her voice, somehow. She could have passed him, if that were the case. Or if he were distracted somehow. Or if he'd fallen and hit his head.

But she went on. She hiked down the meadow and on the wide path through the woods to Hurd's Pond, where there was no sign of him, either.

The sun was fully up, glorious on the fall leaves, by the time she got back to the house. She came in through the front porch again.

Sylvia was in the living room, looking out. "Nothing?" she asked.

Frankie shook her head.

"And no one else has seen him, either," Sylvia said.

"We need some help, I think." Frankie sat down opposite her.

After a moment, Sylvia said, "Davey Swann, I suppose."

"Yes. He'll have organized the odd search party before, I imagine." You read about it every now and then in the paper—usually hikers lost off a trail in the mountains, injured or caught in sudden bad weather. Or a child wandering off. "Not Loren, certainly," Frankie said.

"Good Lord, no. I hope we can avoid him entirely." Sylvia got up and went into the kitchen, where the wall phone hung by the back door.

Frankie followed her and poured herself more coffee as she listened to her mother's voice speaking to Davey. She sounded calmer than she had talking to Frankie—even slightly amused at what she called, to Davey, her "pickle." "Well, I'm not sure how long," she said. "He wasn't around when I got up, and that was sixish."

After a moment, she seemed to be agreeing with him about possible places Alfie might have been going. And then she said, "Though it may be none of the above. He's been diagnosed with a kind of Alzheimer's disease, you know, sort of midstage, I guess, so he may not really remember where it is he's headed."

This led to a long silence on her part, some noises of agreement, and finally the end of the conversation.

"He's coming up," she said as she came back to the table. "They'll start with a group of people searching, I guess the same men who respond to fires."

Frankie stood up. "I'll make another pot of coffee," she said.

The deal was, Davey said, that they could keep it local for maybe three or four hours. Then they'd need to call the state officers in charge of search and rescue and make it official, which would enlarge it quite a bit. Frankie had the sense he'd risked something to get permission to do this, but perhaps not—he was deferential, shy almost, and therefore hard to read. And apologetic to Sylvia, as car after car pulled up outside and parked at the edge of the long driveway. They could see the men and a few women standing around out there, perhaps twenty or twenty-five of them, and Frankie saw how foolish she'd been to make the extra pot of coffee. Though she was having another cup herself while Davey and Sylvia sat at the kitchen table and she went over for him again what she thought Alfie was wearing.

Davey was writing all this down in a notebook he'd brought in with him. He'd turned down the offer of coffee. There was something self-contained about him, so orderly, it made Frankie feel better. Confident.

Yesterday's clothes, Sylvia said. His brown slacks. A striped shirt over a navy T-shirt. And all this, she suspected, over his pajamas, as she hadn't found them anywhere.

And Frankie could imagine it, his getting up and putting on the clothes he'd laid across the bedroom chair without noticing he was still wearing the old print pajamas.

He'd taken his parka, Sylvia said, which didn't yet have the winter zip-out lining in it, and the heavy hiking sneakers he wore most days now. And his old hat, a misshapen beige canvas thing that had once looked a bit like a fedora.

Frankie stood at the back door, sipping her coffee, listening to her mother and watching the group in the yard. They moved around, leaning against one person's car and then another's, some of them sitting inside, turned sideways with their doors hanging open. A few were smoking.

And then Bud arrived. She didn't see his car until after she spotted him walking up the drive. Then she saw that he'd parked it halfway down, behind a pickup that blocked most of it from her view. She moved to the window and stood where he could have seen her if he looked her way, seen her standing there, drinking coffee, hoping to talk to him, to touch him.

But he didn't look her way. Tall, grizzled, wearing a navy-blue jacket she hadn't seen on him before, he moved around among the others, talking, laughing, writing things down.

Well, of course, it made sense not to signal some special relationship. Hadn't they been trying to avoid making that public knowledge?

Davey was asking about the barn now. Did it have electricity? Could they set up tables there? They'd need to make a kind of headquarters, a place to organize things.

Her mother began the apologetic description of the mess out there, and Frankie turned to face them both. "Why don't you use my sister's house?" she said to Davey.

He looked up. "Ah," he said. "Down below, in the meadow."

"Yes. It's got electricity. And a working phone and a big table. A stove. Heat, even—a woodstove, anyhow."

"Well. That'd be helpful. Thank you."

"When you're ready, I can go down with you and show you around. And pick up any of my stuff that'd be in the way."

He stood up. "We may as well go right now. Get that disreputable bunch out of your mother's yard sooner rather than later."

Frankie got her jacket from the living room and came back to the kitchen to follow Davey out. At the door, she turned to Sylvia. "I'll come right back, as soon as they're settled in."

Davey was outside calling out directions, and the assembled few dozen were returning to their cars, starting them up.

Bud came over to her. "Hello, sweetheart," he said, and Frankie felt suddenly tearful. "You want a ride down, or do you have your car?"

"A ride down, please." As they walked back down the driveway, she told him what she knew. In the car, they waited for the line of others to make its way down the driveway and out onto the road to Liz and Clark's. "I've been thinking about you so much through these last couple of hours," Frankie said. "Isn't that strange?"

"I don't know." He looked over at her. "Is it?"

"I feel guilty about it, actually. It's almost as if I welcome this *drama*. Just so I can somehow be with you. Lean on you."

"You don't need a drama to be with me, do you?"

"No. That's my point. Why should I feel so . . . hot for you. In the midst of this?"

They swung into the driveway now, the last in the line of cars. As they turned right down the hill, he said, "I'm glad for the heat anytime, it goes without saying. But maybe it's a way not to think about what might be really"—his mouth tightened—"bad news, here."

Frankie felt stung. She turned and looked out the window at the familiar trees, the last wild asters flowering below them.

At Liz's, the cars were pulling over onto the meadow, some oddly angled, others falling into rows where they could.

As they got out, Bud looked over the top of the car at her. "Where will you be?" he asked.

"I'm heading back up to Sylvia's, once I settle things here," she said. "Are you going to join the search?"

"Yes," he said. "But I'll come find you when I'm done."

"Will you?"

"Yes."

"I'll be waiting, then."

Davey was standing on the back porch, gathering the volunteers around him as they got out of their cars. He had maps he was passing out, areas he wanted different "teams," he called them, to cover. Five-man teams, he said, the usual captains.

There was calling back and forth, laughter, as the teams sorted themselves out. Frankie stood on the porch, too, watching. Someone said, "Hey, Gavin. We still got room," and the lanky boy went over and stood with the small group clustered together nearest her. Some of the volunteers had rucksacks. All wore hiking boots, parkas, hats. Many carried walking sticks. Most of the faces were familiar to Frankie, and she knew the names of about half of them. Kevin O'Hara was there, and Peter Babcock. Dan Stark, Seward Mitchell, John Chick, and Gavin Knox, all of them sorted out into their groups.

Frankie was at first startled to see that Tink Snell was there, too, and then also to see that the others were behaving perfectly normally around him in spite of all the speculation about his possibly being the arsonist. But perhaps they were used to his appearance at events such as these.

Bud had said that he'd continued to fight the fires, too, and that no one commented on that.

In the end there were five groups. Two would start out from here, Davey said, one toward the beaver dam, the other toward the pond. The other groups were to drive to the trails that came at those sites from other directions. When they met, if Alfie hadn't turned up, they'd come back here and see what the next step was.

"We think the professor is probably just lost, probably not too far from here, so we're hoping this'll do the trick. He's got dementia, you should know that, so he may be confused about who you are and where you're taking him. You need to be gentle and careful with him. A lotta explaining, when you find him. If you need help bringing him out, ask for help. He answers to Alfie."

Davey talked about what Alfie looked like, what he was wearing, how long it was thought he'd been out there. He said within a couple of hours, if it lasted that long, there would be food here, at Liz and Clark Swenson's place. Food and extra equipment. That everyone should come back here.

His voice, always, was shy, almost apologetic, but he was clearly in charge. Two men came up to him with their maps, asking for clarification on their exact routes. When he was done, the groups split up. The people in the groups that were driving were starting to negotiate which car or truck would be best to take. Frankie went inside.

She moved quickly around the main room, picking up her books and papers from the table, from the trunk by the woodstove. She started a fire. Once that was going, she went into the bathroom and cleared away her makeup, her toothbrush and hairbrush and used towels. She put everything she'd need for the day into her overnight bag to take up to Sylvia's, along with a change of clothes. She got out a stack of clean towels and set them on the hamper by the bathroom sink.

She could hear that Davey had come in and was talking to someone. When she stepped into the big room, closing the door behind her, there were two men with Davey. They were pushing the table back against the wall. They had set their radios down on it, and stacks of papers—Frankie could see terrain maps and charts, with lists of names.

"We're all set here," Davey said.

"So I guess I'll go back up to my mother's," Frankie answered.

"Yeah, that's best," Davey said. "She can use your company, of that I'm sure. And we'll call, soon's we have anything to report."

Outside the air still seemed cool to Frankie. She could hear the calls starting in the field above, multiple voices: *Aal*fie. *Aaal*fie. She was thinking of her father, imagining him. Imagining him and imagining Bud now, too, walking in the woods, calling Alfie's name. She tossed her overnight bag onto the passenger seat of the rental car and threaded her way out through the maze created by the cars of the searchers, back onto the road. As she reached Sylvia and Alfie's driveway, she saw a car in her rearview mirror, just turning off the road below her into Liz's driveway: Loren's car, with its big star. There would be no keeping him away from the action, she supposed.

It seemed very quiet at Sylvia's after the bustle below. Her mother was sitting in the living room, staring off at the view. She looked up at Frankie as she came in. "Everyone is all set down there?" She sounded determinedly matter-of-fact.

"Yes. They're getting things organized."

"What kinds of things, exactly?"

"Oh, teams, I guess. Search groups. With different assignments. Davey Swann had maps to hand out."

Frankie sat down. She looked out to where Sylvia had been staring and saw a widely and evenly spaced row of figures just entering the woods at the bottom of the meadow.

After a moment, Sylvia said, "Maybe we'd feel more useful down there?"

"I don't think they really want us down there, Mother. I think it's . . . easier for them if we just let them do what they usually do. Tell their usual jokes, you know. Behave the way they always behave."

"I suppose there are jokes, aren't there?" Sylvia smiled ruefully.

"At this stage, anyway. Everyone seemed almost . . . cheerful."

"Well, it's an adventure."

"For everyone but Alfie."

"Oh, it may be for him, too, at this point," Sylvia said. "That's how I'm trying to think of it. That he's out for a walk and is enjoying himself. And he doesn't have the least idea that there are dozens of people out hunting for him."

"If he's not cold."

"Well, yes."

They sat for some minutes more, one or the other of them offering something occasionally. Then Sylvia abruptly decided to build a fire in the fireplace, and Frankie went upstairs to unpack her overnight bag. She stayed up there longer than she needed to, listening to her mother moving around below. She could hear that Sylvia was talking to herself a little, the odd word audible. It was hard to read her, Frankie thought. She seemed to swing back and forth between the deepest concern for Alfie and a kind of willed insouciance. It made Frankie uncertain what her own position should be.

They would find him, was what she told herself. It seemed impossible that they wouldn't. She thought again of the row of searchers moving slowly across the meadow. She imagined Alfie, surprised by the fuss, delighted by the attention. It would be all right. There was no point in worrying.

She went downstairs.

Through the long morning they moved around separately in the house. At one point Sylvia decided to make some cookies to send down to the searchers. Frankie drifted in and out of the kitchen. She ate a fair amount of the raw cookie dough when Sylvia wasn't looking. She tried to read. She borrowed some darning thread from Sylvia and mended a couple of holes she'd noticed in her sweater. They had a mostly silent lunch of canned soup and fruit. They were just putting the dishes in the dishwasher when someone knocked at the back door. Sylvia emitted a little noise, half anticipation, half fear, and, wiping her hands, went over to it. "Oh, it's Bud," she said, her disappointment audible.

She opened the door, and Bud came in a few steps and stood by the table, looking at Frankie. All three of them were standing, Frankie still by the sink, Bud and Sylvia just inside the door. Sylvia had the dishcloth in her hands.

"I bring no news," Bud said. His voice, hoarse as always, surprised

Frankie, stirred her. "My group didn't see anything, and the others aren't back yet."

"Well," Sylvia said. "Well, thank you."

Frankie found herself unable to speak. She wanted to step into Bud's arms, she wanted him to hold her, and she felt very far away from him.

He stayed where he was. "I've got to get a few things done for the paper—I'm late getting it to the printer—but I'll have my car phone, if you need to call."

When Frankie didn't say anything, Sylvia spoke. "That's very kind of you. We *will*. We'll call if we hear anything."

"When will you be back?" Frankie said. Her own voice sounded hoarse to her.

"Late. Late afternoon, early evening. I'll come by."

"Okay," Frankie said. "Okay."

He turned to Sylvia. "I'm . . . I'm just so sorry you have to go through this."

"Thank you," Sylvia said. Frankie said nothing.

"Okay, then. I'm off." Frankie nodded at him. He nodded back. "I'm off."

After another hour or so had passed, Frankie went down to Liz's with the cookies. Two more of the teams besides Bud's were back, standing and sitting around. Frankie went inside. There were two women from town, moving around the kitchen. They were cooking what smelled like chicken soup in big kettles on the stove. Frankie knew one of them by sight—Helen Ardery, fiftyish, stout and red-faced. The other introduced herself as Rachel Stark. She was probably Frankie's age, small as a child, and pretty, in a delicate way. Frankie set the cookie tin down on the kitchen counter. Rachel offered Frankie some soup, but she said she'd eaten.

"I'm so sorry your dad's wandered off like this," Helen said from where she stood at the stove, stirring the kettle, "but I've no doubt Davey's crew are going to find him and get him right back home. And thank goodness it's so mild out. That's a blessing."

"Yes," Frankie said, but she was thinking of the smoke of her breath earlier this morning.

"Now, you're the one who lives in Africa, aren't you?"

"Yes."

"Well, it's so good you've come home to help Sylvia with all this."

Frankie was about to explain herself—she hadn't come home, she wasn't helping—when Helen turned to Davey, who was just coming in, carrying a commercial-sized coffeemaker. "Oh, there. What a he-man. Just put it over there, by the sink."

Davey set it down, and then made a questioning gesture back toward the open door.

"No, no," Helen said. "We'll get the rest. You do what you need to do."

"Can I help?" Frankie asked, and Helen said no, no thanks. They had a routine down, and it was easiest for them just to do it themselves.

"Okay," Frankie said. "Well, enjoy the cookies."

"We sure will. And so will the crew. You just go along. Sylvia will be counting on you for company. We're just fine here."

Davey had gone back outside, where he was standing talking to a couple of the searchers on the porch. As Frankie came out, he stepped over to her. He said that it was seeming more likely that they'd have to call Fish and Game and get more crews on the search. One other team had radioed back with nothing, but they were waiting for the fifth team, which was supposed to meet up with them. This last group was still walking. They had the steepest terrain, Davey said, and he held up one of his contour maps to show her where they were—above Hurd's Pond, heading down to it.

There had been a few things recovered, he said—an old baseball cap, some trash, some tin cans. Nothing that seemed connected to Alfie. He said Byron Morrell would be in touch with them regularly to let them know how things were going.

"My mother would like to come and help down here," Frankie said. She knew Davey would understand this as a question.

"Well, I think it's better she stays right there," he said in his gentle voice. "There's still a chance he'll come back on his own from someplace we didn't anticipate. Or if someone else finds him and calls, she'll be right there, don't you know."

"Yes, that's what I thought, too," Frankie said.

Back up the hill, Frankie told Sylvia about the changing nature of the search.

"Fish and Game? That seems strange."

"Well, I guess they know the terrain and how to move around in it. And they coordinate with other groups. Other rescue groups. Davey says they'll need more searchers. So they'll be in charge of these others. That's mainly it."

"So, we just keep waiting." There was something spiky—irritation, Frankie supposed—in Sylvia's voice.

"Yes. That's our job. Mr. Morrell—Byron—will let us know if they find him. Or if they find, I guess, any signs of him."

"Signs of him?"

"Yes. Pieces of clothing or, you know, something like a campfire." Frankie shrugged. "I suppose he might think of that to keep warm."

Sylvia looked away, as though imagining Alfie cold, needing warmth. "I suppose," she said doubtfully. And then: "He was an Eagle Scout, you know."

"Yes. I remember." In her mind's eye, Frankie saw the photograph of him in his uniform, towering over the smiling little mustachioed man who was his foster father.

They sat in silence for a few more minutes. Then Sylvia said, "I'm going to do some wash. Do you have anything?" Frankie said no. But it was another minute or two before her mother sighed and stood up and went down the hallway off the kitchen.

What to do?

She went to Alfie's chair and picked up a book from the top of his pile. It wasn't one of the books for his precious prize, this one. It was an old book of his about a fire in the mountains of Montana—he'd been reading it, he told her, in connection with the fires here, in Pomeroy. She sat down and opened it. In another life, her father had made notes in the margins in what was then his neat but still almost illegible script, all the vertical strokes so small and so closely identical as to be nearly indistinguishable from one another.

Sylvia came into the room, and Frankie looked up. Her mother was carrying a full laundry basket. "Should we call Liz, do you think?" she asked Frankie. "Shouldn't she know?"

Frankie was flummoxed. She sat silent for a long moment.

"You don't think so," Sylvia said.

"I don't *know*." She set the book down. "If they find him an hour from now, what will have been the point?"

"That she will know what we know."

"But she can do even less than we can."

"Still, she might want to know."

"I think we should wait."

Sylvia's silence was a question.

"See what the end of the day brings," Frankie said. "Call her then if he hasn't been found."

Sylvia set the basket down on the arm of the chair she was standing next to. "What will they do if he hasn't been found?" Her voice was quiet.

"Liz and Clark?"

"No." She shook her head. "The searchers."

"I don't know," Frankie said. "Perhaps they'll wait until morning—it must be hard to find much of anything in the dark."

"Not a *person*." Her voice was full of alarm. "You can find a person in the dark."

"Well, but if he doesn't answer. Or if he's lain down somewhere to go to sleep."

"But he wouldn't be able to sleep in the *cold*."

"He might, if he was exhausted."

Sylvia didn't answer for a moment, and Frankie thought they must both be imagining that version of Alfie—exhausted, frightened, numb, lying down, giving up. Alfie, cold, asleep, dead.

"All right," Sylvia said, turning away. "Let's wait until the end of the afternoon."

Sylvia was up and down the stairs to the basement, doing laundry; and then puttering around somehow in the kitchen, the bedroom. They were considerate to each other, polite, but neither wanted to talk about what she was thinking. Each kept busy trying to keep up the appearance of busyness.

"Would you like tea? A cookie?"

"No. Thanks so much."

"Can I help you fold some of those?"

"No, I'm fine."

After a while, Frankie went upstairs and lay down on her bed with several of Alfie's books, simply because she could think of nothing else to do. She first tried to read *Young Men and Fire* and then a Harper Prize book on Ebola, but in both cases she found herself repeatedly frozen in the text, unthinking, gone, starting a sentence over and over.

At about three-thirty, she became aware of the murmur of conversation downstairs and got up.

Sylvia and Byron Morrell looked up at her as she came into the dining room. They were at the table. Sylvia's hands were folded together as if she were praying. Byron stood.

"It's Frankie, idn't it?" he asked. He was a large man, with a big, round face. He held a kind of hunting hat in his hands.

"It is. And you're Mr. Morrell."

"Byron is fine." He smiled quickly, revealing several missing teeth.

"What's the news?" Frankie asked.

"Well, I was telling your mother here, there's not much. But we're planning on going all night, I guess that's new."

"Ah," Frankie said.

"Yep. It's supposed to maybe rain, and that'd be bad for your father, 'cause it'll be down in the thirties, they say, maybe cooler if he's uphill somewhere, so that rain, that'd be tough. It seemed like it'd be a good idea not to wait till morning. It could be a tough night for Professor Rowley if he had to stay out there all that time." He pressed his lips together.

"That seems right, then."

"Yeah, that's what we thought. So they've got some more teams, some of the mountain club fellas. And then, I think we're hoping that there'll be a helicopter we can use."

"Oh, my God," Sylvia said softly, and bowed her head.

Frankie came and stood behind her mother's chair. "We feel utterly useless up here," she said to Byron. "Isn't there something we can do down at my sister's?"

"I don't think you want to go down there." He shook his head. "There's close to a hundred people going in and out down there, and if anyone can find him, they will. Plus they got a news truck there now."

"Oh," Frankie said.

"Yeah. So you had best just stay up here and wait. You got the hard part, I'd say."

"You know," Sylvia said, after a moment. "I really don't think you need to search very far for him. I mean, this notion of extending the search . . . Well, part of Alfie's illness is a kind of awkwardness. Not immobility, exactly, but . . . Well, I just don't think he's gone beyond where you've been looking. I don't think he could have."

"But why wouldn't he have answered us, then?"

"I don't know. Maybe he's scared, somehow. He has, sometimes, sort of irrational fears."

"Or he could have fallen. He could be unconscious," Frankie said.

"We were pretty thorough. Line searches, you know."

"But if he were unconscious? If he'd fallen?" Sylvia said.

"We should have spotted him. We would have, I think. We was going carefully, the way we do."

"Well, I just thought you should know," she said. She sounded defeated.

"I'll pass it along. Anything else?"

"No, we'll just . . . wait, then."

"I'm sorry," he said, standing up.

Frankie ran a bath. "Hydrotherapy," she said to Sylvia when she excused herself.

"I hope it works," Sylvia said. She was ironing now, in the kitchen.

The water held the palest possible tint of aqua in the old porcelain tub. The drain was set too low, so Frankie had to keep wetting a washcloth and covering her breasts with it to keep them warm. There was a window over the tub, and she looked out at the gathering clouds, the clouds that would deliver rain to Alfie. Only the tallest trees were visible from where her head rested—several pointed pines of a deep, almost black, green—and the unreasonably orange-purple flare of the maple just below them.

And then it came to her. The night when Sylvia told her she didn't love Alfie, when Frankie was sitting with her at the kitchen table, the one light on over it, Sylvia's face half in shadow saying the words.

And the slide of a foot in the hallway, Frankie's quick glance that way, a glance that brought her the sight of Alfie standing outside the bathroom, just beginning to turn away from his wife's voice explaining her distance from him, her resolve to do well by him because she didn't love him, hadn't loved him for a long time. His wife, saying she'd wished for a moment that he were dead so she could be free of him.

In that moment, what Frankie had hoped was that he hadn't heard, what she had chosen to think was that it was unlikely he had. Or that if he had, he would have been incapable of taking it in, what Sylvia was saying. Incapable of understanding how deeply it connected to him and his life.

So she'd turned back to Sylvia, who needed her more right then.

But now, sitting up in the tub, she had the sudden conviction that he *had* heard. He'd heard, and he'd sought a way out, for himself, for Sylvia. *He would disappear.* He would walk away from the house and not be found.

She stood up in the tub and stepped over its edge. She grabbed one of the thin towels that had always been the specialty of the house. She dried herself quickly and dressed again and came down the hallway to her room, leaving damp footprints all the way on the old wood.

She pulled on her socks and shoes and went downstairs. As she passed Sylvia, still ironing in the kitchen, she said, "I'm just going to go down for a minute or two. See how things are going."

"I don't see the point," Sylvia said, reasonably enough. "Didn't Byron as much as tell us to stay away?"

"I guess I'm just having trouble doing that."

Sylvia set the iron down. "Do you want me to come along?"

"No, I won't be long." As though that made any kind of sense.

She walked fast down the meadow under the cloudy gray sky, breaking into a jolting run a couple of times. Around the pond, over the hillock, down again, into the thicket of cars. There was a van with the local TV station's call letters parked there and an ambulance. There were more than a dozen people standing around. There were cigarette butts on the ground here and there.

Inside, the smell of coffee dominated now. All the lights were on. Davey was there, talking to two men in green uniforms. She caught his eye and raised her hand. He nodded to her and, in a few minutes, came across the room to where she'd sat down by the woodstove.

She explained it to him, what she thought. What she said was that Sylvia had been tired that night, talking to her, and said aloud she'd couldn't do it anymore, couldn't take care of Alfie. This was not far from the truth, she told herself.

"And you're sure he heard this," Davey said, when they'd been over it twice.

"I am, pretty sure. I can't be positive because we never discussed it, but I think I'm right."

"Right that he's trying *not* to be found."

"I . . . yes, I think so."

Davey pushed his chair back and sighed. "Well, I guess we'll just have to start all over here."

"I'm sorry," Frankie said.

"No, no. Nothing for you to be sorry about."

"I wish I'd thought of it sooner."

He smiled. "Now, *I'm* sorry about that."

On Frankie's way back across the yard, a woman in a puffy full-length down coat wearing too much makeup approached her with a mike in her hand, trailed by a guy holding a camera, but Frankie gestured her away, waving her hand in front of her, and cut quickly between the cars and into the tall grass that led up the hill, where she knew the woman wouldn't follow her.

About an hour later they heard the helicopter and went to the window to watch it moving back and forth in long, slow sweeps across the hills, its noise steady as a lawnmower for a while, then moving off, growing quieter. Sylvia called Liz sometime after that.

Neither of them wanted dinner. Frankie, who felt vaguely ill after all the cookie dough she'd eaten, had a glass of milk. Sylvia had crackers and cheese and a glass of gin. She looked up and said to Frankie, "Do you realize neither of us has mentioned the fires, all day?"

"That's true," Frankie said.

"What an accomplishment for Alfie." She smiled quickly.

At about seven someone knocked on the back door again. Frankie went to open it. It was Bud. He was back from Whitehall with his papers and about to spend the evening with his helpers inserting the circulars and ads into them. He said he'd stopped below, but they had nothing to report to him.

Sylvia offered him coffee or a drink, but he said he had to get going. They stood awkwardly for a moment, all three of them, and then Bud looked directly at Frankie and said, "Will you walk me out to the car?"

"Oh. Sure," she said.

"Oh, yes!" said Sylvia, as though she'd been stupid not to suggest it herself. "Go on."

The rain had started, lightly. They'd taken only a few steps from the porch when they turned to each other. He held Frankie so tightly that she felt small, she felt engulfed. "I've missed you so much today," she said.

"I know," he said. "I wish I didn't have this fucking civic obligation. I just . . ."

"I know," she said.

"Will you call me?" He pulled his head back to look at her. His breath was warm on her face. "Anytime," he said. "The office or the car or home. Just, if you hear anything, if anything happens, call."

"I will." Frankie wanted to stop him, to tell him she needed him, he couldn't go.

They turned together to walk the few steps to his car, their arms around each other's waists. "I told Davey that Alfie overheard what Sylvia said, about not loving him."

"Because . . . ?"

"Because it seemed to me all of a sudden that he must have heard her that night, and that he may not want to be found. That this may be, really, suicidal, this . . ."

"Yes? You think so?"

"I don't know, but . . ."

They were by his car. He held her again. She could feel his lips, his breath, on her hair, her ear. "Jesus, I'm sorry to leave you. For this ridiculous . . . chore."

"It's all right. Sylvia and I can't think of a thing to say to each other, and you and I would probably just sit there, too. It's just impossible, waiting." She lifted her shoulders and tried to smile. "And maybe he's fine. He could be fine."

"But cold."

"But cold," she agreed.

"I could come back. This'll be a few hours, and then . . ."

"I'll call," she said.

"Okay." He stepped back, and she felt cold. She crossed her arms, hunched her shoulders. He reached out and touched her face. "Sweetheart," he said.

She turned her face and kissed his hand quickly, then stepped away and walked back to the house, hearing the car start up as she went inside.

Byron Morrell stopped by again at nine or so, still with nothing to report, except that the helicopter had stopped for the night. After he'd left, Frankie lay down on the couch with another one of her father's books. Sylvia said she would read, too. In the bedroom, if Frankie didn't mind.

"No," Frankie said. "No, of course not."

And the next thing she was aware of was someone lightly shaking her shoulder. She opened her eyes. Sylvia was bending over her, her face oddly pouched by gravity, by fatigue, saying, "They found him. I'm going in."

"'Going in' . . . ?"

"To the hospital." She had her coat on, she was holding her purse.

Frankie sat up. "Is he all right?"

"He's alive, anyway. Byron thinks he may have had a heart attack or something. He's unconscious. That's really all he knew. They took him in right away."

Frankie was licking her lips, swinging her legs down. "I'll come, too," she said.

Sylvia shook her head. "No. No, no. You stay here. Get some sleep. I'm sure . . . I'll call you, either here or at Liz's, if you want to go back down there. I'd rather . . . I'd like to be alone with him right now."

Frankie looked at her mother. Her face was firm, decided. After a moment, she asked, "Where was he?"

"Not far," Sylvia said. "By the beaver dam. Curled up, under some leaves, they said. Perhaps trying to stay warm."

"Yes," Frankie said, though she was thinking that he was hiding, he must have been hiding.

Sylvia leaned forward and kissed her quickly. "I will, I'll call, first bit of news." She started to move away, toward the kitchen.

"Shall I . . . shall I call Liz?" Frankie asked.

"Oh. Yes." She stopped. "Well, no. It's almost four." She sighed, heavily. "Well, but even if she's trying to sleep, I suppose she'd sleep better knowing. So yes. Yes, call her." And she left.

Frankie called Liz immediately. As soon as she got off the phone with her, she telephoned Bud at home.

"Frankie?" he said. His voice was whispery, sleepy.

"He's alive," she said. "They took him to the hospital."

He cleared his throat. "Where are you?"

"Here. At my mother's."

"Can I come over?"

"It's four o'clock."

"How is that relevant?"

18

~

BUD COULD FEEL IT HAPPENING, the shift in Frankie, starting with her call to him after her father was found. He'd driven over to her mother's house and stayed with her, but only for a few hours—he had to start delivering the papers at six. They'd gone upstairs to the guest bedroom and lain down on the coverlet, pulling the spare blanket over them. Frankie was wired, unable to sleep, alternately relieved, even excited, about Alfie's having been found, and then worried about how he was doing, whether he would recover, and what this episode might mean for him, for his care, going forward.

Bud let her talk, not saying much. He drifted off more than once, but then would wake, wake to Frankie's pressured voice. "I mean, don't you think this is it? That he's just got to have more supervision. That Sylvia . . . that she can't . . ."

And Bud would stroke her arm, her hair, and make his noises of agreement, feeling a kind of sleepy joy. A joy that rode with him through the day—first delivering the papers, and then talking to Davey Swann to get the details of the rescue operation.

Even as he sat in his office in the afternoon and finished the article he'd been working on before Alfie disappeared—even then he could feel it: that she had let go of something that had kept her pulling away from him, away from the possibility of commitment, of staying.

In the evening, he drove over to her house—her sister's house. She'd spent the day with her mother at the hospital, talking to doctors and sitting with her father. At Liz's, he helped her push the furniture back in place and clean up. Then sex, gentle and conventional and sweet, they were both so tired. And in all of that, there was the same newly eased quality to their interactions that he'd felt the night before.

He'd come home at almost midnight. He'd thought about just staying over, but he was reluctant to seem to push anything, to assert any claim. And he was more and more certain he didn't need to. He wasn't going to need to.

So he was moving slowly this morning. He'd just made his first cup of coffee when the phone rang. He almost didn't pick it up, he was so reluctant to start his day. But after three rings, he turned the radio off and lifted the receiver from its cradle.

The voice on the phone was Loren's. He said, "Don't say I never did anything for you."

Bud wasn't happy to hear from him. Bad news of some sort, he assumed. "What exactly is it you're doing for me?" he asked.

"This call. What I'm doing right now."

"What's the big deal?" he asked.

"We've got Tink." Loren's voice was thick with self-satisfaction.

"What do you mean, got him?"

"We're gonna arrest him."

Bud set his coffee down. "Who? Who's going to arrest him?"

"The state police. They're taking him over to Greenwood."

"When did they pick him up?"

"Yesterday. They were waiting for him at the brother-in-law's house there after Rowley was found. Took him down to Black Mountain for questioning. Had him there all day yesterday and into the night and he confessed."

"He confessed."

"Signed, sealed, delivered."

Bud could hear how much he was enjoying this. "Did he have a lawyer?" Bud asked.

"He didn't *ask* for no lawyer. He just confessed."

After a moment, Bud asked, "After how long?"

"How long what?"

"How long were you questioning him?"

There was a pause, and Loren said, "I guess maybe twenty, twenty-four hours or so."

"Jesus, Loren!"

"*What?*"

"This is fucked up. You know that."

"I don't know any such thing." He sounded offended.

Bud told himself to hold it in. After a moment, he said, "So they took him in. Where?"

"They're just taking him now. Greenwood. You get over there fast enough, you can watch it."

"Okay," Bud said. And then, not quite an afterthought, "Thanks."

"I'm always looking out for you."

"Yes, you are." And he hung up.

So much for a slow morning. He'd been planning on getting Alfie's story written. He'd been thinking it would be on the front page. Now it would be pushed below the fold anyway, and maybe farther back. This week would be all Tink. All Tink all the time—for the foreseeable future, anyway.

He rinsed his cup in the sink and got out some bread. While it was toasting, he called Sam Pitkin and Georgie Morrell to see if someone could cover the high school soccer game this afternoon.

The toast had flung itself onto the counter and was cold by the time he reached it. An omen.

And sure enough, it started to rain on the way over to Greenwood. Bud's wipers were not all they should have been, and he had to slow down to see through the streaks they made on the windshield. He had the radio on, listening to the news, but mostly he was thinking of Tink Snell.

He'd gone back and forth in his own mind about the kid's possible guilt. For a long time, as he'd told Frankie and whoever else he was talking about it with, he had thought it wasn't likely. He'd thought Tink was too slow to have eluded the police and the arson investigators as long as he would have had to. But the fire at Sylvia and Alfie's had changed all that, and Bud had been suspicious of him ever since.

And, it was clear, so had the various investigators, since it was after that that the serious surveillance had started. In spite of which there had been six more fires set. On the one hand this would argue against its being Tink who'd set them. How could he, with all that attention focused on him? Though it was also possible that he was pissed off enough at being so closely monitored that he'd been inspired to new heights. And maybe there was an added element to his rage because people didn't seem to have *bought* his heroism at the Rowleys' fire. *After what I did to save the house, you're watching me? Me? Fuck you. See if you can watch me set* this *one, or* this *one. Or this one.*

What Bud wondered was what might have happened if they *had* bought it, presuming Tink had been the arsonist all along. Might that have been gratifying enough to stop him? To heal whatever wound the fires were intended to serve as a poultice to?

Now, monitoring his wipers, trying to keep the white line at the edge of the road in sight, Bud let his thoughts float freely, sometimes turning to Frankie's long white body coiled in the quilt last night, to her legs opening to wrap around him, to his sense of her new ease with him; sometimes to Tink, lost now for sure if he hadn't been before.

The main room at the Greenwood police station was crowded—with other local newspapermen, with a dozen or so people Bud didn't know, with folks from Pomeroy that Loren or someone else must have alerted. Bud saw Harlan and Gavin. Kevin O'Hara. A few others. Adrian was up near the front. Bud had come so late that he had to push his way over to the side of the room in hopes of a better angle. He'd brought his camera.

There was a stir at the doorway, and the murmurs, "They're *here*!" "Here he comes!" And then he watched as three heads moved through the crowd, the two state troopers wearing their hats, and Tink, looking tired and confused, stumbling in between them, visible only in quick glimpses through the crowd. He was wearing his usual outfit, a plaid flannel shirt, jeans, work boots. He'd lost his jacket somewhere along the way, the jacket he'd been wearing in the search for Alfie. His hands were cuffed behind his back.

They marched him up to the counter at the front of the room. A man Bud took to be the arresting officer sat behind it, fat, tired-looking, his glasses swung up to the top of his head.

Yes, now Bud could hear him speaking to Tink, telling him he was under arrest. He looked up sharply, then across the counter, and asked, "Do you understand this?"

Bud couldn't hear Tink's reply. Or very much else the officer said after that. Enough to know Tink was told of his rights, and then several times asked the question again: "Do you understand this?"

It was all over in about three minutes, and Tink was hustled out again. Bud got a few clear shots of him on the way out as people began to move to follow him. By the time Bud also had followed the crowd onto the front steps of the building, Tink was bending to step into a state police car, an officer's hand on his head as he lowered himself. His hands were still cuffed behind his back. Bud took a picture of this, too.

Suddenly Gavin Knox was standing next to Bud. "Where the fuck are they taking him?" Gavin asked. "Do you know?"

"I don't," Bud said.

A man in front of them turned around and said, "Over to the Pembroke jail. For fear of retribution."

Bud recognized him as one of the state cops that had been hanging around Pomeroy for the last month or so.

Bud snorted. "What, you think someone from Pomeroy is going to sneak into jail here and kill him?"

"There've been a lot of threats floating around."

"There are a lot of big mouths with not much better to do than talk to cops and reporters."

"All I'm saying is, better safe than sorry."

"Hey!" Bud said. "Let me write that down."

"Fuck you," the cop said genially.

Back in the car, it occurred to him to call the *Globe* guy and let him know about the arrest, and he did that. Then he drove slowly back to Pomeroy and straight to the town hall. He parked and went around to a small door at the back, the door to the administrative office. He knocked once and opened it just as Emily Gilroy called out, "Come in."

She was turning from the filing cabinet, the light glinting on her glasses as she did. Her face shifted into a warm smile when she saw Bud—she was a person of whom you could say, *Her face lit up,* Bud had always thought.

"Buddy boy!" she said.

"Hey, Emily."

"To what do I owe the pleasure?" She gestured for him to sit in the chair facing her desk, and she went behind it to her own old-fashioned wooden swivel chair. She was plump, and she grunted a little as she lowered herself. She was in her winter uniform already—a turtleneck, a sweater over it, stretchy, pilled beige slacks of some wool-wannabe synthetic fabric. She wore slippers at work; her heavy sneakers were in a basket by the door. She'd been beautiful—Bud had seen the old photographs of her here and there. Now she was jolly-looking, her hair in the usual permed white ridges apparently required of any woman over sixty-five in Pomeroy. She wore bifocals, she had fat rouged cheeks. Mrs. Claus.

"Have you heard about Tink?" he asked.

She nodded. "Loren stopped in, first thing, the bearer of bad tidings as he so loves to be."

"I was just over there for the basic *you're under arrest* ceremony. They said he'll be arraigned in a day or two."

"And they have a confession, Loren tells me?"

He nodded.

"So." She lifted her hands. "That would be that, I guess."

"We'll see. But I'm here to be nosy about him. About his life. What can you tell me?"

Much, it turned out, a little of which Bud already knew. But Emily added detail. His mother was Adrian's youngest sister, the family ne'er-do-well—Mary Anne. She dropped out of high school when she got pregnant, no one was sure by whom, probably least of all she. "She was known for that, I'm afraid," Emily said.

She'd worked for Adrian for a while in the store, but after the baby came, she went on welfare. "She was just big trouble, always," Emily said. "Not the kind of trouble that hurt anyone else but herself. Mostly just men and drinking. But I mean a lot of drinking. We always thought that might be part of why Tink is like he is—you know, a little slow."

Her parents had kicked her out, finally, and she moved to Winslow. The man she was living with there went up to work on the Alaska Pipeline, and she went with him, taking Tink. "He was still little," Emily said. "Maybe one or two. She was up there awhile. It was a wild place then, from what you hear, and apparently that suited her just fine. A couple of other folks from around here went up there, too, for the money, don't you know, and we heard things about her afterward. She was making her living pretty much as a whore, they said. And who knows who was taking care of that baby? Or how much of all that he saw." She shook her head. "Imagine."

She came back to the area when Tink was six or seven. She lived in different nearby towns for a while, with different men. She was married once, for a couple of years. She was busted for drugs a few times. "Then maybe six or seven years ago, Adrian gave her the use of that land and the trailer up by Silsby, and she moved there with whoever she was with then, and Tink. So Tink came back to Pomeroy then and went to the high school in Winslow with the other town kids.

"And then at some point, come to find out she'd left again, without Tink this time. That he was living there all by himself. Had been for a while. I think some teacher noticed the same dirty clothes every day and him getting thinner. It's true he wasn't a baby anymore—he must have been fifteen or sixteen—but still . . . That's not right, you know."

"No," Bud said.

She leaned back in her chair. "Well, Adrian and Lucy took him in, but Lucy said it was hard. Like having a wild animal in the house. You know, he'd never sat down for a meal except maybe the lunch room at school, he'd never been taught even basic manners." She shook her head. "And he's such a beautiful boy. It's just a shame, that's what it is."

He'd dropped out of school, finally, she said. That was when Adrian hired him. At first at the store, but that didn't work out. Then to do some of the odd jobs Adrian used to do himself. People said he was a good worker, Emily said. A hard worker. Just not sociable. "Not socialized, I suppose is what they meant. Though Lucy said she tried. Then when he turned eighteen, he moved back to the trailer.

"He's pretty much a loner. You know how it is with kids. If you're not very bright, it's hard, even if you're as handsome a boy as he is. The girls say he never even had a girlfriend. They kind of made fun of him, he was so shy. I heard that from Carin Knox. That they weren't mean, exactly, but still, teasing. She felt bad about it later, but you know how girls do at that age."

Bud said he did, remembering certain misfits from his high school, the way they suffered.

"So that's pretty much what I know. I guess he's been up there awhile with no electricity and no telephone. That might explain the kerosene purchases that got everyone so worked up."

"I missed that."

"Oh, yeah. Loren and some of the state guys. Adrian had to set them straight. That Tink had let the electric lapse, so he and Lucy gave him a couple of old kerosene lamps. They were all excited when they saw him buying the kerosene. 'Nope,' Adrian told them. 'You're barking up the wrong tree there.'" She shook her head. "I imagine he's devastated," she said. "He really loves that boy, I think. It's hard."

They sat for a minute. "Do you think he set the fires?" Bud asked.

"Well, he confessed, didn't he?"

"Does it make a difference that they held him for almost twenty-four hours?"

"But why would you say you did something if you didn't?"

Bud had read of various complicated reasons you might, but he didn't feel like talking them through with Emily. Instead he said, "Let's say he hadn't confessed. What would you think then?"

She sat silent for a long moment, her lips pressed together. It made her look mean. "You know, I just don't know, Bud. It seems like such a crazy, kinda pointless thing to do, setting a bunch of fires like that. But just think how *mad* he has a right to be. And how few ways he's got to let that out." She shook her head. Not a hair moved independently. "It's just hard to imagine, how you'd respond to such a raw deal in life, isn't it?"

"It's unimaginable for me."

"Me, too," she said.

"This is what I come here for, Emily," Bud said, getting up.

"Oh. Gossip." She lifted her shoulders and looked embarrassed. "Well, I'm sorry. I can't help it, I'm afraid."

"No. Not gossip. Your *take* on the gossip. That's what makes it worth listening to."

She sat a moment, and then she smiled and stood up, too. "You're a nice man, Bud."

"*Finally*. Someone noticed."

And as she swatted her hand in the air to dismiss him, he left.

He sat in the car outside the town hall for a few minutes. It was still raining, but he decided he'd drive over by Silsby Pond and have a look at Tink's trailer, now that he wasn't there.

As he was driving across the valley, the rain slowed. By the time he got to Silsby Pond Road, it had stopped. He drove to the point where he'd stopped before, where the road opened onto the meadow, but this time he continued up the worn double path made by Tink's tires. Grass grew tall between the dirt lines. He saw that the meadow was really an old orchard that was slowly being swallowed by brush and saplings, though you could still see the dark, twisted apple branches through the younger growth. Bud drove up to the high point, where the trailer sat, and got out of his car.

The grass immediately around the trailer was trampled and flattened. He knew there'd been a search warrant after the fire at Frankie's parents' house, but clearly someone had been here again recently, looking for evidence. He turned slowly around. There were sweeping views in all directions, gorgeous even on a day as dark as this.

He turned to face the trailer. It was old, a humped, old-fashioned shape. There was cardboard taped over one of its windows. It sat up on cinder blocks. Scattered around it were tin cans and trash. Tink's firefighting boots were leaned against what constituted the steps up to the door, steps that were also made of cinder blocks. Bud mounted them. The door was metal, with a metal lever rather than a knob.

He stood there, trying to figure out what to do.

If the door wasn't locked, he'd look, he decided, but only from the doorway—he wouldn't go in. Mr. Morally Fastidious. He pulled down on the lever, and the door swung open.

He leaned slightly forward, to see what there was to see.

It was a mess, but there was no way of knowing how much of that was Tink's doing and how much was the police's. Dark rucked-up carpeting covered the floor. Clothing was strewn around on it, and a couple of girlie magazines. Along the wall facing him, a smudgy picture window looked south to the Presidential Range. Under that was a banquette and a built-in table with a Formica surface. There was a small television set on the shelf opposite this.

Dishes were stacked in a kitchenette sink to Bud's left. A little hallway went past that area, and Bud assumed it led to a bedroom—or a bed in a room, anyway—as well as a bathroom. There must be a bathroom. An unfinished picture puzzle was on the Formica table in front of him, and pieces of it were scattered on the floor. An old kerosene lamp with a net filament sat on the table, too, along with a couple of glasses still half full of something, and some more dishes.

The banquette was pulling apart at the top seam. Worn, almost granular foam was spilling out, was pilled over the no-color fabric of the cushioning.

Bud tried to imagine driving from here, from this squalor, down to town, past the well-kept summer homes—empty, unused for most of the year. He couldn't. He tried to imagine coming home to this in the dark every night, and couldn't. It seemed wrong to him, cruel. Maybe it was illegal, actually—there must be zoning laws to prevent someone's living like this in a town like Pomeroy. In the United States of America.

And yet Tink had chosen it. The solitude.

No, the privacy, Bud thought. Over what must have been comfortable and warm, what according to Emily was loving and caring at Adrian and Lucy Snell's.

But you wanted your privacy. You wanted your own home. You wanted to live by your own rules, in your own place. You wanted to fix your own dinner, even if it meant just opening a can. You wanted to sit down and look at the beaver shots in your *Penthouse* and jerk off. Or lean under the light of your kerosene lamp and add six or seven pieces to the puzzle you were working on.

Bud shut the door, pulling it to with the awkwardly small metal lever. He turned around.

The sun was glinting through under the clouds to his left, lighting them a brilliant golden color from below, casting a dramatic, threaded horizontal light across the landscape. Ahead of him, the hill fell away greenly. The ancient apple trees still held the wizened brown fruit the deer hadn't reached, so many homely ornaments. The mountains to the north beyond all this were a distant gray-blue. He looked to the east. Yes, against the brooding dark sky in that direction, a rainbow.

So this was part of what held Tink here. Beauty. After all.

19

SYLVIA HAD WAKED with the idea clear in her head, she told Frankie. It would be better—for her, and for Alfie, too—to be back in Bowman. This was three days before Alfie was to come home from the hospital. She and Frankie were sitting in Liz's house at the table, talking about her plans. He had been in the hospital for four days.

Sylvia said she had started calling as soon as the relevant offices in Bowman had opened this morning. First, the community college where she'd taught. Where, yes—"Oh, fantastic!" the department chair had said—she could come back next semester, certainly to teach one course, and maybe two.

Then she called the housing office at Alfie's college, Wadsworth, which she knew had a small number of shabbily furnished short-term-rental apartments for visiting or retired faculty.

Yes, there were two available now. One on the third floor with one bedroom, one on the ground floor with three. Sylvia said she would take the ground floor three-bedroom.

It was an hour or so later, she said, when it occurred to her to call Barbara Simms about dividing the land on the property here, to ask whether she thought Sylvia could sell perhaps two ten-acre lots up the hill behind the main house.

"With the Lord, all things are possible," Barb had said, and gave her a price range. And just before she hung up, she had also said, according to Sylvia, "This is going to be *fun!*"

The trees outside were at their peak for color, an array that was almost overwhelming in its intensity. The sun was bright on them, and the reflected light gave the room a strange, almost-pinkish glow. Frankie had just come back from a walk—on the road, because the leaves in the woods were so deep you couldn't find the paths, much less the rocks or roots that might trip you on the paths.

Sylvia had been waiting for her on the porch, nervous and excited and eager to talk about her idea.

Frankie had tried not to appear as shocked as she was. Or as hurt, which she only slowly realized was part of what she was feeling. Hurt that Sylvia could so readily dispense with her support, she supposed. Although really, she'd hardly done anything except sit with Sylvia occasionally and listen to her.

But didn't that count? Wasn't that important?

Apparently not, for here her mother was, her face animated into its powerful attractiveness, talking about how much easier it would all be in Bowman. To find part-time care for Alfie (students for now, she thought—always out for what they could make in a couple of hours). To be able to walk to a store—divine! To walk to the library, to walk to see friends. To have colleagues again. To have neighbors close by. "I realized that more than half the reason we came up here was so that Alfie could live the kind of life he imagined for his retirement. Which makes no sense now, since that life is just beyond him."

"Is it really?" Frankie asked.

Though she knew it was. She wasn't even sure why she was asking the question, unless she somehow just needed time to take this in, Sylvia's plan. Certainly she was aware that since the search-and-rescue operation, her father had taken three or four steps more deeply into his illness. He wasn't sure where he was in the hospital—whether it was home or a school he was teaching in. He didn't want to read anymore or, perhaps, suddenly, he couldn't. And his face—his eyes—had that blank look all the time now.

"Oh, I think so," Sylvia said.

"And you think this will work," Frankie said. She was foundering, looking for anything to say.

"Work? What do you mean, *work*?"

"Okay, I don't know. Be manageable, I guess. Not just Alfie, but financially." It was the first time she'd asked her mother anything like this.

"Well, I'll have to look around for a smaller apartment off campus, eventually. And we'll need the money from the land certainly. We may actually have to do some more selling off here and there as we go along. But it's more than one hundred fifty acres in all, even if most of it is in woods at this point. So we'll make it. I hadn't thought of it before we gave Liz her section, but there it is. And no one's ever going to farm it again, that's certain. It's hardly a sad thing, for other people to make use of some of it."

"No. No, it's not sad." Though a part of her wanted to say, *Yes, it is sad.* But she understood even as she had the thought that it was connected to something else. Something complicated having to do with herself, not her mother. Her sense of this farm and its land as in some deep way *her place.* She thought abruptly of the way her colleague, Sam, along with most of the other Africans she knew, considered the villages they had grown up in as their real homes, no matter where they lived at the moment, or how many years they'd lived there.

"When will you go?" she asked after a moment.

"Therein lies the rub. I guess as soon as I can manage it, packing up and getting Alfie ready. I wish I could get down there ahead of time to see the place, to fix it up, but I can't, and that's that."

After a few seconds, Frankie heard herself say, "I could do that."

"Oh, I couldn't ask you."

"You didn't ask," Frankie said. "I offered."

Sylvia looked sharply over at her. "But what would you *do*?"

"Whatever you'd like me to do. Go down, clean it up, if it needs it. See what you'll need. Bedding, I suppose. And kitchen things. Whatever. Do you know what it comes with?"

"No," Sylvia said. "I think those places are all a bit of a hodgepodge, at least according to visiting faculty I've known. Basic furniture, and then some of what any number of people have left behind over the years."

"Well, if it's too dreary, I could try to cheer it up. I'm good at that. Good at making strange digs livable. I could take down a small load of stuff and then let you know what else you'd need. For the short term, anyway."

Frankie could see that her mother wanted to say yes. "So it's settled," she said to Sylvia. "I'll go in a day or two. That way maybe you could actually just bring Alfie directly there from the hospital. Wouldn't that be better?"

"Oh, I think much better. Much less confusing for him." Frankie could hear it, the relief in her mother's voice. "And then you'll come back up here," Sylvia said. This wasn't inflected as a question, but Frankie understood that Sylvia was asking.

"That's something I'll have to figure out," Frankie said. "Maybe once I've finished in Bowman, I'll head down to New York and see if there's something there that compels me. I've been putting off dealing with all that, I have to say. Work. Earning a living. Et cetera. Maybe now's the time."

Her mother frowned and said, "But what about . . . your life? Here?"

"Well, you know. I needed to make some decisions about that anyway." She was thinking of Bud.

And now Sylvia said, "But Bud?"

This had always been the question. "I don't know. I mean, obviously, I care for him." She lifted her shoulders.

"I think you should come back here." And then, maybe because Sylvia heard how assertive she'd been, she said, "If you want to, that is. Maybe you could find something to do here."

"I've tried, Mother." Though of course this wasn't true. Sometimes, in her efforts to imagine a life here, she'd asked about one job or another—an opening at the high school, in the admissions office of the health center she'd gone to visit. But she hadn't followed up on anything. She said, "I can't stay here indefinitely anyway. Clark and Liz will reclaim their house eventually, for one thing."

"But then the big house will be unused. And perhaps someone should be staying there, after all."

Frankie laughed suddenly. "This can't be my life, Mother, staying in empty houses to be sure they don't get burned down. And besides, Tink Snell's been arrested."

"If he is indeed the arsonist. There's plenty of dispute about *that*."

"I know. He has his defenders. Bud among them, actually."

"Is he? I didn't realize that."

"Mostly I think he feels Tink wasn't treated fairly."

"Ah," Sylvia said.

They sat for a while longer, talking about the details. When Frankie would go, when Alfie would be released. What Frankie should take down.

"Well, it sounds as though this is settled," Sylvia said at last, standing. "I'm going to go up and look around and see what needs packing, then."

"Good." Frankie got up, too.

At the door, Sylvia stopped. "I don't know that I think it's helpful to you, that way of thinking about your work."

"What way?"

"*Seeing what compels you.*"

"What's wrong with it?"

"I don't know." Sylvia was frowning. Serious. "I guess there's a lot that can compel you that perhaps can't . . . sustain you. Sometimes those things, the things that sustain you, are more or less accidents. Off to the side of whatever you thought compelled you in the first place."

"I'll put that in my pipe and smoke it, Mother. Thank you very much."

"I didn't mean to try to sound *wise,* God knows." Sylvia made a face.

"And yet . . ." Frankie was grinning, holding her hands up.

After Sylvia had gone, Frankie sat for a while, alone, at the scarred round table. So this was it, then. The kick in the ass. The push. She looked out the windows at the flaming colors. How odd that this was where it should have come from. Alfie and Sylvia. Or Sylvia, anyway, with her sudden drive to seize control of something in her own life again, and in Alfie's life, too. Which perhaps Frankie should have foreseen, her mother had been so at a loss for a while. So not in control of anything.

And beyond that, it did make sense, in many ways. She could agree with the logic of many of Sylvia's arguments for it. It was a surprise, but it wasn't, finally, surprising.

Though it was interesting that it was Alfie who'd set things in motion, with his strange compulsion, whatever it was—to *head out.* To leave, to go. Perhaps to die, which is what Frankie still thought.

No one had been able to get it from him, what he'd intended. When they asked where he was going or what he thought he was doing—Sylvia or Frankie or Liz, who had come up briefly—he couldn't really respond. Once or twice he'd managed to say, "Home." But it wasn't clear to any of them what he meant by that. Did he just mean he was trying to get back to the house here in Pomeroy? Or maybe he had in mind the one they'd lived in for so long in Bowman. Or even, dreaming further back, the one he'd grown up in, in Binghamton.

Maybe none of the above.

Maybe, Frankie thought, *home*—what felt like home—was just a way of being in the world that felt *Alfie*-like to him, like being the person he'd been before the changes that were slowly turning him into someone else began. Maybe by *home* he meant the time when he felt whole, when he felt like himself. The time—and perhaps one of the places—where the world seemed to recognize him in some deep way, seemed to say, *Come in, we've been expecting you. Exactly you.*

And why shouldn't he want that? Isn't that, after all, what she wanted, too?

Bud was startled, and then angry, though he wouldn't acknowledge that at first. "Did I miss something?" he asked, when he'd taken it in, what Sylvia's plan was, that Frankie was part of it. "I didn't realize there was even the possibility of something like this."

Frankie could feel how much she'd sprung it on him. As they talked about it, she grew more defensive.

"But New York?" he said.

"Yes." She didn't look at him. "I need to check it out. I mean, I've talked about that from the start."

"From the start of you and me, you mean?"

"I suppose." She had known he would be angry, but she hadn't known how far away from her that would take him.

There was a long silence. "When was that, I wonder," he said. "I mean, *have* we, even, started? I feel, actually, that you've had the proverbial foot out the proverbial door from the moment I met you."

Frankie wasn't sure what to say.

He was watching her, as though she were a stranger. "What?" he said.

"I suppose I have," she said finally. "Had my foot out the door. In the sense that I need to find work. In the sense that step one would be New York."

He sat back and stretched his long legs out in front of him. "So. A little more temporizing in your life. But temporizing that *slopped over* into my life, too, this time around." He gave the words a mean emphasis.

Frankie said, "I've talked to you on and off about this, Bud. About not seeing a way of making my life here. About needing a life."

He was silent.

"I never misrepresented myself."

"Well, you did and you didn't."

"What do you mean?"

"I mean *this*, Frankie." He gestured around the room. "The way we've been here. Together. I mean, having sex, being loving."

"That wasn't a misrepresentation. I felt that. I feel that."

"But, what? It makes no difference?"

Frankie tried again to explain herself. As she talked, she realized that all along she'd been holding two opposing ideas in her head—that she'd stay; that she'd go. Without examining herself, without taking responsibility for any of it, she'd let herself drift along as if both were true. She'd involved herself here in ways that felt important to her. Necessary. Most of all, with Bud. But in other ways, too. With Alfie and his failing. With wanting to help Liz, who was so tired of being the good daughter. Maybe even the fires had drawn her in: she'd felt a part of the town, listening for noises at night, talking about who might have done it, where it had happened last, where it might happen next.

But she'd also felt that eventually she'd have to go, perhaps not back to Africa, but somewhere *out there* in the world—finally, that was who she was. How she saw herself.

She was looking at Bud, who was listening to her, listening to her intensely, gravely. Honorably. He was such an honorable, honest person. He would never not be dear to her, she felt.

She looked away. She felt tearful, suddenly. After a moment, she turned back to him and said, "I need work, Bud. I need . . . a life."

"We all need work, Frankie. And there's no dearth of work to be done, wherever you look."

"I've *looked*. I've looked here." He was watching her steadily. "Bud. I don't want to argue with you."

"No. Let's not argue." He sounded tired, suddenly. They sat together silently in the twin chairs facing the cold stove for what must have been several minutes. Then he stood up and started unbuttoning his shirt. "Let's just fuck."

And that was what they did, a kind of aggressive, careless slamming into each other that at first excited Frankie and then, as it went on—as he came, arched back above her, his eyes closed—made her feel utterly alone.

Afterward they lay for a while side by side, not speaking. Then, abruptly, Bud pushed up off the mattress, and in the half-light coming in from the big room, he picked his clothes up from the floor and pulled them on. First his pants, then his shirt.

"You're not staying."

"No. I have some stuff I have to do."

She watched him, standing on one foot and then the other to pull on socks, shoes. "I'm sorry you're so angry," she said.

"I am. I'm more angry than you can imagine. I'm angry at everything. But I do have stuff to do." He started to button his shirt, and this made Frankie sad, watching his beautiful bare flesh disappear.

"Please don't be angry."

He laughed, a single abrupt sound.

"What?"

"Just . . . nothing, Frankie. Nothing."

And he left.

Frankie couldn't believe it for some seconds. She'd thought he was going to the bathroom or getting some water from the kitchen, that he'd come back and that they'd finish talking. They hadn't finished. She hadn't finished.

But then she heard the outside door shut, and even as she was standing up on the mattress, stepping across the floor and scrabbling to find her shirt to pull it on, she heard the engine start, the car's loud gargling sound. Just as she reached the door and stepped out into the chilly night air, she saw the car turning out of the driveway, she stood and listened to the sound of it dropping from hill to hill to hill.

The phone was her enemy the next day. Bud wasn't answering or responding to the messages she left, and Sylvia called her almost once an hour, from about eight o'clock on, calls born of her anxiety about every possible aspect of the logistics of her impending move. What to take, what not to take, where Frankie could get the keys, whom she should call if she needed help in Bowman.

Frankie had arrangements to make herself. In between Sylvia's calls and her own to Bud, she talked to Diann, the coordinator in New York. She told her she'd like to come into the offices and talk sometime in the next week or ten days. Diann sounded at first pleased, and then a bit anxious.

She was looking for work here? In the New York office?

Yes, Frankie said.

Well! Interesting. Well, sure. She might as well come in and *talk*.

Frankie remembered then how territorial it was in New York, more so even than in the Nairobi office. How much it was seen as a zero-sum situation—what you have, what you get, is what I don't. She remembered, too, how glad she'd been in the past each time she left New York. How ready she always was after those visits to go back to Africa.

But they agreed Frankie would call a couple of days beforehand, and they hung up. She sat for a while looking out at the trees, at the browning field rising up behind the house. She had to try, she told herself. She was actually good at that administrative stuff. It would be strange and different to be so removed from the work itself, but the aims were the same, and she knew how to implement them. It would be fine, once she was *in it*. She had to try.

By early afternoon, Frankie was packed with what she thought she'd need for what might be a few weeks away, a few weeks that would include the trip to New York, where she would be dressing differently from the way she'd been dressing up here or would be dressing in Bowman. Later she could get the rest of her stuff. She'd thoroughly cleaned Liz and Clark's house, too, in case they decided to come up before she could get to it again.

Once all that was done, she gave herself permission to drive to Bud's house. She couldn't leave things as they'd left them last night. She had thought throughout the day of what she might suggest to him, arrangements friends of hers had made, friends who lived in Africa and had lovers, even spouses, living continents away. Who met three or four times a year in one person's place or the other's, or in some exotic place in between.

Though she'd also thought of Bud's likely answer—Bud, who had talked so often of loving their most ordinary times together, of the pleasures of a daily life with her in it.

She stood knocking on his door for a minute or so, in spite of the fact that his car wasn't there. She could see into the neat kitchen, its counters wiped clean. Bud's home. She was tempted to turn the knob, to step inside, to wait there for him, but she didn't.

Instead she drove to his office. His car wasn't there, either, but another one was parked in one of the spaces. Barb's probably.

And yes, when she knocked, Barb came to the door, wearing a denim jumpsuit with a rhinestone patch above each breast.

Frankie asked where Bud might be.

"Who knows? You can't keep up with that boy. There's some stuff happening with this business with Tink Snell, so he might be over there. But this is the day he takes the paper to Whitehall also, so . . ." She shrugged. Her makeup was very thorough and careful.

Frankie nodded *oh yes,* as though she knew these things and had just forgotten them, momentarily.

"But I thought you'd flown the coop, as Bud says. No?"

"No, I fly the coop tomorrow."

"Out of the Manchester airport?"

"No, I'm driving. I just mean, I leave."

Barb nodded. She stepped forward a little in the doorway and said,

"He seemed a bit . . . down about it, if you want to know. Still good humored—he always is, but . . ." Then, apparently seeing something in Frankie's face, she said, "Oh well. Mind your own business, Barb."

"No, it's okay," Frankie said. "If you could just tell him I stopped by."

"I will." She stood in the open doorway as Frankie walked back to her car. "Say," she called. "Good for your mother! Cashing in on some of that fabulous land up there."

"Yes, it's good she can."

Barb waved vigorously as Frankie pulled away.

Frankie couldn't stand the thought of going back to Liz's, so she drove to the library instead and sat at a table in one of the armchairs there, trying to read *The Mill on the Floss,* which she'd taken off the shelf after a short, aimless perusal of the selection. After a while, though, she felt conspicuous just sitting there, pretending occasionally to turn a page. So she left.

She left, she drove past the news office again, and past Bud's house, looking for his car. Then she drove home, where she lay down on top of the quilt covering the mattress on the floor. And perhaps because she'd had so much trouble sleeping the night before, she felt herself drifting away.

When she woke, it was dark. Dark and chilly. She'd wrapped the quilt around herself sometime during her long nap. She got up and put a log into the stove. She opened a can of soup and set it to heat on the kitchen stove.

After she'd eaten, she drove back to town. She could see the lights were on upstairs in the newspaper offices, and there were three cars parked outside, one of them Bud's. She pulled in and parked off to the side of the others.

As soon as she opened the door, she could hear the voices upstairs in conversation. Bud said something, his voice just a whispering rasp from here, and there was a burst of laughter. Then it was quiet. A boy's voice said, "*I* wouldn't, for one."

And someone, a woman, answered him.

Frankie mounted the stairs and stood in the doorway at the top. The woman noticed her and said, "*Bud.*"

He looked up. "Oh, Frankie," he said. His voice was neutral, cool. There was a pause, and he said, "Did you come to help?"

"I . . . can. Sure."

He turned to the room. The others had stopped for a moment, all but one, the teenager, and he addressed them. "A new recruit, guys." And then to Frankie: "Do you know these folks?"

She shook her head, and he introduced them. Arvilla March, whom Frankie knew by sight; Conor O'Hara, the kid, who looked up quickly and then away; and Gus Moody. Frankie knew his name—he'd worked on her parents' pond a few years back, making it larger.

"See what we're doing here?" Bud asked. And he showed her. The two different batches of advertising circulars. One went into the other, and they both got folded into the center of the paper. "Then you pass it to Conor, who rolls it up and bags it, and counts it out into the haul bags." He was standing next to her, she could feel the warmth from his body, but he didn't look directly at her.

Frankie said yes, sure, she could manage that, and took her place at the table standing next to Gus.

The conversation was intermittent, but Tink Snell was a big part of it. They were talking about the confession. They disagreed as to whether it had been coerced and what that meant about its reliability. Gus and Arvilla were on opposite sides of the question, she certain he hadn't set the fires, that he'd been nearly *seduced,* as she put it, into saying he had. "I mean, think of that boy, without a friend in the world, nearly, and those bullies—there's no other word for them—making him think they were his undying friends, if only he'd do what they wanted."

After a long silence, the shuffling of paper, the *thunk* of the rolled-up tubes into the bags the only noises in the room, Gus said, "Fine with me, Arvilla, if you'll come guard my house after they release him."

Arvilla made a disgusted noise. "Don't you think he's innocent, Bud?"

"I'm agnostic here," Bud said. Frankie was noticing his hands, how quickly, how efficiently, they moved. She thought of how they had touched her, in sex, in affection, and for a moment she felt almost tearful. But she swallowed and forced herself to listen to the conversation, to keep working.

"If he didn't, then who did?" Gus asked.

"Maybe it was a bunch of different guys. Just all of them seeing if they could get away with it," Conor said.

"But the fires stopped when they arrested him, didn't they?" Gus said.

"That doesn't mean a thing," Arvilla said. "I'm with Adrian on this one."

"With Adrian?" Conor asked.

Bud said, "It's Adrian's idea that the real firebug knows a fall guy when he sees one, so he figures this is a very good time to stop."

They worked quietly for a few minutes. Then Conor said, "I tried that thing with the Vaseline and the cotton ball and it was way cool. It just keeps burning like it's never going out." He turned to Frankie. "He did your parents' house, didn't he?"

"Someone burned the barn, yes." Her voice sounded scratchy, and she cleared her throat.

They worked for a while longer. Arvilla asked Frankie about her father, and she tried to sound cheerful. "Oh, he's much better. He'll be home in a few days."

"Well, that's just fine." She hadn't looked up from her task. "Too bad all this stuff about Tink took away from the rescue team."

"They had a good long piece," Bud said. She looked at him, hoping he might look back, but he was working steadily, his hands keeping up the rhythmic folding together of the papers.

"Oh, I know. But it wasn't anything like it would have been, and you like them to get some credit."

And suddenly, they were done—there were no more papers on the table.

While Arvilla and Gus washed their hands at the laundry sink, Conor and Bud carried the bags downstairs and out to the cars. Frankie followed them, hoping this would be her chance to talk to Bud. But he and Conor went back up to get the other bags, leaving her waiting uselessly outside by her car in the chilly dark.

Finally the cars were loaded and everyone was outside saying good night to one another. Conor got in Gus's car, and Arvilla drove off alone.

Bud had gotten into his car at the same time the others did, but he seemed to be waiting for her—he was sitting with the door still open. She stepped over close to him.

He looked up at her. "So, you're leaving tomorrow, Barb said."

"I hoped we could talk."

"Ah, Frankie. There's nothing more to say." He was watching her steadily. "Unless you've changed your mind."

She shook her head, and in response he lifted his hands.

"*Bud,*" she said.

"We're friends, Frankie." His voice was gentle now. "Let's be friends. You're right, you told me from the start you were going to go. I shouldn't have gotten angry. That was wrong of me. I was . . . I suppose I was pretending I hadn't heard you. Pretending to myself, anyway." He shrugged, for a moment a half smile on his face.

And then it was gone. "So you *go*, Frankie. It's what you have to do. I'll stay, and you'll be gone. You'll visit someone up here from time to time, and we'll be glad to see each other." He looked up at her. In the dark his eyes were black, unreadable. "I'll always be glad to see you," he said in his hoarse voice.

"Bud . . . ," she said.

"No, Frankie. I get it." His head made a series of small nodding motions. "It's how it has to be. I get it."

Frankie didn't know what to say. This was what she had wanted in some way to persuade him of, wasn't it?

"Oh!" he said, as if reminded of something, and her heart seemed to move in her chest. He reached over to the passenger seat and turned to her with a paper. "Your weekly news," he said, and shut the door, bent forward to start the engine.

20

~

ON THE DRIVE DOWN, Frankie had been full of anxious self-questioning about what she was doing, so it was a relief to be here, to busy herself unloading the car, carrying in Sylvia's boxes of dishes and books, of bedding, of appliances and lamps and scatter rugs.

The apartment was on the first floor of what once must have been an enormous and graceless single-family home. There was a central common hall with a staircase in the middle. The apartment formed an awkward U around this hall—you had to pass through each room, the living room, the dining room, the kitchen, to get around to the bedrooms, though the last two bedrooms had a short hallway they came off more privately.

The place was old-fashioned but not awful, though most of the furniture was dark and stiff, as though it had been used in the reception areas or offices around Wadsworth before it found its way here. Besides the ugly furniture and some dishes and pots and pans in the kitchen, there wasn't much provided in the way of furnishings.

She went to the mall at the edge of town. The store there was immense. Into her outsize cart she put throw pillows for the furniture, a straw rug for the living room. Bedspreads. A shower curtain and rings. A broom and a dustpan and brush. Cleaning equipment and supplies. White lampshades. Posters. A hammer and nails and tacks and picture hangers and lightbulbs.

At the apartment, she carried her boxes and bags in, dumping everything into the living room. She went around the U to the last bedroom, which was at the front of the house, across the hall from the living room. She made up one of the two twin beds there. The sheets were ones Sylvia had sent down, and as she lifted them and they belled out and slowly sank onto the beds, they smelled familiar, like home. She lay awake on the narrow bed for a long time. She heard several other tenants come in—the door banged shut behind them, and they went up the stairs in the central hall, talking, laughing. The light from a streetlight fell into the uncurtained room. She'd gotten used to the darkness, the stillness, of the woods around Liz's.

That wasn't it, of course. She'd gotten used to Bud.

She let herself think of him. Of his voice, of the nutty, sweet smell of his flesh. Of his long legs, the thighs so muscular and shapely, of his kneeling between her legs, looking down so intently at their bodies coming together. Of his hands turning her, lifting her, sliding her this way or that on the mattress on the floor.

Let's be friends, Bud had said, and sounded as if he meant it. As if he were relinquishing her.

So quickly.

But hadn't she relinquished him? As soon as Sylvia asked her to make the choice she'd known was waiting, she gave him up, didn't she? Hadn't she?

But how could she not? She couldn't stay. She couldn't make Bud her life. She had to have a *life,* after all.

In the ugly purplish light, she tried to quiet her thoughts, her thoughts of him. She focused on something else. Anything. Her mornings in Pomeroy, reading by the woodstove. The way the meadow changed over the summer, yellowed in the fall. The brilliant pink of the maple outside the kitchen window at Liz's house, the sound and smell of rain in the bending, wind-lashed trees. Bud, smiling at her. Turned away from her, crying out in sex. Lying next to her under the shimmering sky of the northern lights. Bud, saying, "Aren't *you* something?"

She spent the next morning cleaning and fixing things up, hanging curtains and posters, making the bed for Sylvia and Alfie, setting out towels. She was aware of herself as a daughter, doing these things for Sylvia and Alfie that she hadn't done before, that she'd left it to Liz to do, for years and years.

In the early afternoon, she shopped, at the grocery store this time, for staples and for the ingredients for dinner—a lamb stew and a salad. She bought Alfie's favorite ice cream, Heath Bar Crunch, for dessert.

It was getting dark by the time they arrived. Frankie had parked her car on the street so they could have the space that went with the apartment. When she saw the Volvo turn into the driveway, she got up and went outside.

Sylvia was already by the car's passenger door, bending down into the space to free Alfie from his seat belt. His hands rose uselessly into the air in front of him while Sylvia worked the latch. When she stepped back, Frankie saw her father—pale, groggy, absent-looking, his mouth hung open, his eyes heavy-lidded and lifeless.

Sylvia noticed her. "Oh, hello, dear," she said. "Here, can you help?"

Sylvia got Alfie to turn in the seat so his feet were on the pavement. Then she and Frankie, one on each side, helped him stand. Together they walked him slowly in, up the porch steps, into the carpeted hall, and then into the apartment. His body, pressed to Frankie's side, was trembling and unsteady.

"Where's the bathroom?" Sylvia asked.

Frankie pointed. "On the left, first real door down that way." She watched as they moved slowly through the shotgun rooms, as they turned into the bathroom together, as the door shut behind them.

She went out to the car to start to carry things in. When she came back with the first of the boxes, Sylvia called to her from deep in the apartment. She went back around the U and found her in the first bedroom, the one with the queen-size bed she'd made up for them. Alfie was sitting on it.

Sylvia came to the doorway. "I'm just going to get him into bed," Sylvia said. "He's exhausted."

"Don't you want any supper first?"

"We stopped for a snack along the way," she said. "Twice, actually. I needed the breaks." She rolled her eyes. "Thank God for drive-through windows."

"Okay, I'll just keep unloading, then."

"If you could get his suitcase," Sylvia said. "The striped one. That and mine are all we really need tonight."

"Okay," Frankie said.

On the way back through the kitchen, she turned the heat off under the stew. And after she'd brought the two suitcases in to Sylvia, she kept working, small loads each time, setting them all down in the living room.

Until Sylvia met her at the front door. "That's enough, Frankie. Come in and sit with me for a while before I collapse, too."

Frankie followed her mother in and set down this last load, a box of what seemed to be desk items. The other boxes were arrayed around the edges of the room and made it seem smaller than it was. Sylvia sank back on the couch with a dramatic exclamation, and Frankie sat in one of the uncomfortable maroon leather side chairs with wood trim, of which there was what seemed to be a set scattered throughout the apartment. Sylvia had taken her shoes off and was in her stocking feet—gray socks. She swung her legs up and tucked her feet under her. She looked more citified than she had in Pomeroy, Frankie thought—the pressed khaki pants and the earrings. In her hand she had a glass filled with ice and a clear liquid—gin, Frankie assumed, and then, yes, she saw the bottle on the end table by the couch.

Sylvia saw Frankie's glance and waggled the glass in her direction. "Want any?" she said.

Frankie shook her head. "Alfie's asleep?" she asked.

Sylvia nodded. "May he sleep through the night," she said. "I'm exhausted, too." She drank and set the glass down.

They talked then, for a while, aimlessly, it seemed to Frankie. About the apartment. About what Alfie's doctors had said. About Sylvia's job.

"So you'll go on working?" Frankie asked.

"As much as I can, as long as I can. I don't think retirement is for me."

After a moment, Frankie said quietly, "What if Alfie died?"

Sylvia didn't flinch. "What if he did?"

"Might you retire then? Move back to Pomeroy?"

Sylvia pondered it, her chin lifted. "Possibly."

They sat for a long moment, and then Frankie said, "Would you think of remarriage, ever?"

Sylvia jerked her head back in mock alarm. "Good Lord! Where did that come from?"

"It's just a theoretical question."

"Well." She sat quietly a moment. Then she said, "Even in theory I haven't done a good-enough job in this marriage to give me much confidence about launching into another, ever."

"I wouldn't say that."

"Wouldn't say what?"

"That you haven't done a good job in this marriage."

"Wouldn't you? Well, you're being kind, then."

Frankie sat, looking at her mother. "Maybe somebody could come along one day and sweep you off your feet."

Her lips firmed into a grim smile. "That couldn't happen to me."

"Why not?"

"Because. Because I'm too afraid."

"Afraid!" This was the last word she would have used to describe her mother. "Afraid of what?"

The line between her eyebrows deepened for a long moment. Then she said, "Just, that when you're my age, it's really hard not to be, in some way you're never in control of, *absurd*. And it's worst when you're happy, when you forget yourself. So you don't, you don't let that happen."

"Because you're afraid of *that*? Of seeming foolish?" Frankie couldn't make sense of this in light of her understanding of Sylvia, of Sylvia's life.

"We're all afraid of something, my dear. You, too."

"What do you think I'm afraid of?"

"Oh, Frankie, you know perfectly well." She sounded impatient. "You yourself said you hold back from life."

"When did I say that?"

Sylvia held her finger up, her eyebrows raised. "*Unavailable,*" she said. "That's what you said."

After a few seconds, Frankie nodded, acknowledging her memory of that discussion with her mother, that feeling about herself.

"Which struck me," Sylvia said, "because you've given yourself so utterly to your work."

Frankie sighed. "It is a paradox, I suppose. Or a mystery, anyway."

"Oh, I don't know. Maybe it's not so mysterious, really."

"No?"

"No. It seems to me that you chose work that asked so much of you that you . . . just didn't have time for all this other, messy stuff. All these demands that seem so unreasonable sometimes. Or just boring. Or I don't know. Trivial. Your life made all this relationship stuff seem . . . dispensable. And maybe it is. Maybe people can live perfectly happily that way."

"Well, I hardly think it's a recipe for *perfect* happiness," Frankie said.

"Happily *enough*, anyway." She poured some more gin into her glass. "Sometimes I think it's just that you didn't have kids. Because kids—you have to give over to them utterly."

"I did that. In my work." She knew her voice sounded defensive. She felt defensive. And she was confused by this turn. When had Sylvia given over to her kids? To Frankie?

"No, I mean, for *good*. And not to thousands of children. That's an abstraction, really. To one child. Or two, or three. Whose pain you feel as yours, whose . . . broken heart, say, is your broken heart. Whose diminishment is your diminishment." She leaned back against one of the bright, patterned pillows Frankie had bought for her. "I mean, look at me now, even with Alfie. Alfie's an adult. And it's true that in some ways I did give over to him. I mean, the way he ran our lives, the way he . . . controlled them, really. With his needs, his passions." She laughed quickly. "His ever-changing passions. And now I have a good deal of, I guess, compassion for him in his situation. But it's nothing, *nothing*, compared to what I'd feel if it were one of you girls." She drank and set her glass down next to the bottle.

"And I still worry about both of you. Probably less about you than Liz, but that's because I've known so little of your life. Until, maybe, this summer."

"You think you know my life now?"

"I know what I see."

"Which is?"

She seemed to take a deep breath—Frankie saw her bosom rise slowly and fall. "That you have . . . too many choices." She made a face. "You can live anywhere." Her arm swept in an inclusive half circle: the world. "You can have . . . men. You can work wherever you choose. It's all so open, there are so many options for you, that you don't make use of what's right in front of your nose."

After a long moment, Frankie asked, "Are you talking about Bud?"

"Not just about Bud, but yes."

"He's a womanizer, Mother." She was teasing her mother, trying to lighten the tone, trying not to be talking about this. "He's been married two times."

"Phht! All that means is he's tried."

"And failed. Twice."

"He *tried*," Sylvia said fiercely.

Frankie was startled by all this. Startled that Sylvia was speaking so directly and with such urgency. Such anger.

And even more startled that now her mother was standing up. "I'm going to have to go to bed," Sylvia said. "My God! I've had it." She walked to the doorway to the dining room. With a hand on its frame, she turned back partway. "Thank you, again, Frankie. For all you've done."

"I'm happy to have helped."

"Good."

She watched as Sylvia walked back through the dining room. She heard her in the kitchen, rinsing out her glass, and then she moved farther back, and Frankie didn't hear her anymore.

21

About fifteen minutes outside New Haven, the train stopped.

"Oh, *God*," Frankie's seatmate said in a weary tone, as though this were all too familiar, or somehow a personal insult.

They sat for ten minutes or so, and slowly, throughout the car, people began to talk, to ask one another questions. *What was it? What could it be? What the hell? What time was the connection to New York again? To Boston? Jesus Christ! Well, here we go again.*

The conductor came into the car. He was perhaps in his forties, slightly overweight and genial-looking. He was in shirtsleeves. His uniform pants were shiny. He stood at the front of the car and loudly announced that the train coming into New Haven ahead of them had lost power somehow. They would have to wait here until someone figured out how to repair it or until they brought a new engine out for it. Frankie heard a woman behind her cry out softly, "Oh, no!"

He'd keep them informed, the conductor said.

As he passed through the car, people had questions. He raised his hands as if to ward them all off; he kept walking and saying loudly, "That's all I know, folks. I've told you all I know."

He went into the next car, and Frankie could hear his braying voice conveying the same news there; and then the same answering hubbub of questions and conversation.

In her car a number of people began calling on cell phones; you could hear them scattered among the seats, most of their voices pitched louder than the conversations between people that had also begun. Those on the phones were explaining over and over, all of them in almost exactly the same terms, that the train was delayed, that it wasn't clear they'd make the connection in New Haven to Boston or New York or Washington or wherever it was they were headed. Frankie had a friend in Africa with a parrot who was good at imitating the telephone sounds of one-sided conversations, and she thought of the parrot now—Helen was her name—saying "Un-*hunh,* un-*hunh,* un-*hunh,* okay, okay, okay, okay, yeah. Un-*hunh,* okay, okay, okay, *bye! Bye!* Bye! Bye! Okay, okay. Bye."

But behind her she could hear a woman saying something else, something real. Saying, "Please, if you get this message, wait. Don't go." Her voice was urgent, passionate, and Frankie was drawn by it, she strained to listen in spite of herself. "The train is late, but I'm coming, and we have to talk. We have to work this out. Please, please, stay. I *am* coming. I'll tell you as soon as I know when I'll get there. I love you. It's crazy to let go of that. I love you. I'm coming, even if I'm late. Please, please, wait."

A little while later, when Frankie got up to stretch, to walk to the café car, she glanced at this woman. She was in her twenties and pretty in an understated way. Willowy. She looked like a ballet dancer—the long neck, the long hair pulled back severely in a low ponytail. She had a high rounded forehead, which was tilted against the window, outside of which were shrubs, trees, their colors at their wildest now, these weeks after fall had come to the woods and fields in Pomeroy.

The woman wasn't looking at any of this. Her eyes were unfocused and tragic. Her face, worried. Her hand rested in her lap, turned up helplessly, the phone lying in it.

In the café car, Frankie ordered tea and stood sipping it at the little Formica counter there, looking out at the graffiti on the cracked concrete wall that ran along one side of the tracks. *Suck my dick. Ronnie L is mine forever, Antwan Visroy King.* There were a couple of stylized wild designs sprayed on the wall, too, what she thought she remembered were called tags. She liked them, their cartoonish quality, their mysteriousness.

Other people came in and out of the car, some to get food to carry back to their seats in little cardboard trays, some to linger, to talk. One or two people asked her about her destination, her timing, and she answered politely, but not in a way that encouraged the conversation to continue. Others, though, seemed eager to share information on where they had to be, and why, and when. On whether they thought they'd make it. There were four or five people talking together in the car at one point, while Frankie, turned away to look out the window, listened. Some of them were resigned, even amused. Others were furious. One man kept saying, "*Fucking* Amtrak," to whomever he was talking to. He was handsome, his hair smoothed darkly to his head. He was wearing what she took to be expensive clothing.

As she sipped her tea and felt the minutes go by, it did seem increasingly unlikely that she'd make her connection. But what she remembered from calling in to ask about the schedule was that the trains to New York from New Haven seemed to leave almost every half hour, so there would be other options coming up. She'd be okay if she could make a connection by two-thirty or three. And if Diann could rearrange her schedule.

But two-thirty might be the last feasible connection, because that would get in around four. Much later than that, and she'd have trouble getting to the office before it closed.

While she was standing there, the conductor came into the café car and announced that they were going to have to wait for parts for the engine, which were coming just now out of New York. It would likely be an hour or more before these parts got to the disabled engine, and then it would take a while longer to do the repair.

The angry handsome man began to argue with the conductor. He wanted to get off the train. He pointed out that they were in a town. "There are bound to be cab stands or cars to rent, and they're *right over there!*" His finger jabbed the air in the direction of the window. Why couldn't the conductor just open the fucking doors and let him out? Him and others, he was sure. They could just hike across the tracks, the man said. If he asked around, probably half the people in each car would rather get out and find their way to New York on their own, forget taking *fucking Amtrak.*

The conductor, who seemed amused rather than alarmed, started to answer several times, mentioning insurance, mentioning the long drop to the tracks, but the guy had wound himself up too tight to listen.

"Why not?" he interrupted. "Why the fuck not? *Look* where we're sitting, like stupid assholes waiting for some . . . rescue by a group of incompetents. All you need to do is open the fucking door . . ."

As he went on, Frankie picked up her empty cup and her napkin and threw them away. She left the car. She passed through the two coaches in front of the café car and entered her own. Before she took her seat, she looked again at the woman behind her. She was in almost the same position, her face a mask of sorrow.

Frankie sat down. After a few minutes had passed, she reached across the aisle and touched the sleeve of the man seated there. She asked if she could borrow his phone. He showed her how to place the call, and she got through to Diann.

Who was so gracious as to seem almost relieved, Frankie thought. "Okay," she said when Frankie had explained to her what was happening. "Well, just call if you're able to get here by, say, four. Four-thirty is probably too late to really have enough time. Actually, four might be. But no," she said. "No, come. Come. Even if it is four when you get here, come."

When Frankie got off the phone, the woman behind her was talking again. Very softly—she must be turned to the window, Frankie thought, but she didn't look around to see. The words, the ones Frankie caught, were much the same. Please. She was coming. She didn't know when. He had to wait. He had to. Because she loved him. She still did. It was her fault. They could work it out. Please.

The man seated next to Frankie caught her glance and rolled his eyes. Frankie smiled and turned away.

When the conductor came through again, at almost noon, Frankie stopped him to ask about the schedule. He asked when her connection was. She said 12:11. "We won't make that," he said, shaking his head.

"No *kid*ding," Frankie's seatmate said.

The conductor got a schedule out of his pocket and unfolded it. Tracing the columns of figures with his fingers, he said that the next train out of New Haven for New York was at 1:18, which would get her in at 2:45. There was another leaving at 1:45, and then at 2:18.

"What time does that one get in?"

"Three forty-five. Then there's one at three-eighteen that gets in at four forty-five, and one at four . . ."

"That's okay," she said. "If I'm later than that, it doesn't work anyway. Thanks," she said.

"Thanks for nothing," the man next to her said, when the conductor had moved on.

But Frankie was listening to the woman behind her, who'd asked the conductor to go over the schedule once more, with her. Then she got on the phone again. She said she was hoping she'd be there at 2:45. She'd call again if that changed. If he got this message, could he just stay? Could he wait? And maybe—she knew it was a lot to ask, given what she'd done—could he call her back?

By now it was harder to hear her, conversation in the car had gotten so general. There were people standing in the aisles talking, as well as the seatmates who'd fallen into deep, friendly conversations, full of personal histories, full of coincidences being remarked on. And, of course, there were people steadily on their phones. Most people in this situation apparently wanted—needed—to talk to someone else.

But Frankie was listening for the woman, and thinking about her. How could it be that so much was riding on this one meeting? Why couldn't she reach him later if they missed connections? Was he joining the army? Marrying someone else? It was hard to imagine that the timing could be so important.

But maybe the woman just liked the drama of it. She remembered Bud—Bud!—in one of their long conversations in bed, talking about Beverly, his second wife, about how she had to keep things constantly stirred up, how, without the drama of that, she seemed to collapse in on some deep fundamental sadness in herself. He had said then, "That's why I like you, Frankie." He was sitting propped up, pillows behind him. The sun made a bright square on the quilt they'd pulled up to their waists. "You just don't go there. You don't look for the theater in life." He had pronounced it "theah-tah."

But maybe that was a weakness, she thought now. One of her many weaknesses. Because surely the *theah-tah* was part of life. The dramatic, real sorrow of the girl—the woman—behind her. The willingness to feel that, to want someone else to know you felt it.

"You're being awfully decent about all this," Philip had said to her near the end, after he'd told her he was leaving, this time for good.

"What choice do I have?" she'd said.

And he'd laughed, ruefully. "None, I expect."

But she *had* had a choice, she was thinking now. She could have behaved like the woman behind her. She could have wept and insisted. She could have said, *Please. Please.*

If she had wanted Philip as much as this woman wanted the man she kept calling.

And for all the good it would have done.

But maybe that wasn't even the point. Maybe the point was you said what you felt, you tried for what you wanted. Maybe the point was that Frankie had taught herself how not to do that, from early on. Maybe some dynamic between her mother and herself had made her believe that's what she had to do—teach herself that. Maybe even her work had been part of the discipline she seemed to have embraced—a kind of daily instruction in the insolubility of human problems, in the unremediability of human suffering.

Did she believe that, as Philip said he did? She didn't know.

She didn't know how she had ended up here.

She looked out the window. Just beyond the trees you could see the backyard of a suburban house, a worn swing set between it and the bushes at the edge of the property. No one had used the swing set for a long time. The chain on one side of one of the swings had broken, and the swing dangled vertically, moving a little every now and then in the breeze. It seemed to Frankie, suddenly, nearly tragic in its expression of desolation, of human loss. She looked away, down the aisle of the car.

Her seatmate had gotten up a little bit earlier, and now he was halfway down the car, deep in conversation with a group of three men, one of whom was seated, looking up at the others. Their faces were animated. They were enjoying their catastrophe. Frankie had a sense, suddenly, familiar and yet new, of her aloneness.

It had to do with the suspension she felt—in time, in place: the no-where-ness of being stuck here. The sense of others around her finding a way to be comfortable with it or else struggling hard against it.

While to her it felt like a sad confirmation of sorts—*You are nowhere, you belong nowhere. There is nowhere you're going, nowhere you're coming from.*

"You have too many choices," her mother had said.

Over to you, Frankie.

She saw the handsome man from the café car come in. She watched him as he spoke to several people, as he slowly drew a small group around him. He was talking intently, gesturing out the window. His plan, no doubt. She could hear the odd phrase. *Outta here. Fucking Amtrak.*

There was an argument, from her seat she could hear one of the men say, "Aw, Jesus, come *on.*" There was laughter, too. But there was also clearly some assent. After a few minutes, the man came up the aisle toward Frankie, followed by a few others—to find the conductor, probably, to talk to him again. They left the car.

It was a little before one when the conductor came back in. He announced loudly as he walked through the car that the train with the repair crew was just arriving in New Haven. That no one knew yet how long it would be, but he would let them know, "the *minute* that I do."

The man in the seat in front of Frankie stopped him with a raised hand and said, "So we won't make the one-eighteen train to New York."

The conductor shook his head. "Out of the question," he said cheerfully.

"What about the one forty-five?"

"I wouldn't know. I don't know any more than what I've told you, okay?" He started to move off. He raised his voice. "I'm hiding nothing, folks! I swear to God!"

The girl behind Frankie leaned forward, her head appeared just over the seat next to Frankie. "He doesn't know about the one forty-five?" she said.

"That's right," Frankie said.

"Okay. Thanks."

Frankie heard her make her call again. Calmer this time. Defeated. But still pleading. She didn't know when she'd be there, but she could stay. She'd stay overnight if she had to. They could meet tomorrow. He should call, or just . . . she'd call again. As soon as anything was clear, she'd call again.

When she hung up, Frankie could hear her start to weep—long, jagged intakes of breath—a sound, she thought, that made you feel your heart was breaking, too. Her own throat cottoned, and she turned to the window so no one could see the tears rising to her eyes.

They pulled into New Haven a little after 1:30 with plenty of time to make the 1:45, although you couldn't have told that from the anxious line of Frankie's fellow passengers forming in the aisle. Or from the way they scrambled off the train when it stopped, some of them actually running toward the station to find out what tracks their trains were on. From her vantage at the end of the line, Frankie saw the handsome would-be mutineer outside pushing his way through the crowd on the platform. Ahead of her the sad ballerina hurried, too, but not as rudely.

Frankie was glad for the fresh air as she stepped from the train, as she walked slowly along the platform. Inside the station, she went to the window for the *Vermonter* and bought a return ticket for the next train back to the town near her parents' new apartment, the town where she'd caught the train to New Haven early this morning.

Then she looked for a pay phone to call Diann, to tell her she wasn't going to make it, that she wasn't coming at all.

22

Is it over? This was the first sentence in Bud's article about the possibility of an ending to the fires, an article he started to write a week and a half after Frankie Rowley had left town.

He stopped and looked at what he'd typed, and then he laughed out loud, a quick bark. "Yes, my friend," he said to himself. "It is."

But he went on typing. *This is what residents of the town of Pomeroy are asking themselves two weeks after the arrest of Tink Snell.*

Though in fact, that question had begun to be answered. Since the police had taken Tink in, day after day had gone by without another fire. People had gradually begun to relax, begun to assume that it was over—the long nightmare—though there was still disagreement about what this meant. There were those who were willing to accede to the obvious: *They arrested Tink, the fires stopped. Good enough for me.* But there were others who argued that the guilty man was still out there. That he had just decided that this would be a good time to stop, when someone else would take the fall. *Well, if you want to have people think someone else was guilty,* the argument went, *wouldn't you stop setting them now? Let everyone make the easy assumption, and there you are, off scot-free, and Tink to take all the blame.*

As far as Bud could tell from his unscientific polling, the split was about fifty-fifty—though even among those who thought Tink must have done it there seemed a surprising sympathy for him. Undefined, a bit inchoate, but still, sympathy that you wouldn't expect anyone in town would feel for the person who'd terrorized everyone for a season. *He must have had help,* some of these people said. *Someone must have put him up to it.*

There was, of course, the undeniable matter of the confession, but again, there was a divide between those who believed, simply, that if you weren't guilty of something, you wouldn't confess to it, and those who felt that Tink had been coerced into signing it, that he'd been chosen because everyone in charge knew he would be vulnerable to that coercion.

Adrian told Bud in the store one rainy afternoon that they'd promised Tink special treatment if he confessed, that they'd held him for hours after Alfred Rowley's rescue, questioning him, that they'd told him—or implied anyway—that he could go home once he signed. Adrian said Tink had told him that he was so tired and confused by the beginning of the second day that he'd agreed, that he would have signed anything they asked him to.

That was crap, the state trooper in Winslow told Bud. They didn't even need the confession, they had so much else. "That confession was just the icing on the fucking cake." He said that Loren had found what he called "ignition materials" in Tink's car, which Tink had left unlocked outside Liz Swenson's house when he joined the search teams looking for her father. These were the same materials found on the ground outside the senior Rowleys' barn the night of the fire there.

Oh, come *on,* Adrian said when Bud asked him about it. It was cotton balls and Vaseline. All the search guys carried cotton balls with Vaseline when they were going out looking for someone, in case they needed to start a fire in tough conditions. Half the volunteers probably had such materials.

"Sure. In their packs," Loren said. "Not fifteen or twenty laying around on the floor of their car."

And so it went. It was interesting, in some ways more interesting than the fires had been. But there was less, actually, to write about, so Bud was back for the most part to his standard material for the fall, the daily small events that constituted the pulse of the town—the recording of which, he reminded himself, was the reason he'd come here in the first place.

This was something he needed to remind himself of, over and over. That he'd chosen this place, that he'd wanted to be here. Even so, he was restless, which he knew was part of his response to Frankie's departure. Since she'd gone, he'd been second-guessing himself, wondering again, as he had in the first days after he landed in Pomeroy, whether he'd made a mistake, whether there might be something retrievable for him in the world *out there,* in the world of greater consequence, as it seemed to him now in these long empty days.

He told himself that the reason for these feelings was just that he was mourning Frankie, that this was temporary. That it would end.

Though it didn't feel as if it ever would, right now.

He tried to give himself permission to do whatever he needed to do to get over her. The problem was that he wasn't sure what that was. He drank himself to sleep every night for the first four or five days after she'd gone, but he felt so crappy the next day that he decided the temporary oblivion wasn't worth the pain. He wept several times—once extravagantly, driving home after bundling the papers the second Monday in October. Louise Hinton was helping that night, and she'd talked to Frankie's mother recently. Frankie was such a help, Sylvia had told Louise, though she'd also said that she felt guilty for keeping her away from her work. "By which she appears to mean New York," Louise had said as she handed one of her newspapers to Conor.

Yes, Bud had said. That was his understanding, that there was work in New York she was eager to do.

Even after he got home that night, he had sat outside his house for maybe fifteen minutes and let himself make the strange grunting, gasping noises that were coming out of him, let his nose and eyes run freely. Until finally it all seemed self-indulgent, and he stopped.

He stopped, he came inside and washed his face, and he went to Pete's house.

He saw Pete more often than he usually did in these weeks. Most times he called ahead, and always he brought two six-packs of beer with him, some to drink, some to leave with Pete. It wasn't good beer, because Pete didn't care whether it was good beer or not, and because Bud was pretty certain Pete would think him a fool for caring about such a thing—though he did. But he also cared, too much probably, what Pete thought of him.

They didn't speak of what was bothering Bud, of why he was suddenly coming by so much. Mostly they talked about the paper. The paper and the news.

Bud had gone to interview Tink in jail, finding him as inscrutable as ever, and he told Pete about that. "I asked him why he'd confessed," Bud said.

"Ya-ah?"

"Yes. He said, 'To get them off my back.'"

Pete nodded several times, judiciously. "*That* worked well," he said.

Bud laughed, aware of feeling a wash of gratitude just for that—to be laughing, to be thoughtless for a moment.

He told Pete about the new regular column he was adding to the paper, a summary each week of the events of the same seven days twenty-five years earlier. Louise Hinton was scanning in all the old files and had the idea. She'd offered to write this piece up each week. Easy enough, she had said.

They talked about what Pete was reading now. He'd finished all of Conrad and was starting on Robert Louis Stevenson, whom Bud confessed he'd never read.

"Lucky man. Some good stuff waiting for *you.*"

"I'm glad to know that. I could use some good stuff."

After a long moment, Pete said, "I'm sorry to hear it."

And that was as close as they came to talking about Frankie.

They talked often about the fires—who was rebuilding, who wasn't. They talked about the developments in the court case. Tink's lawyer was still trying to get him out on bail.

Pete thought this was unlikely to happen, even though there were townspeople who believed in his innocence and were trying to raise the money, to be ready if the judge should rule in Tink's favor.

"Though he's going to get off, in the end," Pete said.

"You think so?"

"I do. They don't have much of anything without the confession, and that's dirty. Take that away and add in all the people lining up with alibis for him." Pete shook his head. "There's nothing there. Like you said in your piece, it's a hard crime to prove, and they haven't." He had some beer. There was a fire going in his fireplace, and Pete had been up often, poking at it, turning the half-burned logs to keep it going. It seemed an activity he enjoyed. "I suspect we're never going to know for sure, one way or the other," he said.

"That'll be really hard for people to take, after all this. They want to know. They need to."

"Too bad. They won't, if he's acquitted on some technicality."

Bud had been watching the fire. Now he looked back over at Pete. "But maybe if that happens, they'll reopen the investigation."

"There's nothing to reopen. They bet the farm on Tink. They've got nothing left."

"Unless there's another fire."

Pete made a dismissive noise. "There won't be any more fires. Whether Tink's acquitted or not, there won't be any more fires."

"What makes you say that?"

"What would be the point? If Tink did them, it *worked*, it worked out for him. There are all these folks willing to stand up for him. There's even some raising money. Sure, it might be mostly because they're so mad at the way the police handled it, but there it is. Why would he put all that goodwill, all that *love*, in jeopardy by starting up again?

"And if someone else did it . . . well, now is the perfect time to stop and get away with it."

It would turn out that Pete was right. That the confession would be ruled tainted and inadmissible after the state police admitted they'd alternately befriended and threatened Tink, after they acknowledged that they told him things would go easy for him if he signed. After they conceded that they had rejected the suggestion by his friend Gavin Knox in their presence that he get a lawyer. After it was discovered that Tink was unable to read aloud or understand a number of the words that had been used in his statement.

But long before all that—and it wasn't until spring that the judge made that ruling, and summer when the quick trial was held and Tink was acquitted—Bud had come around to Pete's way of seeing things: that it was unknowable, though that wasn't exactly what Pete had said. But that was the point, Bud thought. The point of Tink, and of Frankie, too, he'd come to feel. Of the way they arrived together in his life, brought to him by the fires. The lesson was there were things you had to let go of, losses and mysteries you had to learn to live with.

And sometimes, even years later, when he'd see Tink around town—a less and less pretty boy, and then a thickened, balding, middle-aged man—Bud would be aware of feeling a strange sense of connection with him. Of a kind of gratitude welling in him at the sight of Tink—gratitude for his unwitting lesson, for the letting go he had helped to teach to Bud.

It was cold in the mornings now, and Bud decided to change what had been his routines since he came to Pomeroy. Now before he had his breakfast, he built a fire in the living room stove at his house, and he stayed at home for the first half of the day, working at the desk facing one of the big picture windows on the first floor. The window looked down the hill to the northern edge of the village, and from his vantage, he could watch the slow, distant stages of the morning's start down there.

First the dogs came out, freed from their life in their families, rushing to the green to greet one another, to smell one another, and joust and run from one end of the wide lawn to another in barking packs. Occasionally a responsible owner trailed one of them long enough to pick up its shit, then went home, or took the dog for a walk. But mostly the dogs ran and frolicked wildly and freely until they were called back in. And they were all called back in at this time of year—no one let them wander now that hunting season had started.

A little while later the yellow school buses, like old, lumbering animals, made their appearance, stopping every fifty yards or so, heading south with the younger kids to the village grammar school, heading north with the teenagers to the high school in Winslow. A while after that, the townsfolk who worked somewhere else—in Winslow or Whitehall or Black Mountain or even Greenwood—left in their cars and trucks for their jobs.

Then things were quiet. Quiet in a way they never were in the summer, when the summer people moved in and out of town, shopping and visiting with one another. When the kids appeared and disappeared all day in waves, going to the pool, or swooping through on their bikes, or taking up some project on the green itself.

It was quiet, though Bud knew that there were those like him, at work in the old white houses around the green or up in the hills, and he found himself thinking about them, about all of them, doing their jobs. There was a publisher with a tiny press in his barn. There was a weaver, a potter. There was the veterinarian, whose office and kennels were behind his house. Bud had the odd sense as he moved around his own house—making another cup of coffee, standing in the kitchen looking over at the hills, returning to the notes and papers on his desk—of being among them, somehow. Of being *of* them. Of them, in a way he hadn't felt before.

And this feeling held when he stopped in at Snell's for the papers on the way to the office. When he talked to Adrian or Lucy or Harlan or someone also stopping by.

Nothing important, usually. "How's it going?" "Got anything left to write about these days?" It was the same, the way it had always been, but it had changed. Something had changed it for him, and he didn't know what it was. Perhaps the strange relief he felt once the summer people left this year. Or maybe it was the end of the fires. Or the loss of Frankie, who had kept him so much in her orbit.

He didn't know.

The office was empty when he got there at about eleven each day—no Barb. She'd left for a vacation as soon as leaf season was over, and after that she usually came in only rarely through the fall and winter. He worked at his desk and the big table until early afternoon, planning things, calling people, or returning their calls. Then he was out, at the Golden Agers' weekly lunch, or the high school soccer game or wrestling practice. He attended everything—the rehearsal for the high school production of *Kiss Me, Kate,* the fund-raising committee meeting for the volunteer fire department, still strapped for cash, the Haunted House at the town hall. He tried to stay as busy as he could, and it worked, it helped. There was consolation in the very ordinariness of these events, in the conversations he got into, in the sense of belonging he increasingly felt.

And threaded through all this there was the tracing of the slow process of the law in its relation to Tink Snell, for a while requiring Bud's presence in Greenwood once or twice a week, then at more staggered intervals. First his bail appeal. Then the decision about that—*no* was the answer from the judge, just as Pete had thought it would be. Then his arraignment, with more discussion of the bail. Then a hearing in which his lawyer asked that the confession against him be thrown out.

Over these weeks, Bud came to like the Greenwood Courthouse, with its dark wood wainscoting and its uncomfortable wooden benches. The room was always crowded with people he knew, mostly from Pomeroy, though all the newspapermen for miles around also came—Peter Knowlton from Whitehall, Larry Winters from Winslow. Even, twice, Matt Reinhart from the *Boston Globe*.

In all of it, Tink seemed, more than anything, lost. A lost, beautiful boy who might or might not have done any of it. Sometimes, looking at Tink, Bud thought that Tink himself—so blank, so helpless-looking—might not know for sure anymore whether or not he'd set the fires. Could that be?

The drives back and forth to Greenwood were themselves a form of consolation. By now the leaves had finally finished falling, and the woods had opened up to reveal themselves—the bare trunks, the lean, empty branches, everything colorless except for the dark green of the pines here and there and the slowly fading brightness of the leaves that lay heaped over everything. Sometimes, coming around a corner on the familiar roads, Bud would pull over to the shoulder and stop to look at what had always been there but was unseen, unseeable, till now. An old farmhouse revealed on the hill opposite, its smoke curling yellow-gray out of its stone kitchen chimney. A faded red barn visible through the bending white stalks of a naked birch grove. The river, curving where he'd forgotten it was, glinting cold and black behind the bare limbs. These sights did something to him, and he wished he'd made more of all of this with Frankie, that he'd tried to make her see and feel the natural world around them as he was seeing it now. He wished that he'd wooed her with it.

Too late—he'd been seeing only her then.

But slowly through these weeks, as he felt himself giving over again to what seemed fine to him here, he also felt himself letting go of the idea of Frankie just a little, and that made him believe that eventually he'd be able to think of her more easily. Perhaps even as his last, passionate resistance to everything that compelled him here.

And why not resist? Why not resist anything final or definitive in life, anything that said *After this, the doors will not stay open for you here, or here, or here.*

And why not make Frankie, whose yearnings for all the unknowable things that lay behind those doors had seemed worthwhile and serious and noble to him, whose *way* of yearning seemed so real and affecting, even as it seemed to make their way forward together more unlikely, more vexed—why not let her be the emblem of everything *other* that he was giving up, if this helped him? It wouldn't be hurting her or misusing her. After all, wasn't the sex with her, the lying down with her, the talking with her, like a dream of something that couldn't last anyway? Even if she'd stayed, he thought, even if she'd found a way to lead a life big enough for her here, they couldn't have held on forever to the intensity of the passion that drove them over the summer.

Which didn't alter his answer when she knocked on his door one night in mid-November. And wouldn't have altered it, even if he'd known it all, everything that would come. Even if he'd foreseen the restlessness that would sweep her from time to time, that would make her miserable in her life in Pomeroy, that would call her away over and over. Away to New York, for months of work on projects that made her feel alive again, she said to Bud on her return. Away once to Africa for almost a year, a year that made her know one more time that she couldn't stay there but that reminded her of how much she wanted to.

He would have answered the same way even if he'd known the sense that all this would breed in him over the years, a sense of such tentativeness in his approach to her that the moments between them that seemed natural and glad and easy became rarer, more and more painfully dear.

None of this will matter when he hears the soft tapping on the glass in the kitchen on the first snowy night of the fall and puts his book down. When he crosses the living room and comes into the darkened kitchen, when he sees her there through the glass pane, the yellow light over the door falling on her, on the snow moving steadily all around her and catching in the thick, coiled net of her hair resting on her shoulders. When her face changes at the sight of him. When he opens the door and she steps urgently into his arms, and it feels the same. She feels the same—tall, strong, matched to him in every way, limb against limb—and smells the same, and tastes the same.

When, after their long embrace, he says into her ear, into her hair, as he rocks her from side to side, "God, it's you, Frankie. It's exactly you." When she leans her head back to look at him, her whole face a question for him to answer.

When he steps back and up, over the threshold to make room for her to enter.

"Yes," he says. "Yes, come in."

Acknowledgments

THERE WERE A NUMBER of work worlds I needed to inform myself about in order to write this book, and I'd like to thank the people who made this task the pleasure it turned out to be. Judy Muller kindly e-mailed me a prepublication copy of her fascinating and funny book about small-town newspapers, *Emus Loose in Egnar,* and it was more useful than I can say. Sam Allis helped me with newsroom terminology and reporting practices. Kevin O'Hara and Adrian Lakin answered my myriad questions about volunteeer fire departments and how they work, and I'm grateful to them both. Nora Love and Jennifer Martin were more than generous in talking to me about their rich and rewarding lives as aid workers in Africa. The confusion and struggles of my fictional character are not theirs.

My agent Jill Kneerim and Doug Bauer carefully read and commented on an earlier version of the book. Jordan Pavlin, in her editorial wisdom, turned me back into it to do the major revision that made it, finally, much more the novel I had set out to try to write.

Thank you, all.

THE LAKE SHORE LIMITED

Meet Billy Gertz: a fiercely independent playwright, whose
newest drama imagines the story of a man waiting to hear
if his estranged wife has survived a cataclysmic event. As
her life touches three other unforgettable characters, Billy's
play—the emotion behind its genesis and its powerful per-
formance—forms the thread that binds them all together.
A moving love story and a tale of connection and loss, *The
Lake Shore Limited* is Sue Miller at her dazzling best.

Fiction

THE SENATOR'S WIFE

Meri is newly married, pregnant, and standing on the cusp
of her life as a wife and mother, recognizing with some terror the gap between reality and expectation. Delia—wife of
the two-term liberal senator Tom Naughton—is Meri's new
neighbor in the adjacent New England town house. Tom's
chronic infidelity has been an open secret in Washington
circles, but despite the complexity of their relationship,
the bond between them remains strong. Soon Delia and
Meri find themselves leading strangely parallel lives, as they
both reckon with the contours and mysteries of marriage:
one refined and abraded by years of complicated intimacy,
the other barely begun. With precision and a rich vitality,
Sue Miller—beloved and bestselling author of *While I Was
Gone*—brings us a highly charged, superlative novel about
marriage and forgiveness.

Fiction